Sally has been working in the beauty business, theatre and costume design for many years but has always had the desire to write. With a keen interest in drawing and painting, she has combined her talents and produced a book that will delight and entertain all who read it.

I dedicate this book to all the members of my family
who believe in me.
To Mum, a big thank you for inspiring me to go on.

Sally MacIntyre

EARTH, WIND AND FAIRIES THE ROWAN

AUSTIN MACAULEY
PUBLISHERS LTD.

A CIP catalogue record for this title is available from the British Library.

ISBN 9781786127945 (Paperback)
ISBN 9781786127952 (Hardback)
ISBN 9781786127969 (E-Book)

www.austinmacauley.com

First Published (2016)
Austin Macauley Publishers Ltd.
25 Canada Square
Canary Wharf
London
E14 5LQ

Acknowledgments

Mr MacLeod, thank you for your kind permission to use your beautiful Dunvagen Castle and its gardens on the Isle of Skye for my ongoing series of stories.

CHAPTER ONE

LOST, JUST GOLDEN AND BAD YELLOW

W hite, puffy clouds swept over the sky, covering and uncovering the late afternoon sun as Cecee flew to find her way to the top of an old elm tree. She wanted to take a close look at some strange items she had with her before hiding them. Born in these Seven Oaks Woods sixteen years ago, this was her home and where she was formally named 'Carmilina Citrina Foxglove' – it didn't take her family and friends long to shorten this to 'Cecee'.

While cool, eastern winds gently moaned through the elm, Cecee settled down on one of its uppermost branches. Life for her had been easy so far and, being a Royal, she had been sheltered in the comfort of her father and mother's home. She supposed school had taught her enough to prepare her for what she thought life may bring and in two days, it would be September 29th, her seventeenth birthday. This meant quite a few things to her, and apart from leaving school, one other thing was certain – from then on, she would be treated as an adult.

On the edge of the woods and by the cornfields, grew the oldest oak tree, deep in the roots of which, lay the Royal Court with its many rooms and secret passageways. All corridors leading to the Royal Quarters were guarded by the King's Soldier Elves, ensuring the safety of the King and Queen and their family. However, much of the Soldiers' time was spent shooing away unwanted insects and pests! In Cecee's room, birthday gifts were piling high and she longed to unwrap them. However, earlier, she was told to unwrap the two small, but most interesting looking immediately and these were the items she carried with her to the branches of the elm tree, where she thought to take a better look. The mysterious gifts were from her parents and each puzzled her as she sat to study them closely. The breeze blew her long, blonde hair as it continued to whistle through the tree. Cecee held up one gift to the sunlight and peered through the liquid of a tiny bottle while in her lap was the other, a pretty golden pouch. Warnings from her parents left her wondering if these special items did indeed contain magic – the pouch was made from a weave of solid gold, so why did it feel so light in her hand? Cecee could not understand, nevertheless, she did what all fairies do with their most valued possessions – hide them from all! The Sun now sinking and the light fading fast, Cecee edged towards the highest crevice in the elm's trunk. Finding it to be full with dead leaves she scooped these to one side, she peered in. The hole seemed okay, free from any birds' nests or nasty insects, so she hid the gifts inside, covering them with the leaves. She then flew off, back to the comfort of her home and bed.

A new day soon dawned and it was now the eve of her birthday. Excitedly, she washed and readied herself for early today, she was to have her very first secret meeting with the elders of her woods. Off she set to join the gathering where she was invited to sit on a toadstool. Every adult important in her life was there, and after lots of happy birthday wishes for the following day, together with several of her favourite fruit drinks, the King and Queen took Cecee to one side. Secretly, they whispered instructions for the two strange gifts, which she learned were alive and given to her before her birthday so they could get to know their new owner! She must take care never to break the bottle and never expose the Seed to any light for too long – it must be kept safely inside the pouch. Both gifts must be used together in a special way in Seven Oaks Woods on the last day of December at sunrise. Tomorrow, she would be given instructions about what exactly she must do and on no account should she discuss a word of this with anyone. On that December day, she would join with a Human. 'Human...' she wondered, 'why a Human?' Stories at school had taught her most Humans can't see into her World, but the few who could, called 'Seers', seemed easily fooled.

After the gathering ended, Cecee felt very uneasy about where she had hidden the special gifts, so swiftly flew to retrieve them. Alone again and high in the tree, her little fingers hurriedly brushed away the leaves. Feeling inside, she gently removed the tiny bottle and saw it was indeed filled with a clear, purple fluid that had a very strange pearly white swirl and, fascinated, shook the bottle to see if the colours would mix... But they didn't, the swirl simply changing shape. It seemed she could not take her eyes from the mystical object as she removed green vine ties from her hair, tying them around the top of the little bottle which she then hung around her neck. Reaching back into the crevice for the golden pouch, she carefully pulled it out. Dare she open it...? It was so beautiful and she was not at all sure she could resist the urge to look at the Seed inside. Flying off, she settled into a thick clump of ferns where she could hide. Carefully, Cecee opened the pouch... but what disappointment! The Seed didn't look special at all! Peering again inside, even closer this time, in the darkness of the pouch she could see the Seed had a very faint glow around it. She wondered what all this may mean and with a sigh, re-tied the pouch, lacing it onto her belt, and flew back once again to the comfort of her home.

A silver Moon sank into the distance of a star-filled sky, the hooting of owls echoing throughout the night air as Cecee slept soundly in her parents' Quarters. As the Sun rose, the sound of a song bird announced morning had broken and it was Cecee's birthday! She rubbed her large, golden eyes and reached for her Wand... not there! It took her a few seconds to fully wake and realize she had left it yesterday in her mother's dressing room. Although relieved it was safe, she wanted it back, but this was not a good time to disturb her parents. The Sun was just up, and that time was when her parents discussed forthcoming matters of the day. So she brushed aside the problem of her Wand, readied herself for the day and flew off to find her younger sister to help her open her birthday presents. Cecee found Tizzy in her room and already out of bed. Greeting her with a smile, she said, "Morning, Tizzy! Come on, it's time to open my presents – I want to share them with you!"

Tizzy shot a glance her sister's way before returning to the matter in hand. Her pointed ears sticking straight up in concentration, she fought her new Wand which had no desire to sleep, powerful sparks flying out from its crystal in the struggle! Tizzy's Wand was young and undisciplined, full of energy and wanted to practice magic *all* the time. Cecee watched patiently as Tizzy tried to push it into its carrying tube. Finally forcing it inside, she closed the top with a sharp snap and secured the tube to her back-strap. The noise from inside the tube now settled down as the Wand, at last, peacefully slept.

"Phew! Morning, Cecee! I'll be glad when my Wand learns to behave so I don't have to lock it away! Oh, but today is your *special* day. Happy birthday!" she said, relaxing her ears and giving her sister a broad smile and a big hug. She stood back. "Let me look at you. So… how does it feel…? I mean to come of age?"

Tizzy didn't wait for an answer, spotting at once Cecee's golden pouch beneath two others attached to her belt.

"Wow, I love your new golden pouch. Who gave you *that*?" she asked, while reaching to grab it for a better look.

"Mother… father… oh…an early birthday gift. I'll show you the pouch later and as for feeling different… no, not really," she answered, gently pushing Tizzy's hand away from the pouch.

"Oh alright, but will you let me try on that pouch and use it sometimes? It would look great with my new dress."

Tizzy again went to grab it in a playful tease.

"Of course," Cecee answered, this time firmly pushing away Tizzy's hand. She thought she should quickly change the subject so flew up to hover in the air.

"Have you eaten yet and did anything interesting happen yesterday while I was away?" she asked.

"No, haven't eaten and I'm starving! Let's have breakfast," answered Tizzy, as she joined her sister in flight. Taking a sharp turn, they flew off towards the Royal Breakfast Room.

"Did you hear about Nopkin's news?" Tizzy asked, while panting for breath to keep up.

Cecee shook her head.

"Well, the strange 'Weather Elf' told the Court an unusual storm would hit Seven Oaks Woods today but exactly when, he didn't know."

But other things filled Cecee's mind today and Tizzy's news seemed to her a small issue. She answered while flying lower, "When there's any sign of a storm, I suggest anyone caught outside should go to the cornfields where the corn is still high and they can hide."

Tizzy followed close behind, admiring her sister's ability to think soooo quickly! They left the roots leading to their rooms and entered a huge circle of toadstools, 'The Inner Royal Circle'. This was in a deep hollow in the ground and known to all as P.O.H.D.S. It was the centre of the Royal Court and a short cut to their parents' rooms. It was the special place often used by the King and his soldiers, a 'Place of High Decisions'. The two sisters entered another hole in a tree and flew down inside the trunk to the ground where tunnels wound inside a mass of huge tree roots. All were lit by glow-worms and cleverly dammed so they would not flood in heavy rain. The tunnels were difficult to map, very few knowing how to get to the Throne Room or Royal Quarters which had their own maze of secret tunnels and gardens. But Tizzy and Cecee knew their way around everywhere, expertly flying in and out of the tunnels, making their way to a garden area.

The unusual late summer had brought into bloom a few white daisies which Tizzy stopped to pick for a fairy tumbling competition, normally held in the early summer months, but specially arranged for Cecee's birthday party. This was going to take place in the afternoon and, although it could be dangerous, Tizzy's best friend had entered. It was a custom to throw many white daisies into the competition area, as they were soft and would cushion any fall. Tizzy was glad to have found them, but the two sisters were unaware that this simple delay would change their lives forever…

Today, Cecee's favourite breakfast would be served. A delicious feast made by their father's fantastic 'Chef Elf', 'Cameron'. To prepare, he takes one large orange, cuts it in half and scoops out the segments. Next, he lines this 'orange bowl' with his special 'lemon paste'. Once this has hardened, he dips the rim of the bowl into honey and then into powdered coconut. He takes a little orange juice mixed with mango and pours it into the bowl. Following this, he sinks a mixture of large chunks of peeled, honey-soaked orange and lemon segments, blackberries and pitted cherries into the juice until the bowl is full. Then, he tops the centre with a small sprinkling of shredded coconut and finally, drizzles the rim of the bowl with raspberry sauce. 'Honeyed Fruit and Coconut in Juice,' he calls his proud creation and Cecee adores it... not only because it is *simply wonderful*, but coconut is the only nut she can eat without breaking out with a rash!

A bright early morning seemed to be turning into a pleasant day and after breakfast, Cecee sat under the shade of an elm watching her young and carefree sister make daisy chains. Again, she recalled yesterday's gathering and even though she felt excitement, she still sulked about how perfect Tizzy's life would be. Born the youngest into Royalty, she would have all the benefits with little responsibility. While thinking to give her old job of butterfly counting to Tizzy soon, Cecee reached for the golden pouch, untied it and looked inside. She found the Seed with its faint glow still nestled in the dark folds. But then she remembered how she must tell everyone about the expected storm and her cornfield escape plan. Retying the pouch, she called to her sister.

"Tizzy, I'm going to find our friend Tulip, she can send the message about the cornfields in an instant. I'll be half a second, so don't move from that spot."

Before Tizzy could say a word, Cecee flew off.

It's a fact that nature has given female fairies a degree of protection from heat or cold. For most of the time, they do not feel a change in temperature, but a change in air pressure hurt Cecee's ears, and after finding Tulip, flying back to Tizzy proved difficult. The wind had increased, carrying with it fine rain which dampened all the plants, bushes and trees. The bright morning sun now hid behind dark clouds. In the gloomy light, Cecee continued to fly towards the spot where she thought she had left Tizzy. Flying high and low in an effort to avoid the strong, swirling winds, she felt concern having left her sister but she must find somewhere to shelter. Squinting through a fine, rainy haze, all at once a large object appeared directly in front of her – a tree stump with what appeared to be a small opening in its side. She flew onwards to get to the stump but soon realized this was a big mistake as another gust of wind sent her tumbling backwards. Shocked, she managed to steady herself by holding onto a weed just as a voice carried towards her in the wind. It was the fearful call from Tulip.

"Wild, strange weather expected anytime now! Danger! Everyone take cover in the cornfields if you can… if not, try *anywhere*!" Tulip cried.

Cecee froze with fear and so, it seemed, did the wind. In the stillness, she searched for the tree stump, but it had gone, disappearing into a damp mist. Tall trees stood still and silent in the heavy atmosphere, their limbs appearing to point directly at her. "Take cover while you can," they seemed to whisper. Suddenly, something moved on a small mound beside her – flying ants in their hundreds, quickly escaping to take flight from their nest ahead of the oncoming storm. Jagged streaks of lightning suddenly exploded out of the clouds above, cutting through the heavy, moist air. This brought with it a stark reality – the storm Nopkin predicted was directly above! Thunder boomed, shaking the ground beneath her feet, lightning striking the ground next to her as torrential rain lashed through the woods, soaking her hair and wings, making it impossible to fly. Then, quite unexpectedly, the rain stopped. Sitting next to the ant mound, she watched helpless ants floating towards her in streams, coming to rest in puddles around her. Most were dead, or soon would be. Her large, golden eyes squinted as she gazed towards the skies, but what was that? She stared at a strange, dark green cloud with a tail reaching down from its centre, the tip swirling along the ground, twisting in a menacing dance, blowing everything in its way high into the air. But, worst of all, it was heading straight for her! Suddenly, the whirling wind caught her wings, tangling her hair, spinning her tiny body around and around. In the darkness, all her senses seemed numbed.

Cecee was bewildered to see the trees and ground around her covered with snow. Beneath the surface, something made a trail which sped towards a Human boy she knew as Michael. How she might know his name she couldn't understand, but she *did* know him and screamed, "Run Michael, run!" Michael turned and ran towards her but the deep snow slowed his every step. Then horror! Whatever Michael was running from, showed itself in the form of an ugly, little grey creature, screeching, "I want 'Moon' and 'Sun', I want them now! I'm hungry, I want to eat Subros!"

Her wings feeling heavy, flying seemed impossible. Everything except the creature moved in slow motion and while terror filled her whole being, her heart pounding, she watched it disappear back under the snow. Where was it? Was it going to chase Michael again, or was it about to chase her? What was its purpose? What did it want? Michael continued to run towards her, pitifully begging for her help.

"Cecee, I have the Sun *and* the Moon and you have Subros. Help me save them! Please help me!"

But the little monster had caught up and popped its head above the snow, opening its mouth wider than seemed possible for one so small. Sharp, pointed teeth bit hard into Michael's leg as he screamed in pain! Screeeech, screeeech, the sound of the creature's teeth grinding against bone, pierced Cecee's senses, waking her with a start from the awful nightmare! Her heart still racing, she took a long, deep breath to calm herself. Looking around, she could see no sign of Michael, the little monster or any snow. Only clouds, many of them, surrounded her, and out of all the calm, white puffiness, a flock of noisy birds flew past her. Cecee could hear the same terrible screeching as they disappeared into the clouds. She was in danger. The storm had swept her into high, fast moving clouds. Without her Wand, what power did she have? Nervously, she looked to see what else she had with her that might help... two dust pouches and, of course, the new golden pouch. She played with the little bottle around her neck, thinking of a plan to safely escape. Then, her heart leapt with fear as she suddenly thought, '*The Seed! Is it safe?*'

Tiny fingers hurriedly opened the pouch and... relief... the Seed was still inside! She looked around the skies, having no clue where the wind was taking her. Will she be able to plant the Seed? What would happen if she failed? Alone and scared, it wouldn't be long before December arrived. It was then Cecee remembered today was her birthday, and on top of everything else, she was hopelessly lost!

***

Prince Foxglove VII was nineteen years old, the eldest child and only son of the King. He was a head strong elf but a natural athlete, loving any type of sport. He had won many medals, attracting huge crowds when competing in his chosen game. He was a fast flyer, handsome and strong, but did not like being the centre of attention in everyday life. Some said he had a little of his parents in him, sometimes obstinate like his father, but shy like his mother. He grew his white hair long and as the King's soldiers did, he often tied it back with dark green vine. Though his hair grew pure white, it turned almost black at the ends, this unusual look earning him the pet name 'Albatross', later shortened to 'Tross'. A year away from a soldier's formal training, he had not yet encountered serious conflict. As for the study of magic, well, he wasn't at all great with this. But at least he was happy, proving himself in battle-practice throughout the year for which his father presented him a splendid, rose-thorn dagger. Tross was thrilled, going nowhere without it. His love of sport saw him compete in some of the most dangerous. 'Pip-in-the-Pot' was his favourite, involving both bravery and courage which delighted his father as these were qualities expected of every future King.

The King's mind, filled with many concerns, waited at P.O.H.D.S for his son to arrive. Tross entered and headed eagerly towards a conversation being held between his father and their most favoured soldier, Remik… "Our soldiers will enter the woods in search of Cecee…"

Tross quickly interrupted his father.

"Father, since I am Prince, shouldn't I lead the search party?"

"No!" came the abrupt reply. "I don't think you should go at all!"

"But father… TUT!"

"I said NO, absolutely not!" the King insisted. "You're only nineteen and inexperienced – I have enough problems as it is. Even I cannot leave before clarifying a few important details, Tross. Now go and sit down. I will talk to you after I have spoken with Remik and Nopkin and finalised the necessary plans."

Soldier Elves carrying glow-worm lanterns quickly filled P.O.H.D.S, a hush falling over all as the King announced a most generous reward. All who help bring the Princess safely home would be granted their lifelong needs together with those of their families.

A vote as to who would go was quickly counted with the result those chosen would form the search party led by Remik. The selected few left P.O.H.D.S to say goodbye to their loved ones, after which they would meet at the Armoury to receive 'War dusts' of various kinds, including the very rare 'Truth dust'. Meanwhile, the King asked Nopkin if he had any further news of the storm. Nopkin took a deep breath.

"Your Majesty, I have studied the weather pattern and found that a very cold wind from the north blew over and mixed with a warm, southerly breeze, creating a very rare event in these parts."

The King listened anxiously as Nopkin continued to explain.

"The wind was unusually strong, in fact, hurricane force, and spawned a small tornado. Sadly, six of the famous old Seven Oak Trees were destroyed."

Nopkin stopped talking and scratched his head as he wondered how to replace, in the shortest possible time, the vital acorns that would be lost as a result. But the King startled him back to the matter in hand.

"Nopkin, concentrate! Did the storm carry Cecee off and, if so, in which direction?"

Nopkin thought carefully before answering.

"If it did Your Majesty, I think it would have taken her with the wind and clouds now heading north."

The King mused.

'North, hmm... then again, she may have hidden from the storm and is lost somewhere deep in the woods'.

He turned to send his son to take news to the Queen, but Tross had already gone. Nopkin, despite his vast knowledge of all matters concerning nature, had become confused. Restoring the six oak trees had been so much at the forefront of his mind that he had overlooked the obvious. Unbeknown to any of them, the clouds were, in fact, swiftly taking Cecee west...

Tross loved a challenge and was sure he could find his sister. Slipping away, he found his cousin 'Prince Fern'. Fern had partnered Tross before, training their expensive flying frogs which were three of the very best. The game of 'Pip-in- the-Pot' was a costly past time for both. Practicing some of the game's moves with their prized frog called 'Yellow Spec', Fern was high in the air astride the small but strong creature when Tross spotted them. He cupped his hands to his mouth and shouted up, "Ferny, since we are using 'Specs' for the big game next week, can you make certain he is exercised and fed every day?"

Ferny landed, gulping air after his exhausting work-out.

"Hello, Tross… yes of course. Why, are you going somewhere?" he asked, while picking up a bucket of water to throw over 'Specs'.

"I'm leaving to help find my sister, Cecee. You know she is missing?"

"Well, news travels fast and yes, I've only just heard, but should you go, Tross? I am sure your father has made detailed pla–"

Tross interrupted.

"No, not sure, but I think my father is staying here to look after things while his soldiers go into the woods with Remik. Don't worry, Ferny, I'll be back before the big game. All I need to do is find her. How hard can it be – she can't be far. While I'm away, please do my job and keep Specs watered in Seven Oaks Lake and remember, he's our best flyer and ordinary pond water won't give him the energy he'll need to carry either of us. Thanks my friend, I'll see you later!"

Tross thought he had better get something more than his dagger and raced to the heavily guarded Royal Armoury. The guards were surprised to see Tross, not having been informed he would be part of the search party. But no guard dared to question the Prince as he took a pouch of 'Truth dust', quickly tucking it into his belt.

Into the woods he flew, his thorn dagger firmly set in his belt. On his way, he landed in a rough patch of grass and rested beside a stream to make a compass. Placing a blade of grass in his cupped hand he added water, watching closely as the blade floated and turned slowly, coming to a stop. Certain the blade pointed north, he thought, to make absolutely sure all was well, he would check the tree moss as it was said this always grew on the north side. Satisfied he was heading in the right direction he flew off, but suddenly thought he heard rustling in the undergrowth. Something which appeared to be larger than a rabbit seemed to move quickly beneath him. Hovering in the air, he strained his eyes to see what it could be. He could not be certain but reasoned it was probably, after all, just a rabbit. Not wishing to waste any further time, he flew on. His pointed ears remaining alert, he now heard fluttering above, but the sound of voices nearby distracted him and he landed clumsily, narrowly avoiding certain pain from a patch of stinging nettles. But his pouch of Truth dust slipped from his belt and fell into a patch of thick grass.

Quickly hiding behind a nearby tree, Tross could see, sitting under the shelter of some bushes, soldiers chatting excitedly while carving daggers from rose-stems. He had found his father's search party. However, unbeknown to him, Todd Toady, known to many as one of the worst elves in all the woods, sat on a tree branch above, closely watching his every move.

'Wot *wos* that 'e dropped?' Todd thought, as he quietly flew down to look. 'Hummm… a bag of Troof dust! *Wot* a find! Ad better be careful', Todd thought to himself, as he tucked the pouch into his belt. 'The rustle in the ferns earlier and the sound from me wings above, nearly gave me away. 'Ave I stumbled upon somfink? Could that just be Prince Foxglove, Tross? I wonder wot *'e's* doing so deep in these woods? I'd bet the last pouch of me most valuable dust that 'e's farver don't know 'e's precious Prince boy is out 'ere.'

Todd remembered with anger how the King had imprisoned his brother for stealing, and how unfair he thought this was. But revenge is a sweet thing... had the moment come where he could get some for his brother? With the oncoming winter's chill now felt in the mornings, not many Humans were camping in the woods. Todd thought them pests but they had left behind some interesting bits and pieces and spotted an old car tyre hanging by thick rope from a tree branch. Better still, and to Todd's good fortune, it was close to Remik's little group. The tyre twisted around as Todd secretly flew inside to hide. He listened with great interest as chatter from the search party continued.

Tross decided to walk over to Remik who sat carving a new dagger.

"Err ... umm ... hello," he mumbled.

Still looking down with pride at his newly carved weapon, Remik didn't look up to see who the soldier was.

"Oh, hello," he replied. "Not everyone is here yet, so go over there, sign in and wait. The King thanks you again for volunteering."

Tross hesitated briefly. "Right", he quietly said. But how would he sign in and should he let them know who he was? Remik looked up, thinking there was something about that voice.

"Hey, wait a minute. You look like..." He flew a full circle around Tross. 'No, can't be, the King would never allow his son out alone in the woods', he thought, as he called to the group of soldiers, "Hey, we have an elf here who looks *exactly* like Prince Foxglove."

All at once, they flew over to look at the upstart, but one elf suddenly dropped on one knee.

"You're Highness!" he exclaimed.

Remik mildly mocked the soldier.

"For goodness sake, get up. *He* isn't the Prince!"

But the elf looked up and said, "You've been away too long, Remik. If he's not Prince Foxglove, then I'm a snail's dinner!"

Flexing his small but powerful wings, Tross smiled as he saw Remik's face change from mild amusement to utter shock. He and the others now recognized the Royal wing pattern and all instantly joined their fellow elf.

Tross took in a deep breath.

"Oh no, please everyone, get up, I *hate* all that! All I want is to join you in your search for my sister and please, all of you, treat me as one of the group."

"*Excuse me,* Your Highness," Remik replied, while rising. "I really didn't recognize you... You have grown but, Your Highness, may I ask, does your father know you're here, deep in these woods?"

Tross stifled an answer.

"Well, umm ... not exactly..."

Mumbles of concern came from all as they, too, got up from their knees, Remik lifting a hand to quieten them and commanding, "Will everyone *please* calm down! Your Highness, this is a dangerous mission. We must go even deeper into the woods and if any bad elves or fairies find out you are here…"

Tross stopped him firmly.

"Enough! Bad elves or fairies do not know I am here, so stop worrying and, *please,* no 'Royal' addressing. Just call me Tross."

'Hummm,' thought Todd, as the tyre continued to twist and swing. 'E *is* the Prince and 'ow *nice* of 'im… No one to address 'im as Royal… Huh, wot a joke that is!' He pulled a small, sharp twig from his pocket and relaxed back to clean under his finger nails and think… 'Yes, this could be very useful, must fink carefully. I'll get me best elves working wiv me… maybe involve Rush, although there's a risk taking *that* one along! Fings go to 'e's 'ead and 'e could get carried away… dangerous villain! Or, maybe I can grab the Prince for ransom by meself, obviously when the time is right… but wivout 'elp, when will that be?'

For now, Todd had heard enough from the soldiers, so he looked at his nails, satisfying himself they were clean, put his small nail twig back into his top pocket, quietly flew out of the tyre and made his way back to his camp.

Once there, he found everyone in a rare mood. Rush, who was nowhere to be seen, had recently stolen from a bee hive and his gang of elves were busy making mead from the honey Violet would sell in her Inn. Both he and Rush shared in the profit, but resentfully thought it totally unfair that Violet received the most! With that, he decided to pay her a visit.

Walking briskly, he soon came upon a small clearing from where a few more steps took him into a cavern cleverly shaped from dried undergrowth. Night was now upon him as he strolled into the dimly lit Inn to look around. Tiny glow-worm lamps cast a soft light throughout, 'flickering' as the worms moved around inside. Logs lay in a square, the tops having been hollowed out in places and then filled with dried flowers, while inside the square, seven canes had been pushed firmly into the ground. They stood upright and inside was where Violet kept her mead. When this was ready to drink, she poured it into the hollow cane from the top and served it from the bottom when needed – she called them her 'pipes'. There were several different kinds of drink served, but the honey-mead was a favourite. Violet named the cavern 'Two Sevens Inn' and although not her ideal place, seven was her lucky number and she hoped one day it would bring her the Inn of her dreams. She hummed a merry tune as she sat on a log, making new acorn cups. Todd strolled into his usual quiet, dark spot which this night, seemed to match his mood perfectly. Violet put down her cups, filled one with mead and walked over to him.

"Ello, Todd, 'ave some mead, love – you look tired. It'll do you good and maybe warm up that cold 'art of yours."

She laughed as she handed him the drink, but Todd's eyes moved slowly around the Inn, searching every dark crevice.

"That'll be enough lip from you, Violet. 'Ave you seen Rush anywhere about?" he asked, with a hint of menace.

"No I 'aven't, and don't want to niver. Always rushin' round 'im. Expect 'e's up to no good! I'd bet me last pouch of dust on it," came Violet's sharp reply.

"Well, next time you see 'im, tell 'im I wanna talk 'bout some urgent business."

"Righto," she assured him with a happy, carefree shrug.

Todd finished his mead and stood up to leave, but Violet stopped him.

"Hey, hold on a second, Todd! That will be one-tenth of a pouch of 'Ealing dust' for that drink."

"You're getting *very* expensive, Violet!" he hissed, as he threw a one-tenth size pouch at her and walked away.

Violet never trusted Todd so quickly checked the contents then called him back. "Wait a minute, Todd! This is a cheap, old trick, a little 'Ealing dust wiv buttercup pollen mixed in. You fink you can fool me! Remember *who* I am, Todd. Wasn't it me dad that taught yer 'ow to take 'oney from the bees safely?"

Todd snapped a reply. "Oh, I know *who* you are, 'ave no doubts 'bout that, Violet, and yeah, your dad and a mixed-up elf called Bill taught me loads, but a lotta' good it's done me, ay? Me and Rush risk *life and limb* to get that 'oney, me elves make the mead from it and you get most of the profit!"

"Remember, Todd, if it wasn't for me dad, you'd have nothin'. You've been lazy all yer life, you've no skills, you and yer mates are paid very well for the 'oney and you drink up me best mead at a very good price. Now, yer wouldn't deny a fairy a livin', would yer, Todd? So get back over 'ere as quick as a flash or I'll 'ave you locked up!"

Todd pulled out a large pouch he kept cleverly hidden under his wing, grumbling, "Got an *empty* one-tenth pouch, Violet?"

Throwing him a small pouch with 'One T' written on it, she answered with a laugh, "Of course I 'ave, Todd."

Todd caught it and glared back at her, filling it and slamming it down on the table. "There, satisfied now! Take all me 'ard work, take everyfing I've got!"

***

Deep in the woods, Remik's search party received an urgent message from a Court Messenger saying they must change the plan and now head west. But all knew this would take them deep into unmapped, unknown territory, with all its hidden dangers. In the dark, Remik and Tross led the way. Before long, the party came across two wayward looking elves, busily eating the tops off mushrooms and drinking their own cheap, home-made mead. Tross politely approached them. "Excuse me…"

One stopped chewing and, spitting out his uneaten mushroom, pulled out a dagger on the unwelcome pest who he thought would have to be taught a lesson. The other continued stuffing mushroom into his mouth as he stared at Tross. He couldn't believe some young upstart disturbing their eating and drinking – what next! Remik held his breath as in a flash Tross pulled his own dagger, leapt forward and grabbed the hand of the elf who dared to threaten him. With a quick twist, he had him face down on the ground with the elf's dagger flying from his hand and sliding along the grass. Tross knelt on his back and put his dagger to the throat of the thief.

"You want to play?" he asked.

"Ahhh, do what mate? *NO*! Calm down, I was *only* joking!" replied the shocked elf.

Remik interrupted, "Oh, who do we have here then? It's Bertie and George, eating the King's mushrooms… again! Can I see your Food License?"

Bertie nearly choked on a mouthful of mushroom.

"Wot? Oh, yeah… No! I mean… well, we meant to get one but, well, yer know 'ow it is…"

Remik leaned close to him.

"No, tell me how it is… Listen you drunken little weed, I'll forget what I've seen if you can help us with some info."

Tross released his grip on George who struggled up and dusted off his clothes.

"Oh, right," he said with a nervous laugh. "Me mate Bertie's only kiddin'. He, he! No 'arm meant. Wot can we do for yer, then?"

"Have you seen a fairy around here you don't recognize, one with unmistakable yellow eyes?" Remik asked George.

"Nah, 'aven't seen none. Don't know anyfink neiver… *specially* about… well, 'ow to get to 'ovver Worlds and all that. Oh yeah… we 'ave 'erd aaaall about it from a big, weird elf called Rush – *he's* a right badden, 'e is!"

Bertie nudged his friend so hard he nearly fell over.

"George, you've 'ad too much mead!" he whispered.

"Oh, yeah…wot…err…right," George replied, with a wobble, putting his finger to his lips. "Shecret shtuff, shuuuuush… he, he… well, anyway, the shtorm passed and 'at was it, I din't spy no fairy…nooope!" said the elf, as he sat down hard, the drink he had earlier taking even greater effect.

Remik offered a reward, but still no information was forthcoming.

"Okay, you two can go, but take my advice both of you, get the License!" and with a turn, he and Tross left to rejoin the soldiers.

Bertie wiped sweat from his forehead.

"Phew, bloomin' 'eck, 'at was a close'un, and as if fings ain't...err... tough enough! Get a bloomin' *Foooood License,* yeah, right! It's flippin' expensive and... there's aaaaalways a queue as long as a mile."

George studied his rather chubby and also drunk friend.

"Yeah, it's been at *least* five minutes since we ate. Dunno 'bout you but I gotta shober up! 'Ave a date tonite. Can't look sickly and shpesshly drunk, he he. And 'ave you seen 'ow bad *you* look, ha, ha... wot a mess!"

The hopeless pair had a few more mouthfuls of mushroom washed down with the last of their mead before deciding to finally stagger off in the rough direction of their homes...

As Remik and Tross walked together, Remik slapped Tross on the back.

"You handled yourself well back there, Your Highness, if I you don't mind me saying so, I was very impressed by that and glad to know you."

"Glad to know you too," replied Tross, with a laugh, adding, "oh, but please don't call me Your Highness."

Meanwhile, from high up in a tree, Todd Toady and his horrible best friend Rush, had been carefully listening. While spying on the Prince and Remik, Rush whispered excitedly to Todd, "The first plan 'as worked! One of our elves pretending to be a messenger 'as sent the soldiers west instead of norf. Huh! A lost Prince *and* a lost fairy! She *must* be a Royal! After all, why would the King's soldiers be so concerned 'bout an *ordinary* fairy? The opportunity, well, ain't it just golden!"

But Rush, for once in his evil life had, unwittingly, helped by sending them west.

***

The whispering winds of rumour work in much the same way as the winds that fuel forest fires – both waste oxygen to create a cruel and unkind outcome. Spiteful talk that Tizzy had shamefully left her sister alone had circulated the Royal Quarters all afternoon and while the

Queen sat waiting for news of Cecee, she tried to ignore the gossip. Inky skies hugged a distant Moon as evening came upon them, and instead of the wonderful party arranged for Cecee, elf scouts were reporting for duty. In the murky light of the Moon, Tizzy entered P.O.H.D.S. and seeing her mother, thought how lucky she had been to escape the worst storm ever. Taking her place on a toadstool next to where she thought her brother would soon be seated, she looked around.

'Where are Cecee, Tross and father?' she wondered.

At eleven years old, Tizzy was the youngest of her family. Royal blood as white as snow gave her the family's envied creamy skin. She had her father's mint green eyes, and wore her dark green hair long, a bonus for her as, with her wings down, she could hide easily amongst the forest greenery. Though not fully developed, her wings would one day be like her mother's, pure white with striking green peacock patterns, giving her the Royal Mark. The colours all played a part in her formal title 'Princess Snow Pea' and, like her brother and sister, she too, enjoyed a pet name, Tizzy, given to her by Cecee. She was a beautiful young fairy but much preferred her sister's yellow colouring, striving in every way to be like her.

King Foxglove entered with, close behind, twenty soldiers who placed glow-worm lamps all around. The King sat next to the Queen, immediately turning to Tizzy and calling her by her formal name.

"Princess Snow Pea, have you seen Cecee?"

"I beg your pardon, father?" she answered.

Her father frowned and replied sternly, "You should know by now that you must always stay together. Do you know where Cecee is?"

Tizzy nervously tried to recall the series of events.

"I… I…" she stammered.

The King's voice grew louder as he interrupted her.

"What are you trying to say child? When *did* you last see or speak to her?"

"Father, I… I don't know."

The King sprang from his Throne.

"Elves! Where are my Guard Elves!" he bellowed.

Ten elves quickly entered and stood before the King. One bravely stepped forward to speak but the King raged, "Have you searched the entire Royal quarters and gardens as I instructed! Can you account for everyone?"

The elf gulped, spluttering in reply, "Yes, err… yes Your Majesty, but…"

"But what? Have you found my daughter Cecee?!"

A feeling of alarm raced through the elves as another stepped forward.

"Your Majesty. With deep regret, we have not found her and reports from Remik tell that the Princess has not been found in the woods either."

He bowed low and swiftly stood back in line.

"Well, organize yourselves!" the King ordered. "What is the matter with you all? Go and search again! Where is Nopkin? Someone summon Nopkin to attend me in my Quarters, NOW!"

The Queen's wings drooped to the ground as she stood up, the King reaching for her hand.

"My dear, we *will* find her. I promise."

The Queen stared at her husband without answering. Standing as still as a statue, her thoughts strayed to all the things that may have happened. After a short pause, she turned and said, "Cecee has the Seed with her and beyond anything, the 'season' *must* be met. We both know our daughter's life could be in great danger… the pouch and the little vial of liquid could turn against her.

Outside the Royal Circle is unsafe with many hiding places for bad fairies and elves. My darling husband, our beloved daughter *must* be found!"

The King dismissed the court from P.O.H.D.S and hurried away to meet with Nopkin.

Tizzy flew to the comfort of her favourite tree and, in the darkness, sat nervously combing her hair with her fingers. Leaves fell around her like sad tears as she tried to recall the events that took place just before Cecee disappeared. After a while, two soldier elves fluttered into her tree, one announcing, "Princess Snow Pea. You have been summoned to hold audience with King Foxglove VI."

'Summoned?' Tizzy questioned herself. Her heart missed several beats hearing this word as, after all, she had only just left her father. Immediately she obeyed, flying down from the tree and following the elves through a maze of tree roots and into the 'Throne Room' of the Royal Inner Quarters. Tizzy noticed, as well as her father, her mother wore official dress and, what was more, they were both seated upon their formal Thrones.

'Mother and father only wear clothes like that for celebrations or in times of great sadness, and father's look... so stern!' she thought to herself as she walked towards them.

Her father stood and beckoned. "Tizzy, come and sit by my side."

She did as she was asked, relieved he had called her by her pet name, but the King's thunderous voice brought her back to the seriousness of the moment.

"Tizzy, I want you to think very hard. When was the last time you saw Cecee?"

"Father..." Suddenly, out of the sense of great seriousness of sitting in the Throne Room, the chain of events flooded back to her.

"Cecee said that she had to tell everyone to go to the cornfields when the storm arrived. Soon after that, Tulip came and told me also. I flew around to find Cecee, but she had gone. It was then the storm came and I was blown to where mother found me in a..."

"Well," interrupted her father, "thank all the Wizards of Middlesborough you were not hurt, but how many times must I tell you and Cecee never to separate! Fairies must always travel in pairs in case one gets into trouble... the other can then find help. Do you *understand*, Tizzy?"

Shrinking back into her chair, she answered simply, "Yes, Father."

But anger began to well up as she listened to him. She could not help but think how unfair he could be. She always tried so hard to please him but felt she never could. The King dismissed Tizzy to the safety of her room but, she disobeyed. When she and Cecee were younger, they were allowed to go where others were forbidden and she knew secret passages in and out of the Royal Quarters. Finding her way through them, she flew back into her tree and settled down. Tears flooded her eyes which for any fairy was serious...

Meanwhile, the King and Queen made their way to the Private Quarters, the Queen begging the King, "Please don't be too severe with Tizzy, she is, after all, so young."

"I know my dear, but the rumours are all over Court. I will be expected to punish her. She is our daughter but the law is the law. Above anything, she must set a good example and learn to accept her duties and responsibilities."

The Queen argued in reply, "Cecee is missing and Tizzy may not be responsible. There could be something she's not telling us, even afraid to tell us. Our concerns are so great, do we need to add more?"

Reaching their rooms, the King sat down hard in his favourite chair, ordered a cone of peach nectar and sighed.

"I have made my decision. Let her have a good night's rest and tomorrow Willow will clip her wings for one whole day. It will give her time to think about what she has failed to do."

The Queen did not always agree with her husband's decisions. Wing clipping had its own dangers, but he was the King and once he had made up his mind, what could she do?

Tizzy had returned to her room but did not sleep well that night and in the morning, flew out to sit on a branch of an apple tree. Dozens of apples were all over the ground and she remembered the blossom on the tree before the apples arrived, so pretty, and now look, apples for all to eat. The force of nature – everything has its own time and place and all revolves in a huge circle... Tizzy wondered when and where her 'own time and place' was. Why was she here? For what reason? Her life was not going to be like Cecee's whose life, it seemed, had a purpose. These thoughts left her with an empty feeling as the Queen flew to join her, sitting down gently next to her. She took Tizzy's hand and spoke softly. "Tizzy, you have disobeyed again and should not be here. After some thought, your father and I feel that you have not yet understood how to keep yourself safe and as a result, you need more time to think about your responsibilities. We have decided to clip your wings and ground you for a short time."

Tizzy gasped as her mother squeezed her hand and continued, "During this time, you will not be able to fly and easily escape danger, so you must stay close and help me with my duties."

The King stood guard under the tree as Tizzy flew down to him.

"But, father, it was not *entirely* my fault. You are being so unfair and you definitely don't understand..."

"Enough," the King said in a gentle but firm voice. "It has been decided and will be done today. You will go from here to the Royal Apple Orchard to meet Willow."

A very distraught and angry Tizzy flew up to the tree trunk's entrance and disappeared down into its roots. Flying along, she found one arching upward and then down, back into the ground. This special root led her outside and to her parent's gardens where she flew to a small waterfall to drink. Her thirst satisfied, she looked around. Guard and soldier elves were busy with their daily tasks, and although she was used to being stared at by them, it seemed they looked at her differently this morning. She flew to the Royal Apple Orchard where she sat, waiting for Willow. Deep in thought, she watched squirrels run up close to her, grab small fallen apples and scamper away. She stared at them, envying their simple way of life. At that moment, she caught sight of Willow walking towards her and as he approached, he introduced himself.

"Hello, Tizzy," he said cheerfully, "my name is Willow and I think you know who I am and why I've been sent here."

"Yes, I do," she replied with a deep sigh.

"I promise the clipping won't hurt, and the little rest will actually do your wings some good."

A frown of doubt creased Tizzy's young brow as she studied Willow.

"Tizzy, you already know that your brother has this done all the time for 'Pip-in-the-Pot' competitions, and he never suffers any ill effects," explained Willow.

"Yes, but his wings are small and I've never seen it done. What do you actually *do*?"

Willow searched close by for a spider and, satisfied with a small, brown specimen, walked carefully back to Tizzy, the spider crawling over his hand.

"Our little friend here will do all the work and is the exact species I need. I'll watch him carefully as he weaves his fine web… he cannot harm you in any way."

Tizzy looked at the spider sitting on Willow's hand and shuddered.

"They scare me, and I don't like the sound of them… '*Spiders!*' Personally, I have changed their name to 'Speeglades' – it sounds much better!"

Willow responded with a smile. "Here, Tizzy, take him, he won't hurt you."

Tizzy shied away. "I don't know… they *all* look sort of creepy. Their legs are long and thin or short and thick. Then there are the tall ones that make even taller shadows in the moonlight, and those weird spots and jaws. They are either furry, see through or shiny looking… and *totally* unpredictable when they run. Ugh!"

But in spite of all her fears, Tizzy still let the spider run onto her hand. Willow then took it back with a smile.

"I'll be happy to teach you all the markings of spiders and maybe you'll then understand them better. Anyway, Tizzy, think how much bigger you are and how you in fact might frighten them! Now, we'll start by folding down your wings and letting the spider do his work."

Tizzy let the spider start securing her wings, surprised the weaving she could see was, in fact, quite pretty. Just as Willow and his spider had completed their work, Tizzy's mother flew to her to hold her hand and offer comfort, but Tizzy pulled away… 'How unfair my father is, and mother doesn't really care, she can't care! She wouldn't let *this* happen to me if she did!' she thought.

The day seemed endless and Tizzy found it *totally* boring. While helping to arrange tea parties for the elder fairies, she yawned endlessly, so much so that her mother had to remind her that it was rude to yawn quite so often.

'Anyway,' Tizzy thought, 'rude it may be, but I get *no* thanks for all my help! How rude is that?' The only thing that interested Tizzy was a conversation she tried to listen to concerning rainbows, but even then she was shooed away and kept out of the seemingly secret discussion. The elders appeared to be in competition with one another, disagreeing about everything, such as how long they had lived and how much magic each had in her now crooked and overused Wand. One plump and very jolly fairy had a mysterious but fascinating odour about her. She chuckled over everything she said, telling everyone she once knew a famous Wizard called Patrick McCracken. Tizzy did not believe *that,* thinking to herself, 'what a whopper of a fib... even the old ones believe in myths and fairy tales! Don't they know better?'

With her mother by her side, Tizzy walked without worry, but two young fairies who were the twin daughters of a friend of the family, made a habit of hovering above her, staring at her everywhere she went. All day they were there and Tizzy just *knew* they were whispering about her. 'How rude of *them,'* she thought, while holding her head high, trying to ignore the pair. But there was no denying, her heart felt heavy. Sadly, and in spite of everything, she had a wild urge to fly away. 'Mother and Father will be sorry for being so unfair to me. As soon as I get my wings back, I'm leaving!'

Sunrise had come and gone since her wings were clipped but to Tizzy, it seemed a lifetime! The King summoned her to his Quarters.

"Tizzy, you may now have the use of your wings once more. We hope you have learned a lesson by using the time wisely to consider your ways."

"Yes I have, father. When will the web be removed?"

"Willow is here and will remove it later this morning. You are to meet him here with mother."

Later, mother and daughter entered the Royal Quarters.

"Sit there, Snow Pea, and wait patiently," her mother said, gently.

Tizzy sat on a small mushroom and soon Willow entered wearing his usual large smile.

"Well, Princess Snow Pea, it's time to remove the web. But listen, during the first week, your wings will feel stiff, even seem smaller and the colour will have faded. But please don't worry. After a few days and with a little sun, the colour will return and all will be back to normal."

After his reassurance, Willow rid her of the web with his usual expertise. Without thinking, Tizzy tried to fly but, to her horror, she felt nothing but pain. Willow stood back in shock.

"Tizzy, not so fast, you'll hurt yourself... you must be patient child, and your wings will return to normal, I promise!"

Time passed and after a week, Tizzy found herself flying again but something troubled her. She didn't feel as pretty as before – owing to the lack of sunlight, the full colour had not returned to her wings. Growing more impatient with every passing day, an idea occurred to her. 'The old fairies might just be able to help me!' She decided to fly to one she knew to be most friendly and, indeed, quite jolly, and would, she hoped, be willing to help. She was known to all as Florie.

Tizzy arrived at her house, finding her busy and deeply involved with something. Being young and inexperienced in old fairy ways, Tizzy walked in and came straight to the point.

"Hello! Just want to know how long before the next rainbow appears?" she asked without hesitation.

The gentle old fairy looked up from her silk weaving and with a chuckle in her voice, she answered Tizzy's question with another.

"My dear child, rainbows? Why on Earth would a young one like you want to know about rainbows?"

Tizzy replied edgily.

"Because a rainbow or the Sun can help me, and I haven't seen much of either lately!"

Florie scratched her ear, her old eyes gazing into the distance.

"Help you, heh? Well, a rainbow will appear soon, possibly tomorrow afternoon. Yes, I do believe it is to be tomorrow afternoon... but why do you want to know? Don't go flying near it to investigate. You young fairies are much too inquisitive! The colours...especially the ye..."

"Thank you!" Tizzy replied, excitedly, and without listening to what else the wise old fairy had to say, in a flurry, turned to fly away as fast as she could.

However, Florie began to worry as she continued her silk weaving. 'That little one is the King's youngest. Surely she is not going to attempt to go near the rainbow?'

At Court, Tizzy spent her time considering ways to escape, but her chances were few. To make matters worse, those twins *still* following her around everywhere were just plain annoying! But soon, by a stroke of pure luck, her opportunity arrived and she was away, sitting under a huge oak tree, waiting. 'How long will it take for the rainbow to come,' she wondered, 'and was the kindly old fairy right about when it will appear?' The Sun finally peeped out from behind a rain cloud but then disappeared. The smell of approaching rain took her mind back to the day of the Great Storm. Tizzy's thoughts then wandered to Cecee... 'Where in the World can she be?' But all at once, she returned to the present as light rain sprinkled down. Strong, bright sunbeams suddenly burnt through the trees and high above, magic happened. Opposite the Sun, heavy, dark clouds reflected a huge rainbow that arched completely across the sky. Tizzy stared up in awe at the strongest colours she had ever seen. She sprang up and flew straight towards them. Higher and higher she climbed, finally reaching the magnificent colours. In and out she flew, carefully picking pieces of each. Lots of green, a little red, and the yellow, oh how she wanted the yellow – it would make her like her sister, but should she? Pondering whether or not to dare pick the yellow, she felt the colour send a feeling of warmth, drawing her closer. Before long, Tizzy felt hot, then much too hot. Quickly changing her mind, she tried flying away, but the yellow seemed to pull her back! Now panicking, she flexed her wings with all her might but it was no use, the pull was far too strong! Nearer and nearer she came, intense heat burning her arms and legs as the yellow pulled even harder. There was no escape – she was going to burn alive! Then, quite suddenly, something tugged her arm... Florie pulled Tizzy with all the strength she could find, moaning as her wings ached from the strain.

"Tizzy, fly, fly as hard as you can!" she yelled.

Tizzy tried her best but the old fairy's grip was weak and she could hold her no longer... Both were now tumbling out of control as the hungry rainbow pulled them both slowly but surely into the hot yellow. The heat created its own wind and a gust caught Tizzy, sending her close to Florie. This gave her a chance to reach out to the old fairy, but the blinding glare took Tizzy by surprise. She missed the old fairy's arm as Florie screamed, "Tizzy, don't worry about me! Fly into the green, you can do it but do it now, Tizzy, do it now!"

This was the last Tizzy heard from poor Florie as she tumbled out of sight. But Tizzy hesitated – she wasn't sure what to do and was scared. The green seemed thin and lay too close to the dangerous yellow, but the old fairy could suddenly be heard screaming louder, pleading with Tizzy, "By all the Wizards, you took some green. Fly back into it before it's too late!"

Tizzy held her breath and flew as hard as she could, so very close to the yellow but diving headlong into the edge of the green, and then… silence! Quite suddenly, the rainbow melted into a mass of glitter, colours mixing into each other and fading to a misty rain that fell from sight. Now, in the clear sky, her white hair singed and curly from the heat, Florie laughed aloud while puffing out a little smoke, her gnarled and crooked Wand covered in coloured glitter. She exclaimed, "Ha, ha! My Wand may be old, but it's still powerful! My magic works almost as well as it did in days gone by and, little one, with the exception of yellow, your wings now have colours from the rainbow!"

Too shocked to admire her wings' new colours, Tizzy grabbed Florie by the hand and both flew at full speed to the safety of home. But the old fairy was deeply worried – they had escaped and survived the first danger of the rainbow but now there was something else, something that could soon kill them both.

***

Before Tizzy's father planned to leave in his search for Cecee, Tizzy was due to have lunch with him, her mother and a few guests. Tizzy hoped that flying into Court with colour back in her wings would teach those twin fairies not to whisper about her any more. In her room, she prepared to look her best. As she busied herself, something green flashed from the corner of her room. It was her crystal necklace, a gift from her father, brought back from one of his many trips to Middlesborough. She wondered about that mysterious place, with stories of its tall, mauve mountains and why all her father's soldiers repeated the saying, "By all the Wizards of Middlesborough." She contemplated as she combed her hair, 'there is a Middlesbrough, about half a day's flight from Seven Oaks, but the spelling of that is slightly different to where father goes. It's rumoured green crystal from Middlesborough contains special powers – I wonder if my green necklace contains such powers?' But for now, it was enough to just wear and show her father she wasn't angry with him any longer. Content, she flew towards the Royal Circle to take her place on a toadstool, but as she entered, a gasp came from the Courtiers. 'Oh great Wizards, what now?' she thought. Her mother seemed terrified at the sight of her, while her father's eyes fixed upon her with a heavy glare. He stood up.

"Tizzy, those colours, the green is wrong and a little red? They are not yours!" he thundered.

Again, she could barely speak and instantly folded down her wings.

"I… I…" she stammered.

"You have flown alone again and what is more, you have put your very life in danger. It is obvious to me and all in this Court you have flown into a rainbow to take its colours *and*, you know perfectly well, that taking things which do not belong to you is stealing!"

"Yes, but I didn't realize I was *stealing* when I took the colours. We all get our colours from the sky… don't we?"

She looked around the silent Court but could not see Florie.

"I thought anyone could fly through the rainbow. I didn't know *that* was stealing," she mumbled.

The King relaxed a little.

"Tizzy, you are young and still have so much to learn. One thing you must understand is that the colours are vital to us and help us in many ways. Flying near the yellow is dangerous. Fairies do not feel heat until it is too late. Thank all the Wizards of Middlesborough you didn't fly near the yellow…"

Tizzy suddenly caught sight of the now refreshed Florie sitting in a corner, but the old fairy signalled a warning, putting a finger to her mouth and gently shaking her head.

"My dear daughter," the King said softly, "the only time colours are allowed to be taken from the skies is when a special event takes place over Scotland. It is a beautiful, inspiring, mystical sight called the 'Aurora Borealis' and has nothing to do with rainbows – taking *its* colours is quite safe."

Behind her, Tizzy could just hear the irritating, giggling twins. She felt like taking her Wand and… but no, her Wand was like her, young and over enthusiastic and anyway, Royalty should show self-control. She wondered why Florie didn't come forward to explain what happened and how they did indeed fly near the yellow and, in fact, were almost drawn in! Looking again, she noticed Florie had left. Tired of being the youngest at Court, she took to her wings to fly through the room. As she flew at full speed towards the exit, she had to pass the annoying twin fairies and decided she *would* practice with her Wand. After all, it had chosen her and they must get to know one another fully. So she dared to stop and hover above them. Unclipping her Wand from her back tube, she closed her eyes and waved her Wand over the twins, certain that it would know what she wished. She then flew away, stealing a quick glance back before she sped through the roots and out into the woods. Her spell whirled around the twins' heads while they tried to scream. Tizzy's Wand had taken away their chuckles and made their very long hair stand bolt upright and to make matters worse, only Tizzy and her Wand could reverse the mischievous magic! Her parents, while thinking their daughter had again simply flown off to her favourite tree, were left for a second or so, too stunned to imagine who may have been responsible for such misbehaviour!

***

Florie needed to fly home but her wings felt older than usual. They ached and she could now actually *feel* the cold. The 'chill' was upon her already… it had begun. Her wings barely lifted her off the ground as she flew away to make her potions. She must concoct a mixture for the terrible sickness that was about to attack both Tizzy and her. Knowing one part of her potion would be dangerously difficult to obtain, a comforting thought crossed her mind. Tizzy was young so she would not feel anything... not yet at least... and would be easily found in her Royal Quarters, or so Florie thought. However, her main worry was, when would the full effects of the illness some called 'Bad Yellow', be felt by them both?

CHAPTER TWO

OBVIOUSLY DANGEROUS, HOME AND NO MORE!

*S*till trapped inside a cloud, Cecee rested, watching others slowly drift by. Before the clouds melted into thin air, she had to fly, but her left wing ached and she did not want to waste the Healing dust she had with her. Unfortunately, her injury was worse than she feared and she fell fast, landing with a bump on something strangely feathery, rolling clumsily over and onto sand. She sat up to the sound of a deep voice coming from behind. Immediately, she grabbed for her Wand... not there!

"Hello sweetie," a voice said.

Forgetting her pain, she flew up, and in mid-air, grabbed a pouch from her belt. Expertly shaking some Healing dust into her mouth, she blew it onto a big, white bird that stood staring at her in shock. Her aim was to just scare the bird but, of course, the Healing dust, not finding any injury, did nothing but rest on its feathers. The bird was far from relaxed, studying his now glittering chest feathers and remembering how one awful day he accidentally bumped into a skunk. Not wishing to experience a repeat of the awful odour the creature left behind, he urgently asked, "Honey, what was that you just blew over me!? I'm not going to stink for days 'till I'm sick to my stomach, am I?"

Cecee was shocked the bird could speak and replied with a tremble in her voice, "I...I... don't think it will, err, hurt you."

"You don't think... *think*... no, you have to be *sure*! I'm covered in glitter and I'll be a laughing stock. How do I get it off?"

Cecee hovered above the bird and with a wave of her hand, sent the dust shooting back into her pouch before landing next to him. The bird's lower beak dropped.

"Wow!" he said, while holding out his wing, expecting a hand shake. When Cecee didn't respond, he looked at the being in front of him and, folding back his wing, introduced himself.

"My name is Johnny and I live here. Where do *you* come from? *What* kind of bird *are you*?"

Before introducing herself, Cecee looked all around, disappointed to find only sand and sea.

"My name is Cecee. I can't dehydrate and I need to eat. Are there any fruit bushes with berries nearby? I can't see any!"

"De-hy-dr-ate? What does *that* mean?"

"It means I am thirsty and hungry for anything with juice in it."

"Oh, you're hungry! No prob. Honey, I know a great fish place along the beach. It's a Human eating nest with 'All You Can Eat' written right on the door. I'm sure they have berries. You'll have to put on a bit of a show but hey, nothing is free in this World. Fly up onto my back... come on, hop on!"

Cecee thought about this for a second. She could fall from him and her wings were not yet strong enough for her to fly well. But she was hungry and thirsty, so on she climbed and off they flew. Landing safely outside a large, eating area, Cecee noticed something odd – Humans were throwing something into the air.

"What are they doing?" she asked, puzzled.

"They're throwing peanuts for us to catch. It seems to amuse them."

"Peanuts?"

"Yeah, peanuts. Watch my friend Ace, the bird with the grey stripe on his wing. He can catch three peanuts in one swoop!"

Ace soared high into the sky, catching three peanuts cleanly from the air, and then swooped down to land next to his friend. Noticing the company, he announced himself in one breath.

"Hi little bird, the name's Ace, how's it goin'? Have a peanut, you look half starved!"

He dropped two peanuts and shelled the third in a split second, offering it to Cecee.

As hungry as she was, she made no movement to take it. Ace placed it on the sand.

"Come on, don't be shy – eat!"

"I am very grateful, umm… Ace, but I don't eat peanuts."

"Then, little bird, what do you eat?"

"Oh, berries, especially blackberries, they are my favourite. And I like honey – bees give me some when they have extra. Oh, and some rosehip tea would be nice… do you have a chef?"

Ace laughed. "*A chef?*"

"Yes, do you have an elf who cooks for you?"

"I know what a chef is but, little bird, you have *got* to be joking! An elf chef, where have you been? As for rosehip tea, I can personally guarantee we have never

60

heard of it... but berries... well, there we may be able to help you, although it could be difficult... Humans never throw any sweet things into the air, that's for sure. Okay, let me see what I can do."

Flying to the roof of the restaurant, Ace noticed a Human child with a bowl of ice cream and blackberries. 'Hmmm, perfect. Distract the kid and grab some berries... easy as fishing from the sea,' he thought. Moving a little closer, he flew down and perched on the railing by the table. Turning his head left then right, he checked for possible escape routes. Taking a long, deep breath, he flew in and grabbed the berries from the top of the ice cream, flying away in one big swoop. 'What a rush! Brilliant, even if I say so myself!' thought Ace with pride. He landed next to Cecee and said, "There you go, little bird, blackberries with a bit of ice cream on the side. Better eat it fast or the ice cream will melt and you'll miss the best part!"

Enjoying this new, unusual food called 'ice cream', Cecee gazed sleepily at the sea. The treat had been a new experience and she thought to tell Cameron about it when she returned home. Home... how she wished she was there right now. She thought about telling her new friends the urgency of her situation. Could they help and would it be wise to tell them exactly who she was? She decided it was best to say nothing, but now was a good time to find out a few things.

"Johnny, birds can't talk where I come from. Where am I, exactly?"

"You're in 'America' honey, Los Angeles, California to be precise, and we Americans know and can do *everything*!" he answered, while proudly puffing out his chest feathers.

"Oh I see, well, can you tell me if Los Angeles is far from Seven Oaks Woods?"

"Err… ah… let me think…erm, yeah, I think so…"

The vague response troubled Cecee. The bird's World looked promising but then seemed uncertain, while her World was full of woods, flowers and magic – it was all she knew and her only comforting thought. With no Wand and only Healing dust, she wondered if she would ever return home. Even more, had Seven Oaks Woods survived the storm? Ace flew off to investigate further food options while Cecee breathed in the crisp smell of the sea to help her think. As she pondered her problems, she noticed out at sea, Humans riding the waves on coloured planks of wood and, wanting to understand more about her new surroundings, asked Johnny what they were doing.

"They're surfing – you don't know much about Humans do you, Cecee?"

"No, not really, but in the future… maybe it will be one of my duties to protect one."

"Honey, protect a Human, you have *got* to be kidding me! Humans get into all *sorts* of trouble!"

"Umm… no, Johnny, I think th…"

Johnny ruffled his feathers in disgust, interrupting Cecee.

"Personally, I think they're beyond it, always disturbing the balance, quick to kill anything they don't like or understand. Take bees for instance. When are Humans going to realize that they won't get stung if they stop trying to shoo them away. If they lay on the ground and just stayed there, the bees will go on their merry way. A swarm is only trying to find a home to live in…

But oh no, they have to kill them with a disgusting smelling spray. Tut, so cruel, too. Don't they realize that if the bee population is wiped out, then they, Humans that is, will only exist for another six years at a stretch? I really don't get them at all."

Ace returned, and as he landed, Johnny hopped up to him.

"Ace, we have a bigger problem with Cecee than finding food!"

"What do you mean, and *why* are we whispering?"

"Ace, just *listen* for once... I'm not sure she knows the ways of life here... she *can't* stay."

"Ah man... she is so cute though...why not"

"This isn't her World. She needs to be somewhere she knows, where she can find the food she likes. If she is closer to something like her World, she may be able to find someone to help."

Ace shrugged.

"Don't worry, we'll work something out later. Right now, I need some backup. There's a fresh fruit delivery going on at the Human eating nest, all kinds of berries in containers. But just as I was working out a plan to get some, they put lids on top! Now it will take two of us to pull them off."

Johnny worried about leaving his new friend alone, but she needed to eat.

"Cecee, I have to help Ace. Will you be alright alone?"

"Yes, I'll be fine, thank you."

"We won't be long. Hide under this dried kelp and don't move."

"Johnny, don't worry," replied a slightly nervous Cecee.

Cecee sat cross legged and draped the kelp over her head like a cape. With her chin resting in her hands, she studied ladybirds on the seaweed nearby, but a disturbance turned her interest to the shoreline. Commotion came from Human teenagers who seemed upset about something. Aware that some of them might be 'Seers', she cautiously left her hiding place to explore. The teenagers shouted to one another, "Dude, his surfboard knocked him out!"

"Somebody get help!" One cried.

"Call 911!"

"Does anyone here know C.P.R?"

Another came running up to the scene carrying his surf board, wet sand flicking from his heels. He fell to his knees beside his friend.

"Gnarly wipe out... hey... dude... Rory, you okay man?"

He shook his friend, but there was no response.

"Someone help! My friend isn't breathing!" the boy shouted.

Cecee flew close to see the boy's friend lying on the sand, his breathing very shallow. She took some Healing dust from her pouch and sprinkled it over the injured boy, but at that exact moment the other teenagers saw her.

"Man, did you see *that*?"

"Yeah, dude, what *was* that thing?"

"There it is again!"

"Catch it!"

Cecee panicked. 'Great Wizards, they *all* saw me!' Natural reaction made her reach back for her Wand, only to be reminded again that she had foolishly left it at her mother's. She searched her belt for Illusion dust, while a small boy tried to catch her in a net attached to a long twig. She found some! Expertly grabbing the pouch, she tossed the dust into the air creating hundreds of imitation fairies which appeared all around. But the boy with the net wasn't fooled by Cecee's effort to confuse. He saw her as the only real fairy and would not give up the chase. It was then her belt loosened and the golden pouch holding the Rowan Seed inside fell away. Down it went into the sand, and as she watched petrified, a short, swift *'Whooosh'* came from nowhere. On the sand, trapped inside the net, she watched helplessly as her Illusion fairies dispersed into glitter and finally disappeared. Teenagers ran up and peered down at her.

"Come and see *this*!" some called out.

"Wow!" one girl shouted.

"It's beautiful," said another.

The young boy who had trapped Cecee stared at her.

"Dude, I can't *wait* to bring this to 'Show and Tell' at school tomorrow!"

Cecee desperately looked around for an escape, luckily finding the main part of her Illusion dust pouch trapped inside the net with her. Quickly, she managed to firmly grab it. She must drink it down in an effort to change its powers to Forget Dust. Pulling the pouch open, she drank some of the strange, liquid-like dust and concentrated on something she had only witnessed older fairies do. Then, with the biggest breath she could manage, she blew it out, aiming it full blast into the peering faces. Success! All froze, giving her exactly five seconds to scramble out from under the net, grab the golden pouch and fly. One, two, three, four, five… All too soon, the teenagers came out of their frozen state, but any memory of the fairy had been erased and she was able to hover above them invisibly as they continued with their activities. But the boy with the net who had trapped her was a true 'Seer' and not so easily fooled. His name was Tyler, aged about thirteen and he remembered everything. Cecee hovered in mid-air listening as Tyler rambled on to the boy who had been injured.

"Dude, you must have been knocked out, I swear you weren't breathing! Glitter shot around you and man, don't laugh… it looked like…"

"It looked like what?"

"It looked like a fairy flew around you and did something to you with glitter stuff!"

"*Ha, ha! Dude! A what?*" the boy laughingly answered.

"I know… *totally radical*! You should have seen it! I caught it with my net but it got away, a small but strong little thing. Awesome!"

But the boy stared at his friend.

"Ha, ha, Tyler, stop joking with me. Man, have *you* lost the plot!"

Tyler's older brother, Randy, ran up to him.

"Stop telling lies about stuff like that, Tyler! I thought you had a chance to be a solid dude. Well, as a younger bro. anyway, but you are definitely losing it. You're embarrassing, and if you don't shut up, I'll never take you surfing again!"

Slapping Tyler on the back of the head, he walked away, leaving his brother shrugging his shoulders. Cecee had heard enough and decided to fly back to her hiding place under the seaweed. Randy walked with his friends, laughing at his brother's story, but then stole back to sneak another look at his younger brother. This wasn't the first time Tyler had said strange things like this. Perhaps there really was something? But no, it couldn't be… elves, now even fairies? He shut it out of his mind, retrieved his surfboard from the sand and swam out into the ocean to catch the next wave.

Tyler, however, didn't want to surf with Randy and his stupid friends, well, not at that moment, anyway. He may be younger, but *they* needed the practice. He could already surf better than any of them. No, he just wanted to take in the wonder of what had just happened. He stared fascinated while pretending to make shapes in the sand and watched Cecee settle down under the kelp. He recalled a day last year… he'd seen something unusual when camping in the woods with his family. He actually witnessed what looked like an elf stealing two empty glass jars, and in broad daylight! He had tried to tell Randy about that too, but his brother, as usual, thought he was lying. Tyler studied Cecee from a distance. 'What a great thing it would have been if she hadn't escaped my net,' he thought. 'I could have taken her to school… but then, what would have been the point? After they sprinkle that glittery stuff, no one else can see them.' So Tyler decided that any future encounters would be best kept *entirely* to himself.

Cecee, now settled, watched Johnny and Ace land awkwardly with her berries.

"Anything happen while we were away?" asked Johnny.

Knowing they would never understand, she answered, while searching her belt, "No, nothing at all."

She peeked into the golden pouch. '*Phew!* The Seed is safe and still glowing!' she thought to herself. Tying her vine belt extra tight, she was certain of one thing. She must get out of the open as soon as possible as, clearly, it was far too dangerous.

***

A strong wind whistled through Seven Oaks Woods, taking Tizzy far away from the Royal Court. Soon she found herself deep in the woods and, seeing an empty bird's nest, flopped inside, exhausted. She lay back and watched dark rain clouds swiftly moving by, uncovering a full silvery Moon close to which flickered and winked a single star. While she looked on thinking about the Universe and its many wonders, a low, steady hoot echoed through the woods. Her eyes searched the trees and there, sitting on a bare branch at the very top of a nearby oak, she saw the dark outline of an owl. She gazed at it for a while, certain it was staring back at her and mumbled under her breath, "What are you looking at? This is my nest now, go away and leave me alone!"

Her face hidden behind her hands, she tried to sleep, but it didn't take her long to weaken and take another look at the owl. She peeped through her fingers, catching him turning his head around in what seemed a full circle. 'Why is he staying there?' she wondered. In the light of the Moon, she studied the owl's hypnotic eyes, while her own began to feel strangely heavy and, unable to fight the need for sleep, she soon drifted off.

Early morning light arrived and to Tizzy's surprise, the first thing she saw was the owl still staring down at her. But then, quite suddenly, it slowly blinked just the once, spread its wings and flew away.

Tizzy had to find food and water. She was hungry and wasn't feeling well. Flying deeper into the woods, she blamed yesterday's excitement for how she felt. 'I won't go back home,' she thought. 'I'm tired of all the rules and regulations *and* taking the blame for *everything*! As soon as I've had something to eat and drink, I'm sure I will feel much better.'

Flying to a crab-apple tree, she positioned herself on an upper branch and tried to sit and eat. After a few bites, she thought she heard the sound of singing floating up from the ground. She looked down to see a fairy picking one by one the petals of a daisy as she sang such a mournful song.

"He loves me, he loves me not. He loves me, he loves me not…"

Tizzy stared down while the fairy continued until only one petal was left and then, pulling off the last, she moaned, *"Oh, he loves me not!"*

Tizzy flew down closer and came to rest on a fern. Longing for a new friend, she spoke.

"Hello," but the fairy did not reply. Tizzy repeated her greeting, a little louder this time.

"Hello!"

The startled fairy instantly hovered in the air, grabbing a pouch from her belt and, as quick as a flash, Warning dust shot towards Tizzy.

"Who are yer, and why are yer spyin' on me?" the fairy snapped.

"I'm not spying!" replied Tizzy, while darting out of the way of the oncoming glitter. "I just thought you'd *like* some company."

"May be I do, maybe I don't. What do *you* want?"

"Nothing."

The fairy's eyes quickly studied Tizzy, deciding that she was not a typical fairy of the woods. Oh no, this one had a look of wealth and good breeding, and the sound of her voice... soft, like the gentle sound of summer rain. She noticed an impressive looking back tube that clearly must contain a Wand and thought a few cleverly asked questions might drop this pretty fairy's guard. So settling down, she spoke in her best possible accent.

"Me name's Violet, and whommm might you be?"

"My name is Tizzy and I come fr..."

"Well," interrupted Violet, "we look a bit fancy for these parts, don't we? Look at you in them posh leafy clothes and as for them wings, well, I never did!"

Beside Violet was a glass jar filled with honey into which she plunged a finger, pulled it out and, without much grace, licked off the sweet, sticky substance.

"Would yer like some 'oney?" she asked.

Tizzy was hungry.

"Yes please, I'd love some," she replied, gratefully.

Violet stretched out and picked a leaf from a bush. Expertly rolling it into a small cone, she scooped out some honey and offered it to Tizzy.

"So tell me about yerself, Tizzy. Where do yer come from and wot's a young fairy like you doin' in these woods all by 'erself? Can't say as I've seen yer in these parts before and where did yer pinch that dress from? Those wings 'ave *gotta* go if you're staying around 'ere with the likes of me love, far too noticeable by the King's elves when you go stealin'. You'll get caught

71

easy peasy! Oh, yer don't 'ave to put on any fancy airs and graces with me, love. We all 'ave secrets. You can tell me everyfing, it won't leave me lips."

Enjoying the honey, Tizzy told Violet everything from the start of the storm up to where they just met, but for reasons not quite clear even to herself, she held back the fact she was a Royal Princess. Violet, a wood-wise fairy, listened, speechless. Even though Tizzy did not tell her the whole truth, it quickly became clear to her who her new-found companion really was.

"Do you 'ave anywhere to stay tonite, love?"

"I hadn't thought about that yet, but… no," answered Tizzy.

"Well, I fink yer should come and stay wiv me at me 'ome," replied Violet, with a broad, friendly smile.

How Tizzy loved that word 'home', quickly realizing how deeply she missed her own.

***

The elderly fairy Florie rushed back as quickly as she could to her little home in the woods, where she gathered more dried herbs. Clown's Woundwort to stop any internal bleeding. Cowslip to take away any burn. Viper's Bugloss to soothe inflammation. Two parts St John's Wort added to one part Arnica for shock. Blackberry juice to rehydrate and finally Fleur-de-Lys with honey, to sweeten the potion's bitter taste. 'There, I now have nearly all I need', she thought to herself, very satisfied with her efforts. But still she must find that special ingredient, the liquid that would complete the potion but found only in a deep, challenging cave quite far away. She was old and weak. Could she find a way to succeed? Even if she could, she would have to overcome yet another struggle... how to get to Tizzy in time before the King and Queen realized their daughter was gravely ill. She must give Tizzy the potion to drink before it was too late and the King and Queen's youngest daughter would be no more!

CHAPTER THREE

A SOUVENIR, DID ANYONE CARE AND THE JOURNEY BEGINS

Far away from Seven Oaks Woods, Cecee sat on a beach in California. Considering her new friends, she thought about all the secrets and worries she could not share with them.

"Johnny, are there wooded areas in America, or is it all just sand and sea?" she innocently asked.

"No, it isn't all sand and sea. There are beautiful woodlands up north – it's much cooler there – weather's different," replied Johnny.

"Is it far from here?"

"No – a flight along the shoreline and only takes about two to four hours, depending on the wind. What's the matter, honey?" Johnny asked Cecee, noticing her mind seemed elsewhere.

"Johnny, I miss my family and home. If I could at least get to some woods where fairies live, I would feel a lot better."

"Fairies... err... oh yeah, sure!" He nudged Ace. "We *have* fairies there, right, Ace?"

"Fairies, you mean creatures like you, Cecee? Oh yeah... we see them aaaaaaall the time!"

"Johnny, I must go there. They'll help me find my way home."

Holding out his wing to test the wind direction, Johnny agreed.

"Let's finish up here and we'll be off. I must admit, the change of air will do us all good. What do you think, Ace?"

Ace, always ready to do whatever, especially if it involved San Francisco where his favourite fish could be found, answered without hesitation, "Sure man, with you all the way."

It was well into late afternoon when they set off along the shore. To their left, the setting Sun turned the sky's low, wispy clouds into fire, while to their right, dark grey, sweeping cliffs melted like magical mist into the sea. On and on they flew, darkness beginning to descend, when suddenly they came upon a sight looming in front of them which to Cecee, seemed rather strange.

Johnny shouted excitedly, "This is the Golden Gate Bridge, Cecee. We're now in San Francisco!" He looked up at the sky, "It's getting very dark and we should eat. We can rest for the night then start fresh in the morning."

An early morning breeze blew into San Francisco Bay, bringing with it the cutting edge of winter. Although not yet cold enough for Cecee to feel anything, the morning's biting wind felt by the two shivering birds, was a sharp reminder of the oncoming season. All three were now wide awake and Cecee eagerly flew around to flex her wings, happy to find they had completely recovered from the fall.

"Okay, is everyone ready?" she asked.

"Yep, we're ready," replied Johnny.

Off they flew towards the hills, the view below them changing almost by magic. Towering pine trees, the tops of which had already been dusted with a light snow, stretched up towards them. Johnny shouted with pride, "These are the Redwoods!"

Cecee frowned, wondering why things here were named a different colour to what they actually looked and thought to herself, 'Golden Gate Bridge isn't gold, and now Redwoods that look green!' The three flew lower, and at last landed. The trees seemed different from home, but the smell was the same, a smell she had missed so much. She took a deep breath, filling her lungs with the woodland air.

"Johnny, Ace, you can leave me now, but if you ever need me, call me by thinking hard. It takes great patience and concentration, but I promise it works. It's a thing called 'sympathetic vibration'."

The two birds looked at each other with a puzzled frown. Ace politely smiled back at her, not having the foggiest idea *what* she was talking about. He shrugged his wings, told her to take care and flew up into the sky, shortly followed by Johnny who wished Cecee farewell. She watched them fly away in the direction of the coast. The birds now out of view, a single white feather from Ace floated gently down, but before it came to rest, Cecee caught it and tucked it into her hair as a souvenir.

***

As the Moon began to climb into the night sky, an odd, dim light flickered through the trees in Seven Oaks Woods. A fog crept down and around the tall oaks, making it difficult for Violet and Tizzy to find their way. As they flew deeper, Tizzy felt afraid while following Violet, but darkness was closing in fast and the fear of spending another night out alone, made her stay very close to her new friend. Flying through the Moon's misty shadows, they made their way, carefully weaving through the trees when Tizzy heard a scuttling noise in a hedgerow and flew a little lower, Violet following close behind.

"Be careful, Tizzy… Wot's the matter, 'ave you seen somethin'?"

"I heard something."

"Tizzy, look out, it could be the 'Twiggy Men'! Stay close to me love, and I'll see wot it is!"

Violet swooped down close to the ground, relieved to find the scuttling noise was no more than hedgehogs running through the undergrowth. Tizzy, following Violet, could also clearly see them.

"My, they look anxious about something, Violet."

"Yeah love. Todd Toady and Rush 'ave enslaved 'em all. Those poor 'edgehogs are probably on a secret job for 'em right now! Rush is a huge elf who 'ates 'em. Treats 'em all as bad as anyfing. Mark my words, Tizzy, tread carefully around that nasty elf, 'e ain't good."

"Why does he hate hedgehogs?"

"Somethin' about their spines 'aving 'urt him when he was a young'n. Even invented special shoes for protection and sells 'em to others at a huge profit. Always trying to make a quick turn that one, I tell yer!"

"What about Todd?"

"Todd does nothin' but steal from bees. Them two are always up to no good! Okay, we're almost there. It ain't much, but at least it's ''ome-sweet-'ome'."

The two approached a huge hole at the bottom of the stump of an old elm tree and even in the dark, Tizzy could see that on the top, Violet had grown a small garden of moss and tumbling, flowering vines. Violet hovered by the entrance.

"Tizzy, please come in and make yerself at 'ome."

But Tizzy could see two hedgehogs.

"Violet, I thought all the hedgehogs were enslaved by Rush?"

"Ummm, most are," replied Violet, "but Todd gave these to me in payment for a favour I did 'im a long time ago. These two are me friends, Tizzy. That's Porky, 'cos he's so fat, and here's Pine, 'cos he has more spines than I've ever seen on any 'edgehog! The pair protect me at night, and knowing I would never 'urt 'em, they are very loyal to me."

"How do they protect you?" Tizzy asked, fascinated.

"Well, as yer know, they roll into a ball when they sleep to protect themselves against predators, so all they really 'ave to do is sleep in front of me door – nothin' would dare try to get past 'em – their spines would tear anyone or anyfing to shreds!" Violet tested the tip of a spine with her fingertip.

78

"Ouch!"

She looked back at Tizzy while sucking her finger. Remembering her manners, she quickly removed it and showed Tizzy.

"Cor, look at that! See wot I mean, love? Their spines are fearsome. Anyway, it's comfortin' to know I'm safe at night."

Tizzy entered Violet's home. Inside was large and tunnelled underground, making her home feel more spacious than at first appeared. Tizzy's attention was quickly drawn to a pair of jars filled with fireflies, tucked into the hollow roots of the old tree stump.

Violet explained, "It's always dark in 'ere and the fireflies keep me place lit all the time."

Tizzy's eyes explored the room further, resting upon a quilt made of silk, trimmed with rose petals and, testing its softness, seemed to be stuffed with the soft feathers of perhaps a swan. It lay upon Violet's bed looking so inviting, for a moment making Tizzy recall the quilt that lay upon her mother's bed and under which she snuggled at times when she felt the need for comfort. Dried flowers hung upside down and rose stems stood floor to ceiling, their thorns blunted and used as hooks from which hung three dresses.

"Violet, did you make these lovely dresses?" Tizzy asked.

"Yes love."

Touching the soft, silky petals on one, Tizzy admired Violet's talent.

"You can 'ave that one, love," Violet offered.

Tizzy gasped. "Violet, it's gorgeous, but I couldn't possibly take this dress. It must have taken you *ages* to make."

"You need somethin' to change into. Your leafy dress, well, to be 'onest, it's a bit worn."

Tizzy looked down at herself. She hadn't noticed that her dress had torn on something.

"Alright, thank you, Violet, this is very kind of you and I will never forget it."

"Don't worry love, the fairies in the woods 'ave to look after each uver! Now, I'm gonna get another quilt from me friend Rosie, who lives in the next tree over, so make yerself comfy. I won't be long."

While Violet was gone, Tizzy looked around a little more. Her new friend had quite a home – nuts and berries were dried and stored, jars of herbs were arranged all around and seeds were drying to make dyes for her dresses. There were pouches on a shelf, each labelled differently – 'Forget', 'Love', 'Healing' and 'Truth' dust. Picking up a pouch and looking closer, Tizzy mused, 'Hmm, I wonder how Violet has Truth dust in her home… I've heard about this from father's soldiers… very expensive.' A shiver shot down her spine as she noticed a strange looking dust pouch altogether. Picking it up very carefully, she saw boldly written on the front in golden silk the word 'WIZARD,' under which was the letter 'P'. She heard a rustle outside – it was Violet returning! Quickly, Tizzy replaced the Truth dust on the shelf but with no time left, she hid the Wizard pouch in the part of her belt that tucked underneath her wing. Violet entered with another quilt and two more jars of fireflies. Tizzy felt another chill –

was it too much excitement, perhaps? Suddenly, she began to feel unwell – maybe she was over-tired.

"Okay with everything, love?" Violet asked cheerfully.

"Yes, thank you, Violet, I couldn't ask for a better place to stay."

"Well, I think we should make up this extra bed and settle down. After all, it 'as bin quite a day!"

Violet offered Tizzy warm tea and while Tizzy refreshed herself with the enjoyable brew, she noticed an odd looking bowl containing a lot more honey.

"What sort of bowl is that, Violet? I've never seen a bowl that big before."

"It's a coconut shell – comes from a distant country."

"How did you get it?" asked a curious Tizzy.

"Connections," Violet answered, with her nose in the air. "Comes from a place called Hawaii, and it's supposed to be beautiful there." She sighed. "I'm gonna' see it one day with an elf friend of mine. We're gonna' get married and travel the World togever. If only the daisy petals would co-operate and tell me he loves me, but each time I count 'em, they tell me he don't and that worries me no end."

Lying in bed, Tizzy had the strangest feeling – was she actually feeling cold? She thought about the Wizard dust and recalled the events of the day just past. But she couldn't help fearing for poor Violet as it was rumoured counting daisy petals could bring very bad luck. Violet rested in her bed puzzled and alarmed, for it suddenly occurred to her that instead of gaining information from Tizzy, she had told a very young and complete stranger some of her *own* secrets. Thinking a little more, she realized there was something about the young one that seemed so open, honest and vulnerable.

Tizzy tried her hardest but could not sleep. The bed, though comfortable, was strange to her.

"Violet, are you still awake?" she whispered.

"Yes, love, are you okay?"

"What is his name, this elf who you are in love with?"

"His name is Elm and he's a soldier, not one of the King's best, mind you. He doesn't 'ave a fancy uniform and 'as 'ad no training in the secret Middlesborough place, but at least 'e's brave, nonetheless."

Tizzy thought her life so unfair. Everyone seemed to know more than she, especially about Middlesborough, but she didn't want Violet to know that she knew nothing about the mysterious place. So, dismissed any idea of talking to Violet further about it and continued to ask about Elm.

"How did you meet him?" she asked.

"In me place, Two Sevens Inn. I run a bar there and make mead."

"What is mead?"

"It's 'oney wine wot I sell for fairy dust. There's also the craft items I make and sell. It's a living, Tizzy, it's a living. Well, anyway, Elm came in one night, said 'e'd 'eard about the mead and wanted to taste some. As soon as I saw 'im, I was in love which, I 'ave to say, certainly ain't like me. I usually stay away from any attention because Rosie, who I said lives next door, *must* stay low. She's cursed by... oh...err..."

Violet almost got carried away as she chatted on but remembered she had secrets that must never be told.

"Well, anyway," she continued with a little more caution, "Elm and me saw each other reglar like and we used to talk the nite away. Then, late one nite, 'e made a surprise visit to tell me that 'e 'ad to go on a secret job wiv the King's elves, and they would be looking for someone. I dunno who love… he said he would write but no letter 'as come yet, 'aven't seen any in days."

Instantly, Tizzy knew where Violet's soldier friend had gone – news around the Royal Court travelled like wildfire. It was clear now that he had joined the search party and gone on the dangerous mission to find Cecee, and with that disturbing knowledge, Tizzy thought it best to change the subject so asked, "What do you do with all your fairy dust?"

"Oh, I sell it to whoever wants it and it all works out very well for me."

"Violet… I notice you have Truth dust, but you must know it's top secret and only meant for the King's soldiers. I heard it was difficult to get, and very expensive, so how did *you* get it?"

"Look, love, I don't mean to sound rude, but 'ow I get it is my business. It protects me from dangerous fairies and elves. Understand, Tizzy, that when you're out 'ere in the open and not under the shelter of the Royal Court, you must 'ave protection. How I get the dust ain't important. I 'ave it and that's all that matters."

Violet suddenly thought to herself, 'now I've done it! I've let slip I know where this young fairy lives!'

Tizzy thought deeply, now beginning to wonder if she could really trust Violet. She hadn't told her that she was a Royal, so how did she know? The Wizard dust bothered her too, so she decided to keep it under her wing hoping Violet wouldn't notice it had gone missing. However, Violet didn't hesitate to change the subject, kicking herself for slipping-up about the Royal Court…

"Forget dust is important too, Tizzy. Among uver fings, it protects us from the Humans, ha, ha, and aren't they the biggest pests in the woods? Leaving mess behind, causing fires, chopping down trees, making more of those 'orrible Twiggy Men! We use some of their rubbish like this big see-through jar I 'ave 'ere."

Violet pointed to a jam jar resting by her bed.

"They are 'eavy and difficult to fly off wiv, but 'andy pandy!" she said, with a smile. She got up and with great caution, peeped outside. While she was looking, Tizzy asked, "Violet, what are Twiggy Men?"

"They are ghosts, ghosts of angry, bitter trees… very ugly and feared… the unfortunate result of usual Human greed!"

"Why?"

"When Humans chop down the trees to do whatever it is they do with 'em, they take just the main part and leave all the twigs be'ind which lie there rottin'. But on a full Moon, a change 'appens. The twigs mysteriously join togever and walk like the very people who took the trunk away. They come alive, very much alive! They make 'emselves tall and thin, or bent over and fat, twigs sticking out from their backs like big porcupines. The open sores all over 'em drip poisonous sap and they moan like an 'owling wind, or grunt like pigs and throw huge splinters at random from their long, twiggy fingers.

Slowly they creep along the ground leaving trails of sap be'ind to kill the tree roots."

"But why would they want to kill the trees?" asked Tizzy.

"Oh, their anger is a blind rage and their reasoning, well, a bit 'azy. I suppose they fink why should other trees live when they themselves 'ave been cut down? Maybe they fink that if they kill all the trees, Humans would not 'ave any reason to come into the woods. Tizzy, we need the trees – we take care of 'em and live in 'em and the Twiggy Men know it, which makes us a threat too. So, if they see us, they will kill us. I shouldn't 'ave to remind you that it was a full Moon last night. Luckily, they only live for three nights then fade away until the next full Moon when more are born. Urgghhh, they are 'orrible! Oh, and one more fing, they hate rain, so if it 'as been raining, it don't matter what phase the Moon is in, they won't appear. I 'ope you're not frightened by all this, Tizzy? We're in a dead tree stump so they won't bother us – we are safe and we must get some sleep. Daylight will soon be 'ere, so good night, sleep well."

Tizzy lay there thinking how protected she had been at Court. The woods outside her Royal Circle were so very different and so very dangerous! This much she had learned already. Her mind wandered to Cecee and how she was lost somewhere in these very woods, all alone. Did she know about Wizard dust, strange owls that follow you around, ghostly Twiggy Men, thieving elves, and was she trapped somewhere? If so, is she lucky enough to be with someone like Violet? With all these thoughts together with tiredness, Tizzy finally closed her eyes and fell fast asleep.

The next morning, Violet took Tizzy to help her at the Inn, later leaving her there while she fetched Rosie. On the way back, she and Rosie laughed while enjoying a joke, but returning to the Inn, Violet's laughter stopped when she spotted Tizzy. Violet had told her to remain inside and busy herself making acorn cups, insisting that on no account was she to go outside. But Tizzy felt a little better after last night's chill and had gone outside where she found some young woodfairies playing together. Joining in and laughing along with them, she showed them a special dance and one that Violet recognized as a dance taught only in Royal Circles. Concerned, she wondered how long it would take for the wood fairies to possibly guess where Tizzy came from.

"Rosie!" shouted Violet as she shooed away the woodfairies, "take Tizzy back inside the Inn! She is supposed to be making acorn cups… we have a busy day tomorrow."

Back inside, Tizzy felt depressed and tried to shake-off the feeling of missing her home. She realized how free she was there, safe to play and dance whenever she felt like it. Would she ever be able to find home again? Were her parents so angry with her that they had given up, was *anyone* looking for her, did anyone care? Tizzy's head was filled with so many unhappy thoughts, she began to deeply regret ever running away.

***

Deep in the Redwoods, Cecee had slept uncomfortably, her first night alone being uneasy. But now, fully awake, she knew she had to stay alert for the day in front of her. Pangs of hunger urged her to fly further into the thick, towering pine trees. Masses of bushes, heavily laden with fruit, sent out a smell arousing her appetite even more than usual, so she decided to eat before flying around to investigate. Tonight, she needed a comfortable place to rest and after eating, was determined to find one. It was a lovely day as a bright, early winter Sun blazed through the trees.

Flying in and out of the pines, a sudden flash of white caught her attention. It couldn't be the frost or early snow, but something quite different, darting from one spot to another. She wondered if it could possibly be the reflection of a Wand and, if so, whose – was he or she good or bad? Flying down to carefully land upon a fern, another flash caught her eye, this time coming from behind a huge tree trunk in front of her. Hiding in the long ferns, Cecee stared at the tree, watching a strange sight. Slowly, something began to move, a slender horn spiralling upwards, slowly appearing from behind the pine. More and more it emerged until fully visible, shining brightly and protruding from the forehead of a brilliant white Unicorn! As he moved from behind the tree, his sky blue mane rippled like the rolling waves of the sea. Though seemingly young, his body showed great strength – a magnificent male, but there was an unmistakable difference, for this Unicorn had been born with the most powerful wings! Cecee watched him in wonder as he stretched his wings as if to fly, but then folded them back and stood there making a sad, whimpering sound, not the sound she had expected from such a handsome, strong, bold looking creature. Cecee dared to fly nearer, but just at that moment, the Unicorn saw her and their eyes met. To Cecee's amazement, he simply lowered his head and said with a certain amount of surprise, "Hello...Oh...err...yes, hello!"

Cecee, somewhat puzzled by his manner, drew closer.

"Well, hello. What's your name?" she asked.

"My name is Fiero," answered the Unicorn, as he put his nose to the ground and sniffed around.

"Tut, the grass here is *not at all great!*" he added, with absolute disappointment in his tone.

"My name is Cecee. Are you okay?"

With no further reply from Fiero, other than further sniffing around for a tastier mouthful, she tried another approach.

"As you can see, I'm a fairy... I've never seen a *winged* Unicorn before! Where were you born?"

"Oh, I'm a special kind, and lost... well, sort of... it's all so different here"

"How did you get lost and what is different?"

"I don't really know. One minute I was standing with my mother, and the next, not. Strange really, all I can say is she met a friend and they talked and talked. My mother was too busy talking to notice me wandering off. I wanted to explore... I knew there was a forbidden pool not far from where we were... and yes, I know... we'd been warned never to drink the water, but I couldn't see the harm in just going to *look*. I found the pool and stared in, my reflection staring back and seeming to take on a life of its own... very weird! The reflection stayed as still as a rock, even when I shook my head! Well, that made me look deeper and yes, my nose touched the water. And before you ask, no, no one had ever really *explained* to me exactly how powerful the water was so, well, I just licked it off! When I looked up from the pool, *everything* around me was different ..."

Cecee had no idea where this magical water was – she had never seen or heard of it. "What exactly is so different? Please explain." she replied.

"Well, the trees look a bit funny around here and the sky is blue! Above all… only one Sun, so where's the other?!"

Cecee had no answer and thought to herself, 'there is only ever *one* Sun. What does he mean about the sky being blue, what other colour could it be? Maybe he comes from a place where it always rains and the sky is white or grey all the time. No, he can fly… he must know that the sky is blue once you get beyond the clouds.' Stroking his nose to comfort him, she told him about the events that had brought her to this same place.

"So you see, Fiero, I'm also lost and trying to find my way home. Just as you are."

"What is the name of your land?" Fiero asked.

"I come from a place called 'England', and I was born in Seven Oaks Woods," answered a proud Cecee.

Fiero lowered his head. "I come from Middlesborough," he replied.

"Do you mean *Middlesbrough, England?*" Cecee asked.

"No… just Middlesborough,"

"Where?" asked Cecee, with a puzzled frown.

"Oh, you know, Wizards, trolls, reeeeeeeally dangerous fairies, scary dragons… that kind of place…"

Cecee sat down and thought. Her father had mentioned Middlesborough many times… could it be the same? She tried to comfort her new friend.

"Fiero, are you hungry?" she asked.

"Yes, very. I'm always hungry."

"Let's find some food... maybe after we've eaten, we can come up with a solution to our problems."

"Cecee, I have one more thing to tell you."

"What's that, Fiero?"

"My mother is always with me – she doesn't let me go *anywhere* by myself."

"Doesn't let you go anywhere by yourself! Why ever not?"

"It's our custom when found alone, we will be owned by the very first fairy, elf, Wizard or dragon who finds us. Whoever that may be could give us either a very good or very, very bad life! So you see, you in fact now own me, so from now on, I am your responsibility and, I must say, I'm rather pleased it's you who found me. You must keep the special horn on my head sprinkled with fairy dust because it's a bit hard to do myself. Any kind of fairy dust will do, it is only the sparkle we need which goes straight into our blood. You must do it once a month or I'll die!"

Cecee gasped. "But when was the last time you had it done? I am nearly out of dust!"

"Well, luckily, I was topped up yesterday by my mother's owner. We have some time to go, but we will have to find some more eventually. Oh, but it's not all one way. I can be of great help to you, you know. I have powers that can make me appear in one place and then, quick as a flash, appear in another altogether."

He demonstrated this by flashing in an instant from one tree to the next, but being a little too eager, stumbled upon landing and almost crashed headlong into a tree. In spite of this, he trotted proudly back to her.

"I know, it's not as good as it could be but with practice, it'll get a lot better! Anyway, I think you need me. I noticed that you don't have a Wand... dangerous, very dangerous!"

"Fiero, I will be proud to have you as my friend, and I promise I will take good care of you, but I can't *own* you."

"No, Cecee, Unicorns *must* be *owned* – our very survival depends on it!"

"Okay Fiero, whatever makes you comfortable. Come on I'm hungry, and I know you are."

The two wandered around, finding a clearing with lots of luscious, fresh grass. Fiero began to graze, while nearby bushes offered plenty of berries for Cecee. After eating, they rested next to a nearby stream. Cecee brought out the golden Seed pouch from her belt to check all was well. Fiero watched fascinated, seeing for the first time the magical object.

"Is that *the* Seed?" he asked, in awe.

Cecee glanced at him and hurriedly tucked away the Seed.

"What?" she replied, astonished.

"That," he said, "is that the Fairy Rowan Seed?"

"You *know* about this Seed?"

"Yes, of course," replied Fiero.

"Fiero, I honestly don't know what it is called but I think it is vital that this Seed is planted on the Thirty First of December."

"Yes, I know, Cecee, and the fact that you have it tells me you are the eldest daughter of a King, chosen to plant the Seed because your seventeenth birthday is near and falls in a leap year… every reason why I should stay with you."

Cecee stared at him.

"Yes, Fiero, I have just had my birthday, but how do you know about the Seed? It's a secret thing!"

"You'll learn that Unicorns from Middlesborough know about most things that go on in this World of yours."

"But I thought you were lost."

"I am. In spite of the fact I know everything that goes on here, I've never actually *been* here before. Now, if I could find out exactly where we are…?"

Fiero looked at her, waiting for an answer.

"All I have learned so far, Fiero, is that we are in the northern part of California, I mean, San Francisco… actually… to be honest… I'm not sure anymore!" answered a bewildered Cecee.

"Well, don't worry, you've got me. The Seed must be planted as, apart from anything else, the Wizards of Middlesborough Island will be waiting for next year's Wand and Sceptre collection. Once the Seed has fully grown, they'll make these from the Rowan tree's magical branches."

Cecee sat down heavily. Fiero quite definitely knew much more than she.

"Fiero, my parent's warnings were firm. Should I be worried about what may happen if I don't do everything I should?"

"Keep the Seed in the dark, and we'll find a way to get you home. Don't worry about anything, I'm here to look after you."

Cecee retied the pouch onto her belt.

"Fiero, do you know what'll happen if I don't plant the Seed and do you realize, I don't know where to plant it! What if I put it in the wrong place?"

Fiero had heard rumours regarding the consequences of failing this vital duty and shuddered at the thought.

"The planting place has got to be somewhere near your home, Cecee. I promise I will get you back where you will find out more. Fact is, the task *must* be completed."

But the truth was, Fiero silently worried that he was promising far too much. He was lost in Cecee's World with all its strange, unfamiliar surroundings. Would he really be clever enough to keep his word and did he know as much as he claimed? Well, he knew this much, their journey was just beginning and, he hoped, above all, it would end safely for both.

CHAPTER FOUR

HAWAII, DEEP SLEEP AND RUTHLESS ELVES

Who could ever forget that terrible day when, while practicing for battle, Prince Hawthorn of Dean was accidentally stabbed through the heart with a sharp, rose-thorn dagger. On that very day, Prince Ferny swore he would invent something to protect soldiers from such horrible mishaps and quickly set about making a special vest. After countless trials with silk worm thread, he soon realized he needed something much stronger so thought he would find Willow to seek advice and guidance. Willow's expertise with spiders was invaluable and he knew the thread from these creatures would be strong and reliable. Ferny and Willow spent hours training spiders to make long, straight threads and, finally managing to successfully remove the sticky substance, took the thread to Fairy Weavers who produced a tough, strong, reliable fabric they made into vests. Although these could thwart an attack from any weapon, they had overlooked one thing – the vests were not a good barrier against the cold wind. Remik had given one to Tross the previous night and, this very morning, a crisp breeze blew, waking Tross with a start. He stretched and moaned, his body aching whenever he moved. He was strong, but couldn't help envying the fact that female fairies hardly ever felt the cold. As he flexed his muscles, he heard Remik's voice sounding through the woods.

"We must go to the underground tunnels and search there. We have a map which master builder Motley has given us."

Unfolding the map, he spread it over the ground.

"We are here," he said, pointing a small twig at an X on the map, "and the tunnels go off towards the lake and … well, its best if Motley explains."

An impressive looking elf stepped up and stood beside Remik. He wore large eyeglasses cleverly made from the bottoms of Human soda bottles and squinted hard through them as he introduced himself.

"Hello, my name is Motley. Some know me as 'The Mole'. I…"

A rude interruption was suddenly heard from an elf standing to the left of them. "Ask yourselves a question, where did he get that nickname from? I can assure you it wasn't given to him for digging any tunnel. You should *all* know that, like a real mole, he couldn't see a thing when he built the tunnels, and he can't see a thing even now."

Motley turned to see a blurred vision of a scruffy elf leaning against a tree with his arms folded.

"I go on sense and smell and I built all the tunnels in these woods!" answered an offended Motley, while adjusting his eyeglasses for a clearer look.

The upstart of a scruffy elf hopped down from beside the tree and drew close to Motley.

"Yes, but the tunnels are old, and some probably haven't been used for years. They must have changed with root growth and all that. I have excellent eyesight, and I am the best scout around these parts."

Whilst Motley could see only a blurred face, he recognized the voice.

"Aren't you the elf who collapsed one of my newer tunnels last year by trying to rebuild it your own way?" he asked.

"It was a mistake anyone could make, and I still say my knowledge of the tunnels will be a great asset. At least I can see where I'm going!"

Remik joined the argumentative pair.

"Who are you, and where do you come from?" he asked the outspoken elf.

"My name is Bill and I'm from Epsom Forest."

Remik quickly tried to gauge the suitability of the stranger.

"We do need another experienced scout, but the law is the law, and it clearly says that *any* newcomer must be voted in by the soldiers."

"Fine by me, but remember what I have said", Bill answered with a shrug.

The elves busily arranged the vote as Tross joined the group.

"What's going on, Remik? Why all the noise?"

"Ah, Tross, good, you're up. We need your vote."

"My vote?"

"Yes, this new elf here has shown up in camp this morning and although he claims to be a good scout, I am a little worried about him. He says he knows the tunnels well and wants to join us. You know the rules, Tross, he has to be voted in and, *if* he is, I hope we have made a wise decision as our safety will be dependent upon the advice of a stranger."

"Well," replied Tross, "I think we will need all the help we can get. Let's take a vote!"

Each soldier placed a leaf into a pouch, an Elm leaf for a 'yes' and an Oak leaf for a 'no'.

After each had cast his vote, all leaves were counted in front of everyone, after which Remik announced the result.

"Attention everyone!" he called. "The count is eighteen votes for, and fourteen against. I hereby declare that Bill will join us and support Motley as a scout."

Concerned about the newcomer's true ability, Motley made every effort to explain in great detail all he knew of the tunnels. He would make certain, should anything go wrong he, himself, would not be to blame. Motley addressed the assembled party.

"There are food tunnels, important for maintaining our strength, and easily found by the smell of dried fruit. It's true the undergrowth may have changed the look of the tunnels – I was *going* to come to that, given the chance! Beware, tunnels may be blocked off so we must be careful when cutting through as the winter rains and snows may have weakened them. Water may have built up and if the undergrowth doesn't hold together the side walls, they could collapse. And remember, keep a wary eye on the roofs for any movement or weakness. Above all, I urge each one of you to be extra careful and to watch out for one another. Our lives are in each other's hands."

Mumbling could be heard as each soldier looked at another, imagining the unknown dangers which may lay ahead. Remik now spoke up and explained his plan.

"Bill will go with Motley, leading the way. Tross and I will follow. The soldiers will join behind us. If conditions are okay, we will go deeper. Remember, it was a full Moon last night so 'Twiggy Men' could be about. Now, if there are no questions, we should start the search."

There was a brief pause during which no voice was heard.

"Okay then," Bill called out. "In we go!"

"Follow me, Bill," Motley urged, "I'll lead you in and show you the best way to tackle these tunnels."

Bill rolled his eyes to the sky. "Motley, I know *exactly* where I'm going," he replied, indignantly.

But as they made their way deeper, the tunnel walls seemed to close around them. Bill's hand shook a little as he held up a jar of fireflies.

"This will light our way, Motley."

With this, Motley's patience began to wear thin as he whispered, "Doesn't make a lot of difference to me. Remember what you told everyone, Bill, I'm blind. Don't forget, I work on instinct!"

He marched on ahead, leaving Bill struggling to keep up. They searched six tunnels without a problem, and so Remik decided, since they were now very deep inside, he would lead the rest of the way. They had not gone much further when he suddenly stopped, sensing movement in front! Holding up his light, he swivelled around at the very same moment one of his soldiers shouted, "Arms at the ready, we're under attack!"

An arrow whistled past Tross! Two soldiers grabbed him in an instant and, with Motley's help, rushed him out of the tunnel. At this moment, Bill decided to follow them. Remik flew up to the roof of the tunnel holding up his jar to light his way. But what he saw came as a shock. All around, stag beetles flew, their pincers looking particularly menacing! Then the light caught the face of an elf who quickly disappeared into the darkness of a tunnel wall. Remik reached for his thorn dagger, but too late! A fierce burning sensation in his right leg forced him to the ground, dropping both his dagger and light. He grabbed his leg, struggling onto one knee. Then, something heavy hit his wing. He felt a tearing pain surge through his whole body, causing him to topple back onto the ground. A deathly silence settled throughout the tunnels and in the dim light, Remik felt dizzy. He tried to regain his bearings as he looked around spotting his half-empty firefly jar nearby. He reached across and grabbed hold, raising it high, but his heart sank – his soldiers lay all around, but not one moved. His mind raced to one thing – where was Tross? Was The Prince safe?! Through the dim light, a dark shadow appeared. Remik's eyes adjusted quickly to see, staring back at him, a wicked face wearing a grin stretching from one pointed ear to the other.

"Hello. Todd Toady is me name and stealin' is me game. Ha, ha!"

Todd, who thought himself somewhat of a quick wit, stood there expecting some form of response, but none came as Remik tried to move.

"Where d'yer think yer going?" Todd asked. "Not so fast! Relax, yer stayin' right 'ere with me 'cos I want you to meet me friend Rush and he wants to meet you real bad, like."

At that very moment, a giant figure of an elf wearing torn, green clothes, emerged from the shadows, his large ears protruding through a tatty old hat on the front of which was a badge in the shape of a strange looking skull. But what was particularly noticeable, sitting on his shoulder, was a large, black stag beetle Rush had named 'Spikey'. The elf bent forward, peering down at Remik.

"Lookin' at the badge I wear on me 'at, ehh, soldier? I pride meself on the fact I killed a Wizard – well, trying to protect 'imself wiv 'is pafetic magic while I was robbin 'is Wizard dust! What did he fink would 'appen? This skull formed on 'is 'at when I killed 'im, so I took it. After all, he didn't need it no more, ha, ha! I dunno, I sort 'a like it. What d'you fink, soldier? Impressed, are yer?"

Remik did not answer. He knew, without question, with whom he was dealing – the most wanted, evil, grotesque elf 'Rushmore from Stokes', the very one who unlawfully entered Middlesborough to rob and then to commit the ultimate sin... to kill the Wizard Arthur.

Rush brought forward a strange weapon strapped across his back. Admiring it, he recalled the day he found this Human eating tool called a 'fork'. He remembered with pride how he had discovered it. Searching around in the woods one day to see what he could find, he came across this awesome, pronged object lying in the remains of a Human camping fire. What a find! Heavy and strong enough to knock a couple of elves off their feet with a single blow! With such a weapon, what soldier in any King's domain could seriously challenge him! Finding a huge can, he tested the weapon's strength and power by repeatedly prodding it until bubbly liquid squirted forth, some splashing his face. The taste upon his lips was delicious, strangely sweet and even, perhaps fizzy, nothing like he had ever experienced before, definitely a Human 'bubbly drink' of some kind. Even though he knew to drink it was strictly forbidden, he couldn't help himself. Perhaps the King himself knew how wonderful such a liquid tasted and wanted any found to be all his own? His soldiers were under strict command to destroy any cans found, but who was to know? Perhaps they took them back to the King to secretly store somewhere? So why *shouldn't* he just go ahead and sample the contents? Who was around to dare tell him what to do? Rush felt a sense of joy and freedom, gulping down the liquid. 'My King... ohh, I bet 'e experiences this delicious fizzy every day, greedily keepin' all to 'imself!' He brought up a large, satisfying belch before downing the last drop. But then, it seemed all at once, his wings buzzed out of control, sending him shooting up into the air, pulling him this way and that. Suddenly they froze, sending him back down to earth with a heavy bump. He rubbed his head confused, his wings still feeling odd and tingly. He thought the worst was over but seconds later his wings completely erupted, leaving him with a crumpled mess upon his back! He wandered around totally depressed – his wings were ruined! He realized too late why such a liquid was banned to all! Could he see a Doctor about his 'injury', he wondered. No, of course not, he had broken the law. The only answer was to have something done about them, probably unlawfully, as soon as possible. Out of practice of having to walk everywhere and unsteady on his legs, he bumped into an elf who, he discovered, owned a stag beetle farm. The elf stood shocked at the sight of Rush.

"What happened to you? Where are your wings and why is fizzy stuff coming out of your back? Oh no... don't tell me, you haven't drunk 'Human bubbly', have you? Go on, don't even *try* to deny it, ha, ha!"

"Oh no, no, no, no, don't be stupid! It's a war wound and nuffing to worry 'bout. Aven't 'ad no time to see a Doc 'bout it, but when I do, I'll be fine, I'm sure of it!" answered Rush, while trying to brush fizz from his back. He did not like what he saw as a loss of respect from a stranger who even had the cheek to laugh at him! Whilst Rush felt the urge to punch him firmly on the nose, he realized the stranger knew too much which could land him in serious trouble with the King. This forced Rush to promise the farm owner he would help him if he kept quiet, so they came to an agreement. Rush would make certain the hedgehogs, who loved to eat stag beetles, would keep away from the farm and, in return, the farmer would allow the beetles to help Rush with anything he needed. The only problem was, the beetles wings made a clicking noise which may easily reveal Rush's presence under the wrong circumstances... Rush promised himself he would find a cunning solution!

Todd prodded Rush, bringing him back to the matter in hand.

"Rush, stop daydreamin' and concentrate. Wot's the matter wiv yer!"

"Oh, yeah, sorry mate. Almost drifted off!" He leaned closer to Remik. "How can I make yer tell us wot we wanna know?" he asked, with a sickly grin.

But Remik stared ahead in complete silence.

"I see cat's got yer tongue, 'as it? Well, we'll see wot can be done t'get that tongue o' your'n loose and wagging freely!"

Todd pulled a pouch of dust from his belt and showed it to Rush.

"Ere mate, I 'ave this! Found it in the grass, it's Troof dust!"

Rush snatched it from Todd and grinned. "Y'know wot this can do?" he asked Remik. He paused for a moment but again, Remik gave no reply.

"I see, still not talkin'. Well, as yer see, it's Troof dust and y'know wot will 'appen if I use it? You'll squeal like a rat, that's wot, ha ha! Oh, and the after effects when it wears off! I know all about it yer see, 'cos it was used on me once and I got me friend Todd's bruvver put in jail for stealin'. Now, I owe Todd a favour and I don't like owin' nobody nofink'. But for now, I'm gonna leave yer 'ere to think about wot yer wanna tell me without the use of me valuable Troof dust!"

Rush securely tied Remik's hands and led him to a tunnel where he abruptly threw him onto the cold, damp ground. After Rush, Todd and their gang had gone, Remik struggled to sit up, only to see a blanket of darkness. The strong aroma of dried fruit told him he had been taken to a food tunnel, but he was in pain and the smell made him feel ill as he propped himself up against a wall to rest.

The Prince paced up and down. For now he was safe but deeply concerned.

"Oh great Wizards, I need father. There's been no message from him at all and where is Remik?"

He looked at the soldiers who had dragged him to safety, one of whom stood out from the others. Tross was convinced he knew him from somewhere.

"What is your name? I have seen you before, haven't I?" Tross asked.

"Yes, Tross. You came to the award ceremony where your father…"

"Of course," Tross interrupted, "yes, I remember you."

Introducing himself, Elm bowed low before the Prince.

"My name is Lord Elm."

Tross recalled how Elm, in the past, had proved himself a clever and brave elf, saving the lives of fifty soldiers in 'The Battle of Plum Pudding Hill' whilst protecting the Elf King of Nottingham Woods. His loyalty and bravery earned him respect and entitlement and he had been chosen to be a member of the elite band of fearless elves known as 'The Ring of Lords', the gatherings of which were always shrouded in the utmost secrecy.

Tross came straight to the point.

"Elm, I am not at all clear about what happened in those tunnels, but I've a feeling the outcome may not be good. Never before have I dealt with a situation as serious as this. I am in great need of your experience. I've seen no other soldiers come out of the tunnels and as for Remik, I wonder what's happened to him? They could all have been killed or captured! Will you take command?"

Elm thought deeply about the request. 'It certainly is a dangerous mission, but I do have the experience and if anyone is fit to lead, I am. I could earn valuable time off, perhaps enough to take Violet to Hawaii!'

✳✳✳

Meanwhile, deep in the forests of northern California, Cecee and Fiero awoke to a strange smell drifting through the pines and which neither recognized. Unconcerned, they looked around for food, finding nearby ripe blackberries, many of which Cecee soon enjoyed. Fiero, however, found fresh, green grass and, while munching all he could, his mind wandered to Middlesborough. How he missed the juicy, thick blades of home. Suddenly, one of his ears pricked up, followed by the other. Was he hearing bees in the distance? If so, then judging by the noise, they were angry and seemed to be heading their way! Becoming alarmed, he galloped to Cecee, but found her calm.

"Don't worry, Fiero," she said, "It's only a fairy call, but we must follow it."

"Cecee, fly onto my back and we'll go straight there."

Cecee accepted Fiero's kind offer and together, off they flew. As they headed towards the low droning sound, they soon found hundreds of fairies flying towards them.

Cecee whispered into Fiero's ear.

"Wow, Fiero, I wonder what is going on? Just look at all those fairies – I have never seen so many together like this!"

One fairy stopped and hovered beside them.

"Please follow us to the beach, we need help! The Humans have had an accident with one of their seagoing craft and oil is killing the birds and sea-life!"

Fiero and Cecee quickly followed, arriving at the beach to see it covered with thick, black goo, every wave bringing more and more onto the beach. Hundreds of fairies flew around busily blowing or sprinkling Healing dust over the poor, suffering creatures. Cecee's heart stopped as she spotted a familiar grey-striped seagull lying on the blackened sand.

"Fiero, please fly down over there! Take me there now!"

But Fiero wasn't anywhere near fast enough for Cecee, so she flew from his back and soon knelt on the oil covered sand. A bird with broken wings and an entire body sticky and black with oil, lay barely breathing.

"Oh no! *Ace*, please speak to me!" she pleaded.

Grabbing her pouch of Healing dust, she gently sprinkled some over him. Hurt and anger both caused her to raise her voice.

"Why oh why didn't you or Johnny call me!"

Ace began to stir, slowly opening his eyes with a flicker.

"Little bird?" he quietly called.

"Please don't talk. Just lie still and let me try to clean off this awful black poison."

"It's no use, little bird, it won't come off."

"Ace, please don't give up!"

Ace looked so weak but Cecee had no herbs or potions to add to the little Healing dust she had already used. The next few words he struggled to speak, sank her into depths of despair.

"Little bird, Johnny is dead. He caught the worst of it trying to get me out… he's lying over there. You must be very brave."

Cecee's eyes searched all around and soon found Johnny with all but his face covered in oil, his beak wide open as though in the vain hope of a last gasp of air. She turned away from the dreadful sight, tears running down her face.

"Oh no, how did this happen? Please tell me what you need and I will get it!"

By now, Ace could hardly speak, overcome with both weakness and emotion.

"Little bird, keep up your good work, it will help us all in the end, we can …"

"Can what, Ace… Ace! Don't leave me… Ace!"

But alas, it was too late. His whole body lapsed into what looked like a deep sleep, and all too soon his chest feathers lay still. It seemed Ace had stopped breathing. Cecee stroked the feathers on his head and looked out to sea, tears stinging her eyes as she watched black waves bring more and more oil onto the beach. Johnny's words now haunted her. 'Get Humans out of trouble? You've got to be kidding me!'

Fiero stooped low and spoke softly.

"Cecee, I must take you away from here. The poison is on your skin and wings and we must find spring water to wash it away."

Totally numb, the sad fairy blindly flew onto Fiero's back, too distraught to cry any longer. She buried her face in his mane but before Fiero flew off, she glanced back, shocked to see Humans now all over the beach, one carefully carrying away Ace's body.

Fiero swiftly flew from the awful sight. Soon, they settled down next to a spring water lake, deep in the woods. He found mistletoe berries and told Cecee to squeeze the juice from them over the oil and to add a little water. As she did so, the oil began to dissolve. Next, Cecee flew into the lake to wash off the horrible, sticky mess. As she returned to Fiero, she said, "Fiero, today has left me feeling so unhappy, miserable and exhausted."

"Sleep on my back, Cecee," he replied, "you must rest."

Her blonde hair wet and darkened by the water, she flew up and snuggled under his silken mane. Fiero stood guard all night, but Cecee could not sleep. Her thoughts turned to Ace and Johnny as she took Ace's feather out of her hair to study it, her mind full of images of the two seagulls soaring into a crystal blue sky. The thought of Ace catching peanuts from the air brought a brief smile to her face. How she missed the power of her Wand – perhaps it could have saved Ace and Johnny. From now on, she promised herself she would never again leave it anywhere, not with her mother, not with her father, not with anyone. But soon tiredness finally overtook her and she fell into a long, deep, peaceful sleep.

***

In the Woods of Seven Oaks, Elm, having accepted command of the search party, busied himself making plans. It would be dangerous to send the Prince back to

Court and he had only one soldier to escort him, which was nowhere near safe enough. No, on reflection, it would be much safer to take him into the tunnels with them. Scout Bill was fearful of returning back under ground, but agreed to go along anyway – he was not going to be left outside on his own!

The small group ventured back into the dark tunnels and had gone only a short distance when Bill suddenly thought he heard a noise and froze like a petrified tree.

"Elm, did you hear that? Everyone be still!" Was it a clicking sound?

Elm, at the front, listened hard but could hear nothing. Deciding that Bill was becoming a pest and probably better off occupied with another task, he turned to him.

"Bill, I want you to go back to the tunnel entrance, stay there and keep watch."

Bill's eyes widened. "Keep watch! Keep watch for what?" he asked.

"For more of the King's soldiers – he may send reinforcements. I need a scout to show them the way in if and when they arrive."

Before Bill could argue, the others disappeared deeper into the tunnel, leaving Bill suddenly alone where all now became disturbingly silent.

"Think I'll feel better if I whistle," he said aloud. He tried, but fear drying his lips, he couldn't manage a single note. Next, he thought a joke or two would settle his nerves.

"Knock, knock. Who's there? Blue. Blue who? Blew away with the wind!"

'Tut, that was the stupidest joke in the World,' he thought, while staring at his one and only firefly lantern. He had to admit, he didn't know the tunnels all that well. A rustling noise in front of him sent his heart racing.

"Who's there?" he whispered, pulling his dagger, but there was no reply. This time he shouted.

"Who's there!? Show yourself! I have a weapon and I won't hesitate to kill you!"

Whoosh… something cold and slimy jumped out and straight into his face. "Ahhhhhhh!" he yelled, aimlessly thrusting his dagger in all directions. Bill held tighter his jar of fireflies, in a panic flying up and around in circles, bumping his head and wings on the roof of the tunnel. Something made a croaking sound on the ground. He held out his lantern to see what was there.

"A frog! Ha, ha!" he laughed aloud. "A frog, *he, he!* Phew, it's only a frog!"

Heart pounding, he tried to calm himself.

'Okay, okay, everything is fine, just fine. I'm sure I'm only a little way into the tunnel. If the King's soldiers arrive, I know I'll hear them from here. Nothing can harm me if I stay put. It's better than standing in the entrance.'

Promising himself he would never volunteer again for anything, he heard a clunk behind him and carelessly shot around. As he did so, his lantern of fireflies dropped from his hand and crashed to the ground, breaking into many pieces. His only light now disappeared as the fireflies flew deep into the tunnel. He watched frightened and helpless as the light cast menacing, tall, dark shadows that danced and moved about on the tunnel walls and, for a few terrifying moments, changed the shape of the tunnels themselves. Now enveloped in a thick blanket of darkness, Bill whispered miserably, "Noooo, now I am really lost! Come back fire flies!"

He felt for his dagger, but a shiver ran through him. Realizing the weapon was lost and that the clunking sound had been the dagger falling from his belt, he wondered where it could be as he blindly fumbled around on the tunnel floor but couldn't find it. 'Got to find my way to the others or find the exit. What's best?' he wondered, and then remembered with a chilling thought, some of the deep tunnels actually branched off and went underneath the lake, very far down underneath. He'd heard there was a labyrinth under there, wet and icy-cold, where the moles buried their dead. Bill remembered childhood stories of red, glowing eyes staring through damp, white, mouldy webs, and thin, bony paws with long, sharp claws reaching out, and the sound of moaning, moaning to find their way back to the living… With the risk of ghostly looking Twiggy Men oozing sap and firing big, sharp splinters at him above ground, and now fierce, red-eyed, dead moles below ground, reaching out to jealously steal his life away, his wings shuddered with fear. Succeeding to scare himself senseless, he started to feel his way along the tunnel, often touching disgusting cold, slimy moss which seemed to grow everywhere. Edging his way along, the moss became thicker and thicker. Was he getting nearer the exit or going deeper underground? Scout Bill had been a clumsy child and somewhat of a late developer. Learning to fly had been difficult and he was always tripping over this or that as a young adult. So, it came as no surprise, when he stumbled and fell as he made his way along. He threw out his hands to save himself and grabbed what felt like a corner of the tunnel wall. He crawled around it. 'Is that dried fruit I can smell,' he thought, as he stretched out his hand. "OUCH! Hedgehogs!" he called out as something pricked his fingers. Oh joy, he had arrived at a guarded food tunnel! At the risk of tearing himself to shreds, he carefully squeezed between the hedgehogs. Feeling safe, for the moment anyway, he was sure the ghosts of Twiggy Men, or dead moles, would not have any use for this tunnel – food was for the living. Pleased with himself, he felt his way around, intent on filling his stomach and, not bothering to check any further if all was well, he didn't realize that this was the very same tunnel into which Rush had thrown Remik. Tied up in a corner, Remik had heard the noise Bill made. His eyes had adjusted to the dark and he could just recognize Bill's silhouette. 'Thank goodness Bill had survived the attack, but why was he alone, and where was the Prince? I won't call out.' he thought. Cautiously, Remik watched Bill's outline in silence. Bill found some berry pouches, opened one and put the whole contents into his mouth, getting comfortable while he chewed. Content, he began to tuck into the next, but a sudden noise alarmed him. Had the hedgehogs moved again or had someone or something arrived?

"Hello, is anyone there? Motley, is that you?" Bill strained hard to see.

"Stop playing tricks, it isn't funny!"

Was someone, or something, in there with him? He squinted even harder into the dark and called out, "Who's there? This really is *not* funny!"

A clicking sound drew closer, almost next to him. Bill lashed out at once, trying to defend himself, but against what? Then, a mauve glint sparkled in the dark for a split second and spun around him. Bill tried to move out of its way but the sparkle multiplied, swirling about him, making him feel dizzy and confused. Before he fainted and fell to the ground, the swirling abruptly stopped – Truth dust had entered Bill's body!

Remik's attention was now drawn towards the exit where a dull light fell all around. Slowly, a shadowy figure holding a firefly lantern appeared.

"Bill, Bill! 'Ello, Bill, you awake yet?"

Todd shone his lantern close to Bill's face.

"Wot's it they say, Bill? The troof will set yer free? *Ha, ha, ha*!"

And now from behind, a huge figure entered – it was none other than the dreadful Rush!

"Ah, me faifful beetles, they delivered the dust!" he said, as Todd shouted back at him, "Rush, go and get some more fireflies!"

"Go yerself, Todd!" he retorted, taking his favourite beetle Spikey off his shoulder and placing him very close to Bill's foot.

Todd scowled at his partner.

"You're the one payin' the debt, Rush, remember?"

"Oh for the love of a fairy, alright, alright. Don't do nofink while I'm gone, and, Bill, move yer foot one inch and me Spikey will either spray yer wiv some very irritatin' fluid from his bum, or pinch you so 'ard you'll lose a toe!"

Off Rush went, soon returning with three jars which he placed near Bill.

"Now, Bill, you'll soon feel a great deal more relaxed and when yer do, I'm gonna ask yer some questions."

"Are yer firsty, Bill?" asked Todd. "I'll bet yer are so 'ere, 'ave some mead."

Todd thought he was acting kindly, pouring mead down Bill's throat, but Bill spat it out, coughing and splattering several times.

"Oh, Bill, don't squander none. 'Ere, 'ave a drop more."

Rush stopped him. "That's enuff, Todd. In 'is state, 'e could choke to deaff and we don't wanna kill 'im *now*!"

Bill realized with sudden panic that once the grotesque pair got what they wanted, they were going to kill him! Then, he heard scuttling – 'what was that?' he thought. Five hedgehogs entered the tunnel, Rush shouting orders at them.

"Okay you lot, roll up into balls and block the entrance – *don't let no one in!"*

The hedgehogs swiftly obeyed. Spikey didn't like hedgehogs at all and hurriedly flew back to the safety of Rush's shoulder. His master turned to Todd and said, "Righto, we can start."

While under the awful spell, Bill told the two everything, which left Rush as excited as an elfin on his first date.

"Todd, can yer believe we 'ave the chance to capture two Royals *and* take over the woods!"

Todd stared back at his friend in disbelief but nonetheless, nodded in agreement. Rush now started to make even more devious plans.

"Okay, let's fink abou' grabbin' the Prince at precisely …"

Todd turned a deaf ear to the one he now knew for certain to be even more of a mad, reckless, dangerous elf.

"…and if we can find the Princess," continued Rush, "as well as the Prince, we can make the ransom so much 'igher… "

On and on he rambled as he and Todd walked out of the tunnels leaving Bill locked up with Remik. Todd began to question himself. 'Am I in too deep? Is it too late to get out? As much as I like to stockpile fairy dust, crystals and the like, I'd 'ate to see the Princess at the mercy of a mad elf like Rush. 'E could get me locked up for life along wiv 'im! I need time to fink fings over. For the time bein', I'll play along…' He called to Rush, "betta 'ide over 'ere mate. This is where the back-up soldiers are s'posed t'meet."

The two waited for a while, but no one arrived.

"You sure you over 'erd right? Don't look to me like no soldiers are comin'. Any'ow, I 'ave a *brilliant* idea, Todd, me old mate."

Todd's large, pointed ears began to flick repeatedly as was their habit when he was involved in bad deeds, so to calm them down, he curled his fingers around them.

"I'm all ears, Rush." Todd said, with a half nervous giggle.

"We need a scowt 'ho knows these tunnels, and we've go one close by, ain't we, Todd. Who else would wanna' go deep under the lake wiv ghosts about... and it was a full Moon last night. Would you wanna go? Nah, so we send a scout just ahead of us to give the all clear and then *we* go in."

Todd drew closer to Rush. "Mate, you're brilliant! We send Bill in first, right?"

"Right, Todd. But now we must giv' 'im time t'understand 'ow much danger 'e's in, being locked up in that tunnel wiv no one but Remik to 'ere 'is cries for 'elp. It shouldn't take 'im long. Hmm, let's see, an hour or two t'get 'is memory back, and a second after that t'start wailing. Ha, ha! We'll return t'morra and get 'im on our side. As for Remik, we'll deal wiv 'im lata."

A cold night had left Bill shivering, so he huddled himself into a corner and cupped his hands, blowing warm breath into them, trying to keep warm. Shards of soft light beaming across the tunnel floor gave him hope for escape as the hedgehogs started to move. But his heart sank as the now familiar clicking sound from Spikey's thick, strong pincers, told him Rush had arrived. As the hedgehogs moved out of Rush's way, Bill could see from the light shining into the tunnel that Todd was not far behind.

"'Ello, Bill, 'ave a good night, did yer?" asked Rush.

"No I didn't, Rush. Why are you keeping me here? You have no right to do this. Let me go at once. I *am* with the King's men – let this be a warning to you!"

Todd took hold of Bill's arm a little too firmly as Bill flinched – his arm hurting from the fall in the tunnels. Rush sat and said, "Now, let's all calm down.

Bill, yer shouldn't threaten us in that way, it simply ain't nice… be very careful, we could keep yer locked up and forget all about yer. We used a touch of Troof sparkle on yer but really, Bill, it was nufink big and yer know, me 'Ealing sparkle could help yer fix that bruise on yer arm. All we're just trying to do is make a little extra sparkle for ourselves, that's all. It pays the bills and wiv your 'elp, there could be a nice little bit for you too. What d'yer fink?"

Bill glared at them. *'Nothing big!'* he thought, 'is Rush joking, and where did he get that Truth dust? Should I trust them?' In his mind, Bill tried to quickly sum up the situation but Rush, now growing impatient for an answer, was only inches from his face.

"Well, Bill, what d'yer say? Will yer join us?"

It didn't take Bill long to realize that he really didn't care about the Prince and the soldiers. They had given him no respect since he had joined them and maybe doing something like this would change their minds about him.

"Alright, I'll join you," he replied.

"Oh that's sweet, Bill, you won't regret nofink!" Rush replied, with a cynical grin.

Remik, still in his dark corner, could hear everything.

Rush pulled on his hat even tighter. 'At last, plans really are going my way,' he thought. 'There's no turning back for Bill now. He'll be wiv me long enuff t'elp, then … well, maybe I'll get rid of 'im. Then there's Remik. 'Olding 'im 'ostage could prove t'be quite useful if we do get caught.'

Rush's grin grew even wider as he dwelled upon how much he loved to use his evil mind to get the better of everyone.

CHAPTER FIVE

SWIFT RETURN AND DREAM LANDS

I t wasn't unusual for a bitter winter to arrive early in San Francisco Bay. An icy breeze buffeted Fiero, stirring him from sleep. As he awoke, he wondered if Humans had completely cleared the beach of the poor, unfortunate birds and how many, if any, had survived? Cecee, already awake, flew from his back to face him, but saw he looked dazed – had the poison also affected him?

"Fiero, wake up! Are you alright?"

Fiero's eyes lit up in response. "Yes, of course I am. Just slowly waking up, that's all. When I sleep or rest, I'm in a sort of trance, but don't worry, I know everything that's happening around me."

Reassured, Cecee flew to sit on his back once again. Lovingly stroking his mane, she noticed another difference.

"Your mane is changing colour, Fiero. Is that normal?"

"Oh yes, the colour will darken as I age and my coat will turn silver. I think the process has slowed down a bit here, though. Maybe it's the grass I'm eating?"

While debating the changes Fiero would go through, Cecee calmly checked her belt for the Seed when a sudden wave of alarm took over her whole being.

"Fiero! I've dropped the golden pouch with the Rowan Seed inside! Perhaps it's on the beach somewhere near Ace! The Human who carried Ace away, maybe *she* found the pouch?"

In the distance, another fairy call echoed in earnest from a small canyon.

"Fiero, the Seed is missing, and now I hear a call that we must answer!"

"Cecee, don't worry, we'll find the Seed but let's answer the call first. Maybe a fairy has found the pouch. It's golden and unusual, she could be trying to find its owner."

Off the two set in the direction of the call. Nearing a canyon, they heard a sound almost like thunder rolling through the air. Drawing nearer still, they came upon the enormous, deep hole in the ground, the bottom of which was filled with many fairies, all surrounded by a mass of thundering waterfalls. Fiero came to rest at the bottom where, at the centre, sat a fairy who seemed to possess unquestionable authority. She wore a dress of frosted pearls and silver leaves, her white, crystal-like wings appearing to move as they reflected rainbow colours from the falling waters. Her white hair was entwined with delicate crystal icicles and upon her head she wore a Crown of clear, white crystal. She looked as though she were made of ice and a hot sunny day would melt her from existence. Her obvious powers over her realm became clear as, with a wave of her hand, she stopped the flow of the waters, silencing the falls. She spoke in a clear voice.

"Fairies, I have summoned you to discuss yesterday's disaster. I know you are all very distraught, but I will be pleased to answer any questions or deal with any worries you have."

Cecee tried to calm Fiero as he reared up, spreading his wings to turn away. There was no mention of a lost pouch or Rowan Seed and surely something this unusual would have been mentioned first? Fiero felt the fairies had not found them and time was moving on. He definitely didn't want Cecee to be reminded of the terrible sight on the beach, so thought it was time to leave. But Cecee needed some answers and, after settling Fiero, asked the strange fairy, "Why do Humans harm themselves and, worst of all, innocent animals? And why do they need sea vessels that carry such black, sticky poison? Are they not content with what they have on land? Why don't they realize that they risk the lives of many others living on this Earth?"

The 'ice fairy' looked sideways to see who was asking so many questions, furrowing her brow as she spotted Cecee.

"I haven't seen you in these parts before," she said. "You are barely an adult. Where do you come from?"

"I come from Seven Oaks Woods in England. My name is Cecee and I was blown here by a storm."

The strange fairy stared at her.

"Please come and see me once I have finished."

The gathering soon ended and Cecee directed Fiero towards the ice fairy.

"You wanted to see me?" asked an impatient Cecee.

The fairy greeted them both with a warm smile.

"Come down from the Unicorn and sit by me. Let me pour you some elderberry wine – it will calm you."

But Cecee stayed put.

"I see you have a flying Unicorn, so you've been to Middlesborough?" she enquired, holding up a full cone.

"No I haven't. I've heard of it, but I've no idea where it is," replied Cecee, while stroking Fiero's mane.

The fairy put down the cone and turned her face to the Sun, the large, white crystal in her Crown catching its light, forming a strange glow within. She turned back to face Cecee, but the light from the crystal was now so bright, Cecee had to turn away.

"Ouch! Please remove your Crown, its light is blinding me!"

The strange fairy removed the Crown carefully from her head and pointed to the magical stones inserted all around.

"As you can see, there are six coloured stones. The two reds are 'Red Dawns'- war stones, the yellows are 'Yellow Mellows' – go betweens, and the greens are 'Peace' stones. The yellows are vital, for they maintain the balance between the reds and greens. Now…this centre white has wonderful powers. Not only does it allow me to study your aura and see the real you, it has the power to shield anyone who holds it in his or her possession… but only those it chooses to be worthy of such protection."

"Well, I hope what you see in me is *wonderful*, but now we must go," answered an unimpressed Cecee, signalling Fiero to leave. But quick as a flash, a bolt of blinding light shot from the Crown and instantly locked both in a spell. Frozen to the spot, the fairy cautioned Cecee.

"Cecee, I know you can hear as well as see me and I am sorry, but you give me no other choice. I must know exactly who you are and now that you have heard me, I'll bring you out of the trance, but *please* stay calm."

Carefully, she began to blow dust from her mouth over Cecee and Fiero, unlocking the spell. Cecee wasn't going to let the fairy see how much all this frightened her and bravely flew from Fiero to face her.

"Your treatment of us will *not* go unpunished. I am a Royal Fairy, and my father will be extremely angry when he learns of this!" snapped Cecee.

"My dear, I recognize Royal wings when I see them, but how do I know… you could have stolen them…"

"By all the Wizards… *steal wings*? We have no need. If we lose them, they regrow!" Cecee replied, scoffing at any hint that she may have stolen hers.

"Yes, you are right, but I see you have much to learn. Fairies can regrow their wings, elves however, cannot. We can replace them using magic, however, not all soldiers like that method, so the wings of dragonflies are kept by us after they die. These are the only wings that can be joined together and given to injured soldiers who lose their own in battle. We keep them in special places, but bad elves steal them and clever fairies then colour them to copy other wings – each year they get better and better at doing this. Oh enough, sit down for goodness sake and let us talk!"

A little embarrassed by her lack of understanding of such matters, Cecee settled, but when she picked up the cone to drink, Fiero nudged her with his nose. A 'be careful' warning almost written over his face caused her to pause, smell the drink and look at the colour of the liquid. She sipped and waited but nothing unusual happened – she had not been frozen again. A little more relaxed, she took a drink and asked, "What do you want to know about me? I'm not trying to be rude, but I am in a hurry."

"First, let me introduce myself. My name is Icicle and I rule the woods and canyons you see all around. May I ask, Cecee, what is your formal name?"

"I am Princess Carmilina Citrina Foxglove of Seven Oaks Woods... Cecee, for short," replied a young and very proud Princess.

"Please eat some berries," Icicle said, holding out a bowlful, "and tell me what happened to you and how you reached my canyon."

Icicle's calmness left Feiro feeling uneasy, and as for that wry smile of hers, he wasn't at all sure what her intentions may be. He scraped his front hoof on the ground and tossed his mane in an effort to warn Cecee who simply calmed him and carried on talking.

"Icicle, I must go back to the beach and look for something I have lost."

Icicle leaned forward. "What is it? Maybe I can help you."

"Unfortunately, you cannot help me at all and I must go back as soon as possible."

Icicle knew she must let them go – a wise fairy treads carefully and Icicle is *very* wise indeed. As she watched Fiero prepare to fly, she knew when, where and how to use her magic on them both, but this was not the time...

"Alright, Cecee, take your Unicorn and go – I look forward to your swift return. Good luck to you both."

As Cecee and Fiero took to the air, Icicle watched, again that same wry smile appearing across her face…

***

A fine, icy rain swept over Seven Oaks Woods, the kind that seeps deep into the pores of elves, but it wasn't the rain that bothered Rush as he sat alone on a tree stump. Spikey rested on his knee ready to take orders but Rush took the beetle and placed him on his shoulder. He felt completely fed up and depressed. Yes, he had plans, but for him, nothing seemed to move forward quickly enough. He thought a drink at Violet's may help him see things differently, so off he set. Owing to the severe injury to his wings, all he could do was walk. On the way, he bumped into Todd and Bill who had no choice but to walk with him. Bill folded down his wings and strutted alongside the two rogues. Now in the company of this infamous pair, he felt no one would dare bother him. In fact, maybe some might even show him a little respect. Todd Toady hated walking.

"'Bout time you 'ad yer wings fixed, Rush," he said with contempt. "We could get 'round a lot faster."

"Can't do it, mate."

"Why not?"

"There ain't enough dragonfly wings big enough to join togevver for me."

Todd clucked in disgust as they wandered into Violet's Inn, but she wasn't there.

"Rosie, where's Violet? We want some of 'er best mead and we've got plenty of 'sparkle' to pay for it," demanded Todd, as the three sat at Rush's favourite table.

Rosie stood behind the bar alone. Ignoring Todd's request, she signalled to one of the helpers to fetch Violet, but before he left, Rosie had a quiet word with him.

Violet and Tizzy were sitting together, talking in her tree home when the messenger elf flew in.

"Violet, you must come to your Inn now. Rush, Todd Toady and an elf called Bill are there demanding you serve them your finest mead. Before I left, Rosie pulled me to one side and said to tell you she had a feeling they're up to no good!"

Violet shot up.

"Tizzy, stay here, I'll be right back," and off she flew with the messenger.

Tizzy, feeling unwell again and not wishing to be alone, secretly followed.

Entering the Inn, Violet flew to face Rush.

"I don't want no trouble 'ere, Rush. Wot d'you want?"

"Tut! Just drinks, Violet. Calm yerself, we all need a drink after an 'ard day's work."

But Rush's attention was swiftly drawn to a new fairy.

"What do we 'ave 'ere then, Violet?" asked Rush, his head to one side, looking behind her.

Violet spun around to see Tizzy hovering some way behind her.

"Tizzy, I told yer to stay 'ome! This is no place for yer!"

Rush stood up.

"Why's that then, Violet? Come 'ere fairy and let us see yer proper."

Tizzy flew and stood beside Violet after landing gently on the floor.

Rush looked her over.

"Cor, them feavery wings make yer fly with such grace... nice...you'll 'ave to tell me where you got 'em made. I'd pay a good price for that kind'a work."

Tizzy instantly folded down her wings.

"I... I didn't have them made."

Violet stood in front of Tizzy, blocking Rush's view of her.

"She's me new 'elp, Rush. Come on now, Tizzy, let's go back 'ome, we 'ave training t'do. She *can't* stay 'ere in the bar Rush, she's not trained yet and barely old enough. D'you want me to lose me license!"

They flexed their wings to leave, but Rush grabbed Violet's arm.

"'Old it, she's stayin' right 'ere! Now, do as yer told, Violet and get us some mead!"

Violet hesitated, but then turned away to get the drink as Rush sat back down.

"Now, I was asking where yer got them wings."

"They're mine, I was born with them."

The giant elf leaned close.

"Born wiv 'em were yer? And where exactly was that then, where were yer born, eh?"

Violet brought cones of mead filled to the brim, hoping the heady liquid would calm the three trouble making elves. Although it was against the law for her to own Wizard dust, today she decided to risk everything and if she must, she would use some. Todd finished his drink in one gulp and leaned back, wondering why Violet had given him such a generous measure. Rush carefully picked up his drink, not wishing to spill one drop and, with a noisy slurp, savoured the taste.

"Ummm, that's real good, Violet. Fanks, fanks a lot!"

Violet disappeared into the cellars of her Inn to get more while Rush refocused – this was without doubt, some of Violet's very best mead.

"Now, where was I... oh yeah, you fairy, what's yer name again?"

"Tizzy."

"Tizzy, is it. Unusual name. How did yer get that one, then?" replied Rush before taking another gulp.

"My sister gave it to me when I was small."

"Aw, 'ow very sweet, and 'oo might I ask is yer sister?"

Violet reappeared with a fresh pipe of mead.

"Ere, 'ave some more mead."

She pushed the pipe into the ground and offered to top up their cones with some more of her oldest and most potent brew. The excellent taste of this rare mead was obvious to Rush.

"My, my, Violet, we *are* extravagant with yer triffic mead today and the taste… wow, wot'a kick! Now, yer wouldn't be tryin' to pull a fast'un on me, would yer?"

He tossed back his head, laughing so hard the point of his tatty old Wizard hat bent forward with the force. Violet wasn't quite sure – did she see that awful scull badge on the front of Rush's hat wobble? She was certain that the badge was embedded into the hat, so how *could* it move?

"Yer know I can drink any elf under the toadstools, let alone the table, Violet! I can 'old me drink with the best of 'em," said Rush, while pulling his hat straight.

Violet laughed nervously.

"Don't be stupid, Rush. We're oversupplied and I have to get rid of it before it spoils. You just 'appened to pick a good day to visit, that's all."

Rush could never afford the mead he drank so heartily today, and remained blissfully ignorant that Violet's rarest mead would render *anyone* mindless. Violet shot a glance at Tizzy, wishing the liquid would hurry and take full effect.

"Come on, Tizzy, I need something from me 'ome so let's go now. Rosie can take over from 'ere."

But before Violet knew what was happening, she was on the ground, stunned from a smack delivered by the horrible, loathsome Rush, so harsh it shocked even Spikey who flew from his master's shoulder and landed on the nearest twig. The soft, gentle lights in the Inn flickered as Rush bellowed, "Not so fast, Violet, she ain't goin' nowhere! Tizzy, sit 'ere next to me, I 'aven't finished talking to yer!"

A very shocked Tizzy immediately sat near the huge thug.

"Now, you was saying that yer sister gave yer name to yer. *'Oo's* yer sister then?"

Tizzy couldn't bear to see anyone else hurt so quickly answered, "Cecee, her name is Cecee."

Rush's mind surged, ideas flooding his devious brain. Was it possible for his luck to have turned so beautifully?

"Cecee… as in, Carmilina Citrina Foxglove?" he asked.

"Yes."

He stroked her long, green hair, his large hand moving underneath it and to the back of her slender neck.

"Gorgeous 'air you 'ave," he said, tightening his grip, twisting his hand to wind her hair around it and with a quick pull, said, "You're comin' wiv me."

Tizzy's eyes glanced towards Violet while Rush grinned menacingly.

"Oh don't worry about Violet. Lucky for 'er, I didn't 'it 'er that 'ard!"

Holding onto Tizzy's hair, he dragged her out of the Inn and over to a disused mole tunnel hidden deep in the undergrowth and known only to him. Without any concern for the young fairy's wellbeing, he pushed her into the tunnel. He called to two nearby hedgehogs and ordered them to roll up and block the tunnel's entrance. Todd and Bill followed, by now panicking as they began to realize who this fairy may really be.

"Rush, wot *are* yer doin'?" asked Todd.

"I'm doin' wot I must. Anyone can see, even though they ain't developed yet, she 'as Royal wings! I fink she's the youngest Princess, but I promise I'll find out exactly 'oo she is later."

"Rush, you're messin' with female Royalty mate. We could all *die* for this!"

Rush stopped in his tracks.

"Are you two weasels in or out?" he barked in reply.

Bill and Todd stood rigid and stared at him.

"What d'yer mean, Rush?" asked Todd, with a fake, wide-eyed innocence.

"I mean, Todd, are yer wiv me or not… well, I'm waitin', in or out…?"

Bill and Todd both knew they were in far too deep and knew too much. Rush could easily kill both of them where they stood, and would if he had to. With this in mind, Todd stole a cautious look towards Bill and answered nervously, "Relax Rush, relax mate. He, he, of course we're in… we're in!"

The three returned to Violet's Inn. Entering, Rush and Bill collapsed onto the nearest toadstools, the mead now taking full effect. But Todd flew straight to Violet and whispered, "Violet, wot were yer finkin', tryin' to trick us, especially Rush, you know 'ow 'e can be."

"Only cowards 'it fairies, and I won't let the likes of 'im get the better of me!" snapped Violet. "Where 'as he taken Tizzy? Rush is not the only one wiv fairy dust or the know'ow to use its magic." She pulled out Tizzy's Wand and threatened, "Yer see, Todd, I 'ave to watch out for meself, too!"

Gasping in shock, Todd flew back, realizing she had actually stolen a Wand, a very serious crime, but he would not back down.

"You're a bold one Violet, but yer in *no* position to demand a fing. Remember, both me and Rush know exactly 'Oo you and yer friend Rosie *really* are. Now go and get us some mead before I forget meself and tell the King's soldiers wot Rosie's family 'ave done."

Rush tried to focus his eyes on Todd and called out, "What's going on 'ere, Todd?"

"Nofink mate, everyfing's under control. Just sortin' out the next drink, that's all."

Bill lifted his head from the table, having no idea what was happening. Violet disappeared but returned almost immediately with some cheap mead and while she poured it, a voice sounded from behind her.

"That's right, a fairy must do as she's told. It's the way of fings, especially for you, Violet. The sooner you learns that, the better off you'll be," said Rush.

He sat down again, heavily, his glazed eyes trying to focus on Bill.

"Now, Bill, in the mornin', we're goin' into the tunnels to search for the Royals and you'll go in first to scout, then me and Todd will follow... whatever yer do mate, don't lose the plot... er..."

He fumbled through his back pocket, eventually taking out an old, tatty piece of crumpled paper across which notes were scrawled. He unfolded it, trying to take out the creases, but the writing was illegible.

"Oh flip, can't remember me plan exactly, but we'll go over it tomorrah."

"Oh… yes, Rush, of course," replied Bill, knowing when the time was right he'd run for his life. Todd sat playing with his empty mead cone thinking about what would profit him the most. It wasn't too late to betray Rush to the King's soldiers. He tossed away his empty cone and said goodnight. Bill also took the opportunity to leave. Rush eventually managed to stand and stumbled out of the Inn to make his way home. On his way, he convinced himself he could still drink anyone senseless…

Tizzy found herself locked in a cold, dark, underground tunnel, with the ever-obedient hedgehogs guarding the exit. A disturbing feeling had come over her and she did not feel at all well. Her stomach ached and a cold sweat enveloped her whole body, making her shiver. She sat crouched in a corner as time ticked slowly by. 'How long have I been here?' she wondered. It felt like hours when she suddenly heard the faint hoot of an owl. Comforted by the sound, she called out, "Is that my owl out there?" But no reply came so she covered her face, sobbing so hard she forgot what she knew to be true, 'A crying fairy is a dying fairy'!

Left all alone in the tunnel, Tizzy longed for home. She was ill and in pain, feeling freezing cold and her wings felt strangely heavy. Moisture was quickly escaping through the pores of her skin which frightened her. Again she heard the hoot of an owl.

"Owl, are you there?" Tizzy called out.

This time, the owl softly replied, "Hoooo…"

"It's so dark I can't see you anywhere."

A feathery wing brushed by her shoulder as she reached out in the darkness.

"Can you please help me?"

All she could make out in the gloom were enormous, luminous eyes.

"Hello. How did you get in here?" she asked. "Where do you come from? Why have you chosen to follow me? Can you guide me to the Royal Court? I am in desperate trouble…"

The owl's head turned as if to survey Tizzy's very surroundings and as she asked questions, a stream of glitter magically and gently blew from the owl's beak, sparkling in the dark as it spread throughout the tunnel.

Hours later, she awoke to find herself warm and comfortable. Someone or something had thoughtfully covered her in a blanket of leaves. Feeling a little better, she sat up and brushed them away. Then, she heard a noise at the entrance. Busy clearing a path through the hedgehogs, Rush cast a huge shadow from the light streaming from his firefly jars. Fearing the evil elf would kill her owl, Tizzy's eyes scanned the dark to find it, but the bird was nowhere in sight and Rush, it seemed, was alone.

"You're comin' wiv me," he growled, grabbing hold of Tizzy.

"Where are you taking me?" she cried.

"To see someone yer might know."

He dragged her for some distance, much deeper into the tunnel and roughly threw her into the entrance of another. Tizzy stumbled as the smell of dried fruit filled her senses, Rush's gritty voice breaking the dark silence.

"Remik, take a close look at this fairy and tell me 'oo she is and where she comes from."

He held up a pair of lanterns and the two prisoners instantly recognized each other.

"Well!" Rush shouted, as he put down one lantern, "D'you know 'er…?

But no reply came from Remik.

"I'm warnin' yer, Remik, this silence ain't clever. We'll see 'ow yer feel 'bout talking after I 'ave left yer both 'ere a few nites. If the cold don't get yer, thirst will get 'er, and the Twiggy Men… out and about tonite – wouldn't want 'em to sniff yer out and find yer 'ere!"

But Remik remained silent, leaving Rush in a blind rage as he stormed off, accidently leaving behind a lantern. When Tizzy was sure the huge elf had gone, she picked up the light and held it to Remik's pale face, gasping, "I know you, you're my father's *top* soldier. But by all the Wizards, what have they done to you!"

"Never mind me, Your Highness. You look very ill! What's the matter with you? Tell me how you feel and what is happening out there. Do you know where your brother is?"

"Remik, I don't know, but I feel very cold and weak and my skin is wet all over."

Remik struggled, but could do nothing. Tizzy sat beside him and tried pulling apart the tangled vine knots around his wrists.

"There's no way I can release you, this vine is too tight and I have nothing sharp enough to cut it."

Without thinking, she reached for her Wand, but realized it wasn't there! Remik looked weak and drawn. Tizzy had to do something, so with the aid of the lantern, she scraped through the gravel on the ground trying to find something sharp, her tiny fingers finding only a small pouch inside which were a few berries. She offered them to Remik, but he turned away.

"Thank you, but I can't eat," he said, weakly.

"You must try, Remik. Berries have juice – they will give you strength."

But even as she spoke, she knew how he felt. She, too, could not face the berries and the sweet smell in the tunnel made her feel sick. They both sat silently in the dim light, and as the hours drifted by, the night began to draw in. She ran her right hand up and down her left arm and was thankful it felt dry. It was then she again heard the sound of an owl in the distance.

"Remik, can you hear that?"

"No, Tizzy, I can't. What is it you hear?"

"Am I going mad? The hooting of an owl. Don't you hear it?"

"No, sorry."

"Are you *sure,* Remik?"

"Yes, I'm sure, Tizzy."

In their prison and from out of the dark, another hoot could be heard, this time louder. But neither prisoner realized an owl was close by as glitter once again filled the air. Under its spell, both fell into a deep, restful sleep, a magic sleep that carried them to that far away, safe place the Wizards call 'Dream Lands'.

CHAPTER SIX

MIDDLESBOROUGH AND ETERNAL LONELINESS

Cecee held tightly onto Fiero's mane as he flew full speed towards the beach, but returning to where Johnny and Ace met with a terrible accident, awakened a painful loss. The Humans had cleared away the awful black, sticky mess, and there was little left to eat for the hungry seagulls that squabbled over the smallest leftovers. As Cecee and Fiero settled upon the beach, each looked around for a sign of the pouch but neither could see anything – the Humans appeared to have removed everything. Cecee took a last desperate look all around when, to her complete amazement and surprise, she noticed the intense sparkle from an object in the beak of a lone seagull resting upon the beach.

"Fiero!" she cried, "Look over there! That bird's picked up something! It's shining like golden fire! It could be the pouch containing the Seed!"

Unbeknown to Cecee, the bird was a female and placed its prized possession upon the sand. Standing guard, she squawked a severe warning as Fiero and

Cecee approached. Fairies with wingless Unicorns were not an uncommon sight, but Fiero was a deep concern – he could *fly*! And with that horn on his head, he could prove a formidable predator! As Cecee cautiously approached, it became obvious in no way would the bird allow her to come near, quickly picking up the pouch and flying away.

"Fiero! Follow that bird! It has the pouch in its beak!" screamed Cecee.

With Cecee firmly holding onto his mane, Fiero chased the seagull as it flew out to sea. On and on they flew until they reached a lonely, rocky island where they saw three nests, each at a different height. From one, noisy, baby seagulls with beaks wide apart, cried hungrily for food. The female bird landed near one of the nests, dropping the pouch into it. With that, Cecee flew from Fiero in a state of panic. "Fiero, it's too late! The seagull must be a female and has fed the Seed to her babies!"

"Calm down, Cecee, the Seed is inside the pouch," replied Fiero. "She'll have to find a way to get it out so she can feed her babies, which gives us a little time to think."

"Fiero, if we throw something into the air, do you think she might leave her nest to catch it? But what *do* they eat while they are nesting? There is nothing here."

"They go searching for whatever they can find and so must we," said Fiero, with a worried frown.

It didn't take long for Fiero to persuade Cecee to leave the island and go back to the beach in search of food. They decided the best place to try was the nearest restaurant but once there, they found a sign on the door saying, 'Closed for oil clean-up'. Fiero trotted around to the back and, finding a bin full of useless peanut shells, tipped it over and sorted through the remains where he discovered eight whole peanuts.

"Cecee, come quickly, look what I've found! Let's fly back to the island with them."

Cecee quickly flew over to him.

"That's wonderful!" she cried. "I have seen how seagulls love to catch these from the air. I could throw them while you hide behind a rock. When she tries to catch them, you can go to the nest and get the pouch!"

Off they flew back to the nest where the female gull stood guard over the golden pouch. One after the other, Cecee carefully threw seven of the nuts into the air, but the female bird didn't see them, she was far too busy guarding her new found treasure. Other gulls, delighted that once again peanuts were being thrown for them to catch, caught every one. Cecee couldn't be sure but was certain one gull caught a few in one go! She studied the one remaining nut in her hand, realizing with a sinking heart that this one had to do the trick. Just as she looked up into the sky to throw it, a voice interrupted her.

"Hi little bird, have a peanut, you look half starved!"

Cecee instantly recognized these words and swung round to see a sight she couldn't believe. There, standing on the rock proudly holding a peanut in his beak, was none other than her beloved Ace!

"Ace! Ace, by *all* the Wizards *how*…?!"

Ace dropped the nut.

"Well, you know it had to be me. Who else do you know who can catch three peanuts in one go? But, had to please the wife, so flew off to give her two. Yep, that's my wife you're trying to throw peanuts for, and those in the nest up there are my newborn kids. Careful, she's a fiercely protective mother and takes no prisoners!"

Cecee could hardly contain herself with the joy of seeing Ace and explained hurriedly, "Ace, she has something of mine – a pouch that is extremely important. How can I get it back?"

"Do you have any more of those peanuts?"

"Yes, but only the one!"

Ace picked up the nut he'd dropped and gave it back to her.

"Now you have two and this is the plan. Throw them for me to catch and when my wife sees I have more food, I'll call her to me this time. She will fly from her nest knowing I will pass them to her in the air. That'll give you the chance to grab the pouch as she takes the nuts from me, but keep the flying Unicorn out of sight."

Cecee threw the peanuts which Ace expertly caught. He called to his wife who left the nest to collect them – the plan was working well. From a short distance, Fiero watched impatiently and with the female gone from her nest, thought this would be *his* chance to help. It was now or never, so up he flew and yes, there, in the nest, was the pouch. Down he swooped to grab it, clumsily knocking the nest so hard it almost fell from the rock! Immediately the babies squealed and squawked with fear, instantly sparking anger within the mother, an anger so fierce she flew towards Fiero with head and beak thrust forward, wings outspread as wide as possible, screeching a terrifying challenge. Fiero, who could easily pierce the bird with his horn, didn't wish to fight, so flew to a now angry Cecee who hovered in the air as he flew past her with the pouch safely in his jaws. Thinking quickly, Cecee caught up with him, grabbed his flowing mane and away they sped, leaving the gull to tend her wailing young. Ace followed Cecee and Fiero, all landing on the beach where Fiero proudly presented the pouch to Cecee. Too relieved to tell him off, she opened the pouch but a sudden wave of sickness gripped her stomach. The pouch was empty! Cecee sat down hard in the sand, feeling totally helpless. The Seed was lost – she had failed all who trusted her. What will happen to her World now, and if she ever found home again, how would she answer to all? She looked pitifully at Ace who had tried his best to help.

"Ace, your wife has given the Seed to your young, I just know it."

"Don't give up little bird. As tired as we are, we must take a chance and return to the nest."

Even though Fiero was fed up with going back and forth, he readily agreed, the three returning to the same spot on the rocky island where Ace's wife continued to stand guard over her babies.

Straining his eyes, Fiero said with alarm, "Cecee, I think the gull has the Seed in her beak!"

"That's it! It's getting too much light!" replied Cecee, "I'm flying straight over there now!"

But Ace stopped her.

"Wait! I'll fly up to her, she'll listen to me."

With the Seed in her beak, the gull dipped her head into the nest – who should she give the food to, her babies were *all* so hungry. In an effort to share it among them, she tried to split the Seed and struck it as hard as she could against the rock. The helpless and horrified look on Cecee's face was too much for Fiero to bear. He had noticed the life-glow had almost gone from the Seed, forcing him into another swift decision. He flew up to catch the gull's attention, and realizing the terrifying predator was back, this time she wasn't going to leave her babies helpless. Forgetting she still had precious food in her beak, she swung her head around hard to let out a vicious squawk. One split second of pure anger and the Seed flew from her! Cecee seized it mid-air and the three turned away to escape back to the beach. The bird thought Fiero far too clever. He and his fairy friend had tricked her and threatened her babies very lives... they could no longer live! This time, she was going for the kill! Flying hard, she quickly caught up with them and began to peck at Cecee's legs and then her hands. Pain surged through her as the bird then flew to attack Fiero's throat. Ace watched in horror – he had to think quickly! It seemed only a kill would now satisfy his enraged wife! He flew in pretending to attack Fiero and Cecee, the bold move instantly quietening his wife. She broke free knowing her faithful husband would take care of the vicious predators. Remembering her babies were alone and unprotected, she sped back to the nest. Cecee, Fiero and Ace continued flying to the beach where they quickly came to a halt, Fiero almost falling over in his haste. Cecee ignored her injuries, all that mattered to her now was that she had the Seed once more. She examined it, realizing its life had vanished. Her mother's warning echoed in her mind, 'Don't let the Seed into the light. Keep it inside the pouch.' The only hope was to tuck it back inside as fast as possible. She placed it inside very carefully and retied the pouch. Now all she could do was to hope and wait. Sitting on a pile of kelp, she waited for a while before daring to peer inside, a sigh of relief escaping from her as she did so. To her utter joy, the Seed once again glowed with its life-force.

Ace hopped up next to her.

"Little bird, are you okay?"

"Yes Ace, a few scratches, but I'm fine. Thank you for asking."

"I don't know much about your World, but I know enough to realize that Seed must have some *im-por-tance*! You could have been killed!"

Cecee hugged him.

"Ace, you are the sweetest."

She released him from her embrace and took his old feather out of her hair.

"This is yours, Ace. I thought it was all I had left of you and Johnny, but here you are alive, so I can return it."

Ace took back the feather gladly.

"Wow little bird, thanks, I can make use of this. Yep, the wife is busy feathering yet another new nest… we're having more kids!"

With the feather in his beak, he flew upwards calling out, "You know us Americans do everything in a big way! Oh, and honey, don't be too hard on Humans, they saved me in the end. Took me to a place called a 'bird sanctuary', looked after me and honey, they did a fine job! Keep up your good work, maybe we can…"

"Can do what, Ace, what can we do?" Cecee called, with a warm smile.

Ace swooped down and flew past, struggling to hold onto the feather.

"Save the World little bird, save the World!"

Cecee's smile broadened as she watched Ace fly up again and out of sight.

Fiero nudged her.

"Come on, we must go too. Ace is closer to the truth than he can ever imagine," he said.

She flew up onto Fiero's back as he spread his wings to fly away and reunite with the mystical fairy called Icicle.

**

Finding Icicle's beautiful home was easy. Waterfalls cascaded once again, boiling around rocks before spilling into a beautiful, silver lake, the whole scene appearing to be alive as Cecee sat beside Icicle. It was the perfect time to ask the whereabouts of the mysterious Middlesborough. However, Icicle's answer came with plenty of warning.

"Cecee, should you choose to go there, you *must* be alert at all times. You see, High Wizards began building Middlesborough almost two hundred years ago. It is an Island with surrounding waters much fiercer than they look. The Wizards needed somewhere which could be protected, so made the waters appear calm, but they contain many hidden dangers. This ingenious idea came from a Wizard who lived in Middlesbrough, England – his name was Roddy. He wanted somewhere where magic could be placed into crystals in secret and to keep them safe. The place he and the High Wizards created was the Island called 'Middlesborough'. In memory of Roddy, you will see the letter 'R' displayed in many different places. Sadly, he died long ago and over the many years, Wizards have looked after the Island, keeping it protected and safe from harm. It has grown since Roddy knew it, with further schools built, all with different teachings. There are flying schools, schools for sports, schools teaching the art of writing Wizard, Latin, Gaelic and Welsh, schools for writing in the air with glitter, and more. I could go on and on, but what you need to understand is the larger the Island grew, the more others wanted it for its mysterious and magical powers.

There is now much jealousy among a few who live there. Fairies, elves and other creatures who have evolved, were born in Middlesborough, and until twenty years ago, they all lived and worked together in peace. But since then, some have turned bad. There aren't many there who have chosen a wayward path, but those who have, are extremely dangerous. Please be aware that the Island itself is constantly on the move which can bring about change in the strangest way… It's all too easy, however safe you think you are, to suddenly find yourself in a very unforgiving place. But there is somewhere you will always be safe, Patrick's Castle called 'Tiddlesworth' which once belonged to Arthur. This sits high on a mountain, overlooking the sea and what is so important, it doesn't move at all. Patrick is the Head Wizard, the chief of all Wizard Headmasters if you like, and carried on after Arthur was so brutally struck down.

Cecee listened, intrigued. "How do we get there?"

"Well, I and certain others whose names I cannot tell, can send you, but without any of us, if you happen to be by any lake, concentrate upon your reflection. As you stare, do not move your focus at all and take a little drink of the water. If you do this and you are by a true 'Window Lake', of which there are a few, you'll soon find the reflection below actually becomes you and what is above is just a shadow of yourself. You will be drawn into a mysterious purple hole, a 'Window', in the centre of the Lake, one which can even defy the speed of light itself. It is a dark energy, nothing bad, but all good. This energy warps back on itself and pushes anything along at tremendous speed! Cecee, it's difficult to fully explain now, but you will be taken to the Island in an instant. From this World, you will enter Middlesborough, but be warned, you must have a genuine purpose in mind. You may see hypnotic lights bobbing up and down on the surface of some. These are from the underwater dwellers, the 'Sidhe', beckoning you to follow – not even I know in which Lakes they live. Seeing you from the deep, they will think you are creatures from a neighbouring lake, come to take over theirs. Do not follow their lights – it's a trick and you'll lose your way, swimming through dangerous waters which will drown you both. This is one of the many reasons the Lakes are forbidden. To enter without strict instruction would be foolish. The water of the Lake presents a great barrier for it is the only connecting path to Middlesborough. Be very aware, once there, your journey will not be an easy one. There is so much for you to learn. There are parts of the Island which you should not visit, nor should you ever *want* to. One such place is Viperla's beautiful caves. Should you find yourself there, be very careful – she is an extremely dangerous fairy, full of hate, menace and impatience. She has been imprisoned and no one except a Wizard called Ian knows where. Dragons and Pixies protect her caves. Remember, one great advantage you have over Pixies is they cannot fly, but give one the chance and he'll poke you in the eye with a sharp stick! Another part of the Island is the furthermost, northern region called 'Thunderbird'. It may be the home of the fearsome Thunderbirds, but it is also a breeding island for beautiful butterflies that migrate from there to the mainland once a year. You must *never* play with these butterflies, Cecee. Oh they're beautiful and hypnotic, but they suffered a curse in the 'The War of Wands', and are now deadly to anyone who touches them."

Cecee stared at Icicle captivated, a little scared of the answer she may receive to the question she was about to ask…

"Can we communicate with our own World once we are there?"

"The Wizards send back many signs to us, Cecee, signs we couldn't possibly miss, especially from the air. Carved into cornfields, they tell us of the affairs in Middlesborough."

"Can we send signs *back* to them?"

"Yes, our World is mirrored in theirs and when we make our cornfield signs, they see them in Wizard's Eye Lake. If cornfields grow by a lake, you will know that it is a 'Receiving Lake' through which messages are sent to us."

'How amazing!' Cecee thought, her mind racing away with itself. 'Of course, there were lakes by Seven Oaks Woods, and the cornfields where all were going to shelter from the storm were right next door to the Royal Quarters. Her father would receive messages there!'

"Cecee, are you listening?" Icicle asked.

"Yes," replied Cecee. "Sorry, I was just trying to take in what you were saying."

"Cecee, it is very important that you listen to me… You will notice something else strange to you. Two Suns and two Moons, one Sun and Moon is actually there, the others are reflections of the Sun and Moon from our World."

Fiero listened, spellbound. Icicle's story of the Lake… it's how he came to be here! He hadn't seen any lights bobbing up and down on the surface of the Lake, he was certain of that, but he knew one thing – lights or not, he wanted to return home.

"Remember, Wizard's Eye Lake in Middlesborough is the only entrance to, or exit from that World, but is cursed by two Troll families. You must take care not to…"

Icicle's explanation came to an abrupt stop as Cecee interrupted her.

"Icicle, I've heard enough and I don't have a lot of time. Please take us to the nearest place to enter."

"Are you sure you want to go, Cecee? The dangers are endless, and you could be caught in a labyrinth…"

Cecee knew she had no time to spare and couldn't listen to any more that might change her mind. She had to get to Middlesborough without fail. Her father spoke about it all the time and it could prove to be her pathway back home and whatever the cost, she must find a way.

"Yes, thank you Icicle, but we really must go!"

"Remember something else, Cecee, dragons can be your best friend or your very worst enemy, so never turn your back on one."

Icicle removed her Crown and held it carefully.

"This Crown I wear was given to me by Arthur who was killed by an English elf named Rush. All I have left of Arthur is this Crown and my beautiful castle which is hidden behind the waterfalls. But now, prepare yourselves, I must use my magic to send you to Middlesborough. Remember, look for the purple Window at the centre of my Lake, and be on your guard for the bobbing lights of the Sidhe."

Cecee and Fiero now understood that Icicle's large, ice-blue lake was indeed a Window Lake. It looked magical as distant little ripples danced and sparkled in the late afternoon sunshine. But Fiero was concerned, wondering if those sparkles would confuse him. Could they in fact be the threatening, bobbing lights of the Sidhe – he hoped not!

After thanking Icicle, Cecee sat on Fiero's back and both waited for whatever Icicle was about to do. She began to chant a language neither Cecee nor Fiero understood, as quite by magic, a black, glowing wand appeared in Icicle's hand. She lifted from the ground, turning around slowly in the air, a bright glow from the wand now appearing all around her. The more she chanted, the faster she turned and the stronger the glow grew. Then, suddenly, all stopped. The wand flew from her hand, light streaming behind it, and hovered over the centre of the Lake sending down a bolt of brilliant, white light. It then spun back through the air and into Icicle's hand.

"Fiero, I've awoken the Window! Take Cecee over my Lake! Go *now*!" Icicle called, before slowly descending to the ground.

Off they flew. Looking down, Fiero searched all around but saw nothing. Then suddenly, he spotted something.

"Cecee, is that it? The purple patch to our right, much smaller than I had imagined. Are you ready to go in?"

"Yes, Fiero, that must be it! Let's go!"

Fiero's wings swept the air as the Window from the deep started to swirl. Captured by its magic, Fiero folded his wings and shot headlong towards it. Cecee, holding on for dear life, took one last look back at Icicle, still surrounded in a faint glow, as Fiero plunged into the swirling waters. The last thing Icicle saw of them was Fiero's blue mane and Cecee's golden hair flowing and twisting in the strong current. Hoping it wasn't too late, Icicle removed her Crown and, mustering all her energy, and in a burst of sudden light, threw it out and over the Lake. It flew through the air as she clearly called, "Shield companion, unstoppable energy, fly like an arrow!"

The Crown spun violently through the air, hitting the centre of the Lake with a splash. Immediately the shape of the Crown changed and now an awesome, silver eel with sparkling, jewelled eyes, swam at the speed of light down into the abyss with just one purpose... *seek and find the Princess Cecee!*

Darkness lay heavily upon the woods of Seven Oaks, a chilly tension hanging in the air. The sky was clear and full of stars, but this gave a false feeling of calm as in the distance, a snowstorm drew nearer. A full, silvery Moon cast its image over the icy waters of a lake, its light catching drowsy ripples as they softly danced in the breeze. Tross flew down for a drink, heartened to see a lucky omen – a pair of swans, one black, one white, moving gracefully over the water. But once again, if only Tross had known. Hidden in the high branches of a nearby tree was Todd, watching the Prince's every move. He couldn't decide whether he should betray Rush and tell the King of the elf's evil plan, but then again, with Rush's devious mind, their gang could easily capture this small and tired band. Todd decided to quietly leave the tree but as he did so, an unexpected hoot from an owl broke the silence of the cold night, sending a shiver through his body.

Flying towards home, he admitted to himself he was more than a little scared of Rush. He was several years older than him and his wings and body ached, but what could he do? At his age, he needed comforts and only a lot of sparkle could bring those. It was too late for him to start all over again, far too late. Whilst contemplating his future, he heard another owl call hauntingly through the bleak, winter woods, sending yet another chill down his spine. 'These owls, all over the place tonite…givin' me the right shivers!' he thought.

Elm, deep in thought, sat on a rock, wondering if they'd missed something in those tunnels. Tross settled by his side.

"Tross," said Elm, "I'm going to take us to a fairy who I know will feed us. It's now dark and the perfect time to travel. I think our morale will improve once we have eaten."

Tross agreed.

Motley's scouting job was complete, so he said his goodbyes, and left to venture back to his home. The remainder headed west, deciding to walk to save their energy. It was cold, dark and silent but Violet's Inn was not far. Elm watched between the trees for any movement, while icy twigs crunched underfoot. As they struggled through the tangled undergrowth, Elm heard a cracking sound to his left, about two trees away. He stopped, his heart beating faster.

"Tross, did you hear that?"

"Yes, and it didn't come from our footsteps!"

The little group peered intensely into the darkness. They heard a growl and in the moonlight, saw a slight movement. Was there a shadow of something bent double, hiding behind a tree?

With a whisper Tross asked, "Elm, what *is* it?"

"A Twiggy Man, and where there is one there will be more! Stay grounded! Don't fly up anyone, you could easily put yourself in their line of fire!"

Elm searched his belt for something while Tross and the soldier kept watch. He took out a small piece of wood around which long vines were wound. He carefully unwound these as Twiggy Men, glowing hideously, began to appear from behind every tree. A ghostly, green glow of what had once been leaves surrounded them, cruel looking twigs protruding from the back of their arms and legs. Holes in their bodies opened and closed, breathing in air but blowing out waste, poisonous gas. Yellow sap oozed from every crack in their small, twiggy, trunk-like bodies. Some creaked and cracked as they moved, while others moaned or made angry, snorting, pig-like sounds. Soon there were many moaning, grunting hordes, the tall and thin, the short and fat, the ones bolt upright and those bent double, all slowly heading towards the elves. Elm couldn't give them another moment! Holding the vines, he hurled the piece of wood attached high above his head and began to whirl it around and around until the wood hummed and whistled its strange song through the air. Louder and louder, waves of sound were sent far into the distance, making the Twiggy Men stop to look to the sky, their breathing-holes working harder and harder, sap oozing everywhere, they could see nothing of what was soon to happen… Snow clouds, hanging low and heavy, didn't bother them at all as they shifted their gaze once more towards the elves, resuming their slow but determined walk. Creak! Crack! Closer and closer they came, while the chant from Elm's spinning wood grew louder and louder. Brave Elm made no attempt to shield his body from what would soon be an attack from long, flying splinters sharp enough to run through a tree. He continued whirling the wood around his head at an even pace, sending forth further waves of throbbing sound.

Suddenly, Elm stopped and began to wind the vines around his wrist, bringing the wooden piece back into his hand. Tross stared at him, bewildered to see him give up so quickly. Clearly, whatever Elm was doing, could not be working! But then, through the snow clouds, came a sudden, deafening, dark, strange sight. Woodpeckers, in their hundreds, swarmed down, their beaks relentlessly pecking the Twiggy Men until the evil creatures collapsed into motionless twigs. Seeing the remains of the Twiggy Men all over the ground and certain their task was complete, the birds flew noisily away, one leading what seemed to be an enormous dark wave, up and out of sight. A deep and eerie silence followed. In the stillness, Tross looked around fearfully.

"Elm, what on this Earth were *they*?" he asked.

"They were ghosts, threatening ghosts of trees now long departed. There's no time to explain now Tross, but you are innocent of many things that happen out here in the woods, away from Court. Just remind me to make you one of these."

Elm held out the piece of wood for Tross to take a close look. Moving the vines along it a little, Tross studied a beautiful, oblong carving. Elm explained.

"It's a 'Thunder-spell' or 'Buzzer'. One of these attached to strong vines and used correctly, will always keep you safe from the Twiggy Men. Either this or loads, and I mean loads, of water will kill them." He looked up to the sky and added, "A snow flurry or two won't do it!"

The storm arrived and soon snow lay thick upon the ground. Approaching Violet's Inn, Tross saw elves busily clearing away snow from the entrance. Upon entering, the place seemed in complete chaos. Violet, spotting Elm, ran to him and sobbing, fell into his arms.

"Elm, thank all the Wizards you're 'ere! A Princess was 'ere secretly staying wiv me. Rush, Todd and another elf come in for drinks, saw 'er and demanded to know where she come from and now they've taken 'er away! We must *do* somefing, I think they mean to 'arm 'er!"

"Violet, calm yourself. Don't worry, we'll sort this out."

Tross, overhearing their conversation, asked, with both hope and dread in his heart, "Did you say a Princess was here? Was her name Cecee?"

"No, 'er name's Tizzy!" came Violet's quick reply.

"Tizzy," Tross blurted. *"Tizzy must have flown into the woods alone!* Elm, *both* my sisters lost, and where on this Earth is my father!"

Violet thought to herself, 'He must be Tizzy's brother, the Prince, so his other sister must be Cecee and both lost! If only I could say something, but I daren't! If I do, they will soon discover who I am and the terrible crime Rosy's family has committed. Oh, what shall I do?!' Poor Violet, what an awful dilemma she found herself in.

The wind picked up, moaning through the snow laden trees. Dark clouds continued to hide the Moon and stars. In the dimness, and on the highest branches of the trees, the black silhouettes of five owls loomed, their feathers ruffled by continual flurries of snow. The wind easily carried their secret, hooting messages throughout the woods, from one owl to another. Violet's voice also carried without effort as she called to Rosie who was busy cleaning her home in the next tree over.

"Please, Rosie, come and 'elp me make somefing for the soldiers to eat."

But Tross interrupted.

"We haven't time to eat now! We must go back and search. It looks like more heavy snow will fall and those tunnels will be buried. If Cecee and Tizzy are in there hiding, they will die!"

He flexed his wings to leave but Elm flew up to stop him.

"Tross, don't panic! It's bad if we lose control. We must eat first to keep up our strength. We'll return to the tunnels immediately after we've eaten."

"What if my father has sent soldiers and we've missed them? We're wasting time!" But Elm stood firm.

"Tross, we *must* take a few minutes to eat, it's not going to change anything. Forgive me, but I must insist. Please sit down, you have put me in charge so now do as you're told!" Elm said, hoping he wasn't taking too much of a liberty with the Prince...

A little snow had blown into Violet's Inn, lightly covering some of the toadstools. With frustration, Tross cleared snow from the top of one and sat to eat berries without further argument. Watching the Prince, Elm's heart quickened, having never before in his whole life spoken like that to Royalty. When this was all over, he wondered what would be reported to the King.

Violet had disappeared but returned with unusual 'gifts' for Elm.

"Elm, me and Rosie made these weapons. Please take 'em wiv yer. They're very effective, but please be extremely careful," she said, inwardly hoping Elm would accept without too many questions. Elm's initial feeling was one of guarded caution as these weapons really did seem to him to be out of the ordinary. However, he gratefully accepted, warmly embracing Violet. With that, he and the others left the Inn.

Later, all arrived at the camp near to the tunnels, where Elm closely inspected Violet's 'gifts'. Thick, wooden twigs bent and tied with strong vine… just ordinary bows, or so they seemed. He pulled an arrow from a roll of twenty, realizing as he did so, he had never seen one quite like it before. It was very sharp but had no quill, as light as a feather even though it seemed to be made of pure silver. He placed it on the vine, drawing it back as far as he could, aiming the arrow at a small branch of a distant, large tree, bathed in moonlight and only just visible.

Releasing it, the arrow flew at tremendous speed and without effort to its target, scoring a direct hit! Elm was an excellent bowman, but not that good! Positive that an ordinary arrow at that distance would have definitely missed such a small target, particularly in the darkness, he loaded another and purposefully aimed it away from the same small branch. Releasing the arrow, it shot forward, curved to the left and then to the right before flying forward, hitting the branch dead centre once again! It seemed the arrow had read his very thoughts which to Elm, was more than a little unsettling. Violet must have put magic into them! Elm was not at all comfortable with this. Keeping his thoughts to himself, he nevertheless handed the weapons to the others. Each with a few arrows tucked into his vine belt, bow over his shoulder, firefly jar at the ready, the three cleared away the snow and entered the tunnels. After a thorough search, it was, alas, the same story – there was no sign of either Cecee or Tizzy. As they made their way back towards the exit, Elm noticed in the dim light, hedgehogs huddled together.

"Halt everybody, I have a strange feeling those hedgehogs may be covering the entrance to another tunnel!"

While Elm and the others were deep inside, Rush, Bill and Todd met at the tunnel entrance. Rush whispered, "Right then, Bill, in yer go. Check the first four tunnels and report back. I'll wait for me army of elves to arrive. Some 'ow, we're gonna find that Princess and 'er bruvver."

Bill made no move.

"All by myself?" he asked.

"Yeah, Bill, all by yerself, mate," Rush answered, peering at him impatiently. But again, Bill remained where he was.

"Well, what yer waitin' for, Bill, off yer go!"

Bill racked his brains for an excuse.

"Why don't you send one of *your* gang to scout the tunnels, Rush?"

"I don't fink so, Bill. You'll go in furver or you'll die. You choose…"

Bill gulped.

"But it's so dangerous, and there are *dead* soldiers in there! We should all go in together and…"

"You're lucky you ain't a dead'un too, Bill. I 'ighly recommend yer go mate or, err-ummm, maybe I should turn yer over to the King's soldiers… remember, yer left yer post, naughty, naughty!"

Bill knew it was no use arguing so he took a deep breath and flew in, counting the dark, musty tunnels as he went. 'Two, three… where did all the dead go?' he thought to himself. Now feeling *very* scared, he flew back towards the second tunnel… mumbling, he could hear mumbling! He came to an immediate stop and pressed himself up against the tunnel wall to listen. He could hear Tross and Elm in the second tunnel and they were about to leave – they may see him at any moment. Then, before he could think any further, he found himself face to face with the Prince!

"Bill!" Tross hissed through tightened lips as he grabbed him, pinning him against the wall, his dagger at Bill's throat.

"Before I slit you wide open and make one horrible mess, tell us why you betrayed our trust, you little weed! What are you doing here, and why did you desert your post?"

"Have you seen anyone, Bill?" asked Elm.

Not taking his eyes from Tross's dagger still thrust at his throat, Bill whimpered, "No, hush, one at a time please, one at a time. I … I got lost, and err, thank all the Wizards, I bumped into you, that's all!"

Tross turned his thorn dagger towards Bill's left wing.

"I know full well you pulled a disappearing act on us. You ought to be arrested. Why, I should carve off a wing right here and now!"

"No, you really don't understand!" Bill whined, shaking in his boots. "They captured and tortured me!"

"No names, Bill, only they? Oh give me strength! Don't worry, I'll let you live. It'll give you time to invent some other ridiculous story. We could all do with a hearty laugh!" said Tross, putting away his dagger.

Rush, still waiting outside the tunnels, paced up and down.

"Where's Bill... e's bin gone ages! What's 'e up to?"

By now, Rush's gang had arrived and, determined to find the weedy elf, decided to lead them into the tunnels to search for him. They made their way, passing the second where Tross and company held Bill. Rush raced through, past the fourth and as far as the sixth but found nothing. Tripping over all sorts of obstacles and avoiding pesky insects whilst fighting through undergrowth in search of the hopeless Bill, was not his favourite pass-time. Enraged beyond belief, he decided to turn back and head for the exit. At the same time, Tross and the others had left their tunnel to venture deeper in. Now both groups were on a dangerous course to meet one another...

As they headed onward, Bill had a strong feeling they were bound to encounter Rush and Todd, but when? He kept going, trying his best to stay close to Elm, hiding in his shadow as much as possible. Then, without warning, he was certain he heard a voice!

"Hey, did anyone hear that?"

Everyone stopped to listen.

"I didn't hear a thing, Bill," replied Tross, who then asked, "did anyone else?" to which both answered, "No!"

Suddenly, Elm yelled, "Tross, to your left! An armed elf, right side tunnel!"

The elf saw Tross, backed into the dark and shouted, "Rush, they're over here!" Elm immediately shouted his orders.

"Drop and load your bows! Fire at will!"

Rush and his group threw their lanterns down to take cover, silver arrows now quickly flying everywhere. Elm looked for Bill who had disappeared in the confusion, but had no time for distraction – his only concern right now was for the Prince. Suddenly, he saw Todd run in the direction of the exit.

"I fink some of our gang 'ave bin killed, Rush! Run for it!" shouted Todd, as, along with some of the gang, he made a dash out of the tunnel. Rush's army of beetles now emerged from the depths, gases blowing at random from their rear ends in defense – the air was thick with obnoxious odours. Elm choked on the fumes but saw his chance, flying fast to catch up with the old elf Todd who was now far behind the gang, catching him in his right leg with his dagger, bringing him down hard into the snow. Following close behind, Tross pounced onto Todd, pinning him to the ground. But at the same moment, both Tross and Elm watched helplessly as Rush left the tunnels and escaped into the darkness.

"Elm, Rush is getting away! Should I go after him?" asked an eager Tross.

"Phew! Am I glad to see you safe, Tross, but no, I'll get some vine and we'll tie up Todd. Then we can find out if they have hidden Cecee, Tizzy and Remik. Todd will give us the information we'll need, won't you, Todd." But Todd made no reply.

What was left of Rush's gang, now emerged from the tunnels, coughing and spluttering, their eyes streaming from the effects of the obnoxious gases from Spikey's army of beetles. Wiping their stinging eyes, they flew off to disappear into the woods. Close behind, followed the dreadful insects. With snow covering their usual hiding places, they had nowhere to go and, to add to their fear, Rush had vanished and taken their leader Spikey with him leaving them to fly aimlessly around.

Bill knew exactly where the food tunnel was – a perfect place to hide and think and, what's more, he could get there quickly. On his way, he found a bow and a very smart looking quiver of silver arrows which Elm had dropped in the tussle, both of which Bill picked up and secured to his back.

If he could move those annoying hedgehogs far enough away to get into the food tunnel, no one would guess he was in there and he could vanish once everything settled down. To his surprise, as he reached the nest, one hedgehog moved a little and, accepting cutting himself on the spines was certainly better than dying, he squeezed past. Once inside, he sat down quietly to wait. Tizzy and Remik silently watched Bill enter but no one seemed aware that an owl had quietly hidden himself in a large hole in the tunnel wall.

Elm and Tross stood over Todd.

"Do you know where Princess Cecee, Princess Tizzy and Remik are?" Elm asked.

In reply, Todd blurted out, "No, I don't! It was all Rush's idea. *He* 'id 'em, not me!"

"You had better say something worth listening to, or you're one dead elf!" threatened Elm.

Todd cringed.

"I've no idea *where* they are, but if yer capture Rush, 'e'll know. 'E did it I tell yer. Try the food tunnel, maybe they're in there. It's easy to find 'cos when Rush locks anyfink up, 'e covers the exits wiv 'is 'edge'ogs!"

Elm knew it! That hedgehog nest was covering the food tunnel. They secured Todd to a tree and left him all alone. Returning to the tunnels and entering, Tross noticed an unusual number of owls, but ignored them and headed towards the nest.

Outside, Rush watched from a distance, unable to hear anything that had been said between Todd and Elm. Staying very low, and when all was clear, he crawled over to Todd and untied his vines.

"Rush! Oh, good one mate, them vines were tite!" Todd said gratefully, hoping more than anything, Rush had not heard a word he had said against him.

The two villainous elves together again, Rush quickly told Todd of his latest scheming plan...

In the tunnels, Elm tried to move the hedgehogs while Tross and the soldier, finding two firefly lanterns, stood guard. All at once, the creatures moved aside, clearing the way. The three entered, their eyes slowly adjusting to the darkness, Tross straining to see who or what the black shapes in the dark corner may be. Holding up his lantern for closer inspection, he found Tizzy and Remik huddled together! Tizzy didn't look at all well and crawled along the ground towards Tross who put down his lantern and knelt beside his young sister.

"By all the Wizards... my darling, Tizzy!"

"Tross, please help me, I feel really ill," she weakly replied.

The wet coldness of her skin had returned and as she put her arms around her brother, her touch filled him with horror. He looked closely at her and found her beautiful wings torn and falling apart which meant only one thing – Tizzy was dying!

Elm put down his lamp by the side of Remik to cut loose his ties, when suddenly his attention was drawn towards the exit. Dark shadows moved in the murky, damp haze from the lanterns. Elm again grabbed his light for a clearer look, only to see none other than Rush and Todd!

"Well, well, well, wot' do we 'ave 'ere, then?" Rush asked, scornfully.

Elm flew to help the Prince guard Tizzy, but Rush did not recognize Tross in the dim light and pushed them both aside to grab the young Princess. Hiding in the corner of the tunnel, Bill faced yet another dangerous situation as he saw Rush take the human fork from his back-tube and hold the sharp prongs to Tizzy's throat uttering a warning, "Now, everyone will do as they're told, or she'll die!"

Slowly, he began to withdraw with Tizzy. Bill panicked, wondering whether to stay where he was or go with Rush. He unhooked the bow from his shoulder and stepped out of the shadows where Rush could see him.

"Bill! Well, well, well, I am glad you're 'ere to cover us and wiv a weapon too! I've never been so 'appy to see anyone in me life!" said Rush, with a large grin across his loathsome face.

Carefully, Bill slowly took out a silver arrow and loaded it onto his bow. He pulled back the vine tightly, seemingly aiming the arrow at Tross, then, in the next second, he turned his head to face Todd, remembering how truly evil this elf was and all that he had done.

'Perhaps this is my chance to make good for what *I* have done wrong. Just look at how these two elves have treated poor Tizzy and Remik! Todd deserves to be killed!' Bill's mind was set and Todd was his last thought as he turned to aim the bow at him! Rush hollered at Bill to break his concentration, "Bill! You worthless little weasel! What do you think you are doing?!"

All at once Bill's fingers slipped from the string, releasing the arrow. Even in the dim light, it glinted brightly as it whistled through the air towards Tross. But while all were gripped in hypnotic terror, the arrow stopped in flight, turned and wavered as if undecided where to go, then shot at lightning speed straight into Todd's chest, killing him outright! It all happened so fast that Rush, shocked at the sudden death of his friend, dug the sharp prongs of his weapon even harder into Tizzy's throat. Silently, an owl appeared from one of the many nooks in the dark tunnel and, spreading his mighty wings, flew out, straight at Rush. The evil elf found himself snatched up in the owl's powerful talons with such force that he let out a huge gasp, immediately losing hold of Tizzy and dropping his weapon. Before he knew what was happening, the owl had whisked him through the tunnels and out into the open, taking him high above the clouds and out of sight...

Owls now appeared from every corner. All those lost were once again together and the chance to escape had arrived. Plucking them one by one, the strong birds carried them out and off to the safety of the Royal Court. But, above the clouds, the owl holding Rush tightened his grip even more while changing direction and flying far away. Flying over Seven Oaks Lake, the owl's keen eyes expertly found the purple Window and Rush found himself heading straight towards it. With a splash, down they went into the eerie darkness where the swirling waters carried the two deep into the Lake's core. Rush, stricken with horror, realized all too quickly that the owl carried him to a place he had been before, 'Middlesborough'! He struggled to free himself as they left the surface of Wizard's Eye Lake and flew northward over Moderf Island. Changing course again, the owl flew northeast over Hagarty Land, then turning southeast to fly high over Viperla's caves, veering eastward, over the northern part of Serpent Lake. Then the owl sped towards the towering turrets of Tiddlesworth Castle, turning again for a final descent. He entered a large window at the top of the Castle's magnificent central dome, heading onwards to pass through a long, dimly-lit secret corridor. Paintings of Wizards, past and present, one after another, passed by Rush's line of vision. Finally, the owl had arrived at his destination, 'Coney Hall'. Two great, black doors in the shape of a Wizards' hat stood in front of the owl as he placed Rush upon the ground, hovering above him, still tightly holding onto Rush's shoulders. The elf stared spellbound at a large, golden crest of Middlesborough that had been placed in the centre of the doors, with a sign to the right which read, 'Clenworth Judging Chambers'. The owl sent out three distinct hoots. With a groan, the great doors slowly opened wide. A voice from inside spoke a language Rush did not know at all.

"I read a writ of Habeas Corpus for the elf, Rushmore!"

Rush was then swiftly taken inside where an enormous round table faced him. There the owl carried him to its centre, carelessly releasing his grip so that the oversized elf landed with a thud. There was an unnatural quietness as Rush looked around. Then, another door opened with an unnerving creak as Rush watched twenty hooded figures silently enter to take their places around the very table he had been so ungracefully placed upon. Their faces were dark and cast downward as all stood perfectly still. Rush peered at them trying to see a face, any face! One by one, they lifted their heads, white beards cascading down their chests. Rush's gaze was drawn to one pair of eyes, the eerie glow radiating from within hypnotizing him. He found the energy to pull his stare away, only to be drawn to another pair of penetrating eyes!

With the smell of magic filling the Chambers, it was clear the figures surrounding him were the elder Wizards of Middlesborough! Uncomfortably aware that the Wizards' beards looked exactly like the one Arthur had worn, Rush finally managed to tear his eyes from the mesmerizing stare to see yet another disturbing sight. The Wizards Circle of Power was broken by one space, a space that, without doubt, demanded his utmost attention. The owl who had brought him to this awful place had left, but now returned holding something in his talons, laying down whatever it was in the darkness of the empty space. Rush's stare was fixed upon the object which now became clearer. Lying there, was a folded purple and yellow cloak. One of the dark figures called, "Enter, Blackette-Ord!"

Through the same creaking door, a small elf entered, carrying a Wizard's Sceptre which he placed by the side of the cloak.

"Exhibit A," he exclaimed in a forceful voice, before promptly leaving. Rush instantly recognized 'Exhibit A', his mind racing back to the moment of his terrible crime.

'Arthur's magic Sceptre, the very one I used to kill 'im!' he recalled. 'The Sceptre 'ad so much blood on it that I 'ad to leave it and run!' Unable to stop himself, the foolish Rush yelled out, "Arthur's Sceptre!"

The elder Wizards stared at the murderous creature as he sat in the middle of the table, their eyes piercing him to the very core. A voice boomed forth, "The accused recognizes the exhibit. The trial shall commence!"

Another Wizard spoke out. "The Wizard Ian is not present – I will act in his place!"

These were terrifying words to Rush. He looked to each Wizard, searching for any sign of pity as each pulled his Sceptre from its tube and aimed the powerful crystal end towards him. Accusations repeatedly came forth in low voices throughout the fearful Chamber.

"You wear the mark of a Wizard killer! Rid yourself of it and you will be set free!"

At first, Rush did not understand, stuttering, "I… I…" then realized what they meant – the badge he wore so proudly on his hat! For the first time since his horrible deed, he cast aside the hat, happy to rid himself of it. He looked to them and smiled slyly, 'they will have to let me go now!' he thought.

But Rush could not be more wrong. The image of the skull moved from the hat and magically passed through the sleeve of his coat. A terrified Rush quickly rolled back his sleeve to find the scull was now on his arm! His own flesh! Desperately, he tried to rub it away but it wouldn't budge. His heart pounded, fear gripping his throat, leaving him to look around in horror, as he saw each Wizard's face had changed. Through their dark hoods, ugly shapes of the skull he once wore so proudly peered back at him. The time had come for judgement to be passed. Holding their Sceptres high with one hand, the Wizards all pointed bony forefingers with the other at Rush. Lightning instantly flashed out of every Sceptre shooting up to the ceiling and rebounding to surround Rush, almost paralysing him! Confusion made his head spin, as before his eyes, Arthur's old and tatty Wizard hat had renewed itself! The badge in the shape of a scull which Rush had so proudly displayed, had changed back to the Crest of Middlesborough and now in its rightful place, a magical glow shone forth, almost blinding him. He managed to shield his eyes while an immense energy seemed to surround his whole body. Suddenly, everything seemed to grow larger and larger! By contrast, he felt much smaller and of little importance, but worst of all, completely vulnerable, particularly when he saw the clothes which once fitted him now covered him like a gigantic tent! To add to Rush's disbelief, he could actually see his nose growing and projecting forward, his ears shrinking close to his head. But it didn't stop there... sharp spines now quickly sprouted from his head and body! He scuffled out from under his old clothes and saw an ant running along the tabletop, a strange feeling overcoming him. He wanted to eat it, the very thought making him feel sick! The Wizards had changed him from the tallest and strongest of elves feared by all, to a small, insignificant, insect eating hedgehog! Exhausted, he shuddered, thinking his punishment far too harsh. With no time to think further, an owl whisked him up and out of the Chambers and back to Wizard's Eye Lake. Through the water they went until they emerged into Seven Oaks Lake.

In what seemed like just a few moments, he was back home in the woods. The owl placed him in the old food tunnel with the other hedgehogs and left him. The others sniffed and snuffled around the newcomer and, recognizing the smell belonged to cruel Rush, they turned away from him, leaving him to fend for himself. Worse still, he did not dare venture out for fear of an elf kicking him around with the very shoes he had invented and sold for huge profit. But another blow was to come... His favourite pet beetle, Spikey, refused to come anywhere near him. Because of this, his once loyal army of beetles also stayed well out of his way. From now on, his only company would be irritating fleas that would make his back itch, a horrible itch he could not possibly reach to scratch! But his real punishment was to come. Throughout his life, Rush had brought nothing but fear to many. The wise Wizards of Middleborough would now bring to *him* his very worst fear of all, a fear from which he could never escape... eternal, helpless, loneliness...

CHAPTER SEVEN

THE CORNISH COAST, ROYAL QUARTERS AND ARREST HER!

In the secret depths of Seven Oaks Woods, Florie returned to her circle of old friends. She had her herbal mixture, that was the easy part, but for the potion to save Tizzy, she needed a very special ingredient. Furthermore, she must transfer to Tizzy some of the magic learnings handed down to her long ago, learnings that over the ages had proven to help strengthen any fairy. As for the special ingredient... well, that comes from the deepest caves in Cornwall. Finding this would present a challenge only very few would accept. Florie was old and wondered if she had the energy to journey to the Earth's core, find what she wanted and then return. If only at this very moment she could find the magic to make her just twenty years old, full of life and energy...

Green crystals cast a soft, eerie light upon the faces of the old and trusted ones as they gathered in a secret place known to them as 'The Umbra'. All sat ready to discuss the magic Florie wanted so desperately, but a stern warning came from her best and most trusted friend, Emily.

"Florie, as you know, we're doing this at great risk. Once we have performed the magic and given you the years you desire, you will have only six hours before the magic will reverse. When it leaves you, you will be thirty years older than you are now. Remember what this will mean, Florie, as you are already seventy years old... there's other magic we could use, not as powerful but the lasting effects will not be anywhere near as drastic."

Florie stared into the peaceful, green glow of the crystals and thought. She had lived and learned so much but had let herself down. Reflecting upon how tired she always felt, it seemed she slept a little too long these days. Florie had sensed Tizzy was going to enter the rainbow that fateful day and should have been more decisive, perhaps calling her back to explain all the dangers. Was it her advancing age that made her act so slowly? If anything happened to Tizzy, Florie would never forgive herself. Her gaze still fixed upon the crystal's light, she answered her friend with conviction.

"Yes, Emily, I know what I must give up, and I know what will happen to me – it *is* powerful and *very* frightening magic!"

The day was set for when they would all meet again, the day Florie would be given the magic she so longed for. It was sunny but cold as Florie said goodbye, leaving her circle of faithful friends. Holding a list of do's and dont's, she read aloud the dont's as she flew towards home.

"Don't fall into the bat pooh and get stuck, you might get eaten alive by cockroaches! Don't fly near the fat glow-worms' silk threads, or stare at the alluring

blue light glowing from their bottoms! Don't fly out with the bats or the hungry falcons might eat me! Don't go near the cave dwellers. Don't be tricked by mysterious under-waters that look as though they have air above. And last, but not least, don't go too near slimy, hanging snottites!"

Her Wand safely strapped in place, she flew as fast as her old wings could carry her. Florie had convinced Emily that the magic used must make her *and* her Wand only twenty years old. She giggled to herself – it had been a challenge convincing the others to agree to make her Wand as young as she wished, but she had succeeded. Her old, crooked Wand with its dwindling powers, would be of little use where she was going. Florie knew it would be the last thing the two of them could ever do together and would use the magic to its full effect. After all, when it finally leaves her, it will also leave her Wand, perhaps crumbling it into dust.

The day arrived and Florie returned at The Umbra where the elders were seated around a huge pot into which all their crooked old Wands had been placed. A roaring fire had been lit beneath, and Florie was asked to place her Wand inside with the others. As she did so, the potion within immediately bubbled and boiled, steam rising to fill The Umbra. The Wands danced around inside as if they wanted to escape, sparkles and coloured bubbles flying everywhere. As Emily chanted her magic, more and more sparkles and bubbles burst and popped, the mass of energy now spinning around and around as Emily repeated the chant over and over again. The spinning mass all at once descended around Florie's head, twisting faster and faster before quite suddenly entering her very being! Florie shrieked as a strange hot then cold shiver ran through her. She gasped as she looked down to see a young, unwrinkled hand, smooth and perfect. Even Emily could not believe how quickly the magic had done its work as all looked on in awe. With a new and youthful over excitement, Florie reached into the pot for her revived Wand.

"Noooo, don't do that, it's far too soon!" Emily screeched. "Not yet, you *must* wait!"

Florie felt terrific, truly alive and for the moment, free from the ill-effects of the rainbow! She had a tremendous urge to fly all around with her limitless energy, but this was not to happen. Emily fully understood Florie's youthful enthusiasm but needed to calm her. She carefully took Florie's Wand from the boiling liquid and instructed Florie to be very, very careful as it would take several hours before it was completely cured. She blew over the Wand with a magical icy breath to cool it and then passed it to Florie – it too was young once again. She now held in her hand a straight and flawless Wand, full of powerful magic!

The elders looked into the boiling pot for their Wands but all had gone – they had given every bit of magic to Florie's. Florie again could not help but think failing to warn Tizzy had been a dreadful mistake. The cost had been dear and her friends had just given all in an effort to save Tizzy. How could she repay them? A simple thank you was not enough. She bowed to them respectfully, said her goodbyes and flew off.

On her way home, she saw her reflection in a lake and gasped at the young fairy staring back at her. Soon she landed outside the entrance to her home and walked in, admiring her rejuvenated Wand. Upon entering, she sat and pondered over what she needed to take from the caves. The special liquid was a countless number of miles down and to get it, she would have to go through very narrow tunnels, some called 'squeezes', and into the Earth's core itself. Youth, for the moment, was on her side, and she could not wait to re-visit the breathtaking place in the caves known to the fairies as 'Sparkles Keep'. Searching her room, she found a small vial with a capped top... perfect! Before leaving, she took a last look at her home and thought about her very uncertain future. But, when was the last time she visited the caves? Was it really fifty five years ago? Oh that seemed unreal, all those years, where had they gone? With a deep sigh, she thought how she must now prepare to fly to the Cornish Coast.

***

The owl carrying a sleeping Tizzy, carefully took her to her tree. To him, she did not seem at all well – her breathing was weak and shallow. But in her slumber,

Tizzy was certain, in the distance, she could hear the call of a second owl, a call that for some reason seemed so comforting to her. As it grew louder, she was determined to open her eyes and as she did so, even with a confused mind, she was aware that two owls were peering down at her. Her eyes now fully open, she saw one owl turn, and with a powerful leap, fly from the tree. The remaining owl stared straight ahead, a strong puff of glitter suddenly leaving his beak to swirl around his body and, with a blinding flash, explode in the air! There before her, was none other than her father! The King reached forward to pick up his daughter, but as he did so, one of her wings fell away like a petal from a dying rose.

"Tizzy, my darling, precious daughter, what have I done!" cried the King.

Seeing her once delicate, pale skin now tinged with a grey hue, he deeply questioned his judgement. Tears stinging his eyes, he whispered, "I knew you ran away but I was the owl following you – I have kept a *very* close watch over your safety all these days. Oh, Tizzy, what have I done! I used you, but I *had* to. We needed to catch that evil, murderous elf Rush and we still haven't found Cecee or Tross. Please, please forgive me!"

He gently rocked her in his arms as he had done when she was a baby. Wiping her wet hair from her brow, he said aloud, "Have I failed you! By all the Wizards, what curse is upon you? When and how did this happen? What did I miss?"

He held his beloved daughter close but could find no answer.

***

The now young Florie flew over miles of winter-frosted land and on towards the sea. Reaching the edge of land, she found a small crack in the ground where she came to an abrupt stop. She hovered above as the smell of lime-rock drifting up from deep beneath, took her mind racing back to her childhood. She peered down into total darkness, thinking back to the time when she reached seventeen, the age of 'responsibility', and how she had so many choices. Even though she had returned to a twenty year old, the wisdom she had gained throughout her life, she hoped remained. 'As we grow beyond seventeen, we must accept the consequences of the choices we make in life, after all, they define who we are. Who am I and what have I become?' she wondered. 'This awful thing happening to Tizzy isn't the Princess's fault. Poor little thing, she's only eleven. And now, at my true age of seventy, I find myself in a terrible mess. I must prove my worth for Tizzy's sake and, before it's too late, for my own.' With these thoughts, Florie closed her wings and dived head first into the abyss.

Down and down she plunged, freefalling into blackness until the sound of running water met her ears – time to spread her wings! She ordered her Wand to give light as she flew along a deep, dark tunnel. In the soft glow, she met her first encounter – caves with many hundreds of hanging worm threads, some twisting and looping around the worms' prey which struggled to escape. Florie watched as fat worms slowly squeezed down inside their thin, dripping threads to reach their poor victims. Although this was part of all that was nature, it made her shudder. Avoiding them with great care, she flew onwards over huge mounds of bat droppings – they were so much higher than she remembered and seemed alive, writhing with thousands of cockroaches! She headed on into a small tunnel, a 'squeeze', that twisted and turned, bringing her through to the 'Falls'. The power of the water, the danger, the damp enclosed stillness and the smell of the caves, once again took her mind racing back to her youth. The excitement made her heart race as on she flew, reaching an old time favourite spot. Through the wet mist from the falls, Florie stopped to stare at an amazing sight, the 'Sparkle Walls'! She giggled, remembering how long ago she visited this spot with an elf friend who boasted that there was nothing down here to be scared of.

"Oh," he said, "I know the caves well and will show you around – there is nothing to fear."

With great bluster, he mistook the 'Wall' for a sparkly void and flew into it with a loud thud! How Florie stifled a giggle as he slid down in total confusion – the poor elf! With no time to waste, she turned to fly on, soon arriving by the 'Two Tone Pools'. These were formed in two layers, one of fresh and one of salt water. But they could be deceiving as the top layer appeared like air but was, in fact, water. This illusion had fooled many a poor victim who chose to explore these wonderful and inviting but unforgiving caves. However, the tranquil sound of running water soothed her nerves and the beautiful sight that glimmered through the still blue water, took away her breath.

Glinting in the light of her Wand, hundreds of blue and emerald stalagmites, formed long before the caves flooded, stood proud, some reaching far out of the water, some only half the size, but all emitting their own colours and energy. She journeyed over them, disappearing headlong into a tiny tunnel. Down and down she flew until a little glimmer of light beckoned her into another space.

Now she was very deep in the caves, gazing at a vast open expanse, enormous frosted, crystal cones dancing in the light of her Wand, dwarfing her almost to a speck of dust. She flew between huge, thick shards of crystal growing in every direction from the ground, shining so clear she could see her reflection as she flew. Growing from the walls, delicate, feather-like formations of gypsum extended for miles. Florie landed on the tip of a crystal to take in the magical, breathtaking sight. She sat for a brief moment before following the stream that would finally bring her to where the dreaded 'snotties' hung with their dripping, burning acid. The obnoxious smell of gas coming from the acidic water grew stronger as she approached the long, slimy hangings. Below these was where the 'White Water' flowed – this was Florie's final destination! She needed exactly six drops of the water, but to obtain these would prove perilous as the effects of the drippings could be fatal. They were everywhere, all different widths and lengths, their acid dropping at random. But succeed she must and to avoid breathing in too much of the toxic gas, Florie took a few deep breaths before flying down.

She weaved her way through the dripping acid, before skimming across the water to carefully scoop up a few drops with her little vial... Success! She had more than the vital six drops and flew to rest on a lime rock where she could study her prized haul. The little water she had captured was full of the rare, precious, white sediment. Florie was delighted – after she had taken what she needed, Emily could use the remainder for her healing potions.

Lost in thought, she flexed her wings forgetting all caution. From beneath the water, something strange and eerie, pure white in colour and with no eyes, sensed her movement. Unaware of any danger, she pondered, 'Oh, what joy to flex my wings without the pain of old age!' She folded them down, the tips just entering the water. Stretching contentedly, she took a last look all around at the beautiful, enchanting sight. Little did she realise, behind her, resting on a crystal under the water, lay a blind, white, salamander, its gills like lettuce leaves wavering in the gentle current. Its head swayed in slow motion, its senses feeling movement from above. Cold, white, finger-like little toes crept nearer and nearer to Florie. One final step and like lightning, it leapt from the water – SNAP! Florie spun around to see a white cave dweller had tightly gripped onto one of her wings! Shocked, she tried to fly, struggling to free herself, but the creature held fast! It tossed its head violently, flinging her around, trying to drag her under the water. Florie had no choice but to drop the precious vial.

Taking her Wand in both hands, she aimed it straight at the creature, zapping it down to a mere speck! Brushing from her now torn wing what remained of the horrible creature, she looked down to see the vial smashed into tiny pieces! She had to think fast – time was running out! Her only option was to find a crystal in the shape of a cone. It was forbidden to remove any from the caves, this she knew, but again she had no other choice.

She felt immense guilt as she broke off a piece which must have taken millennia to grow, but convinced herself she was doing this for all the right reasons – if they ever find out, perhaps her King and the Wizards would understand and forgive her. Florie once again braved the dangers of the dripping acid, finally recovering just enough of the special water she so desperately needed but, in so doing, lost all sense of time. Back through the dangerous caves, tunnels and squeezes, she found her way to the exit. The six hours in which she had to complete her task were rapidly fading. In the time that remained, she hoped her wings would have enough strength to take her all the way home…

***

"Emily, I have it! I have the water!" exclaimed Florie, as she entered the Umbra. Taking the crystal cone, Emily smiled warmly but thought to herself, 'A *crystal* cone! What has Florie done? I'm sure she had a very good reason for this!' Emily reached for her special mixture of herbs, delicately sprinkling some onto the cave water which straight away bubbled, fizzed and foamed – the potion was at last complete! Florie suddenly realized she had just thirty short minutes before the magic that made her so much younger would reverse. She flew as fast as she could towards the Royal Quarters, holding close the mixture, not wishing to lose one, single, precious drop.

King Foxglove carried Tizzy home, taking her to the Royal Bedroom where he lay her upon the bed. As the Queen sat quietly sobbing by the young, dying Princess, the King turned to speak to one of his personal guards.

"Bowood, please bring what I need – immediately!"

Bowood hurriedly left. It wasn't long before a buzz hummed through the Quarters concerning the ill-fated Princess.

Florie reached the entrance of the Royal Quarters, but with so many guards, would she be able to easily enter? She pleaded and begged with them to let her pass, explaining she had a potion that would save the Princess from certain death! But not one recognized the young, over-excited fairy. They looked at one another asking, "Who could she possibly be?" Florie was now desperate – she had to think of another plan. Suddenly, she remembered the secret entrance she and her friends used as young fairies, when they dared each other to sneak into the centre of the Circle to mingle with the Royals and then disappear again! But where was it? She must find it – time was running out! The Royal Circle was immense but when she was young and full of energy, she would fly around the outside many, many times as if it were a small garden. She recalled, to the rear of the Royal Circle, an overgrown bush with a small gap and after a little searching, there it was, the old secret entrance! With a steady hand upon the crystal cone, she crawled through and into the Royal Circle, making certain no one had seen her. Brushing herself down,

Florie quietly made her way through the gardens, trying her best to blend in with all those there. Reaching the rear of the Queen's Chambers, the 'Peace' rose she so clearly recalled, had grown enormous, hiding all trace of any entrance to the Queen's rooms. For a better look, Florie pretended to admire the delicate cream and pink colours.

Then, from nowhere, she heard a guard yell, "HEY, YOU THERE!" Despite all her caution, she had been seen! She could wait no longer, flying straight into the rose bush. Making her way around inside, the prickly barbs scratched her arms and legs but she knew, somehow, she must find a way in. Finding an old, open window, she flew through it and to her surprise and great relief, she found herself inside the Royal Bedroom itself! Before anyone realized what was happening, including the King and Queen, Florie sped to the Princess, lifted her head from the pillow and poured the magical liquid into her mouth. With no time to spare, she took her Wand, spinning it around her own head. Coloured streams of light shone from her eyes and into Tizzy's then, as fast as everything had happened, it was over...

Fearing for her daughter's life, the Queen screamed, "Arrest that fairy!"

Immediately, guards held Florie fast, thrusting sharp daggers at her throat, preventing her escape! But now everyone's attention fixed upon Tizzy who coughed, choked, spluttered and began to slowly open her eyes.

"Urrgghhh, oooohhhh, where am I... eeeeewe, I think I'm going to be sick!"

Tizzy struggled to sit up. Without any understanding of what had just happened, the King and Queen stared in amazement at one another.

"Who *is* that fairy!" demanded the Queen. But no one knew.

For now, all the Royal Couple could do was to hug their weak, precious daughter, so very relieved she was alive!

Florie felt herself rapidly losing strength. Her time had run out – the magic was now leaving her. She had given Tizzy everything, her knowledge, her strength, in fact, almost her very life! Agony gripped her like an ice-cold curse as she stared down at her now shrivelled, bony hand, still clutching the empty crystal cone. The change – how fast and painful it was! Now the warning from Emily was taking real effect. She had grown old, very old, long past her years and the ill-effects of the rainbow were now attacking her entire, frail body.

Bowood rushed to the King.

"Your Majesty," he whispered, "the Wizard dust! I have it!"

The King snatched the pouch, now in a complete dilemma. For the first time in his life, he felt unsure of himself. He had made a mistake with Tizzy and did not want to make another. Turning to his Queen, he asked, "My darling, what should I do? This dust alone could save Tizzy, but she *seems* to be recovering! If she *is* and I use it, it may be too much for her young body to take and I may end her life!"

The Queen looked at her husband knowing something was wrong. He was usually so very strong minded, utterly decisive on matters, especially when it came to their children, but seeing Tizzy's life reflecting like fire from her eyes, the Queen gently took his hand.

"No, my darling," she said softly, "don't use it. Look, Tizzy is getting better by the second."

The King turned to the fairy who had brought the magical potion. But what was this! How could she age so rapidly before his eyes! And it was then he recognized her. The fairy was none other than a very old Florie! For a second, he stood there stunned, realizing the magic she must have performed would surely kill her. Why would she give up her life to save his daughter's?

Guards loosened their grip as Florie's body shrank further. Bent double, she finally collapsed to the floor.

"NO!" the King's voice thundered. "Whatever is happening? By all my powers, I will not allow it! She has saved our child!"

He threw the Wizard dust all over Florie's weak body. The frail fairy struggled for breath as the dust entered her, but was the King too late? As if by a miracle, life-bringing air slowly filled Florie's feeble lungs as she gasped and began to crawl towards her King.

"It's all my fault!" she cried, gasping for breath.

"What's your fault, Florie?" asked a shaken King. Distraught at the sorrowful sight before his eyes, he bent down to help the poor fairy to her feet.

"Tizzy flying into the rainbow. She flew too near the yellow and caught 'Rainbow Flu'. I failed to warn her of the awful virus!"

"You *knew* my daughter was entering the yellow of a rainbow!"

"Yes. I beg your forgiveness, Your Majesty. I know I have done wrong."

The King watched as Florie regained more and more strength – the Wizard dust had worked its wonders. But it was then he saw what he knew was a terrible misdeed – the empty crystal cone still in Florie's hand was surely from 'Sparkle Keep'! To make matters worse, a few of his personal guards had seen the crystal cone, also realizing the old fairy was guilty of a shocking crime. This left the King little choice. As much as he wished he did not have to, he ordered his guards, "Arrest this fairy!"

CHAPTER EIGHT

SUCH A THING, SILLY DREAM AND DR. L

Doctor Lessenoftencoughandichew, better known as Dr 'L', suggested Remik rest, maybe go home to Scotland for a few days which he willingly agreed to do.

Tross, Elm and Bill found themselves placed by the owls in the Royal Circle where they waited patiently, for what, they were unsure, but it was a stern and serious King who sat in his Quarters busily writing. Soon, he would prepare his magic for a trip to Middlesborough. Unfortunately, the earliest he could put this into practice was midnight tonight, but this would not bring forth what he needed until tomorrow afternoon. How he wished this very second he could seek help from the Wizards to find Cecee. Whilst they were reluctant to interfere with the King's World, they may, on this occasion, agree to help in what had become his 'Great Matter'. He sat writing on parchment for a small ceremony he planned for early tomorrow morning, hoping this would improve morale for all but also, to some, it would teach a valuable lesson. As he walked from his Quarters towards P.O.H.D.S, he knew this much – reading the parchment would certainly cheer him up. Once there, he joined his son to discuss the events that had happened so far.

Tross quickly approached his father.

"Father, we searched *everywhere* for Cecee. I am *convinced* she is not in Seven Oaks Woods!"

The King stared at his son and, though relieved to see him in one piece, he was still angry he had left without his permission. He mused, 'one day, my son will make an excellent King. Although he disobeyed me, he has proven to have a brave and true heart. Despite what I have written on the parchment, should I still punish him?' Quickly, he decided what should be done. For now, he would discuss matters no further. Tomorrow morning he would reveal at the ceremony, to a rather wayward Tross, his decision. He told everyone to retire, leaving the Prince in a state of doubt, wondering if his father was angry with him, hoping, above all, he was not!

A new day began. By now, the whole of Seven Oaks Woods knew about the ceremony. Some spoke about Bill and how he had prevented the capture of Royalty, bravely saving the day. But, as all assembled where the King was to speak, others told stories of Bill's weakness and cowardice. One thing was certain, everyone secretly wondered what the King would do. Elm, Tross and Bill had risen early that morning recalling, over an enjoyable breakfast, yesterday's events, but silence fell over them as they were interrupted by one of the King's Elves.

A stern voice announced, "Prince Foxglove, Soldier Elm and Scout Bill. You are summoned at ten o'clock this morning to hold audience with King Foxglove V1!"

Elm glanced at Bill whose mood instantly changed to one of sheer panic.

Elm tried to give some comforting words.

"Bill, it'll be fine. The King has heard about your conduct and I'm sure he is more than pleased."

Bill's mind quickly recalled memories of his own father who he so longed for. Since his untimely death, he had felt very much alone. However, his friendship with Elm made him think about his life and he wondered if, at last, he dare dream of happier times. But his real concern now was would the King punish him for killing an Elf and if so, what would it mean for his future?

The sun had cast its ten o'clock shadow – the time had arrived for the three to appear before their King. Escorted into the Royal Circle, they found it full, alive with subdued excitement. Violet sat quietly at the back, sharing a toadstool with Rosie, overjoyed Elm had returned safely. Motley and his crew sat in total disbelief, listening to rumours of Bill's great bravery. Tross, Elm and Bill were directed to toadstools at the front where they sat, an air of nervousness descending over all three. The waiting was over as all in the Royal Circle stood and bowed while the King and Queen made their grand entrance, nobly making their way to sit upon their thrones. The crowd now sat, a silence falling over the entire Circle. The King immediately stood.

"We greet every one of you and thank you for your attendance. I must begin by announcing my eldest daughter is, regretfully, still missing. This afternoon, we will start a further search. I trust each of you will lend whatever assistance may be asked of him or her. For this, the Queen and I offer our sincere appreciation."

Mumblings of where on Earth to look next carried throughout the assembled group.

The solemn King took up a parchment.

"I am deeply saddened to announce the loss of those brave soldiers who gave their lives in the search. Once I have read their names, I would ask that you show your respect in the customary manner. I now ask you all to stand."

All immediately stood, their heads bowed low as one by one the King read the names of the fallen, after which followed a minutes silence. Due respects having been paid, the King and Queen now sat and requested all to be seated.

"It is now time to pronounce reward or judgement upon a few of my subjects."

When Bill heard the word "judgement" he gulped, stifling the urge to run, fly or hide from the scene as quickly as possible!

"I now call upon an elf by the name..." the King looked at his parchment to make certain he had the correct name of the new elf... "Scout Bill!"

The King's eyes looked all around with interest. Who would step forward?

Bill looked up, not believing he was hearing his name, but he was, and oh how he did not want to be the first out of the three to approach the King! Surely someone else should go first, maybe Elm, so that he, himself, could hear what the King would ask. He stood and tried to step forward but feared his legs would collapse beneath him.

"Elm," Bill whispered, "Help, I can't move!"

"Get a grip, Bill, take two deep breaths and go!"

Bill gulped in air and took several uneasy steps to stand before his King. The King spoke aloud.

"Scout Bill. I have heard conflicting reports concerning your conduct!"

Silence followed. Bill thought he was going to faint or even worse, *die* on the spot!

"Well, what do you have to say for yourself?" The King boomed.

Bill stuttered, nothing but nonsense coming from his mouth, all his senses numb as he looked at the King.

"Oh enough, you did *very* well, Bill!" said the King, while heartily slapping him on the shoulder. "Saving my daughter and son from dangerous elves was indeed an act requiring outstanding bravery, an act no one will ever forget."

Recovering with a cough and splutter from the firm but friendly slap, Bill stood amazed while the King held up a scroll. Expertly flicking it open to let the leaf unroll, he read aloud for all to hear.

"Scout Bill, I, King Foxglove V1 and Queen Citrina 111, grant you a free license to eat from the Royal Woods for life together with the use of six pouches of Fairy dust, the choice of dust being entirely yours. We also offer an invitation to you to join our soldiers and train as a Master Bowman, and should you choose to do so, you will be trained to the highest level. We assure you, Scout Bill, the life of a Master Bowman is most rewarding in many ways and will give you a purpose about which you can feel proud. We recovered all the bows and arrows left in the tunnels by the fallen soldiers, and Elm has returned them all to me. I am happy to say, you have our Royal permission to own one!"

A very relieved but shaken Bill could not speak, bowing low and accepting the scroll before the King sat down. All in the Circle applauded and heartily cheered as Bill again bowed before returning to his seat. For him, all had happened too quickly! He wanted to re-wind to the start of the ceremony, to enjoy the moment again and to properly take it all in! He almost choked with happiness and excitement. He could now hold his head high for the first time in a long while and he felt great. His mind raced back to the incident that had earned him this honour of the highest order. Even though he felt remorse having to kill Todd, he also felt content, Todd was indeed an evil elf who had chosen to live a bad life! Bill wished his own father were alive today – how proud he would have been to see him honoured by the King and Queen. Bill wiped a tear from his eye and decided now was the moment to make a choice for himself, he would join the soldiers and learn how to fight *everything* evil.

The King's smile broadened as he stood and announced, "I call upon Lord Elm."

Elm proudly approached and stood before the throne.

"Elm, you are a special soldier. In your usual manner, you have performed above and beyond the call of duty. The Queen and I award you twenty pouches – the choice of dust is yours."

Elm was now wealthier than any other untrained soldier in the Kingdom.

"We have also decided to send you to Middlesborough to receive official training. Upon your return, you will join my most trusted soldier Remik. Do you have anything to say, my fine fellow?"

Elm accepted his scroll with a low bow.

"Your Majesties. I am so very grateful and indeed honoured, but I must inform you there is a fairy among us who should be known to you. Without her help, we would all, most certainly, have been killed."

The King leaned forward a little puzzled but very interested to hear who this fairy might be. He prided himself that he would never be unaware of anyone's efforts. Elm then demonstrated the awesome weapons Violet had given him, hitting a seemingly impossible target with the greatest of accuracy.

The King smiled.

"I see you have quickly mastered these most effective weapons. So, tell me, who *is* this fairy?"

"Violet, Your Majesty," replied Elm.

A command was made for her to step forward but she was nowhere to be seen.

"Vi, why are you leaving!? Where are you going?" asked Rosie, as she flew after her friend.

"Rosie, I *can't* go before the King – those silver arrows were stolen and I'm sure the King has realised!"

"Did you steal them, Vi?" asked a shocked Rosie.

"No, Rush had them – told me they were stolen from a place called Middlesborough and ordered me to hide them. What's more, he knows our secret, Rosie, and blackmailed me. How can I explain it all to the King, knowing how he feels about stealing? I wonder about the

King. Although we have dropped our titles and Scottish accents, and never attend Court, he *must* know we are the cursed Royals from Scotland. Why has he never asked me where we're from and why we choose to live in the woods? I lied to Elm too, telling him we made those weapons. I have put you at great risk and we both know our secret must not come out. I'm so sorry, Rosie. I long for the day when all will be well and then, at last, I can lose the false accent. We are from Scotland and I find it a wee bit tiresome to make convincing!"

Their secret was certainly a grave one and their story a weighty problem. Violet was indeed the great cousin of a fairy Princess from Dun Vegan, Scotland, who dared to marry a Human. The story tells how the fairy Princess's father did not agree to the marriage and told her that because the King she wanted to marry was a Human, the marriage would bring nothing but disaster to both Worlds. But the Princess was headstrong and went ahead with the marriage but on condition it would last for only one year. Within the year they had a boy child. After the year had past, she left all behind including the child, returning to her own World. Then, late one night, the wind carried her baby's crying to her. Unable to ignore his cry, she secretly returned to give him a magic shawl for everlasting protection. In fairy law, this is strictly forbidden. Her terrible act was discovered and it is her family's responsibility to find the shawl and return it to their own World. Until they succeed in doing so, the family is shamed into hiding. Rosie's family line however, was even more direct than Violet's, as she was the great-granddaughter and must, on no account, reveal her true identity.

But Rosie argued, "Violet, giving up the weapons was a good thing... after all, you were only trying to help them."

Violet had no answer. She had a more pressing concern... She still had Tizzy's Wand and had to find a way to return it. If she was discovered, that too, could result in ruin! She flew into her tree to think of a way to resolve the mess and Rosie, not wishing to return to the ceremony, followed her, wondering if there was anything she could do to comfort poor Violet.

The King had all but finished the ceremony. Only one Elf remained to be rewarded, his beloved son. "I call Prince Albatross Foxglove V11."

Rather shyly, Tross approached his father.

"My son, you broke your King's command! What do you have to say for yourself?"

Tross gulped.

"Err... Your Majesty... I did what I thought would help find Cecee. I... I have since learned my action placed everyone in great danger, and for that, I am truly sorry."

"I repeat, you disobeyed my command." Nonetheless, the King's stern expression relaxed as he held up the last scroll. "However, it has been reported to me you showed great bravery and despite the severe dangers you faced, continued to do your utmost to find your sister. For this, I shall reward you."

As the King rolled up the scroll, the attention of all was drawn to an elf flying into the Royal Circle, coming to rest in front of the King. Placed across his arms and carried with great care was a silver stick, similar in appearance to a long, thick, knotty twig. On one end, held in place by a small sliver owl's claw, was a clear, blue crystal, sparkling in the morning light. Handing the scroll to Tross, the King carefully took the Royal Sceptre in both hands and presented it to his son.

"My son. This Sceptre has vast powers and magic and was presented to me by a Wizard when I was your age, but on the strict understanding it was to be used only when essential. Before you ever find the need to use it, you will require much advice and guidance. I will personally give a little to you prior to our journey to Middlesborough and on our return, provide you with full instruction. One day you will become King and your reign will require you to make so many difficult decisions. Knowing how and when to use the Sceptre will prove invaluable."

Tross bowed low, his heart ready to explode with excitement as he returned to his toadstool. He could not believe his father was soon to teach him the powers of his new Sceptre as well as take him to that magical land called Middlesborough!

The ceremony over, a short celebration was held. Every elf and fairy attended but with two exceptions, Violet and Rosie. The King and Queen then left to address more pressing matters. Elm could not fully enjoy the occasion – Violet was not present and soon he would be leaving with the King. He longed to spend his remaining time with her and flew to Tross.

"Tross, have you seen Violet or know where she has gone?"

"No, sorry, Elm, I haven't seen her at all," came the disappointing reply.

Elm decided to leave and fly to Violet's tree. He found her sitting quietly with Rosie.

"Violet, what are you doing here? Didn't you know the King wished to see you? Why aren't you with the rest of us, enjoying the party?"

"Elm, I don't know 'ow to explain to you why," answered Violet, looking at Rosie for support. Then, after a short pause, she could contain herself no longer and sobbed, "The weapons I gave yer were… *stolen!*"

Elm glared in amazement. "Violet, what do you mean!"

"I *mean,* Elm, they were stolen! Rush 'ad 'em and gave 'em to me to 'ide and, forgive me, I did wot 'e asked!"

Elm was stunned. He needed to clear his head and think.

"I need to go… maybe I will see you later," was all Elm could say in reply.

Violet watched him leave without a word and, for the first time in her life, felt so very alone…

Elm flew back to the Royal Circle where he sensed an air of complete excitement. He spotted Tross and Bill and ventured over. "What's going on?" he asked, straining to hear the gossip all around.

An eager Tross answered, "Two soldiers from our neighbouring woods saw a rather small but interesting cornfield carving which, when decoded, reads, "HELP, CECEE!"

The King's pace quickened as he re-entered the now silent gathering. His voice thundered through the silence.

"We have received a message from Middlesborough, but we cannot determine if it is definitely from my daughter or from someone who could be trying to trick us. I demand all soldiers prepare – there can be absolutely no delay. We *must* leave now for Middlesborough!"

Tross, Bill and Elm, together with all the soldiers, hastily prepared for the ensuing journey while a nurse elf flew to the King, whispering in his ear, "Your Majesty. Remik has returned and offers his thanks for his time in Scotland. He wishes you to know he is fit and ready to accompany you."

The King instructed the elf to thank Remik and to ask him to meet with him and the others in his Royal Quarters in fifteen minutes. All gathered as requested to receive their orders. As the King entered, Tross noticed something which left him bewildered. His father carried a large, shining, Sceptre at the top of which, a huge silver owl's claw gripped a perfectly round, clear, green, brilliant crystal. He had never seen such an impressive looking object and could only imagine what unknown, magical, perhaps even threatening, powers it contained!

***

On the eve of the departure to Middlesborough, Tizzy slept fitfully in her tree. She had lost her Wand and dared not tell her father. Thankfully, he was far too busy to notice anyway, but there was something else on her mind – where had the soldiers taken Florie? Though she had lost her wings, she told Dr. L she felt much better and now believed him when he said, "Patience lass, you're very young and your wings will grow back and be even more beautiful than ever."

Yes, she had nearly died, but it was not the fault of Florie who, surely by now, should be forgiven! Tizzy removed and opened her pouch of Wizard dust and thought deeply. Should she try its magic? No, definitely not! The powerful, multi-colour sparkle from within, scared the young fairy so much she quickly closed the pouch and retied it to her belt. As she lay relaxing, a gentle voice called to her, "Tizzy, before it's too late, return what is not yours."

'Am I hearing things!' thought Tizzy. 'Has that awful virus left me imagining voices?!'

Startled, she grabbed her firefly lantern, climbed down from her tree and looked all around but could see nothing. Not one owl peering down at her, no single, mischievous elf threatening her and as far as she could see, no fairy calling to her. 'I *must* have dozed off!'

Tizzy thought. 'There is nothing here to harm me. Return what isn't *mine*? It was a dream, that's all.'

***

Though it was cold, the afternoon had brought to all who had gathered at Seven Oaks Lake a rare sight. A large, red winter sun cast its magical light through the trees and across the water, any remaining snow on the shores glinting in its path. The Queen witnessed all from high in a tree, but was deeply concerned. It was the first day of November and time was running out for her daughter. The Queen, like Cecee, was the eldest daughter of her father, King Clover V111, and so, as was the custom, passed the duty of planting the Seed to her eldest daughter. But Cecee had vanished, so she could not tell her all she needed to know. Looking down, the Queen watched her family and the soldiers preparing to leave. She called to her husband who at once flew to her side. Her hand gently caressed the side of his face as she looked deep into his eyes and asked a question she was not sure she wanted answered.

"My King, my love, the cornfield carving. If it is from Cecee, then how on this Earth did she manage to get into Middlesborough? She may be trapped there for months, and the Seed must be planted soon. I have borne two daughters it is true, and if our darling Cecee is… perish the thought… dead, the only way for Tizzy to plant another Seed is after she has been through a long, tiring ritual with the Elders. Would that allow enough time to plant the Seed and secure our future?"

The Queen could contain herself no longer. She broke down and sobbed with pure anguish for her daughter, while her husband comforted her in his arms.

"I don't know how, or even if, she entered Middlesborough, my sweetheart, but please stop crying – you know to shed tears is dangerous. Please rest assured, if Cecee is there, I will find her and bring her home."

Tears continued to fall from the Queen's eyes but the King knew he must leave her. He ordered elves to bring a flower cup containing equal measures of blackberry and cherry juice. While he was away, they were to make certain the Queen drank the mixture at least four times a day. Above all, she must stay under the close care of Dr. L.

CHAPTER NINE

GREATEST RESPECT, TELL NO ONE AND UNTIL WE RETURN

*B*eing with his father filled Tross with great pride. His father's acceptance of him as a volunteer meant so much to Tross who felt he must now be seen as more than just a young elfin Prince. Before rejoining the soldiers, Elm returned to Violet but only to say goodbye and to tell her he needed more time to think about what she had done. With sorrow, she thought he was unaware that she loved him beyond anything else in her life...

Excitement was at its highest as the small army prepared for the journey into the strange and mystical land about which they had heard so much. Standing by the Lake, Tross studied his new gift. On closer inspection, he saw it was a small Sceptre, definitely more powerful than a Wand but just how powerful? Perhaps soon, he would know for certain. The King had arrived but Remik was late, so he had some time in which to instruct, even warn, his son about the Sceptre's powers.

"Tross, you must listen carefully," said the King. "The Sceptre must be worn strapped tightly to your back. It contains powers beyond your understanding. I have no time to instruct you fully but listen when I tell you, it must be used with extreme caution."

With that, the King flew with him to a more secluded place where he spun Tross around in the air, checking every strap and buckle, and then checking again.

"You are to keep the Sceptre in its case on your back."

"Yes, father, I understand, but when will you show me how its powers work?" an eager Tross asked as he watched his father check once again the straps of the Sceptre's case.

"The Sceptre cannot obey orders from within the case. However, once removed, it will follow all commands given by only you."

Tross carefully removed it from the case and looked at it with pride.

"I *would* like to try it out father."

"Always make sure the straps are secure," warned the King.

Impatiently, Tross watched his father once again test all were secure.

"Father, may I *please* try it?"

But the King could not stress enough.

"Should it become lost and fall into the hands of bad elves in Middleborough…"

"Yes, I *completely* understand, father, but may I try it *now*?" interrupted an even more impatient Tross.

His father thought for a moment, and knowing they were high up in the trees away from prying eyes, sighed, replying, "Tut, alright, Tross. Do you see that rabbit at the foot of the tree?"

"Yes, father."

"I want you to make it motionless."

"You mean you want me to freeze it, father!?"

"The rabbit will come to no harm and when you release it from the magic, it will remember nothing."

"Do I have to say anything?" asked Tross.

"No, just concentrate with all your power on what you want to do while pointing the Sceptre – it will be directed by your last thoughts. I repeat, you must always concentrate with all your power and its magic will do the rest. And remember, hold the Sceptre as tightly as you can!

Tross pointed down the crystal end, aiming it straight at the rabbit. Concentrating as hard as he could, he said to himself, *'Freeze rabbit, freeze!'* The Sceptre shuddered in his hands, hot light suddenly bursting from the crystal! Tross was caught by complete surprise! Losing his grip and concentration, he looked towards his father thinking, 'Father! What should I do?!' He was about to call out but it was too late. The bolt of light struck a nearby tree, instantly rebounding and striking the King, freezing him rigid! Now unable to control his movement, the King plunged downwards through the trees landing, fortunately, on top of a toadstool which greatly softened the blow. The King toppled backwards and lay still on the ground. Tross, now in total shock, immediately flew down, throwing the Sceptre to one side, while a very puzzled rabbit twitched his nose several times before hopping away.

Tross knelt by his father's side.

"By all the Wizards! Father, are you alright!?"

But the King was frozen in time, simply staring blankly upward towards the empty sky. Tross stood up and stepped backwards, his mind searching for an idea. He picked up the Sceptre, panic confusing his thoughts.

"Oh no, what have I done!" he called aloud.

Holding the Sceptre before him with trembling hands, he pointed the crystal end towards the King. Concentrating with all his mind, he pleaded. '*Bring back my father! Please, I beg you, please do your magic and bring back my father!*' Tross tightly closed his eyes as, once again, light shot from the crystal, but nothing seemed to happen. Tross opened his eyes to see the stream of silver light wavering in mid-air, failing to reach the King. It seemed to shudder as if frozen in its own space. All Tross could do was concentrate even harder, this time with his eyes wide open. And then, without warning, the bolt shot forward, striking the King fully in the chest! A very nervous Prince ran towards his father. He bent down beside him crying, "Father, *please* speak to me!"

Slowly, the King began to stir, awakening from the spell. Entirely unaware of what had just happened, he sat up confused, rubbing his forehead, wondering how he had reached the ground so quickly. Tross wiped the sweat from his own brow, utterly relieved his father had survived the mishap!

"Father, is everything alright?"

"Of course everything is alright. Don't look so worried! I think you must have missed the rabbit, that's all," replied a bemused King as he looked around for the creature. "We all make mistakes now and again. Please don't fret. All it takes is lots of concentration and practice. Trust me, you will soon learn how to harness the full powers of your Sceptre."

Promising his father he would, in future, pay full attention when using the powers of the magical instrument, Tross securely returned the Sceptre to its case. From that day forward, he knew it must be handled with the greatest of care and respect.

***

Tizzy rose very early that morning and before going to the ceremony, sat beneath the spreading limbs of a plum tree. She again took the pouch of Wizard dust from her belt. It felt so strange to her. Even the bare branches of the tree seemed to point accusingly at her. She wondered where Cecee was as she opened the pouch and pondered what she was going to do with the dust. Wanting to study it further, Tizzy peered inside. Colours seemed to swirl around each other as she dared to take a pinch. She placed the small amount into her cupped hand but, as she did so, a sudden, gentle breeze blew it from her. What happened next, would take her breath away. In an instant, standing before her, was Cecee talking to a beautiful, bold looking, winged Unicorn, both of them surrounded by mauve mountains! What gave her the special powers to see this? Cecee and her companion seemed completely unaware they were being watched. Tizzy held out her hand to touch her sister, but it went

212

straight through what was no more than just an image. She squinted hard, straining her eyes, studying the hologram still forming in front of her. Suddenly, she felt a strange presence, and with it came a peculiar but not unpleasant odour. The smell was familiar, but from where? She quickly turned to look, but there was no one there. Turning back again, the picture of Cecee and the Unicorn had vanished. Certain this time it was not a dream, she trembled, attaching the Wizard dust pouch to her belt before hurrying away. Reaching her tree, she climbed up and sat at the top, deep in thought. 'Cecee is in a strange land! I know it now and saw it through the Wizard dust. Could this strange place be Middlesborough? Is that where Cecee is? But I can't tell anyone! I've used stolen dust, Wizard dust! What would my father say? No, I can tell no one…'

***

After Dr L's lengthy check that the elf was fit and well, Remik finally arrived. As the last soldier elves gathered by the Lake, the King called for the attention of all.

"I wish to demonstrate the mighty power of this Sceptre. Tross, please come with me." Facing the Lake, they stood together for a short while without either speaking a word. The silence was broken when the King, pointing his Sceptre towards the water, asked his son to watch the Lake and to listen to what he may think no more than mumbled words. Tross watched and listened intensely as his father spoke vaguely, the bright, green crystal at the end of his Sceptre sending forth a mighty rainbow-coloured bolt that streaked down through the

Lake's water and into its depths. The powerful glow awoke a small, purple patch from the deep as a whirlpool began to swirl around and around. Faster and faster, wider and wider it spun, until a huge, dark shadow from its centre spiralled upward. In no time at all, from within the vortex, a massive sailing ship burst onto the Lake's surface with a mighty splash, water cascading from her decks as all looked on in complete awe and wonder.

Even though the ship had emerged from the deep, one hundred fit and able 'Middlesborough Monitor Elves' had somehow survived the ordeal and were already expertly trimming the vessel to bring her under control. There was no uniformity of dress, each elf having his own individual style. However, they did have a few things in common. They wore a feathery badge on their sleeves and around their necks, tied with fine vine, were small, pointed crystals, many wearing six or seven. Some were of varying lengths and different shades of green. As well as the crystals, some wore roughly cut black onyx or blue lapis bound in leather around their wrists. Many elves were strikingly adorned with a mass of multi-coloured feathers attached to one shoulder of their jackets. Even though all had painted faces ready for battle, it appeared strange they seemed to carry no weapons at all. One of their first duties was to drop anchor before hoisting the remaining huge, white sails. This they executed with well-rehearsed, expert precision, each elf knowing precisely the duty he had to perform. The sails soon billowed in the strong wind but the ship was held back by its mighty anchors.

"Task completed?" an elf yelled from the top of the main mast. All on deck nodded to one another and, looking upwards, returned the cry, "Task completed!"

Each elf flew to his position, his small wings pointing downwards. All stood still, one behind the other in perfect rows on either side of the ship, now fully prepared as she rocked to and fro upon Seven Oaks Lake.

From a distance, those on shore could clearly see the vessel's beautiful golden shields lining her sides and glinting in the winter sun. Bill stared at the impressive crest of Seven Oaks embroidered on the centre sail billowing in the wind. Remik had witnessed the breath-taking scene once before but Tross stood agog at the sight, while Bill, uncertain of the whole episode, slipped quietly through the group until he stood at the very rear,

215

asking himself all the while if he was ready for *such* an adventure.

The King spoke. "Before we board our ship, there is something I must give each of you. Tross, will you please pass around these small pouches of dust. But be warned each of you, such dust carries great powers. Once in your possession, guard it with your life!"

Bill, not wishing to be excluded from the King's attention, ran forward, blurting out, "Oh, I know what it is, it's Truth dust!"

A deathly hush descended upon the group as they awaited the King's reaction to this impertinent interruption. But all were mystified when he simply replied in a gentle manner, "Well, Bill, in a way, you are correct. This is a powerful dust and very special, for it belongs to the Senior Wizards of Middlesborough. You see, it is dust that was once in the possession of now dead Wizards and has been temporarily entrusted to us by the Seniors. Whatever we do with it, it will always return to them."

A deep murmur passed through the gathering, soon fading to silence.

"I must add," continued the King, "it is, in fact, the *most* powerful dust in existence and must be used with extreme caution. It is capable of changing any living being into anything. I call upon you all to watch while Remik demonstrates its powers. Remik, will you please step forward?"

This time an even deeper murmur spread among the soldiers.

"Please be silent!" ordered the King.

Remik stepped forward and turned to stand in front of the assembled soldiers. Searching for a 'volunteer', he thought who better than the Prince himself. Asking Tross if he would kindly take part, the Prince could do no other than agree. Taking the dust and placing a small amount in his hand, Remik quickly blew it in the direction of the Prince, who though a little surprised, stood bold and ready to face whatever was to come.

As the dust settled over Tross, Remik closed his eyes and focused upon what he wished the King's son to become. Magically, Tross's appearance began to change. First, a silver helmet with a fearsome point jutting from the mouthpiece, formed upon his head, a plume of black and orange feathers adorning the top. Next, a yellow, fluid-like material spread over his entire body to form a suit of impenetrable armour. Around his waist, a leather belt held a dagger more fearsome than his own, while across his back, glinting in the sunlight, hung a silver bow with a sheath holding silver arrows. Remik took another pinch of dust, throwing it upwards and allowing it to fall upon himself. All at once, a winged, silver coated Unicorn stood in place of Remik. The creature reared up, throwing behind him a jet black mane while spreading enormous dark wings. With a mighty snort, he shook his head and settled next to Tross. Together, the pair appeared invincible, a match for anyone or anything.

Loud gasps escaped from the onlookers. Bill's mouth fell wide open watching the King perform the same action with the dust to return Tross and Remik back to their former selves. This was the first time Tross had been part of magic quite like this. Despite feeling shaken, he quickly stood beside Remik, the pair bowing low to the King before rejoining the soldiers. Bill could not wait to learn more so ran to Elm.

"Elm, do you think that was painful? I mean, that *had* to be painful, didn't it?"

Elm replied with a slightly edgy tone.

"I don't know, Bill, hush and listen!"

The King stepped forward.

"Now that you have all witnessed the magic of the dust, be strongly advised... on no account ever change yourselves into anything while you are alone. Be certain there is always another, ready and able to use the dust to reverse the magic... remember, Unicorns have hoofs, not hands!"

In response, the soldiers laughed nervously whilst heeding the Kings advice.

"Once we arrive in Middlesborough," continued the King, "you can practice the art of Wizard dust transformation! Now, please follow me, I bid you all to board our ship. She will be our home until we return."

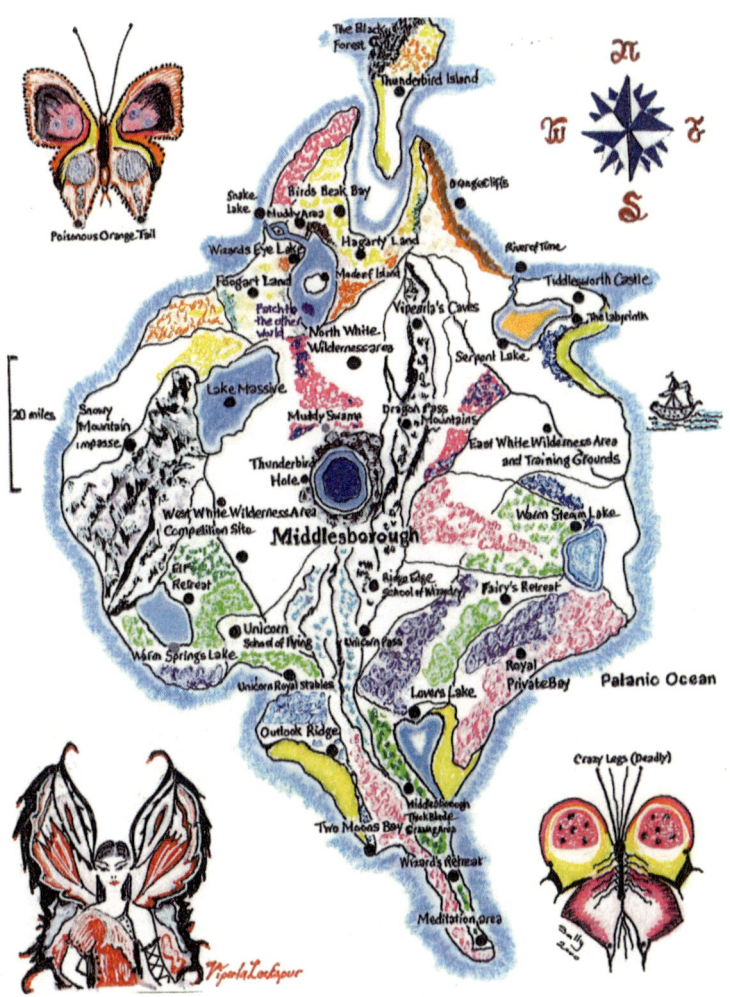

Poisonous Orange Tail

The Black Mass Forest

Thunderbird Island

Snake Lake

Birds Beak Bay

Muddy Area

Hagarty Land

Orange Cliffs

Wizards Eye Lake

Foogart Land

Mad elf Island

River of Time

Tiddlesworth Castle

Patch to the other world

Viperia's Caves

The Labyrinth

North White Wilderness areas

Serpent Lake

20 miles

Lake Massive

Muddy Swamp

Dragon Pass Mountains

East White Wilderness Area and Training Grounds

Snowy Mountain impasse

Thunderbird Hole

West White Wilderness Area Competition Site

Warm Steam Lake

Middlesborough

Elf Retreat

Ridge Edge School of Wizardry

Fairy's Retreat

Unicorn School of Flying

Unicorn Pass

Warm Springs Lake

Unicorn Royal Stables

Lovers Lake

Royal Private Bay

Palanic Ocean

Outlook Ridge

Middlesborough Dark Bridle Crossing Area

Two Moons Bay

Wizards Retreat

Meditation Area

Crazy Legs (Deadly)

Viperia Larkspur

219

Chapter Ten

Mission and Powerful Piece of Magic

Tizzy sat in her tree and took out the Wizard dust pouch. She wanted to try it again but, as before, felt reluctant. Was it perhaps guilt because it did not belong to her? Suddenly, she saw a figure below, a tall, giant male with a long, white beard. He wore a mauve and yellow hooded robe and held a long Sceptre which seemed to keep him upright as he leaned heavily upon it. Gazing up at her with hypnotic, crystal blue eyes, he gently spoke.

"Hello little one. I am glad to see after your illness you are much better. The dust you have, you must give to me. I do not wish to frighten you but please come down from the tree."

He held up his hand towards her. But fear ran through Tizzy. She hid behind a thick branch and shut her eyes tightly! Hoping the strange giant would disappear, she opened them and breathed a sigh of relief for he had indeed vanished.

***

Excited chatter filled the air as everyone began to board the ship. Bill flew to catch Remik, curiosity getting the better of him as he nervously approached.

"Remik, what did it feel like to be a Unicorn? To change into one of those *must* have been painful!"

Remik, who had his own worries, flew next to Tross, trying to ignore Bill's unwelcome attention. Elm walked along beside them, his mind elsewhere. He was an experienced soldier having fought many battles and very little caused him any concern. But this search for Cecee seemed to him, for reasons he did not understand, to be quite different. He felt very uneasy about the whole mission…

A pair of Trolls from the Hagarty Clan sat on the east bank of Wizard's Eye Lake. It was a perfect day for fishing. Once their rod was set up, one prepared a catch-net while soaking his furry feet in the Lake's soft waters. His friend played hypnotic music with a flute to draw the fish towards their bait. Very soon a small ripple moved across the water. Their line pulled tight, while the water began to swirl and then... success! They had already caught a fish! But the water swirled faster and faster, forming an eddy which grew larger and larger, sucking down the Trolls' line and rod! The two stared at each other, knowing what this could very well mean – the arrival of the Other World visitors, and they definitely did not want to meet whatever or whoever may emerge from the watery hole! Cursing the loss of yet another good fishing rod, they quickly ran to hide behind a rock from where they watched a water spout gush high into the air. From the top of this bubbling, roaring, watery column, a magnificent winged Unicorn burst forth, carrying upon its back a beautiful fairy. With Royal blue mane flowing freely behind, Fiero's wings spread out to meet the new World. Cecee tightly holding his mane, he flew towards the shore, overjoyed to see two Suns brightly shining in a pink sky. At last he was home! Feeling as fresh as a daisy, Fiero landed on the sandy but rocky shore, Cecee instantly flying from his back, surprised to find neither were wet. Fiero drew in the air as though to quench a long endured thirst.

"Well, do you like my World, Cecee?" he asked.

Cecee stood gazing at the splendid view of the tall, mauve mountains surrounding them. Each peak came to a point, some piercing small, white clouds which formed a perfect circle around the very tip. Fiero explained to her as he took another gulp of air.

"The two mauve Suns shining brilliantly reflect different colours depending on the weather. The little clouds circling the mountain tops mean there will be no rain for at least a week."

Cecee had to admit, "It is *sooooo* beautiful, Fiero," looking in wonder at the furthest, tallest mountain. Fiero, meanwhile, admired the tranquil Lake when, all of a sudden, another eddy began to form, spinning more and more and funnelling up into the air. From out of the top leapt a strange silver eel with jewelled eyes, wings shooting from its sides as it flew through the air, straight towards Cecee and Fiero! From behind their rock, the two inquisitive Trolls could not believe their eyes. As their heads turned to look at one another, one said, "I just *knew* something terrible would happen one day! Come on, *quick*!" The two lost no time running for their lives.

"Fiero – what is that!" screamed Cecee, "it's heading our way!"

Fiero immediately stood in front of her as the eel shot over his head and landed on a large, blue bush growing behind them. Writhing around a branch, it instantly changed shape, and there, hanging before them, was a crystal Crown!

"Fiero, it's Icicle's Crown!" Cecee exclaimed as she flew to retrieve it. Taking it from the bush, she realized just how heavy it was. Looking at the Crown, she noticed the centre stone, instead of being pure white, was now as clear as ice. Turning it over, Cecee noticed writing around the inside, a language she had never seen before. Placing the Crown upon her head, she was surprised to feel that now it had no weight at all.

"Fiero, what do you think? Is it definitely me?" asked Cecee, as she twirled around in front of him.

"Gorgeous, Cecee, it's simply *gorgeous*," he replied, bending his neck to take a drink from the Lake. But yet another ripple moving along the edge of the water was shortly followed by another, then another, followed by a tremendous thump that shook the ground. Fiero's head shot up.

"Cecee, fly onto my back now!" he ordered.

The fear in his voice obvious, she immediately obeyed. The brave Unicorn lifted his wings to hide her, lowering his head to charge forward with his horn. Then, from behind a boulder, a grotesque head set on the end of a long, scaly neck peered at them through glittering red eyes which turned to black slits as the creature intensely studied Cecee and Fiero. Without warning, it reared its head upwards, filling its lungs with air. Then, just as quickly, its head shot downwards, firing a white-hot ball of fire which flew over their heads, instantly incinerating something behind. Cecee and Feiro froze in terror, watching the monster rear its head again, but this time, with a tremendous roar, it shot a huge gush of steam high into the air, shaking the ground under them. Slowly, it brought down its large, scaly head right in front of them.

"Phew, you *obviously* didn't see those Thunderbirds, *did* you!" the monster pompously remarked.

"P… Pardon me?" Fiero questioned.

"Three of them crept up behind you and would be digesting you this very moment if *I* hadn't toasted them to a pile of ash! Don't you know they hunt in groups and just *love* a tasty morsel or two, just like the pair of you! What were you thinking, standing out in the open like *that*? Well… are you just going to continue to stand there gawping, or thank me for saving your lives?"

As Fiero lowered his wings, Cecee flew from him, landing close to the monster, bravely standing her ground.

"We are very grateful! Thank you, but what *are* you?"

"I am a fire breathing dragon and my name is Drucid. Good job I was coming along. Didn't you hear me? I usually make enough noise, being *my* size."

He leaned closer. "Before you go running off *all* scared, I promise I am the gentler kind of dragon."

He waited for a reaction, but when none came, he repeatedly taped the tip of his tail on the ground in disappointment.

"Well, *obviously* I don't scare either of you. Tell you what though, you *do* need to be careful of the small winged variety of dragon, oooohhhh, they are particularly unpleasant!"

However, Fiero still did not like the look of this particular creature.

"Cecee, come on, we must leave and find a place to stay."

But Cecee lifted her hand in protest.

"Just... one... moment, Fiero," Cecee replied. "Drucid, do you know a safe place where we can stay for the night?" she asked.

"Well, let me see ..." he replied, again tapping but also swishing the tip of his tail, this time in a puddle, carelessly splashing wet, muddy sand over Fiero. Unaware how annoying this was, he resumed.

"You could try our 'Welcome Inn'. It's over the hill in front of that tall mountain and was the first Inn built here. It's a great deal of fun, if you like that sort of thing."

While Drucid pointed his tail in the general direction of the Inn, Cecee flew up to take a look.

"Where is it, Drucid, I can't see anything?"

"Oh, it will be there. You just have to catch it at the right moment." Looking to the sky, he exclaimed, "The Suns and Moons must be perfectly positioned, as indeed they are now. We will have to leave at once if you want to stay there tonight."

By now, Fiero had decided he did not like the dragon, thinking him just plain annoying and so irritating with that tail of his! Turning his head to brush off the

226

muddy sand, he thought to let Drucid guide them as far as the Inn then, somehow, lose him, and the quicker the better…

As they made their way, Drucid explained the various Inns of Middlesborough. "We have so many. For example, 'Roam Inn', 'Dream Inn' which is, come to think of it, a little too close to Nightmare Lane, *not* a good choice. Then there's 'Glow Inn', 'Charm Inn' – you really do need to think carefully about the name before you choose. You'll need a map to find your way. There are places you should avoid, and the Lake you have come from is one of them."

"Why?" asked an inquisitive Cecee.

"There are wars being fought for the so called 'ownership', the Lake being the only way to reach the other World. The Foogarts and the Hagartys are two opposing Troll families fighting for the right to *actually charge* a *huge* amount of…"

Drucid chatted away, but neither Cecee nor Fiero paid much attention. As they walked onward, a dense, cold fog suddenly surrounded them, only to disappear as quickly as it arrived. Now before them, in the distance, stood a vast, sprawling Inn.

"Ah, there it is, the 'Welcome Inn'!" announced a proud Drucid. "Come on, there's not much further to go."

After walking for a short time, they arrived and entered through a large archway, finding themselves in a magnificently lavish reception where funny little furry servants, with far too much energy, busily hurried around, chatting to all. One stopped in front of them, pointing a forefinger upwards in front of himself as if to prevent anyone going further.

"Before we take each of you to the room *we* feel will suit you best, please rest assured, we can change it if you *don't* happen to like it."

He brought his finger to his lips, his eyes raised as though deep in thought.

"In fact, if you wait for just a minute, we can change it to your own requirements with the power of our minds. Just let us know your wishes… Would you like a 'Story Teller' before bed?" he asked, hurrying them along a glass corridor with many doors, each with its own number. Room '8' was Cecee's. Upon entering, the first thing she noticed was the domed ceiling made of glass and, with complete darkness almost upon them, the stars shone through – perfect! A strange looking vine with a bright orange tassel attached to the end, spiralled down from the ceiling, coming to rest above a large bed. Doors next to a beautiful bay window in the far wall led to what would be Fiero's room, in the middle of which was a patch of his favourite grass, 'Juicy Middlesborough Green'.

"Well, do you like your rooms or not?" asked the furry little servant.

"Yes, these will do nicely, thank you," replied Cecee. Fiero nodded in agreement.

Cecee and Fiero soon settled and in no time at all, Cecee was lying on her bed, studying the two distant Moons shining through the glass ceiling. In this strange World, the Suns had still not quite set so it was too early for sleep. There was just enough time to take a tour of the Inn. Without realizing it, Cecee and Fiero had left all reality behind. Everything seemed unimportant, cares and responsibilities had vanished just like the earlier fog. With so much time and fun to have in 'Welcome Inn', they certainly meant to have as much as they could.

Fully content, they walked through two massive arches covered in fragrant pink and yellow vines. The path along which they wandered veered to the left. Finding a large garden filled with excited guests, a water fountain appeared to be the centre of attraction. They ventured nearer. Buttons, the shape of letters of the alphabet, were arranged over the ground surrounding the outer part of the fountain. Fiero saw one of the guests step on the letter 'D' which activated from within the fountain's spray holograms of dragons. Fiero reared back, watching them breathe balls of fire towards the audience, certain he could feel the heat, while others watched, screaming with delight. Without a care, the two wandered on further, stopping at a strange looking track which carried along a little way further, but then seemed to shoot straight upwards, disappearing into the night sky. An elf standing by shouted, "Ride to the Stars and see the Planets as you have never seen them before!"

"Fiero, a ride to the Stars! We *have* to go!"

"Err... no, bad idea!" replied an uncertain Fiero.

Cecee approached the elf and asked if she could go alone.

"No", the elf said, "must ride two to a car, health and safety and all that!"

Before Fiero had a chance to breathe a sigh of relief, a guest from the garden suddenly appeared, offering to accompany Cecee. The temptation was too much so Cecee gratefully accepted and waited excitedly for a carriage to come down the track. It wasn't long before one stopped in front of her, and Cecee watched two very happy passengers step out.

"Fiero, wait here for me! I'll be back soon!"

She stepped in with her new companion. As soon as they sat down, the car doors shut tightly with a swoosshhh! The carriage moved along slowly but then roared along the track and shot up into the sky. But there they seemed to stop abruptly and float around in a strange stillness surrounded by Stars. Quite suddenly, they shot forward again, flying this way and that, shooting around the Planets, whizzing out of the way of oncoming comets! Next they made their way around the Moons and then found themselves ducking and diving through the rings of Saturn. Ceceee watched in disbelief as black holes sucked in giant meteors! On they flew, bursting through Galaxies and seeing Stars so close that Cecee felt she could just reach out and touch one. Before she knew it, the carriage turned around, hurtling back down the track and to the ground, finally screeching to a halt. The doors clicked open to let out an elated Cecee with her companion.

"Oh, it was over *far* too quickly," she screamed with excitement as Fiero galloped up to her.

"By all the Wizards, Fiero" she said climbing out, "you have just *got* to come on this ride with me! My friend told me they have special carriages for Unicorns and I can join you in one!"

Fiero, upon seeing her friend looking quite ill from the experience, replied, "Err, well… no. Thanks for asking, but I think not."

"Fiero, don't be scared. Come with me. Let's get on!"

"I think the elf is closing now. It's getting late and we should go to our rooms."

"You're scared!" Cecee insisted, with a definite smile.

"No, I'm not scared. Let's just go?"

"Alright, Fiero… but you *are* scared!"

Off they went, Cecee teasing poor Fiero all the way. Arriving at their rooms, Cecee, still wide-awake from the excitement, took off the golden pouch and placed it on her bedside table, washed and found a change of clothes that had been left for her. She had some berry juice and got into bed. After Fiero had enjoyed a good helping of 'Juicy Middleborough Green', he entered Cecee's room and suggested something to help her sleep. She agreed and pulled the tassel to order a 'Story Teller'.

"Will he know stories from my World, Fiero?"

"Yes, I suppose he will"

"Alright, I will see you in the morning – scaredy-cat!"

"Cecee, I was *not* scared. I would never have fitted into *any* of their carriages, special or not! *Good night!*"

In a huff, Fiero headed towards his room while Cecee settled in her bed and pulled the tassel again. Sure enough, a small furry helper ran in.

"What can I do for you?" he asked.

"I ordered a Story Teller. When will he or she be here?" asked Cecee.

Obligingly, the little helper pulled a crystal from his belt and shouted into it.

"Send Micky to the Glass Ceiling Room," and then he left. Almost instantly, a small human-like being hobbled into the room wearing a grey bowler hat, grey suit, pale green silk shirt and a grey tie. Tucked securely under his arm, he held a large, dusty book and spoke with an Irish accent.

"Top o' the evening to you, lass. So it is a story you'll be wantin', is it? And what would you like a story about? Go on, anything you like, lass."

Cecee, being in a teasing mood, put him to the test, asking for a story to explain why it always rains over Loch Lomond in Scotland.

"Righto", he said, as he sat awkwardly upon a stool.

"Ahh me back … 'tings ain't what they used to be, to be sure!"

As he opened the big book, dust flew from it and onto his clothes. He clucked as he stood up to dust himself down.

"And here, I put me best stitches on for ye. Are ye comfy now, lassy?"

"Yes, thank you," replied Cecee.

"Before I begin," he said, sitting back down, "I'll be puttin' a wee mist in front of ye, but don't blow on it, it'll spoil the pictures as I tell the story. Now, I hope ye are ready."

"Yes, I'm ready," answered Cecee.

He flicked through blank pages, text appearing from nowhere as more dust rose in the air to form a misty cloud in front of Cecee, and from within, a beautiful scene of Loch Lomond appeared.

"The story is called 'Tears over Loch Lomond'" …

Cecee awoke, recalling a touching tale but couldn't remember when she had fallen asleep. Fully refreshed, she got out of bed and walked to the window where a soft breeze blew a delicate fragrance into her room. A goblet of strawberry juice standing on a breakfast tray, suddenly rippled as a thudding sound shook petals off the vine around the window. Fiero looked up from his grazing, and trotted over to her room.

"That noise *has* to be horrible Drucid!" he said.

Drucid's large, scaly head soon appeared at the open window.

"Good morning. I hope you both slept soundly. Have your juice now, Cecee, because we must be out of here as soon as the Sun's have fully risen over the outside wall of the Inn. By that time, as the Inn is always moving, we will be in a place called 'The Knoll'. There, we'll leave the Inn. It's safe, but you must let me guide you to your next destination."

Fiero was sure he could find his way home and politely declined Drucid's help.

"Drucid," asked Cecee, "before we arrive at The Knoll, is there anywhere I can fill my pouches with fairy dust?"

"Fairy dust? I really don't think you can get *that* anywhere *here*."

Unable to think clearly, she asked, "But, I should have dust for Fiero to sprinkle over him regularly… shouldn't I?"

Drucid's eyes focused on her head.

"The Crown is all you really need. The clear crystal with the light of a Wizard inside, is right there at the centre. Try using your Crown's power, that's better than any dust."

Cecee reached up, removing it from her head to take a look.

"Wow, I forgot all about that. I must have slept all night with it on my head!"

She looked closer, studying the circle of letters engraved around the inside, but again, unable to understand them, shrugged her shoulders and replaced the Crown.

Drucid, seeing the two Suns now fully above the wall, said, "It is time to leave. If we don't, we'll be taken with the Inn to somewhere else. Cecee, have you remembered everything? If that golden pouch by the side of your bed belongs to you, you'd better get it."

The Inn's effect had made Cecee forget the tremendous importance of the pouch "Oh yes, it's mine" she replied, and without any cares, flew to retrieve it. Tying it to her belt, she could not believe she had forgotten something so pretty. She flew onto Fiero's back and the three left through the great archway of the Inn. Having gone only a short distance, they looked back to see the Inn slowly fading into a fog until not a trace could be seen. With its disappearance, something even more peculiar happened. All the thoughts, concerns and worries she had before entering the Inn now returned to her mind with a rush. She thought of the Rowan Seed and immediately checked her pouch. With a huge sigh of relief, Cecee found it still in place.

"Drucid, I forgot all my troubles while staying at the Inn. What happened to me, and where did the Inn and fog go? I have lost all sense of time! What date is it?"

"Cecee, it is November the 14th. Oh, and the Inn and fog have simply moved somewhere else."

Cecee was stunned, realizing she had been away from home almost three months. Time was rapidly running out!

With a doubtful tone, Fiero asked, "So, where are all the other guests, then?"

"The guests are still inside and went with the Inn to another place. As for the carefree feeling, I invented it, and I'm really glad to hear it still works. You see, I built it for those still in shock from what they saw in the 'Great War of Wands'. They need a place to forget, a place to get away from all the badness, a place where perhaps they can recover."

Fiero peered at him. "Drucid, I was born here and I don't remember *anything* like that."

His patience waning, Drucid turned away to allow a full blast of steam to escape his nostrils before swinging his head back to face Fiero.

"You are a young Unicorn, Fiero, and it is my guess you have had a sheltered life. The curse upon this land came *before* you were born. I know all about the Inn because *I created it*… and no, I can't go inside for what should be obvious reasons. To start with, just look at my size!"

A confused Fiero continued to stare at him.

"A dragon, Fiero … would normally scare anyone off … I'm not really a dragon though, I'm a Prince. Yes,

I know, you may have heard that one before, but believe me, it's true. I have the curse of a wicked fairy upon me and, unfortunately, a simple kiss from a fairy Princess won't lift it from me! Let me tell you, sadly, there's another dragon trapped in a huge, deep, dark lake known as Loch Ness. It's found in Scotland which is part of the 'Upper World'. She was going to be my wife, but the same curse sent her there... Oh, it's all such a long story... I could write a book! You'll get used to life around here. One last word, I forgot to give you a map, but don't worry. If you get lost, look for the signs. With everyone asking directions, the Wizards decided to put up *loads* of them. Should you bump into a Wizard, remember, you can still ask him the way. The Wizards will always help you. This is their Island and they are proud of it. It's in their veins, and I do mean that literally. They carry a special little pouch of dust, and when they want to find their way in a hurry, they shake it onto their inner left arm. The veins magically come to the surface, and by a simple thought process, they alter shape, forming a map. I first saw this about eight months ago, but I'm sure you've seen it too, Fiero. Isn't it amazing to watch?"

Not ever having heard of, let alone witnessing the magic, Fiero gave an assuring nod to Cecee and said, "Oh yes, seen it *loads* of times. In fact, *I* first saw it two years ago!"

Drucid knew the magic, at the most, was only a year old. Was the Unicorn trying to impress Cecee, or did he simply not like his company?

"Okay, I can see you don't need me, but take good care, and whatever you do, look out for the Thunderbirds!"

"We will, Drucid," Cecee assured him, "and thank you for all your help, but before you go, what is your real name?"

"I am Prince Larkspur of Middlesborough, the eldest child and only son of Perla Larkspur who was once Queen of this land. But all the powers bestowed upon her changed her for the worse and made my mother very bad. The Wizards now call her Viperla!" And with this, he said goodbye, and left.

Fiero was glad to see the back of Drucid, even though he may actually be a Prince! One thing was certain, he wasn't going to tell Cecee he felt more than a little uncomfortable with all that steam and fire!

They journeyed on, running into patches of fog here and there, and while the two discussed if this may have a special meaning, they came upon a sign by the side of the road which read, 'The Knoll'. Here, they rested.

"Is there anything you recognize that could help you find your way home?" asked Cecee.

"No, I've never been around here before," Fiero replied.

Cecee decided to sit and study the Crown again. Noticing a small but strange light now glowing within the centre stone she asked, "Fiero, Icicle's Crown obviously contains powerful magic. Should we try it?"

"Why not give it an order and see what happens?"

"Okay."

Cecee placed it back on her head and thought she would recite a poem.

"Crown, Crown, upon my head, change all the blue flowers before me to red…" Nothing happened. "Um, how about… crystal light with all your power, make all the trees around me flower…" Still nothing happened.

"How about one last go. Let's just try, HELP, CECEE!"

This time, Cecee concentrated even harder. Now, a barely audible hum came from the Crown. But once again, disappointment – nothing more than that happened.

"Oh well, Fiero, I can see I'll have to think a little harder about how to use the Crown. Let's fly around, you never know, you may see something familiar."

The Knoll was a peaceful place with trees, lakes, hills and waterfalls, tiny colourful birds darting here and there, enjoying the morning sunshine. Cecee stopped to drink from a small lake nearby, savouring its refreshing, apple flavour. She looked around and noticed a haze in the distance. 'I wonder if that leads somewhere?' she thought.

"Let's fly towards that haze, Fiero. How strange it should be here on such a clear day."

Fiero looked towards it, puzzled.

"I don't know. Do you think it's wise to fly into it? It seems fog or something like it always appears wherever we go. Suppose it leads somewhere dangerous? What do we do then?"

"Oh come on, Fiero, let's at least have a look. If it looks dangerous, we don't have to go any further."

Against Fiero's better judgement, off they flew, but a damp chill quickly filled the air. As Fiero cautiously entered the haze, all at once it changed into a solid, murky fog. He landed, turning his head to look behind, dismayed to see most of his body had disappeared!

"Cecee, I can't see you. Are you still on my back?" he anxiously asked.

The fog muffling Cecee's voice, she answered, "Yes, don't worry, I'm here."

Fiero trotted around in a full circle, but he had completely lost his sense of direction.

"Cecee, the fog is too thick. I can't see a thing. I think we're lost!"

Cecee strained her eyes to see.

"I can't see a thing either, and with no Wand, I can't make light!"

Fiero, concentrating with all his powers, thought he would try something he had never done before. All at once, the horn on his head began to glow and then shone brightly as he pointed it into the fog.

Cecee gasped. "That's really amazing, Fiero! How did you do that?"

"Concentration, Cecee. Just like all magic, it takes a lot of concentration. Humm, but it isn't working as well as I thought it might. Look, the light is just bouncing off the fog."

He cautiously took a few more steps forward. Quite suddenly, looming out of the fog, appeared a large sign which read, 'Nightmare Lane'. But then their attention was immediately drawn to silhouettes of three Thunderbirds coming to rest on top of the sign! Ruffling their feathers, they stared down at Fiero's shining light. Their hearts pounding, Cecee sat rigid while Fiero somehow dimmed the light of his horn, slowly moving backwards to try to disappear into the fog. But now, to add even more to their fears, the fog quite unexpectedly lifted, which was the last thing either of them wished for! One bird gave an ear-piercing screech as it swooped down to attack Fiero, pecking at his head, whilst another flew to claw his face. Cecee tightly gripped Fiero's mane as the third creature swooped low to grab her in his talons.

"Hold on tight, Cecee!" Fiero yelled, as he reared up to shake off the relentless attack. Violently tossing his mane, he accidentally flicked Cecee from his back, leaving her hovering in the air. To Cecee's amazement, she felt Icicle's Crown change shape, forming a protective helmet over her head. The centre crystal shot forth a beam of blinding light so powerful, Cecee was thrown backwards. It instantly struck the bird that threatened to grab her from the air! A second beam immediately split in half, striking the other two birds. All three had been reduced to smouldering piles upon the ground. The crystal continued to radiate as if awaiting further danger, but sensing none, dimmed to a gentle glow while the helmet returned in the blink of an eye to its former shape, Icicle's Crown!

Cecee, too dazed to understand what had just happened, once again flew onto Fiero's back.

"Fiero, are you alright?" she anxiously asked.

"Yes, I think I'm fine and hope you are too. I tell you what, I'm beginning to really, really *hate* birds! Didn't Drucid say something about 'Nightmare Lane'? Let's get out of here before anything else horrible happens!"

They flew away as fast as they could, flying over three small lakes each of which had an air of silence, fog eerily swirling above the surface of each. On they flew, reaching the far edge of the third lake where they landed by a large grove of dead trees. Thick, knotty, barren branches reached outwards through the dense, white swirls of fog. Cautiously, Fiero trotted on. Soon, another sign came into view which read, 'Walking Woods. Quiet *PLEASE!*'

Cecee leaned closer to Fiero's ear and whispered, "*Walking* Woods, they all seem dead! Do you recognize where we are?"

"No, Cecee, I don't, and what's more, I have no idea how to get out of here, let alone get home. Even worse, remember, I need fairy dust put over me and soon. I have been trying to save what's already in me, but I know that light I made must have used up a lot."

On they ventured, but Fiero had an uncanny feeling… Were the trees only sleeping? Did he hear one of them snore? Perhaps they were actually *watching* them?

"Cecee, we must be quiet! The trees aren't dead, I think they're *asleep*!"

Asleep they may be, but knotty eyes seemed to follow Cecee and Fiero as they walked further into the grove. The deeper they went, the louder the snoring became, creating a strong wind. Soon it became so powerful it blew Fiero and Cecee in different directions, carrying Fiero to the very edge of the grove where he stumbled to the ground. It was then he saw Cecee's Crown hanging on a branch nearby. Alarmed, he flew to retrieve it and, spearing it with his horn, shook it onto his head. But where was poor Cecee… she was nowhere to be seen!

Cecee looked around bewildered, lost once more in another storm. 'This can't be happening again!' she thought, while clambering out from under a dense bush. Shaken but thankfully unhurt, she looked around for Fiero. The sound of voices suddenly coming from a group of strange looking, noisy young Trolls scared her, so she quickly hid inside a pile of logs.

As the trolls came near, she could hear them talking loudly while they formed a group around her shaded hiding place. They laughed and chatted together busy setting fire to twigs they had piled on top of her logs! The fire grew, smoke and the lack of air soon choking her. Cecee was in trouble and had to think fast. The Crown! Surely the Crown would help! She reached up, shocked to find it was no longer on her head! In a panic, she looked around for an escape but could find none! All around was bone dry and the fire grew faster and faster, becoming out of control. Trees began to sway with anger as they witnessed sparks breaking free and falling near to dry bushes.

Delighted with what they had done, the mischievous trolls ran to hide, wishing to see from a safe distance what they knew would happen next. The trees moaned and frantically waved their branches, the earth exploding upwards as their roots ripped themselves from the life-giving soil. One tree lunged its huge trunk towards the fire, bringing down heavily a massive root in an effort to stamp it out. Another tree soon followed, smashing down its huge roots, coming very close to crushing Cecee! But the flames licked upwards even more, leaving the over excited trolls to look on wide-eyed from afar, clapping their hands and laughing aloud. This was exactly what they wanted to see... fire had such amazing power, completely awe-inspiring to watch! Sparks darted forth, filling the air and catching fire to nearby bushes, engulfing them in seconds. An old elm swayed in the fiery wind, certain it had seen something fly under the logs and was sure it could see a little being among the burning embers.

Risking its own life, it bent its great trunk to stretch forward, spotting a fairy under the logs, but the aroma of the Seed Cecee carried, sent it into dread. It was the 'Rowan Tree Seed' and was somewhere under there! It had to be saved at all cost! Reaching its smallest, finger-like branches into the embers, they became like kindling and caught fire which quickly spread along the small branch to its trunk, causing the tree to pull backwards. Its higher, larger branches began flailing wildly, sparks flying into the air, catching light to young trees which burned to cinders in seconds. The fire was now completely out of control, flames soaring upwards and outwards, consuming everything their path! There seemed no hope as the flames whirled high into the air. The trees in the Walking Woods were all going to die and along with them, the most important tree Seed in the World. Waving their branches in sheer terror, they called to one another, *"What to do! What to do!"*

A grand, old elm signalled to a birch, waving all its branches and sighing in the burning wind. "Breathe in and hold the air, all breathe in now, together!"

This was the last resort. At the risk of destroying other beings in the woods and to save the Seed, the trees all acted as one, swelling their trunks full to capacity, sucking in all the air from the surrounding grove. The fire struggled, still continuing to burn as long as it could but finally, with no oxygen from the air to feed it, in a dying protest, billowed out huge amounts of smoke, flooding the area as if to spitefully choke the life from any remaining creatures. At last, it was all over – finally, the fire was extinguished.

From a safe distance, the trolls had seen enough, running away, completely satisfied with their terrible deed. Again, a tree branch reached under the logs to pluck out a seemingly lifeless fairy. The smell of the Seed was about her as the tree carefully took her little body upwards from one branch to another, lifting her to the highest point. Still holding her safe, the tree, along with all the others, breathed out the air with such force, they blew away all the ash and smoke. Cecee gasped and spluttered as she filled her lungs. But the sudden release of air from the trees had swept Fiero into a huge tree which moved along the ground with a hefty thud, bringing him to Cecee who now lay in a total daze on the ground where the tree had placed her.

"Cecee!" Fiero called, as the tree lowered him next to her.

"Are you alright?" he asked with great alarm.

Cecee couldn't speak, smoke still burning her lungs. The Walking Trees bent down great trunks, their strange, knotty eyes carefully observing Cecee. The oldest elm whispered, "This fairy is the 'Chosen One!' She is to plant the Rowan Seed for this year! She is in urgent need of water!"

Long, thin, finger-like branches from another oak, once again plucked the poor fairy from the ground and, holding her firmly, all trees plodded west towards the low mountains. Fiero followed as they took Cecee to the bottom of a mountain where a small, silver lake sparkled brightly in the sun. The tree placed Cecee on the shore, all then turning their gigantic trunks to make their way back to their grove. Fiero settled by the lake as the Walking Woods trudged past him, but one young tree bent down the very top of its trunk, as it made its way along. It seemed to smile at him as it whispered, "You know what you must do."

Fiero gently nudged Cecee who sat up coughing.

"Cecee, take a drink then get into the lake and bathe." he said.

She cupped her hands to take a few sips of the refreshing, raspberry flavoured water after which she entered the lake, her long hair flowing backwards in the gentle water as she washed away the soot and grime. Recovering slowly from her ordeal, she flew up to stretch her wings and sat next to Fiero to dry herself in the warm sun. The little vial of liquid still around her neck was intact, but suddenly she thought, 'the Seed!' Once again she quickly searched her belt finding it safe and dry inside the golden pouch. Fiero passed her Icicle's Crown, knowing exactly the meaning of what the tree had said to him. Even more important than his own life, he must protect and keep safe this very special fairy!

He went to have a drink and to clean his coat. Trotting out of the lake, he shook himself down and lay next to Cecee. Together, they closely studied their new surroundings. At the top of the highest of several tall, narrow mountains, stood a castle. Even though it was a long way in the distance, Cecee counted seven, dark purple turrets.

Fiero softly touched Cecee with his nose and suggested, "If you're feeling up to it, maybe we should try to make it to that castle?"

"I don't know about that Fiero. It looks so beautiful and may belong to a Wizard, but this Island is dangerous. Just think what we have already been through and who knows what dangers there may be in those mountains. They look peaceful, but I wonder!"

They continued to stare in silence, both wondering what to do next. After a short pause, Fiero made up his mind.

"Well, I don't think we have much choice. It can't be any worse up there than it is down here. I'm sure it will be difficult and dangerous to get there, but rest on my back and let's go."

Cecee agreed and climbed onto his back and the two set off towards the distant mountains.

Fiero was right. The journey was both difficult and dangerous, flying across foggy lakes and deep canyons. At times, it seemed they were gaining no ground at all. Strange looking birds flew all around, searching for what or even who would be their next meal. Large, ugly snakes bubbled up from below the waters of lakes as Fiero and Cecee flew over. To their left, a group of small-bodied dragons flew low, their unusually large wings casting huge shadows over the waters below. Fearsome talons at the end of their wings and very sharp, black horns jutting from their heads, told Fiero and Cecee these were very different creatures to Drucid. Red and white striped fins fanned from behind their ears, as they lowered their heads to spew streams of white-hot fire from their mouths in a terrifying show of power. Fiero whispered to Cecee as he lost his balance a little, "that's called 'deadly spray'!" Then, with a mighty roar, the dragons turned away to slowly disappear into the distance.

"Cecee, that's it, I have *definitely* had enough! Hold on tight, I am heading at top speed towards that castle!"

***

At home in Seven Oaks Woods, Tizzy couldn't wait to discover how far her newly grown wings could carry her. Finding a secluded place within the Royal Gardens, she cautiously flexed them, and with a degree of nervousness, flew from the Royal Circle, soon realizing there was no way she could fly for more than a short distance before needing to rest. She had to find a safe place where she could hide the Wizard dust. Anywhere – a hole in a tree, a rabbit's warren, even an old bird's nest she could easily fly to, in fact, *anywhere* close to her home would do. But *should* she hide it? It did not belong to her, after all. Indeed, should she find a way to return it to Violet? Tizzy thought deeply about her options, deciding this would be the safest, so off she set to Violet's home.

It was a blustery day as she struggled on foot and needing to shelter for a while, she settled into the roots of a tree to regain her strength. As she sat there, she noticed all the leaves had been blown from the trees, forming a colourful carpet, hiding any familiar markings that would lead to Violet's. Even if she could now find her way to Violet's home, she was uncertain if she could enter without Violet knowing. Even if she tried, would the hedgehogs let her in? She took the pouch from her belt and holding it in her hand, felt very uncomfortable. Her mind wandered to her father… how firm he was with anyone taking anything which did not belong to him or her and she was now beginning to understand his feelings. As she sat there, and without warning, she suddenly felt a presence. She turned to see, standing behind the very tree she sat under, the same strange, imposing figure she had seen earlier. Leaning calmly upon his Sceptre, he stared down at her, the tip of his spiral hat almost touching the first branch. She thought her heart would leap from her chest and continue beating upon the ground, right there in front of him! For a brief moment, Tizzy stared back at him, petrified. Sensing her great fear, he gave a warm smile and gently spoke.

"You have something that belongs to me, my little winged one," the stranger said.

His manner was kind and soothing. Tizzy, now a little less scared, stuttered a reply.

"I…I have n…nothing of yo… yours. Go away and p…please leave me alone!"

"You have Wizard dust that belongs to me," he insisted, firmly.

Tizzy looked at the small pouch in her hand.

"This dust isn't yours. It be…belongs to my friend Violet!" she replied, beginning to regain a little confidence.

"No it doesn't," insisted the stranger. "Please give it to me child and relieve yourself of your obvious guilt."

Why did this Human-like being think the dust was his and not Violet's? Tizzy's mind racing with many thoughts, bravely stood her ground.

"Who are you, and why should I give you something I don't think belongs to you?"

The spicy odour surrounding this strange being grew stronger as he drew closer to introduce himself.

"I am Patrick."

"Who?"

"I am the Wizard, Patrick McCracken."

Tizzy gasped with surprise, recognizing the smell. Her father *always* had that odour about him when he returned from Middlesborough, and the same mysterious smell lingered about Florie who had confessed to know Patrick! Was it the smell of magic – very *powerful* magic? Feeling much less threatened, Tizzy replied, "Forgive me, but I thought Wizards existed only in storybooks!"

Patrick smiled as he sat down next to her.

"Well, I am not like those you may have heard about in tales of old... and I have less powers than some but more than others. Now, settle down little one and talk with me a while."

All the same, Tizzy still felt uneasy, but how could she escape? It was obvious he wanted the Wizard dust, but why? Is he *really* who he says he is? Apart from the strange odour, why should she believe him? The problem of the pouch was hers to deal with, but could she alone? She looked behind her and was reminded of something missing – her Wand! What if she needed it? The two dust pouches she wore today held only Healing or Forget dust, and she had a feeling Forget dust would have absolutely no effect upon this Wizard.

Patrick told her many things about himself, including how well he knew her father. He explained the place called Middlesborough where he, himself, had polished the very crystal she wore around her neck, a gift from her father. But the biggest surprise of all was Patrick explained, even though Tizzy was young, how she possessed magical powers beyond her years, offering help at any time if she felt troubled by such great responsibility. Above all, he gave her a severe warning – on no account should she ever try to use such powers without prior instruction. This caused immediate concern for Tizzy as she recalled the time she used the dust alone and saw Cecee talking to a winged Unicorn! Should she tell Patrick? In fear of further trouble, she decided not to...

"I have magic powers beyond my years... what do you mean?" she asked, with a puzzled frown.

"Florie saved your life and gave you all the powers she possessed. She's old and blames herself for not warning you of the dangers rainbows hold, and felt she placed in peril a Princess not old enough to know better. Even though she has been forgiven by your father and the Elders of Middlesborough, she finds it hard to forgive herself."

"I don't care! It wasn't all her fault. I want to see her, talk to her and tell her it's okay. Where is she?"

"She is in a place where we take very good care of her and she is happy."

"She is with you?"

"Yes, well, in a sense... She is in a place called, 'Skye'. It's in the Highlands of Scotland where elder fairies go when they know they are coming to the end of their lives. There they watch lights dancing in the sky and gaze into crystals... to see and reflect upon the lives they have lead and to prepare for the lives yet to come."

"What do you mean? What are all these 'lives'? My father arrested her. I saw it... She's in prison."

"No, Tizzy, she isn't."

"Well, all the same, I don't like the sound of the place!"

251

Patrick smiled at her. "Tizzy, I am pleased at your age you do not like the sound of such things. You are far too young and have your whole life in front of you. Florie will be reborn and the long life she has known will become a memory!"

He raised his Sceptre towards the sky.

"She will become part of the Sun as, indeed, so will we all. Together with countless others before her, she will shine upon the Earth, helping to create new life – this is the natural order of things. Without this constant cycle little winged-one, our planet will die."

Patrick lowered his Sceptre…

"Keep the memory of dear Florie in your heart, for those we keep in our hearts become a part of us and can never be taken away. Look to the Stars when you feel the need to talk with her and she will hear you. Now, please cheer up, Tizzy, Florie would not want you to fret. Let's discuss the Wizard dust."

After much conversation, Tizzy had a greater understanding of life and why, indeed, she should return the dust to Patrick. As a reward and to help her, he would teach her how to safely practice by herself one very powerful and useful piece of magic…

CHAPTER ELEVEN

TIDDLESWORTH CASTLE AND EARLY EVENING

Fiero flew with determination and soon they arrived at the foot of the mountains. The Castle was now much clearer. To the west, a sea lapped against the bottom of towering turrets. The only road they could see wound its way east. Close to them stood an upright, crooked sign which read 'Warning! Poisonous Butterfly Season Starts Next Month!', whilst another, which had fallen over, was harder to read as the weather had faded the writing. All Cecee could make out were the words '…. worth… brid…' Fiero decided to follow the road for almost half a mile where they came upon tall hedges which Fiero tried to fly over or around, but as he did so, they grew taller and wider. Whatever he tried, he couldn't get past. Then, quite suddenly, within the hedge directly in front of them, appeared a gate.

"Look, Cecee, a way in!" exclaimed Fiero. But a sign in front of them read, 'All Who Enter Are W…' Again, as with the last, the remaining letters had worn away. "We need to be careful, this could be an entrance to a labyrinth just as Icicle warned, but before we try, let's see if there's a another way to the Castle."

With Cecee safely on his back, Fiero trotted down the side of the hedge, one way and then the other, but each seemed to go nowhere. It appeared they had no choice but to enter through the gate. Cautiously opening it with his nose, he and Cecee passed through. With a crash, the gate slammed shut behind them and vanished, leaving them with no hope of going back. A path ahead seemed impassable as yet a further hedge blocked their way. Cecee looked along the path.

"Now we are inside, maybe it's possible to fly over the hedges, Fiero?"

Fiero decided to walk along to see what was actually there. Reaching a hedge, he found the path split in two, each going in an opposite direction, one to the right and one to the left, both with its own sign – one read 'Right Path to Sadness', the other, 'Left Path to Happiness'. Of course, Fiero and Cecee chose to follow the 'Left Path to Happiness', but they looked at one another, both wondering, could this be a trick? They made their way to a square from which three other paths lead north, east, and west and in the centre stood a further sign which read, 'You Have Entered This Labyrinth at Your Own Peril!' By the side, stood a beautiful white oblong shaped crystal with writing down one side. Cecee looked closer to try to understand the meaning but what happened next, made her and Fiero jump with surprise. From within, came a piercing whistle, followed by a faint voice.

"Ca… you… h…r … me?" it asked.

Fiero answered, "Did someone speak?"

"Can you hear ... e ... ow?"

"Pardon?"

"Plea...tou... the crystal!" answered the voice.

Cecee reached forward and touched the crystal.

"Can you hear me *now*?" the voice inside asked, this time as clear as a bell.

"Yes!" Cecee and Fiero replied together, while staring at an elf glaring back at them from within.

"At last you can hear me! These confounded channels are getting worse and worse by the day! For your information, the sign written on the crystal reads.

"All Who Have Entered Are Warned..." The elf stopped mid-sentence to impatiently ask, "Tut, you couldn't find the Safe Bridge? There is a sign outside you know, if you can read."

Cecee stared at the elf.

"Your signs need repairing! The writing on those we've seen has worn off and can't be read!"

"Oh we know, but that's expensive and times are hard at the moment... we do what we can! Well, you are in now...There is a trick to finding your way through this labyrinth, and there are clues all around you, but, *next* time you visit, *please* walk down the side of 'Feared Serpent Lake'. After about a mile, on your right, you'll find a bridge called 'Whitworth's Crossing' which will take you safely over the horrible lake and *around* this labyrinth. Be warned, you have entered somewhere that can change very quickly. Anyway, glad it's you and not me. It's been nice talking to you. Goodbye!"

Cecee's golden eyes widened as the elf faded from the crystal.

"Wait! Please don't go! We need your help!"

Again she touched the crystal but to her disappointment, the elf did not return.

"He's gone, Fiero! As you heard, there's a bridge outside, further on! *Now* he tells us! What good is that?"

They walked on turning to the left, then to the right and then left again until they reached a dead-end where a few tiny, furry animals with soft, pale-pink fur, ran along underneath the hedge. Cecee took a closer look at the adorable creatures, with their large, pink eyes and long, dark green eyelashes. Some approached her but Fiero warned, "Don't touch *anything*!"

But unable to resist their sad, drooping eyes, Cecee picked up one which snuggled against her, its large, innocent eyes staring up at her.

"Please get berries for us. Last winter cold and berries red! Can you get berries to eat?" it asked.

Cecee looked at Fiero. "Ahh, they speak and they're so sweet!" she said, as she put it back down to scamper away.

Fiero shook his head. "Be *careful*! Remember, the elf said things change around here!"

"Fiero, we were warned about poisonous butterflies, not these cuddly things."

They retraced their steps, exploring other pathways but getting nowhere. Fiero suggested Cecee rest while he explored further and left her to sit alone. Once Fiero had left, the little pink animals returned, keeping Cecee company whilst they scuttled around her feet. One ran off and rested under a nearby sign which read 'Feed The Animals'. Another quickly jumped into her lap.

"Poor little thing," she said, stroking its head. "Why can't you get your own food?" It turned its eyes upward and whimpered, "Cannot fly, cannot climb, last winter cold making berries red and delicious. Must wait for wind to blow, no wind for long time, fairy fly up get some. Red berries only, green make ache in tummy!"

Despite Fiero's warning, Cecee couldn't see any problem. Surely these were only babies? What harm could they do? She put down her adorable new pet and flew up. Of course, the higher she flew the more the hedge grew, but this did not bother Cecee as her only interest was the berry tree, the top of which she soon reached. Busily picking the reddest, juiciest berries she could find, she looked down to see even more of the little animals, all looking up at her with large, hungry eyes and wide open mouths. Not satisfied with the berries she had collected, she saw a large, ripe bunch higher in the tree. Heading straight for it, her attention was caught by the white flash of Fiero's coat, charging back to where she had left her furry friends.

Overloaded with so many berries, some fell to the ground where the little animals rushed towards them. On her way down, she caught her wing on a branch as she saw Fiero skidding to a halt and crying out, "No, Cecee! The sign reads, '*Don't* Feed The Animals'!"

She tried unhooking her wing, but lost grip of the berries which tumbled to the ground where the little creatures gobbled them up as fast as they could. In their greed, they scuffled with one another, biting ears and scratching faces as each screeched, "Mine! Mine!" while fighting for the ripest, reddest berries. Cecee and Fiero watched in horror as the once sweet little beings swelled, their pink, fluffy fur coats turning as red as the berries they scoffed.

Their innocent eyes now yellowed, the round, black pupils turning to thin slits. Sharp teeth protruded from what had become huge mouths, their tiny, furry paws growing vicious, razor-sharp claws. Spotting Fiero, they attacked him without mercy. Cecee screamed in shock as she tore herself free from the branch and flew swiftly down, pushing and pulling away the ghastly little creatures. Fiero lay with a terrible wound to his side, his precious silver blood pumping out with every beat of his heart.

Now the horrible little monsters greedily licked the blood on the ground then, to Cecee's horror, hopped onto his body to feed from the wound. Before they could devour any more, Cecee flew up to gather as many green berries as she could carry, then hovered above to distract them. They viciously snapped at her as she tossed the berries into their gaping jaws. In all the confusion, they greedily ate what they thought to be their favourite red berries. Instantly, they returned to the lovable, little pink, furry animals they had been only moments ago. Staring up at her with the same huge, innocent eyes, they soon realized that no more berries were to be had, so they shrugged their shoulders, fluttered their long green eyelashes and with perfect little smiles, all brought forth an appalling noise... "BUUUUUUURRRRPPP!" With that, they leapt from Fiero and scurried away, disappearing under the hedgerow.

In a daze, Fiero struggled to stand but couldn't. His injuries were serious and he had lost a large amount of his precious, silver blood, but his life wasn't going to slip away in front of Cecee who thought she had the situation under control.

"Fiero, don't try to move. I'll use the Healing dust!"

But, searching for her pouch, she suddenly remembered using the last on the Human boy! A wave of fear enveloped her as at that very moment, a blue, cloudy drop of liquid from one of the stones in her Crown, mystically rose into the air. She watched spellbound as it floated over Fiero, settling into his wounds which magically began to heal! All at once, a beam of light flashed from the centre stone of Cecee's Crown, turning any remaining blood on the ground into a mass of silver glitter which spun upwards, twisting in the air. Spreading out like a small cloud over Fiero, it melted into his body. Fiero began to stir.

"Fiero! Are you alright? I was so worried!" Cecee gasped.

"What happened? Why am I on the ground and where are those disgusting little creatures?" Fiero asked, alarmed he had no recollection of what had happened to him.

"They've returned to the hedgerow," answered Cecee, as she quickly checked they hadn't reappeared. She removed the Crown to take a look.

"How *do* you work?" she asked. But of course, there came no reply. She kissed it quickly and once again replaced it on her head. Fiero stood, shaking himself all over, feeling as strong as ever, unaware that only a few moments ago, he was close to death. In fact, the whole incident seemed to have strengthened him. But Cecee's own strength had dwindled. She was exhausted and flew onto his back to rest. Closing her eyes, she soon slipped into that place between awake and sleep where sounds seem to echo in a misty distance. She could hear Fiero lecturing her for having fed the little animals... "Cecee, please don't touch, feed or stroke anything ever again... it is so..."

Along the path they went, while a mysterious mist crept through the labyrinth. Another sign appeared in front of Fiero which read, 'Twenty Three Thousand Feet above Sea Level'. Fiero snorted. "We *can't* be that high up, it's *impossible*!"

They ventured on, alarmed snow was now quickly settling on the top of the hedges and lay so deep on the ground that Fiero found it difficult to trot. Yet another sign appeared. Fiero asked Cecee to fly from his back.

"Sit and wait and *don't* move or do *anything*!" he insisted.

She flew to a branch, jutting out from a hedge. Fiero plodded through the snow, drawing nearer to the sign.

'Thirty Six Thousand Feet above Sea Level' it read.

He called to Cecee to join him, "Look at this!" he shouted, as she flew near. But something made her stop, hover and glance behind. Far behind them, a little creature popped up out of the snow, greedily eating something. Captivated, Cecee fluttered higher to get a clearer view, but it spotted her and quickly disappeared back under the snow. She flew to Fiero and whispered nervously, "Fiero, I just saw something pretty awful dive under the snow back there."

He turned around to see the snow, pure white and undisturbed.

"I can't see a thing," he said, a little frustrated. Turning back to re-examine the sign, he could now see a map he hadn't noticed before. 'Am I seeing things?' he thought to himself.

All the while, Cecee's eyes had not moved from the spot where the creature had vanished. Then, sure enough, there it was again!

"Fiero, there it is!" she screamed, as Fiero turned to see a tiny creature eating something which he could not quite see. But Cecee could see quite clearly as the creature devoured in seconds a very large snake, at least ten times its own size! Then, without warning, it once again disappeared.

"Cecee, you're right! There *is* something in the snow and it looks *grotesque*!"

Whatever it was, popped up again, but this time closer, much closer. Was it seeking Fiero? Perhaps, but upon seeing him, it dived back down. Cecee flew onto Fiero's back.

"Fly away from here, Fiero! Fly!"

But Fiero seemed in a trance, unable to move. Cecee tried to yell again but her voice had gone! Then thankfully, a miracle! Fiero's legs sprang into action, galloping at full speed as Cecee held on as tightly as she could. But a root hidden in the snow, tripped Fiero who fell with a tumble. Soon the trail of the little monster hidden under the snow caught up with them. Fiero almost froze but managed to stand and trot along in the deep snow while Cecee hovered in the air. Now Fiero found himself trapped against a hedge and could go no further. The little monster lifted its head above the snow, opening jaws which seemed much too large for its head. Seeing Fiero's leg, it shot towards him letting out a hungry snarl. Fiero screamed, "Cecee, Cecee, please do something! Cecee, *Cecee*!" The jaws of the creature were about to close around his leg, then... SNAP!

Hearing her name, Cecee awoke with a start. Now wide awake and trying to gather her thoughts, she found Fiero bent over her. "Cecee! Cecee! Are you alright? You fell asleep on my back. Wow, you were all over the place and fell off! You must have been having a nightmare."

"Fiero, by all the Wizards, I had another terrible dream! It's always about a crazy little creature who seems to want to eat everything!"

"It was only a dream. You're here with me and you're fine."

But Cecee was far from rested and could not help but wonder why she had this recurring dream about a frightening little monster that seemed to live under the snow. She felt weary of it all. 'When are we ever going to escape this *endless* danger?' she thought.

As the two walked on, Cecee began to hate the Island and wondered how Fiero could possibly love it here, full of traps, horribleness and nasty little beings! Apart from his food, what was there to love? She missed her home and wanted to return, not only to plant the Seed, but just to return to all she knew and adored. They turned into another clearing with a small lake, tiny, colourful frogs hopping around and jumping in and out of the water. Fiero spotted a nearby sign which read 'Frog Pond' and thought to himself, '*NO*, reeeeeally?'

But to Cecee, it was a refreshing sight, one that reminded her of her childhood back home. She approached one of the frogs…

Fiero warned, "Cecee, please be careful of little things that appear harmless. Haven't you learnt *anything*?"

"I'll be very careful and promise I won't feed any."

She sat by the pond watching one frog which had caught her attention, while Fiero tasted the water.

"This water is excellent! It has a peachy flavour and we should drink all we can. Who knows when we will get another chance?"

"Alright, Fiero, but first I want to say hello to this little yellow frog."

She offered her palm for it to hop onto. Everything about it seemed fine – it felt heavy and cold in her hand, just like the frogs at home.

"If I kiss you, will you change into a handsome, brave Prince?" she asked, with a giggle.

To her complete astonishment, the frog answered, "No, but here are some directions! From here, you go twenty steps right and thirty left, where you will see a birch tree. Go around it and straight on. You will come to a fountain, which you must ignore. Walk straight for exactly fifteen steps, then turn left. This will lead you to a roundabout with seven exits. Count four from your left and go down this a little way, where you will see what looks like a dead end. There you must say, 'Red frog, show me the way – and don't forget, pling-plong'!" The frog then hopped onto a lily leaf and floated off.

"Fiero, the frogs instructions may be a clue. Did you get all that!?"

"Yes, I think so, but maybe you should call him back just to hear it again."

Cecee beckoned to the frog who gladly returned and hopped onto her hand once more.

"Would you mind repeating those instructions, please? We want to make sure we understand."

But the frog simply answered, "Information all gone."

It then jumped from Cecee's hand and disappeared into the pond.

"Oh no! Fiero, can you remember it all?"

"I'm sure I have it!" Fiero replied with confidence.

Losing no time, they left, finding their way to the dead end.

"Okay, Fiero, here we go. Red frog, show me the way!"

A red frog jumped through the hedge. "Password?" it bluntly asked.

Fiero tossed his mane. "Password? We don't have a password!"

"Well, for the record, you must have a password."

"But the frog didn't give us a password, and he's out of information. So how are we going to get it?" asked Cecee.

"Don't know, not my problem," replied the red frog, before jumping back through the hedge. Cecee's wings drooped with disappointment.

"Fiero, what are we going to do now?"

"I wish your Crown would do *something* when we want it to. It seems to choose the worst times not to work! Let's go back – maybe we can then remember all he said. All we need do, is reverse the directions and return to the pond."

Reaching the roundabout, Cecee sat by the hedge to review word for word what the frog had said.

"Okay, Fiero, let's try to recall the frog's instructions."

"Cecee, didn't the red frog say something at the end? Something silly and simple? Was it 'ding-dong'… no, not that. How about 'fling-flong'? No, not that either. I remember! 'Pling-plong!' It was *pling-plong*!' He meant, don't forget to *say* 'pling-plong' after 'Red frog, show me the way!' That must be the password!"

They hurried back to the hedge where the red frog willingly hopped out. Fiero repeated the words, "Red frog, show me the way."

"Password?" asked the frog.

"Pling-plong," replied the two together.

The magic was instant. Down fell the tall hedges, leaving nothing but green, rolling fields before them and high up on one of the mountains, majestically stood the Castle, its large, colourful flags flapping gently in the breeze. Without a backward glance, Cecee and Fiero hurried towards it. Up a narrow path they flew, eventually making their way straight to the Castle. Reaching the top Cecee had a great desire to ask Fiero something as she gazed at the wonderful site.

"Fiero, why is Middlesborough so very, *very* dangerous, and why do you love it so much here?"

Fiero thought it time to tell her the little he knew.

"Fly onto my back, Cecee, and I'll explain … I had not seen danger in my life until now and this is a different part of the Island. What I've heard, and this *is* only hearsay, is during 'The Great War of Wands', a wicked and jealous fairy turned all the animals, and any other living creature she could lay her spells on, into evil beings, all to aid in her greedy quest. The Wizards were eventually victorious in the War… well… sort of. They are *still* trying to correct all she did wrong!"

"But didn't she spare *anyone or anything*?" asked Cecee.

Fiero sighed. "I'm not sure, it was all *before* I was born. I suppose Drucid was right. I have been sheltered. I know he has the Queen's correct name 'Viperla Larkspur'. She was the ruler here and cause of the War. Thinking about that, I feel sorry for Drucid if she really is his mother… just think! Anyway, that really is all I know, apart from the fact that she has a daughter too, very young and I hear very, very spoiled. Well, we both know now that *something* here went terribly wrong. Maybe the answers lie within the walls of this Castle."

Certain there would be safety inside the Castle, Fiero flew towards the entrance. Shortly, a sign came into view. Sick to *death* of signs by now, he read with a deep sigh, 'To every brave heart who has made it this far, WELCOME.' Then in brackets below, Cecee read 'It's safer to come here via the bridge, though.' Cecee stared at it before an angry sigh escaped her and said with certainty, "They *do* have a habit of telling you things a little too late here!"

Before them stood two massive, crystal-studded doors, each having in the centre a wooden 'R' entwined in silver. The many crystals sparkled in the sunlight, and as Cecee and Fiero wondered what awaited them inside, the doors groaned and slowly opened. They had reached the threshold of 'Tiddlesworth Castle'.

***

For many of the soldiers, this was the first time they had boarded the King's ship. Morale was high as they chatted excitedly about the journey and what may lie ahead. They secured themselves in hand-carved, teak chairs below deck and looked around in awe as the Monitor Elves shut tight the doors ready for departure. Silence fell about the ship while on deck, and unseen by anyone, the King pointed his Sceptre at the water below. He remained there as it began to violently swirl. Then, with his Sceptre, he spun a protective shield around himself. Light flashed and thunder roared as the mighty ship disappeared into a bottomless, watery abyss. Not a hair out of place, the King stood laughing aloud, his senses alive from the spectacle he had created! Then, in what appeared to be no time at all, the ship slowly revolved and rose from the depths, emerging into a new World with great majesty and a mighty splash! Water cascading from the decks and down the sides, she rolled from side to side, making her way through the mighty waves before finally coming to a graceful calm – they had reached their destination, Wizards Eye Lake, Middlesborough. Life returned to the whole ship, shouts coming from all around.

"All safe below deck?" shouted one of the Monitor Elves.

"Yes, all safe! Is the upper deck dry?" cried the sailors.

"Yes, completely dry!"

"Safety shields in place?" asked the sailors.

"Yes, all in place. Doors now ready to unseal. Stand by!" replied the Monitor Elves.

The doors were unsealed, letting in a rush of fresh air.

Bill couldn't wait. Unclipping his belt, he flew on deck to survey the surroundings while the King, with a grand wave of his Sceptre, released his protective shield and went to find Remik.

Alone, Bill peered over the side to view the South Bank of Wizard's Eye Lake. He breathed in the fresh and unusual smell of his new surroundings. The pointed mountains around the Lake, well, he had never seen anything like them in his life. He looked up to the sky, fascinated to see two mauve Suns shining brilliantly. All this was far too much for him to take in at once. While he enjoyed this welcome break, a group of Trolls from the Foogart family ambled along the beach, chatting and enjoying their day. But their conversation came to an abrupt stop when they noticed the strange, mighty ship afloat upon *their* Lake. With great astonishment, they turned and ran back to tell their family.

Soon, dozens of them had arrived to see this unwelcome spectacle, all hiding behind boulders and trees on the shore to spy on the ship with its many flags flying in the breeze. They debated with each other if the ship they saw in front of them belonged to the Senior Wizards, or if it was a pirate ship from the Other World up to no good, trying hard to disguise itself. The three who first discovered the ship were certain they saw a very ordinary looking elf cautiously peering over the side and reported this to the Head of the family. On hearing this, the Head Troll quickly judged the ship to be a pirate vessel which definitely had no right to be here and must be sunk at all cost!

On deck, free from official wear, a relaxed King stood discussing with Tross his new Sceptre. Remik and Elm arrived together, studying a map of the surrounding area. A sudden whooshing noise heard coming from the shoreline, drew the attention of all on deck as they looked to see lethal spears heading straight for them! One whistled past, dangerously close to the King's head. Alarmed, he shouted to everyone, "We're under attack! Grab the shields to protect yourselves!"

Monitor Elves flew to retrieve the shields lining the sides of the ship, but Bill struggled to release his. Elm wasted no time, quickly raising his just in time to thwart a spear heading straight for Bill's chest. As it struck, it melted into the shield, completely disappearing. All over the ship, the same was happening to the spears thrown by the Trolls who soon realised this form of attack was useless. They needed to find something much more effective against these pirate elves. They had brought with them a sling-basket which they attached to very elastic vines hanging from nearby trees. Filling this with as many sharp stones and small rocks as they could find, they stretched the basket back as far as they could, taking careful aim at those on board the ship. TWANG! A deafening cheer rang from the Trolls as the stones and rocks flew high, raining down upon the ship's deck. A shout of "Fire!" rang out just before arrows filled the sky, hurtling towards all those on board.

The King grabbed his Sceptre, pointing it to the sky and shouted above the terrible noise, "Father of the Four Winds, blow us north!" Monitor Elves hurried to change sails as warm, strong winds blew from south to north. The sails billowed, sending the ship with a sudden jolt northward at an incredible speed of 75.34 knots, just as the King had planned. He stood by the ship's wheel, recalling from his previous visits why the Trolls had acted as they had. He shouted to all, "That was one of the two Troll families, fighting for sole ownership of the Lake. They think it's theirs and death to anyone who stands in their way! That's why they attacked us. When will they ever stop this senseless squabbling?!"

Now, far from the menacing Trolls, their brief respite was soon over. With no warning, two fearsome dragons flew low over all onboard who dropped their shields and gazed up in total shock. To everyone's relief, the monsters resumed their flight straight ahead but then turned and headed back to the ship! They came to a stop and, with deafening roars, hovered just above the water. Streams of white-hot fire now spewed from their mouths, so fierce the water beneath boiled. Were they about to attack? There was no time to find out. The King took his Wizard dust and covered himself head to foot. The transformation was instant – a terrifying, roaring monster now stood in place of the King! With several flaps of its huge wings, it lifted from the ship's deck and flew to engage the menacing pair.

Anxious sailors and Monitor Elves stared in disbelief as fearsome teeth gouged out large chunks of flesh. Blood poured down as sharp black claws tore at scaly bodies in a fight to the death.

Hideous screams came from one dragon as it fell from the sky, hitting the water with a gigantic splash, sending several waves crashing into the side of the ship. All onboard quickly steadied themselves as the ship rocked from side to side. No one could tell if the slain dragon was in fact their King. But then, one of the two remaining beasts flew away, leaving the other to land on the deck of the ship. All held their breath as it folded back its powerful wings, sending forth a huge ball of fire onto the Lake. Standing in horror, all prayed the battle-scared creature was in fact their King. Remik cautiously approached, trying his best not to unsettle the already agitated monster. The dust he had would either kill or change the dragon back to his King. Remik quickly blew it as accurately as he could in the direction of the fearsome giant. Then, a huge cheer sounded from all Tross stood in astonishment. The change from dragon back to his father the King, was so quick that his emotions changed from total fear to complete relief in the same second. Several Elves flew to the top of the main mast, while others peered over the side of the ship, all watching the slain dragon slowly sink beneath the surface of the Lake.

An angry Remik flew to the King. "Sire, that whole episode could have been avoided! Why didn't you use me? I could have fought in your place! Suppose you had been killed! What then!"

The King brushed himself down, replying, "Remik, it was my duty to defend all on board. I had no other choice. I am sure you understand."

"Sire, next time, *I* should take the risk. Tross is hardly ready and able to be King!" The King often indulged Remik in these short exchanges, simply because he held him in such high regard. Even though he would sometimes dispute Remik's advice, he valued it. After all, Remik was sometimes right! No other soldier could or would ever dare speak to the King the way Remik did. Together, they discussed the best way to protect the ship and all on board as they sailed steadily on across the waters. Tross had heard enough from Remik. He would definitely have to prove himself and soon, prove he is worthy of the highest position which would one day be his. He left his father's side to find Elm and Bill. As he flew past the centre of the ship, he heard sounds of pain coming from a seriously injured soldier who lay on his right side in the dark shadow of the main mast. As Tross landed, he could see two sharp stones embedded in the soldier's back, his left arm severed from the shoulder and his wings badly torn. The poor being was covered in so much blood, he was

273

difficult to identify. Tross knelt by his side and gently asked, "What is your name, soldier?"

"Hello, Tross," the wounded soldier whispered weakly. "It's me, Bill."

Tross almost choked.

"Bill! By all the Wizards! Don't worry my good friend, you are going to be fine!"

He called for help as he looked around for anything he could use to stop the blood flowing from Bill's terrible wounds. Finding a square of spider-web fabric, he quickly wrapped it over the awful injuries.

"Bill, that should stop the bleeding for now, just rest while I get help."

"But, Tross, my arm feels so weird."

Bill's strength draining away, he lifted his head to take a closer look. When he saw his left arm was missing, he fainted. Tross quickly flew to find his father. Weaving in and out of busy Monitor Elves, he couldn't believe the mess the Trolls had caused. The Elves were busily hurling sharp stones and any remaining spears back overboard as well as replacing shields onto the sides of the ship. Tross found the King.

"Father, Bill is seriously injured! His arm has been severed and he has two sharp stones lodged in his back!"

"Where is he?"

"He's centre ship, under the main mast. Follow me!"

The two soon reached Bill where the King knelt by his side.

"Bill, can you hear me?" the King asked.

Bill stirred a little.

"Bill, you've lost quite a lot of blood but it isn't as bad as you might think. You're going to be fine, I promise."

The King looked into the crystal of his Sceptre and called for all Doctors on board. Two arrived immediately. After they tended Bill's wounds, he was carefully taken to the 'Care Room' where the Doctors removed the stones, dressed his wounds and gave him potions for the pain. The King demanded that Bill be treated as a Royal and made as comfortable as possible. He would need all his strength to withstand the magic the King was going to use to restore his lost arm. Before leaving Bill's side, Tross reminded him, "Bill, please *listen* to my father. All you have to do is rest and trust him!" But Bill was so weak, he was unable to reply and fell into a deep, peaceful sleep.

Arriving back on the upper deck, the King and his son rejoined Remik to inspect the damage which they found not to be as bad as first feared. A few holes in the port side, a few torn sails and a minor crack in the main mast could be repaired quickly. The King sat and rested from the turmoil, swearing to himself that before he died, he would do everything in his power to put an end to this needless war between the two Troll families. If he couldn't, perhaps he would create an island upon which the Trolls could fight it out between themselves and leave others in safety and peace!

The Lake's waters were peaceful once again as the King turned the vessel to sail north past Moderf Island and then north west. Eventually reaching the entrance to Snake Lake, Remik ordered the sails to be taken down and to drop anchor for the night and told everyone to rest. Early tomorrow, they would complete repairs, set sail along the narrow 'Snake Lake' and into the 'Palanic Ocean'. The King had decided not to take the easy route north around 'Thunderbird Island' as it would mean sailing directly past the 'Black Forest' where dangerous butterflies bred. Once on the Ocean, they would change course and sail north east and then south into the safer 'Bird's Beak Bay'. Once there, they would head north, and then take a southerly direction past the 'Orange Cliffs', along the 'River of Time' and finally into 'Serpent Lake' where they would set anchor. By early afternoon, they would disembark and go on foot to 'Whitworths Crossing' and then onwards to Tiddlesworth Castle. The weather reports from Nopkin were perfect and Remik estimated they should reach Tiddlesworth by early evening.

Chapter Twelve

Get Me Out of Here!
And Evening Sky

Fiero and Cecee entered through the great doors of Tiddlesworth Castle, finding themselves in a bustling market. Fiero stopped a passing fairy carrying a basket filled to the top with berries.

"Excuse me. My name is Fiero and my friend is called Cecee."

"Hello, I'm Faye."

"Pleased to meet you, Faye," Fiero replied. "Do you know where I can top up with fairy dust and perhaps a place where we could sleep for the night?"

"Oh yes, the 'Glow Inn' on Cherrycot Hill," she said, pointing a finger to the west. Susan looks after the Inn but she's away, so ask for Darcy who will take good care of you. If you prefer a room with an ocean view, be sure to tell her Faye sent you. Oh, and you don't need fairy dust to feed your blood, the Wizard's crystal on the front of your friend's Crown has been doing that for you while you sleep."

Fiero looked totally surprised, "You mean it's the *Crown* that's kept me alive? How do *you* know? We've never met you before!" he asked.

"Your friend is your owner and without her knowing, the Crown has done everything to keep you alive. Fiero, fairies from Middlesborough know the powers of the Crown your friend wears. I can assure you, you won't need fairy dust while your friend has it!"

Fiero and Cecee thanked Faye and set off to find the Inn. Climbing a steep, cobbled path, they found what they were looking for, the 'Glow Inn'. A massive desk adorned with colourful flowers greeted them as they entered. Among this floral array sat a beautiful fairy with large, smiling, brown eyes. Over her shoulder, she carried a green, leather pouch which held two crystals, one green, the other pink. She stood up to address her visitors.

"Welcome to 'Glow Inn'! My name is Darcylina, but you may call me Darcy. I can assure you, your stay here will be a *blazing* one."

A puzzled Fiero and Cecee looked at one another, wondering quite what a "*blazing* one" really meant.

"Oh," Fiero replied, "we were told to ask for you."

Dipping the sharpened tip of a small feather into a pot of fairy dust, Darcy said, "I need to take your names…"

Fiero gave their names which the fairy then 'glitter wrote' in the air. Cecee watched, fascinated, as their 'glittering' names suddenly shot into Darcy's crystals.

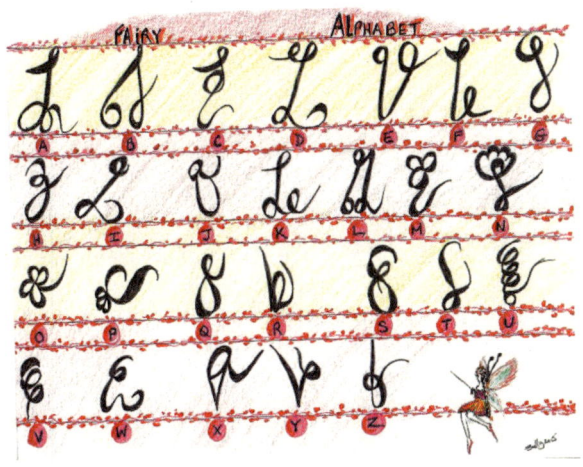

"I know Faye sent you here and I am to make your stay a *blazing* one. I will do everything I can to make that happen. Faye recognised your wings... high Royalty, a Princess, and a winged Unicorn... a rare combination, I must say. According to Middlesborough etiquette, the Wizard Ian must meet you. But first, we must tidy the pair of you as you both look, well, if you don't mind me saying so, rather shabby!"

Three firm taps on the green crystal, immediately brought forth three fairies accompanied by three elves.

"These attendants will be yours and, Princess Cecee, should you require a hairdresser to cut and style your hair, this can also be arranged. Fiero, you will be expertly groomed by Richard and his two assistants. I will note your meal preferences now. You will dine with Ian when you are both presentable. Now, Princess Cecee and Fiero, how else may we serve you?"

With feather pen in hand and dust-pot at the ready, Darcy waited to record their wishes in the same manner as their names. Cecee and Fiero looked at her, somewhat overwhelmed by her over-efficient manner. Cecee said with a smile, "I would *love* to have a bath and to wash my hair but a hairdresser won't be necessary, thank you."

A look of disappointment crossed Darcy's face as she wrote the order – she really wanted to restyle the Princess's hair as she knew this would bring much needed business to her Inn! A starving Fiero could think of nothing but food, but before he could order his favourite supper, to his surprise, the three elves whisked him away. The fairies escorted Cecee to a large room with a perfect view of the sea. In the window, hung a large crystal through which the Sun's rays reflected, setting the room ablaze with warm colours. Cecee thought to herself, 'Now I understand what Darcy meant by a "*blazing* one". This is truly magical!'

A stand containing oils of all kinds had been placed within easy reach of a generously filled bath. Cecee took her time bathing, refreshing herself with the oils full of wonderful aromas. Once dressed, she was taken by the fairies through a large, glass archway, alight with many shining crystals, and out into a square. As they walked across, Cecee asked, "Where are we going, and where is Fiero?"

One fairy answered, her manner somewhat haughty, "We are going to the 'Great Hall of the Seniors'. Don't worry, Fiero is waiting there for you."

At the far side of the square, stood two very impressive doors, to the side of which was a silver plaque with a crystal surround. Upon this was engraved the letters, 'G.H.O.T.S' (Great Hall of The Seniors). As they approached, the doors magically opened wide before them.

The fairies asked Cecee to wait a moment and with a flurry, disappeared inside. Soon they reappeared and lead Cecee in, formally introducing her.

"May we present the Princess Carmilina Citrina Foxglove."

Cecee entered a huge, softly lit room containing a pleasant odour which reminded her of apples and nutmeg. There stood Fiero, his mane now royal blue, faintly shining in the dim light. It had been arranged in one thick braid that reached almost the entire length of his back, and around his neck was tied a bright blue and silver ribbon. Cecee approached, finding a very unhappy looking Unicorn. He already had a major issue with the Inn having received no supper… and now, the way he had been presented, was just about the last straw!

"Thank all the Wizards you have arrived!" he said to Cecee. "This braid is so tight it's *killing* me, and please help me remove this silly blue bow – I feel ridiculous!"

"Yes of course, Fiero" Cecee replied, trying very hard to hide a giggle.

In a generously sized chair sat the Wizard Ian, his long, curling, white beard reaching almost to his waist as he stood to greet them. Dressed in a purple and yellow robe with five layers of fabric cascading down the back, he held a Sceptre in one hand, greeting them warmly with the other. However, Fiero's mind was still firmly set on food, thinking of nothing else and gently nudging Cecee with his nose.

"I don't know about you, but I'm *starving*. When *are* they going to feed us!" he quietly whispered.

Ian pretended he had not heard Fiero and pointed his Sceptre towards an empty part of the floor just in front of them. Fiero soon contented himself as a large patch of juicy 'Middlesborough Thick Blade' suddenly appeared. Then, with a quick wave of Ian's Sceptre, a table appeared on which was arranged a meal fit for a Princess.

"Please, sit and eat," invited the Wizard. "I am very glad to see you here and have so much looked forward to our meeting. As soon as your father arrives, you'll be home within the hour, Cecee, leaving you plenty of time to plant the Rowan Seed."

Cecee nearly dropped her goblet of juice.

"How do you know about me and my mission, and exactly how long do I have?"

Ian stroked his beard, deep in thought.

"Humm… two weeks," he replied.

"Is that all I really have to do… plant this Seed? That seems the easy part. Getting back home could be the hardest!"

"Cecee, along with your father, I can help you find your way home, but planting that Seed may not be as easy as you think… Anyway, everything is in my crystal ball. Come and look for yourself. You will see your father and brother preparing to enter Middlesborough as we speak."

At the side of Ian's chair, was a stand in the shape of a silver owl's claw holding a large ball of pure, green crystal into which Cecee gazed. As she drew closer, she saw what seemed to her, a clear image of Seven Oaks Lake! On the shore, her father and brother stood together, talking. The image of them, together with the familiar surroundings of home, tugged at her heart. Impatiently, she looked at the Wizard.

"If you can see everything by looking into this ball, why didn't you find us before now? You could have saved us from a terrifying journey to your Castle!"

"I'm sorry, Cecee, but by the time I knew where you were, you had entered the Labyrinth. Visibility there is limited owing to the tall hedges and the blankets of fog which appear at random. However, Icicle told me you had the Crown, and I knew it would protect you from danger."

Cecee took a deep breath and sighed.

"Ian, can you deliver a message to my father now?"

"Not until he has entered Middlesborough. Please don't worry, your father is very experienced in the art of Wizardry and we can easily communicate with each other. Unfortunately, at this moment, he and the others are entering through Wizard's Eye Lake. For them, the journey will seem quick but it actually takes nine hours, so we must be patient and wait."

"Does Cecee's father know she is here?" Fiero asked Ian.

"Her father learned of a message sent from Middlesborough, carved into the cornfields at Seven Oaks Lake which, when decoded, read, 'HELP, CECEE!' This is the way only she writes her name, so he knew it was his beloved daughter and immediately set upon a journey to find her."

Fiero took another mouthful of grass then swung his head around to meet Cecee, mumbling excitedly, "Your message *was* sent! The Crown *did* send your cry for help!"

Ian smiled. "Ah yes, Arthur's Crown," but then looked a little puzzled. "May I take a closer look?"

"Yes, of course," Cecee replied, as she handed the Crown to him.

He carefully took it to investigate.

"Do you know there is a stone missing?" he asked, now with a look of great concern.

Cecee took back the Crown and could see that a stone *was,* indeed, missing.

"We *must* find it!" the Wizard warned. "It's a Red Dawn, a war stone, and could easily be a dangerous weapon in the wrong hands! Can you remember where you may have lost it?"

"The last time I saw it was in the Labyrinth. In the struggles we had, the stone must have worked loose and fallen out!"

"Cecee, let me explain the magic of this mysterious Crown. You see, it works as an extension of yourself. It has all the senses you have when you wear it, so when you sense danger, for instance, it will also. But more than this, it knows when you need protecting and will take over and keep you safe from harm." Ian paused to give her a few moments to try to understand before continuing. "Although the stones work together, some can also work independently of one another. Each has its own name and purpose but when the Crown has a stone missing, it cannot perform all its magic. However, a Red

Dawn is one that can work alone, it is a war stone and must be found at all cost!"

Cecee now understood its immense power and the responsibility upon her to find the missing Red Dawn.

Fiero and Cecee bid farewell to Ian and left to investigate the grounds of the great Castle. Even though the Seed was still to be planted and the missing stone had to be found, Cecee felt she could relax a little. Her father was on his way, and all would soon be well. Leaving behind the Great Hall, they wandered through the grounds and to the rear of the Castle where they came upon a steep hill which they began to climb. Reaching half way, they could see further on a tall tower surrounded by a wall with steps leading to a large window. They also noticed the back of the Castle had another tower that jutted out into the Ocean. The weather was calm and out across the water, floating in a silvery mist, were many large sailing vessels, armed and ready for battle. But strangely, one appeared unarmed, shimmering magically in the mist and boldly displaying the name 'CIGAM' upon its side. Cecee realized, with some degree of guilt, that she had previously miss-judged Humans. Her World also seemed to have the need to venture out onto the vast expanse of the Seas and Oceans.

"Fiero, why are those ships out there, and why isn't the ship in the centre armed?"

"Those ships belong to King Elves from your World, and there are usually many more. The one ship you see in the centre is very special – on board lives 'The Blind Keeper'."

"Who on Earth is 'The Blind Keeper'?" asked a curious Cecee.

"He is a dragon of pure silver whose eyes are made of clear, green crystal, and who guards all the crystals the Wizards have implanted with magic. The name on the side 'CIGAM' simply means MAGIC."

"Oh I see! So 'CIGAM' is 'MAGIC' spelt backwards, so we can understand when we see the reflection of it in Seven Oaks Lake!"

"Yes, Cecee, exactly."

"Everything backwards... that seems almost too simple."

"Cecee, don't tell a Wizard that! Simple or not, they do things their way and are easily offended!"

"But if the silver dragon is blind, how can he take care of the crystals?" asked Cecee.

"All I know about Cigam's dragon is, he judges the intentions of all 'visitors' with his acute sense of smell, allowing any who dare, to come aboard and enter the 'Crystal Room'. But, unless you have the odour of a Wizard or a King, he will sting you with his lethal tail, ensuring you will never leave! So you can see, only Wizards and Kings can board the ship to retrieve the valuable crystals. The other ships look after your World as well as mine. All except CIGAM, have exactly one hundred elves to look after them. How many elves are on board CIGAM, I do not know, and neither do I know what the dragon eats to stay alive – only the elves know this…"

As they chatted, a soft breeze blew, carrying with it the sound of a fairy's sad cry.

"Fiero, did you hear that mournful cry?" asked Cecee.

"It must just be the sounds carried on the wind… I can't imagine it could be anything else."

"Fiero, let's go up a few more steps. I want to listen carefully to see if I can hear the cry again."

They climbed a little further but a giant, thorny, bramble bush blocked their way. Down below, fierce waves now began to angrily flood over the rocks and pound against the wall of the tower. To Fiero and Cecee, this truly was proving to be a very strange and spooky place.

"Fiero, I wonder why this part of the Castle now seems so menacing?"

"It does give that feeling. Maybe we should leave!" replied Fiero, as he looked up at the tower window. "Cecee, don't you think that window has a dark and ominous look about it?"

"No, let's not leave. That window does look eerie but I heard crying and we should find out where it came from. Who knows, there may be a fairy who needs our help. If we find nothing, *then* we can leave."

"Cecee, I'm sure it was just the breeze you heard."

"Come on, Fiero, I admit we've had a few scares, but we're in Ian's Castle now. It'll be alright, we just need to find out where that cry is coming from."

Again the cry came, this time sounding more anxious.

"Fiero, there it is! We can't ignore it! Let's fly over the bramble to the other side so we can see if there *is* a poor fairy there. If you refuse to take me, I will go by myself. I am *sure* a fairy needs help!"

Fiero sighed deeply. "*Alright*, I will take you, but don't leave my sight when we reach the other side, and no touching anything!"

Though Fiero was careful, taking Cecee over the huge bramble proved dangerous. In the breeze, long, thick stems with large, sharp thorns, seemed to deliberately stretch out to catch them. A thorn suddenly caught Fiero in his leg while another tore at Cecee's hair, scratching her head. Was it their imagination or did the bramble seem to whisper an unnerving warning? "*Stay away... stay away!*" Finally, Fiero took a flying leap, arriving at the other side. Trotting further up the steps, he stopped as a shiver crept down his spine.

"Brrrrr, it's freezing cold right here and on such a beautiful day! I'm now *very* concerned about where we are, Cecee."

"You caught a thorn, Fiero. Maybe it's stuck in you and is poisonous, making you feel cold?"

"No, it fell out too quickly so it can't be that," Fiero replied.

Over the tower walls nothing grew but clover which crept all the way up to the ledge of a barred window. Cecee flew from Fiero's back to take a look inside.

From below, Fiero called out, "You be careful, Cecee. You've no idea what may be up there!"

Cecee, however, desperate to look inside, ignored Fiero's warning. To her bitter disappointment, it was too dark to see anything, so she turned to leave, but a sudden, strange, bright, single flash of light from within, hit the bars of the window with a loud crack! Cecee's curiosity got the better of her as she spun round. This time, she pressed her face up against the bars to peer into the blackness when, from out of nowhere, something reached out and grabbed her!

"Help, Fiero!" she screamed. "Something's in here and it's got me!"

Fiero flew up and carefully with his jaws, tried to pull her from what seemed like a long, black and red snakelike tentacle, but its grip was too strong and he could do nothing! The bars now mysteriously widened as Cecee was dragged through by her throat, disappearing into the darkness. Fiero tried to follow when all at once, the bars snapped together again, preventing him from entering!

A terrified Cecee could see nothing as the tentacle pulled her down onto a cold, stony floor where it suddenly released its grip.

Fiero strained his eyes to peer through the bars.

"Cecee! Where are you! Are you alright? What's happening? Speak to me!"

Rubbing her throat, she flew up to the window.

"I'm fine… I… I think," replied a shaken Cecee, her face a ghostly white.

Fiero was so relieved to see her peering back at him. If only he could release her. For a second, Cecee looked past Fiero at the sea behind, peacefully glinting in the sunshine, a stark contrast to the fierce waves crashing against the tower walls below. The thick bars at the window left narrow gaps, making escape impossible. Whatever force had pulled her through, how and for what purpose, she could not imagine.

Fiero, quite unsure what to do next, bucked and flew one way then another.

Cecee called through the bars, "Fiero, please! I need you to remain calm… come here to me."

He hovered close and faced Cecee.

"I *told* you this was not a good idea, Cecee! How can I get you out? That force…unreal! When are you ever going to *listen* to me! Can you see what's in there with you?!"

"Fiero, calm down! I can't see much at the moment. The best thing is to go for help and I will investigate while you're gone. This force may have imprisoned some other poor, unfortunate creature in here which might explain the cries we heard earlier!"

"Cecee, I will go for help. Do *not* explore further. Stay right where you are! I mean it!"

"Alright, Fiero, go now but *please* hurry back," replied Cecee, trying to hide her deep feeling of dread.

Fiero flew off leaving Cecee to turn into the darkness alone. She fumbled around determined to overcome her suffocating fear when once again she heard the cry, but this time it was closer. A damp breeze caused a strange prickling feeling on her arms and her voice trembled as it carried through the blanket of darkness.

"Who's there? What's your name? Are you hurt... can you talk to me?"

"My name is not important," a voice replied with a soft whisper.

"I will help you but where are you?"

"I'm here, almost next to you," the mysterious voice said.

Cecee squinted hard, peering into the darkness but still failed to see anything. She gingerly held out her hand and asked, "Can you see me or touch my hand?"

"Yes, I can see you and I know you are unable to see me, little one. It takes quite a while to grow accustomed to the dark."

Still waiting for any touch, Cecee asked, "Do you know what pulled me in here?"

"It was the same force that pulled me in a long time ago. It's magic, magic only wicked fairies perform."

A thin, cold, bony hand reached out and touched Cecee's arm.

Cecee stepped backwards and asked, "Was it a bad fairy who left you in here? Is she still in here with us?"

The reply was definite. "Oh yes, a very wicked one, some say the wickedest ever, but let's not talk about her now. Did you bring in any of the clover? No, I am glad, I hate it, especially the four-leafed variety. It brings out the ugly fairy and we don't want that! Since we are safe at the moment, can you help me escape this damp, horrible tower?"

"My friend Fiero has gone to get help and will be back soon…"

Fiero flew like the wind over the now subdued bramble bush, its long, thorny stems still and quiet. Down the long hill he flew and into the streets of Tiddlesworth Castle, up Cherrycot Hill and finally into Glow Inn. Puffing and panting, he asked the first fairy he saw, "have you seen Darcy? I must speak to her immediately!"

"Yes," the fairy answered, rather surprised. "Try to calm down! She is over there, talking to her sister!"

Darcy loved to share a joke, and Fiero found her laughing at a private one that only she and her sister could appreciate. Fiero flew to them, words tumbling from his mouth.

"Come quickly! Cecee, it's Cecee! She's in a tower. Something horrible pulled her in and she is trapped, trapped inside. We must rescue her now!"

"Fiero, *please*!" Darcy said firmly. "You're talking much too fast, I can't understand you!"

"I *told* you, it's Cecee. She's trapped in a tower!"

Darcy turned to her sister.

"Sorry, I have to go and sort this out. Clearly, something has happened to Princess Cecee and I must find out what it is. Should anyone need me, call me on my pink crystal. Before we leave, I must speak with Ian in his quarters. Call me anyway, and we can meet up later for tea." She then looked back at Fiero. "Come with me, Fiero, we are going to see Ian."

Fiero felt helpless.

"This is wasting precious time. We must go to that tower now!"

"Please, Fiero, settle down. Nothing will be accomplished if you don't. Now, Ian is the only Wizard here at the moment as the others are making new magic at 'Ridge Edge'. However, you are in luck as Ian is Head Wizard and will know exactly what to do, so please do as I ask and come with me."

She flew off quickly, giving Fiero no choice but to follow. Arriving at Ian's room, Darcy knocked softly on the door. Unsettled and anxious at receiving no reply, Fiero nudged her.

"Knock louder! Maybe he can't hear you?"

"Fiero, *please*! Just let me handle this," she replied, while opening the great door.

They found Ian sitting cross-legged, meditating. A deep, purple mist twirled from a pot in front of him, forming pictures above and creating soothing sounds to help him relax. Fiero peeked from behind Darcy, nudging her further into the room.

"Go on, Darcy, speak to him," he urged.

"Alright, Fiero, don't push me!"

She flew close to Ian and whispered his name. He looked up at her, a far away expression in his eyes.

"Ian, you must come out of your trance. We need your help and quickly."

Calmly reaching for his Sceptre, Ian waved it over his head with one expert stroke and, breathing deeply, became fully alert.

"Well, Darcy, what is it?"

"Ian, it's Cecee. Fiero say's she's trapped in a tower of some kind."

Ian, his face paling, fearing the worst, nervously asked, "Where? Which tower?"

Fiero spoke, once again words spilling from his mouth.

"It's at the rear of the Castle where the waves crash against the tower wall, four leaf clover, *loads* of four leaf clover, and a huge bramble bush grows there, difficult to fly over, thorns grab at you, Cecee is stuck on the other side, pulled through a dark, barred window high in the tower!" By now, Fiero was gasping for breath.

"Fiero, be calm. Did you hear anything from within the tower?"

"Yes, we heard what seemed to be a cry for help. I thought it was the wind, but it wasn't!"

Gasping with shock, Ian replied, "By all the Great Wizards of Middlesborough, that wicked fairy has no doubt used that confounded light to trick Cecee and drag her into 'Turncoat Tower'! She has captured Cecee! Believe me, we have no time to spare!"

Darcy knew nothing of what Ian feared and watched stunned to see such a powerful Wizard almost panic as he grabbed his Sceptre, complete determination in his eyes.

"Fiero, we need to ride on your back. Please use all your powers to get us there as quickly as you can. We have no time to lose!"

Ian expected Fiero to move in a flash, but Fiero had not regularly practiced moving anywhere in an instant!

But he would do what he could as they went outside the Inn where Ian and Darcy climbed onto his back. As Fiero flew to the Tower, Darcy held on to his mane with all her strength, Ian's white beard and purple robes flying behind.

Cecee's eyes slowly grew accustomed to the darkness as she sat on the cold floor waiting for Fiero's return. She thought it might be a good idea to talk to the fairy again and, peering through the dimness, she could now see her white face shining back at her. It was like the Moon on a clear night, her black eyes matching the darkness around her. Spreading her dark black and red wings as though in anticipation of a long awaited flight, silvery sparkles along their edges magically glinted, almost menacingly in the dim light as she drew closer to Cecee.

"Now that you can see me young fairy, what is your name?"

"My name is Cecee."

"What an unusual name. Where do you come from?"

"I come from a place called Seven Oaks Woods in England," replied a nervous Cecee.

"England... hummm...What are you doing here in Middlesborough?"

"I am waiting for my father to find me and take me home. I got lost in a storm."

"You poor thing, and so young... Well now, Cecee, I wonder, have you already been gifted with any powers?"

"Powers... No, not really, but I do have this splendid Crown."

"A Crown, ah yes, I see. Let me look at the wonderful thing!"

Her long, thin forefinger pointed to the Crown. Suddenly, a steam of light lifted the Crown from Cecee's head and carried it into the white, sinewy hand of the mysterious fairy.

"He, he, he," she cackled, while caressing and taking a very careful look at the precious object. 'Well, he, he, this could spell the end of my lonely, wretched, unjust existence! Freedom at last!' she thought to herself with great cunning.

"Cecee, I can make the bars of the window widen to let someone in, but I can't make them wide enough for us to get out. Perhaps your Crown could help us? Are you brave enough to try?"

A now suspicious Cecee quickly replied, "So, it was *you* who dragged me in here, then!"

"Of course it was. Don't be foolish, do you see anyone else in here? Anyway, now you are here, you will command your Crown to get me out of this cold, forsaken Tower! I have to leave. I am in here only because I know too much magic – the Wizards are jealous of me. I used to be the Queen, but they are cruel and have put a wicked spell on these bars. I can't budge them to get out. Believe me, I have tried everything!" The fairy changed her tone to almost a whisper. "My name is Viperla Larkspur. Some who are daring enough, call me the 'Fallen Queen'. It has taken all the Wizards of Middlesborough to summon magic strong enough to hold me — *ha, ha!*"

Cecee's heart turned to ice, recalling Drucid's talk of his evil mother, Viperla. She knew at all cost she must not anger her, but Viperla was easily roused.

Cecee tried to disguise her great fear, calmly replying, "Viperla, too much magic is not a bad thing, it's how you use it that really matters."

It now became clear just how quickly Viperla could be angered, her face changing to a scowl, her wings turning completely black and the silvery edges now a dull, lifeless grey. Her long, thin fingers slowly caressed Cecee's face but then squeezed spitefully as she hissed through tightened lips, "What do *you* know! Are you trying me? You dare tell *me* how to use *my* magic! I've waited a long time for a little fool like you to venture my way! NOW HELP GET ME OUT OF HERE!!"

"I…I don't know if I *can* help," a trembling Cecee replied.

"WELL TRY!!" Viperla shrieked, as she forced the Crown into Cecee's hand.

Cecee, shaking with fear, placed it upon her head. Trying to remain as calm as she could, she thought intensely about the bars opening but, as hard as she concentrated, nothing happened. Suddenly, a hard slap came from nowhere, knocking her to the ground and the Crown half off her head! For a moment, she lay there stunned, before hearing Viperla scream once more. "YOU ARE NOT TRYING HARD ENOUGH, *CECEE*! HURRY, TIME IS OF THE ESSENCE! CONCENTRATE WITH ALL YOUR POWER, YOU *HOPELESS, YOUNG, NAÏVE, USELESS FAIRY!*

This time, Cecee begged, 'Crown, please help me! You must help me to open the bars!' This time, the Crown's centre stone glowed and slowly but surely, the bars began to creak and bend apart… Viperla laughed hysterically, clapping her hands with delight.

"Well little fairy, maybe you are not so *useless* after all! What great mastery of that Crown and such excellent magic from one so young! Now, out of my way and let me see if I can squeeze through these bars to my prison!"

Pushing Cecee aside, Viperla found herself on the other side of the bars in no time at all. Seeing the Tower wall covered with four leaf clover, she laughed aloud.

"Look at the pathetic efforts those Wizards have made to keep me locked away! But I must be very quick – I don't want the ugly fairy to appear! *Ha, ha, ha!* I'll show you all proper magic! *My* magic!" With a flick of her hand, all the clover burst into flames and was gone within a few seconds. All that was left was a great, charred mark on the side of the Tower and a plume of smoke curling upwards, darkening the sky.

She again laughed aloud. "Ha, ha, my magic has returned and I am free again!"

The hideous fairy hovered, peering back through the window.

"Okay, Cecee, thank you *so* much for your assistance. Out you come! I'm taking you to meet my wonderful sisters! They'll simply adore you *and* your Crown…"

Her cold, ghastly hand grabbed Cecee's wrist, pulling her between the bars. Holding her tight, she flew through the last remains of the smoke and disappeared into the distance.

As Fiero headed as fast as he could towards the Tower, Ian's heart sank to see a thin trail of smoke slowly climb high into the evening sky…

CHAPTER THIRTEEN

HEADACHE!
AND WOW!

Aboard the ship, all was calm and quiet. However, Bill, in his quarters, could not sleep. Convinced he'd had enough rest, he got up to take a look out of the porthole. He saw two huge, misty Moons hanging low in a violet sky, and thought he could reach straight out to touch them, but this only reminded him of his missing arm. His body was healing and, feeling a certain energy, there was no way he could return to his bed to rest. Wide awake, he walked to Elm's cabin and knocked on the door.

"Elm," he called, "are you asleep?"

Elm turned over in his bed.

"Well, I'm not anymore! Who is it?" he asked, stretching and managing to disguise a wide yawn.

"It's me Elm, Bill!"

Elm, still not fully awake, stumbled out of bed and opened the door to see a blurry vision of Bill. He rubbed his eyes. "Bill, what are you doing out of bed? In your condition, you should be asleep!"

"Well, I've run out of juice and the Doctor said I'm supposed to drink loads...."

Elm turned round half awake and went back into his cabin to get Bill a drink. Bill followed Elm, closing the door behind himself.

"I don't know, just can't sleep and thought I would at least come by and thank you for saving me from those spears."

"Well, thanks accepted. Now, good night, Bill. Go back to bed, you must heal those terrible wounds. Here, take this juice with you."

Bill took a drink and turned to leave, but another knock sounded on Elm's door.

"Great! Who is *that* now?" He poured more juice for himself while the voice of Tross sounded. Uninvited, Tross opened the door and walked in.

"Hello. Heard talking and thought you wouldn't mind if I joined you..." He noticed Bill in the soft light.

"Bill, you shouldn't be up and around. How are you feeling?"

With a grunt of annoyance and a wider than normal yawn, Elm grabbed the jug of juice and another cone, grudgingly inviting them both to sit around his table.

"I've been thinking," Bill said, then taking another mouthful of juice.

"About what?" asked Elm.

"Why don't we try out the Wizard's dust, just to get me back to normal?"

"No, Bill, I've heard the King's promise. He will take care of you," replied Elm, before taking a long gulp of his drink.

But Tross thought on the idea... maybe *he* could do it – save his father the trouble. The idea wasn't a bad one, and if the Wizard dust didn't work, then his new Sceptre might do the trick. He suggested this to Bill.

"Err ... no, Tross, it's okay," answered an uncertain Bill.

"Oh come on, Bill, I could turn you into anything you want."

It wasn't long before Tross had persuaded Bill and Elm to leave the ship and try out his idea. After gathering their weapons, they rowed ashore in a small boat as Bill was too badly injured to fly. After landing on shore and securing the boat, Elm lay down to rest but instantly fell asleep. This gave Tross a chance to practice on Bill without argument from Elm.

"Okay, Bill, stand by that boulder," Tross said. "Instead of using the dust, I think I'll use my Sceptre!"

"Shouldn't I sit?"

"I don't know, Bill, I haven't done this before and I am sure there will be a few teething troubles!"

"Tross, I think we should use the dust," replied a nervous Bill as he removed his prized bow and arrows.

"Sorry, Bill, I must have been half asleep, I forgot to bring any! Elm might have some with him but he's fast asleep."

Bill ventured over to Elm anyway, but Elm was in such a deep sleep, Bill could not wake him, so he searched his pockets and found his dust.

"Here, Tross, we can return what we use of it when we get back onboard."

"Okay, Bill. Now, what do you want to look like?"

"Well, I want my arm back of course, but I want to be handsome. I don't want big, grey, floppy wings like an old elf who hasn't worked out all his life. I want small, really strong, brilliant white wings, dark hair maybe, and tall, yes, I want to be tall."

"Bill, that sounds like Remik! You want to look like him?!"

"Well...erm... yes, why not!"

"Bill, I can't do that. You can't look like my father's right-hand man!"

"Well, can I *almost* look like him, then?"

"I will do my best, but I can't achieve miracles!" said Tross, while taking out the dust. "Bill, you heard my father's instructions. The only change I'll make is before I blow it at you, *I'll* think what you should look like, and don't *you* do any thinking, alright?"

"Okay!" agreed Bill, with much excitement about his impending makeover.

Tross concentrated with all his mind while blowing the dust which circled around Bill, all at once entering his body. Then, what's happening! Surely not! It can't be! Not this quickly! Everything Tross imagined was taking immediate effect. Bill's legs became muscular, his waist grew thinner, his chest expanded, his neck thickened and his height increased by several inches! And by magic beyond even Tross's belief, a replacement arm appeared, growing with his other in perfect proportion to the rest of his new body. His chin became

chiselled, defining a strong jaw-line. His eyes turned
from a dull brown to a sharp, striking blue and his hair,
once limp and lifeless, was now dark, shiny and tussled.
From his back, sprouted small but incredibly strong,
snow-white wings. But it was then, Bill's transformation
came to a sudden stop! He felt more than a little dizzy as
Tross blindly stepped back in amazement, only to
accidently trip over Elm who awoke with a start.
Without saying a word, Tross nodded in the direction of
Bill. Elm gasped so much he almost choked. He sprang
to his feet seeing a totally new Bill, his new clothes,
given to him by the King only recently, now somewhat
tight and torn!

"What have you pair been up to while I was asleep?" asked Elm, knowing what the answer would be. "Bill, by all the Wizards of this Kingdom, you look fantastic!"

"Elm, now don't get angry," said a worried Tross, "I didn't use my Sceptre, I…err… used some of your Wizard dust!"

Elm stared straight at Tross. "You used my *Wizard dust,* Tross? I don't think your father meant it to be used like this! He will *not* like that one bit! Anyway, we all heard him say, he was going to help Bill! We have got to return Bill to his former self before we re-board the ship! My dear, Bill, how do you *feel?*"

"I feel GREAT!" bellowed an over-joyed Bill, showing off and flexing his well-developed muscles as he replaced his bow and arrows over his shoulder.

Elm was very concerned. "How are we going to undo all this?"

As they debated the, no doubt, challenging reversal of Bill's new physique, a soft voice came from above.

"Hello there."

Together, they looked up to see hovering close to them, the most beautiful fairy each had ever seen. With long, silver hair and sky-blue wings, she gently settled like a feather onto a bush next to them.

"If I may ask, what are you three handsome elves doing here?" the fairy asked.

Tross noticed two other fairies flying towards them, one in pink with blonde hair, the other in green with red hair, each as beautiful as the first. Bill stared at them as they came to rest next to the other and thought to himself, 'Well, my new looks have already brought about some promising results!' He nudged Tross.

"Say something, Tross. You're the Prince and the one in charge!"

Tross stifled an uncomfortable cough. "Err ... isn't it dangerous for you three to be out alone at night like this?" he asked.

The silver-haired fairy disguised a giggle.

"No, we're just fine and I can assure you, we can take good care of ourselves. Let me introduce you to my sisters."

The elves bowed low while the fairies looked at Bill with deep admiration.

"My sister in pink is Sevilla, the other in green is Elmiva and I'm Levira."

Elm could not take his eyes from Elmiva, thinking what a strange coincidence it was their two names were similar. Questions raced through his mind as Elmiva turned her charms toward him. Could he already be falling in love with this fairy, after all, a vision of such perfection, how could he not? However, his conscience pricked him as he thought about Violet at home waiting for him – he hadn't forgotten how she had helped him and the others with the weapons.

"We're going to have some tea. Will you join us?" Levira politely asked.

Tross, always ready for an adventure, couldn't see any harm. Elm couldn't resist either and Bill, so enamoured with his new-found looks, couldn't wait to show them off. The fairies took flight and, although it was the middle of the night, the three elves followed close behind. They flew inland which worried Elm – were they going a little too far away from the ship? But he reminded himself there were three of them and they could take care of themselves, so he shook off the worry as they all reached the spot where the fairies had previously prepared tea. The hour was advancing and the wind began to moan, while far away in the distance, they could hear the frightening screams of dragons...

Tross and Elm started to feel a little light-headed, thinking they may have eaten too many honeyed blueberries. Elm shook his head, which only intensified the feeling, while a strangeness over-took Tross, who began to feel quite separated from himself and sat perfectly still trying to make sense of what was happening. Bill, standing a little distance away, laughed at them both, while in his hand, he raised up and down a heavy rock to exercise his new arm.

"What are you two doing sitting?" he called, but no answer came from his two friends. He put down the rock and walked towards them, but through the darkness, an even darker, ominous cloud caused him to look upwards where he caught a glimpse of two fairies riding the now howling wind, one dressed in fire-red, and the other? His eyes squinted to focus as the yellow hair became vaguely familiar. But no, he couldn't recognize either of them. Suddenly, before he could make sense of it all, the ground rushed up to hit him square in the face!

Viperla landed near her sisters, keeping poor Cecee firmly in her cold, tight grip.

"Viperla!" the sisters cried aloud in unison, "How did you escape!"

"Well, my sisters, I coaxed this little fairy into helping me and, excellent news, I *still* possess my *extraordinary* magic! Flying safely over 'The River of Time' without getting caught in its warp, proved *that* beyond any doubt...*Ha, ha!* Cecee, let me introduce my sisters, Sevilla, Elmiva and Levira," said Viperla, pointing to each in turn.

She swung Cecee around and into the hands of Levira.

"Viperla," Elmiva said, as she pointed to the unconscious elves, "we have these three, and were planning to use them as ransom for your release. What shall we do with them now?"

Viperla stared at Cecee.

"Oh, I don't know. Let's think about that later for right now, a celebration is in order!"

A while later, Tross awoke seeing Cecee for the first time since the storm. He called to her, but Levira held her back before Viperla intervened.

"Oh no, Levira, let the poor little darling go to her friend. What else does she have in her final moments of freedom...*ha!*"

Levira begrudgingly loosened her grip on Cecee, allowing her fly to Tross.

"Cecee, the side of your face is so red. Are you alright?" Tross whispered.

"Don't worry I'm fine, but how did you get here? Is father with you? Is he here?" replied a hopeful Cecee.

Tross looked Cecee over and quietly said, with more conviction than he had ever felt in his life, "You *are* hurt! They will pay a high price for this, I promise!"

He noticed the crystal Crown on her head and asked how she managed to find something so unusual. She whispered back, "Tross, don't say or ask too much. They don't know we are brother and sister and Royalty. I will explain the Crown to you later. Where is father?"

"He's on the ship, Cecee, and I don't think he knows we've left!"

"Father has a ship? What ship?" But before Tross could answer, Cecee quickly added, "Don't say any more Tross, Sevilla and Viperla are heading our way!"

The two sisters strutted towards them, Sevilla fixing her eyes on the Crown and whining, "Viperla, I want that fairy's lovely Crown!"

"Then take it, sister. *I* have no use for it… I now possess more magic than the strength of three Crowns like that put together, and as for the *pathetic* weapons they carry… a couple of daggers, a bow, a few arrows and a small Sceptre, HA! Ignore them, they are no match for me! *Ha, ha!*"

Sevilla glared, demanding, "Give me that Crown, Cecee!"

Cecee reached up to remove it, but it held fast to her head.

"Cecee, I told you to give me the Crown. I am asking you nicely, but don't push me or else!"

Cecee tried once again, even harder this time, but still the Crown would not move. It seemed to have become a part of her and Sevilla might as well have been asking for a limb. The spoiled sister reached across to grab the Crown, twisting and pulling with all her strength, but there it remained. Viperla watched her struggle and flew nearer to help, demanding with a real threat, "Reverse the magic you have placed on that Crown Cecee, and remove it! *I will not ask you again!*"

"Viperla, I haven't used magic! It has a mind of its own! It refuses to come off!"

Viperla's eyes glowed red as she raged, "*Are you trying to test me, fairy?*"

"No! You have to believe, I am not!"

Tross, Bill and Elm flew up to protest, but Sevilla immediately blew a spell from her mouth, freezing them in mid-air. Cecee suddenly noticed clover growing on the ground and quickly reached down to pick a four-leaf, holding it up in front of her. In the darkness, Viperla was too slow to notice. Her nose became too big for her face and her once smooth skin was now scaly and wrinkled. In place of her hair, green snakes twisted and turned wildly on her head, venom dripping from their fangs, hissing wildly as they reached towards Cecee. Viperla cast an ice-cold shadow in the moonlight as Cecee hurriedly took several steps backwards, almost stumbling over as she did so.

"Oh, little one, don't be frightened. You found a four-leaf clover and I wasn't quick enough. Now you have succeeded in revealing the true me. I must say, I'm very impressed!"

The three sisters laughed aloud at the new, scary snake 'hat' on Viperla's head. How wonderfully inventive she was, and so quick to think, a true mistress of magic! But how quickly the sisters' moods changed as they looked at one another to see that they, too, had returned to their ugly, horrible, true selves. Cecee dropped the clover and instantly the terrible fairies' false beauty returned. Sevilla grabbed at the Crown and with one mighty twist, off it came, her entire face triumphantly shining with satisfaction!

"Well, that's more like it!" she exclaimed, while carelessly waving her hand to bring the elves out of her spell. But her happy state was short lived as she whined, "Oh no, there's a stone *missing*! I suppose now *I'll* have to find another to put in its place… come to think of it, I do have a purple stone at home which should fit. Oh, I can't wait to put the Crown on. Made of crystal, how unusual but soooo very gorgeous!" She then sniggered, "I must say, Cecee, it will look better on me than it did on you!"

Then, with an air of complete arrogance, she placed the Crown on her head, flying over to a nearby small lake to admire her reflection in the moonlight. Very pleased with herself, she returned to the others. Viperla smiled at the youngest of her three sisters – she liked to see her happy and contented. After all, Sevilla looked so much like her own beloved and much-missed daughter who was now 'in the care' of Tiddlesworth. One day, she would seek her brother Avilbert's help to free her. One thing was certain, as weak and untrustworthy as he was, he was a true master at fooling people into believing he was something he was not. Such a quality would, one day, prove invaluable to Viperla, but everything in its own time...

"Sevilla," Viperla said, "since you have brought the *brave* soldiers out of your spell, we must take them to our home. I think they will be quite comfortable there, *ha, ha, ha...*"

Elmiva secured the wings of their prisoners with a spell and while doing so, she noticed Cecee's golden pouch... a very pretty adornment but should she draw attention to it? Certainly not she quickly decided, just in case Viperla gave it to the spoiled Sevilla! No, her plan was simple – she wanted it and would get it later while the others slept.

Poor Cecee. Trapped, time was no longer on her side. In fact, she had lost all sense of it but had a definite feeling December the first was just around the corner. Would she have enough time in which to plant the all-important Seed? Would her father still be able to find and rescue them from these evil sisters? Cecee had so many questions but could not find the answers...

Sevilla loved her new Crown. She studied the huge, white centre stone as they walked towards Viperla's caves, but was it her imagination... *did* it emit an energy that gave her a strange feeling? She really didn't care, smugly placing the Crown on her head once again. As they all arrived at the entrance to the caves, Sevilla still wasn't entirely happy and moaned aloud, "This Crown is too *heavy*… it's giving me a *horrible* headache!"

***

The ship rocked peacefully to and fro upon the gentle waves of the Lake. King Foxglove awoke from a restful sleep to find a beautiful, still, sunlit morning. He summoned a Monitor Elf to wake his son but he returned all too soon and, somewhat distressed, informed the King that Prince Tross was absent from his cabin. The King gave orders for Elm, Remik and Bill to attend him at once. He was soon dressed, pacing his room, awaiting his faithful elf soldiers, but Remik came alone and in great haste to inform the King the ship had been searched from top to bottom but Tross, Bill and Elm were nowhere to be found…

"How can they just disappear!" the King growled. "We all retired early last night, and I am unaware of anything happening since then."

Remik, very concerned, looked out of the porthole.

"Majesty, I hope they did not venture out last night. I do remember Tross saying something about his Sceptre, and how he wanted to practice with it… maybe they went ashore to do just that?"

The King's face grew purple with rage.

"Once *again* my son has left without my permission! How could he do this when he knows what deep and troubling concerns I have! Is my son a fool! Remik, they must have gone ashore, where else could they be? He and the others have *got* to be found! There is danger and it doesn't take much effort for an innocent to fall into the hands of an evil being!"

The King stormed out of his cabin, but not before yelling behind him, "Remik! Call every sailor and Monitor Elf to top deck immediately. I need to address all!"

"Yes, Majesty, at once!" Remik quickly answered.

Hastily making his way alone to the deck, King Foxglove's thoughts were so focused upon those missing that he failed to realise the deck would be wet with morning dew and, stepping onto it, lost his balance. He fell back, hitting his head hard. Confused, he struggled to right himself, but the ship suddenly dipped and he slipped again. Flailing around and grabbing at the air, he slid across the deck and fell overboard with an undignified splash! Unseen and unheard, he was sinking fast. Questions raced through his mind. *'Did anyone see me fall or hear the splash?'* Now, deep under the water, thoughts of his childhood entered his head. How busy he had been learning Royal duties expected of him as an adult. In fact, he had been so pre-occupied by all this, he failed to learn one of those basic necessities required by all, even Royalty – how to swim! Although cold and extremely tired, he felt cocooned in the water's icy grip, surely this would not be the end! Then, from out of nowhere, he found the strength and determination to push his way upwards, legs kicking as hard as they could and arms pulling at the water. Breaking the surface of the Lake, he splashed wildly, gulping much needed air. A few Monitor Elves leaning over the side of the ship, cried out and waved their arms to attract the King's attention.

"Your Majesty! We are coming to save you! Don't panic! Try to keep calm and concentrate on catching our legs as we fly over you – we will then be able to lift you out of the water!"

But the dazed King failed to understand, water lapping over his head as he tried in vain to hear their cries. His vision blurred and his strength now much weakened, down he sank once again, deeper and deeper. Without considering any danger to themselves, the Elves plunged overboard, diving deeply in search of their King. Alas, there was no sign of him, and although they were fit and strong, they were no match against the Lake's dangerous undercurrents. As hard as it was for them to accept, they had no other option but to give up and struggle back to the ship. On board, all rushed to see what the urgency was about. Rumours had spread already – the King had drowned! As the sailors and Monitor Elves began to quickly assemble on the top deck, Remik had momentarily gone to his cabin just below, but the abrupt, noisy stir, caused him to return. He walked on deck as an Elf shouted from centre ship, "Come quickly! The King is here and alive!"

All ran to where the King lay unconscious, soaked through, shivering from head to toe but breathing – he was indeed alive! Remik flew to his side, his eyes searching for immediate answers, but nothing could explain the King's situation. He questioned aloud, "*What happened here? Can anyone explain? Stand clear everyone, the King must have air!*"

At that moment, a voice shouted, "What's that up there?"

315

All looked to see a small, white cloud, floating just above the ship. Remik was taking no chances – the safety of the King came before anything else. He flew upwards, dagger drawn at the ready. As he approached, the mysterious cloud faded, and in front of him, hovered a fairy! Remik stared in disbelief.

"TIZZY!! By all the Wizards, is it really *you*?!" He looked around. "Where *have* you come from?!"

"Remik! I used magic which made me invisible," the young fairy answered.

"*What!* Where did you learn magic like that?"

"A long story, but I took Wizard dust from Violet when I was staying at her tree house. I traded it with Patrick and he taught me a little magic."

Remik looked at Tizzy, mystified as she persisted, "I may be young, but I want to help find Cecee too, so when I saw the ship rise from the waters at Seven Oaks, I used the magic so you couldn't see me and jumped aboard to sail with you. When we reached Middlesborough, I just thought to look around, still invisible of course. But then I saw father fall into the Lake. I didn't want to reveal myself and get into trouble and was about to help, when I saw him come to the surface. Watching the Elves trying to save him as he sank again, I could see they wouldn't be able to. So I jumped into the water, the magic forming a large air bubble around me so I could breathe. It was sooooo weird! I could actually fly under the water! Down I flew in the bubble to find father sinking fast. I held out my hands and it was then something very strange happened! Lightning shot from my finger tips to surround father in light, magically lifting him to the surface of the Lake and then to the safety of the ship!"

"Well, that's *some* story!" replied a very impressed Remik. "You had better follow me. We must go to your father immediately."

Still lying upon the deck and surrounded by Doctor Elves, the King coughed several times, spluttering water from his lungs. He opened his eyes and realized he was facing Tizzy!

"My beloved daughter! What has happened and why all the fuss! Where am I and why am I wet through?"

Remik helped the King lift his head a little.

"Majesty, you fell overboard and almost drowned. Tizzy saved your life!"

"Tizzy saved my life!" exclaimed a confused King, sitting bolt upright.

Looking at his surroundings, he then remembered where he was.

"Remik, help me to my feet. How could Tizzy possibly be here?"

Before he moved further, Tizzy knelt beside her father.

"Father, I wanted to help find Cecee too, but no one takes any notice of me, well, only when I'm in trouble! So I smuggled myself aboard with magic that made me invisible!"

Her father looked hard at her and thought, 'Magic, she is using magic? This young child of mine, always doing things she shouldn't! But without her today, I would surely be dead!'

"Tizzy, my darling child. You acted so swiftly, putting yourself at risk to save me, a truly brave and selfless thing to do. It is time you knew more. This ship

317

is a gift to my dear children. You, along with Tross and Cecee, would have soon known about this surprise, but then the storm arrived, causing all this terrible upheaval. My dear child, when are you ever going to understand what you mean to me and your mother who must be frantic with worry! We must get word to her you are safe and well and with Tross and myself."

Deep down, the King understood Tizzy's frustrations. He remembered well his own formative years when he learned so much. The early stages of life can be difficult with many setbacks, but a strong character will help us recover from life's stumbles.

Remik wrapped a blanket around the King then looked at Tizzy with a warm smile.

"Tizzy," he said, "you must eat. We will soon be going on foot to Tiddlesworth Castle where we will meet with one of the Wizards."

A Monitor showed Tizzy where to eat, and soon she satisfied what had become a ravenous hunger. Now contented, she gazed through a porthole next to her table, pondering why growing up a fairy Princess should be such a daunting process. She thought about how she had saved her father's life, and remembered how the magic came straight from the same fingers she now drummed upon the table. Wondering if she should try a little more magic, her eyes searched the cabin to find she was alone. She spotted a glass on a table some way from her and, concentrating with all her powers, she pointed her right forefinger towards it and commanded it to rise. As quick as lightning, a stream of light instantly surrounded the glass which lifted high above the table! But just then, she heard voices and her concentration was lost! The light left her finger and the glass fell, shattering into pieces. A few Monitor Elves busily chatting and laughing aloud, entered the cabin. Fortunately, they had not heard the glass smash. Tizzy's green eyes sparkled with excitement as she stared at the broken pieces. 'What awesome magic!' she thought to herself. 'WOW!'

CHAPTER FOURTEEN

SPECTACULAR SIGHT AND ELM

Fiero, Ian and Darcy stood gazing up at the dark, menacing window of the Tower. Thunderous waves continued to crash against the Tower wall as Ian realized the cause of the smoke and his anxiety. To his horror, all the clover covering the Tower wall had been burnt to a crisp. How he had failed! Viperla had regained her magic, and he hoped above all she would never again use the herbal mixture to make those terrible bubbles which he recalled so well, the red being the worst. The situation had become dire so Ian asked Darcy to use her crystal and summon the Wizards, calling them back from Ridge Edge. He thought the sea air would help him think more clearly so decided to take a peaceful stroll along the beach, far below the other side of the Tower. To get there quickly, Ian mumbled a few strange words of magic, before he and Darcy stood on the first of the steps leading down to the beach. Instantly, it changed into a large stone slab which hovered in the air before descending rapidly to the beach below. This left Fiero with the chance to practice his, as yet, unperfected art of flashing from here to there. So with all his concentration, off he shot and, to his great surprise, landed almost instantly upon the sandy beach! 'Humm, not bad,' he thought, as he shook himself. 'I think I'm improving!' Darcy approached him with a smile.

"Fiero, I have an idea. You could summon other winged Unicorns. They will be of great help against any dangers we may face."

"Me, summon the Unicorns? How can I do that?"

Darcy looked towards the sky.

"Look at something you wish to change by using the power of your mind. Perhaps those," she said, pointing to a small cluster of clouds. "Now watch me carefully, Fiero."

Staring at the clouds and clearing her mind of all thought, for a moment, she sent herself into a deep trance. Slowly, each began to change shape, one into a tree, another into a frog, and a further into a rabbit, all floating high above. Darcy laughed to see Fiero peering up at the sky, his mouth wide open. She flew up and tapped his nose.

"Fiero, only you can summon other Unicorns. Look at the waves, so large and full of foam, perfect for your task."

Fiero stared at her while Ian listened to Darcy. He was very proud of her – his teachings had not been in vain. While Fiero stood gazing at the Ocean, Darcy met his gaze.

"Fiero, look at me. You must think only of your mother, imagine where she is and what she may be doing at this very moment... then call to her. Use the power of your mind."

Fiero thought deeply about where he had come from. In his mind, he saw his mother grazing at home and thought, 'Mother, this is your son, Fiero. I hope you can hear me. I am in desperate need of your help.'

He now clearly saw not only his mother, but also his father. Seeing them both, his heart ached, making him lose concentration. A tear fell from his eye as all at once they disappeared, but looking across the water, longing for the vision to return, he could not believe what he saw. Foaming waves began to build, gaining more and more strength. Towering above him and with the sound of thunder, they repeatedly pounded the shore. Suddenly, before his eyes, pointed shapes formed within the white, bubbling foam, protruding upward and with the next crash of waves, a herd of white, winged Unicorns burst forth onto the beach! Immediately behind them came another mighty swell of the Ocean. Bounding out from the thick, foamy water, came something so bold, majestic and beautiful – it was none other than Fiero's parents! With grace and elegance, his mother galloped onto the beach, shaking water from her silky coat before trotting to her son.

"Fiero! Where *have* you been? Your father and I have been so worried."

"Mother, I am very sorry. I drank from a forbidden lake…"

His mother shook her head.

"Mother, I know, I know. I can see now *why* they are forbidden, but we must talk about something that simply cannot wait."

His father, after a short, formal greeting with Ian, also trotted over to him, immediately suggesting what he should do if he became lost once more.

"Fiero, let me tell you about the White Horse in Wiltshire. He is there for our lost ones and will guide them home. Of course, we couldn't hide him from Human sight as he was, long ago, carved into the side of a hill. He has certainly remained a mystery to those poor Humans who wonder why he is there and what purpose he could possibly serve!"

Fiero listened, irritated. He could not understand why his father didn't immediately grasp the seriousness of the situation. Surely he must know there was a good reason for performing the amazing magic that brought him and mother here, not to mention practically all the flying Unicorns in existence, and he just knew his father was leading up to a telling-off! Why else would he bang on about being lost! He raged at his father.

"*Father, not now!*"

His father stood back, stunned.

"Fiero, your biggest problem is that you do not stay calm in the midst of trouble. Show some respect for mother and me! We are here to help with whatever trouble you are in. Now, calm down and tell me all about it."

"Father, *I* am not in trouble, but I do need help to get a fairy friend out of the clutches of an evil fairy."

As he spoke, Fiero looked for support from Ian and then looked at his mother. Time was of the absolute essence and he did not know where to begin.

"Ian, will you please try to explain it all for me," he begged.

Ian hurriedly walked back towards the Castle with Fiero's mother and father while explaining what had happened. Fiero flew with Darcy to join the Unicorns, absolutely thrilled to do so, as dozens flew over the massive wall of the Castle. Descending into the town, there could not have been a more spectacular sight!

***

Even though they were helpless, the tense journey to Viperla's home gave Cecee, Tross, Elm and Bill a little time to think. But all too soon, they approached a craggy hill to the side of which large rocks were scattered all around. They followed a twisting, uneven, stony path as they finally approached Viperla's huge, dark, foreboding caves. Before entering, fearsome looking guard-dragons scrutinized all, spewing white-hot streams of fire from their bright red mouths as if to demonstrate to all their undeniable power. However, none of this fazed Viperla or her sisters. On the contrary, all four found the spectacle quite entertaining, and hoped their 'guests' would also!

"Oh, don't worry about them," Viperla said flippantly. "I control them. In fact, I have complete control over all dragons on this Island! As long as you stay close to me, you will be safe. They rely on me and my sisters, the hopeless fools, always burning their food to a small crisp, failing to realize the object of a kill is to cook and eat enough to stay alive!"

The dragon's eyes followed the prisoners in whilst together they blew a fierce blast of hot, white steam close to the terrified captives.

Through a number of adjoining passages, Viperla and her sisters took their captives along a corridor, passing small caves, each lined with different stones – diamonds, sapphires, quartz, amethyst, amber and many others. Each cave was guarded by a small, sinister-looking pixy, sitting upright in its entrance.

"Don't even look at those caves! They are mine and mine only. You dare even look and I will set a curse upon you for all eternity!" Viperla hissed as she hurried them into a cold, dark cavern at the very rear of her lair. She pushed them inside, securing them by locking a large, metal gate.

Elmiva sniggered, "You will be comfortable here, I am sure!"

Then, cackling between themselves, the four evil sisters departed.

Cecee paced the floor of the cell.

"Elm, what *are* we going to do?"

Elm, deep in thought, caught her helpless gaze while Tross brought out his Sceptre, proudly holding it high.

"I have this! There must be a way to use its magic to get the Crown away from Sevilla and then, I am certain, with both Sceptre and Crown, we will have some power over Viperla."

Bill too, had an idea.

"Tross, we obviously cannot get to the Crown, but suppose we use your Sceptre to instruct the Crown to come to us! It must be worth a try!"

Elmiva crept around each of her sister's bedrooms to satisfy herself each slept soundly. Certain they were, she turned on her heels and headed back to the prison. However, unlike her sleeping sisters, the prisoners were wide awake.

"Hello. Ahhh, can't we sleep?" asked the sarcastic creature.

All four captives focused upon her.

"Cecee, that golden pouch you have about you, I want it! And I mean *now*!" she forcefully demanded.

Cecee looked at her, astonished.

"You can't have it!" she replied "I... I... it's special only to me... a gift from my parents! You're not having it!"

Tross leapt to his feet.

"Cecee", he whispered, "father will get you another. We don't want to anger any of them even more!"

"No, Tross, she can't have it. Not this one!"

Tross stared at her in disbelief. This was not the sister he knew. They were less than two years apart in age and had grown up together. The old Cecee would *never* hold on to such a trivial object, however pretty it may be! He tried again.

"Cecee, give her the pouch! Have you completely lost your mind? She will call for Viperla and we don't want that, do we!"

"Tross... you don't understand, she *can't* have it!"

Elmiva's patience, wearing thin, thrust her hand through the bars.

"Give me the pouch!" she hideously shrieked. "Do you want me to melt you into your own shadow, or should I change one of your companions into a toad?"

Cecee ran to the bars and gripped them with both hands.

"You cannot have the golden pouch, but I will give you anything else you want. Here," she said, letting go of the bars to expose two other pouches on her second belt. "These two are Royal. They are empty but you can have them both. Two instead of one must be much better!"

She quickly took them off and passed both through the bars. Elmiva took them and carefully examined each. 'This fairy is Royal!' she thought to herself. 'I should tell Viperla. But first I must admit these pouches are indeed very beautiful and I want them for myself!'

"Well, Cecee, since you offer, I will keep them, but I *still* want that golden one!"

Tross could hear no more and crept behind his sister.

"Cecee," he whispered, "Elmiva will *now* wonder where you got those pouches from! You have just hinted to her you may be Royal!"

Her vine belt tied at the back, he skillfully slit it apart with his dagger. In a split second, the golden pouch dropped to the ground and Tross kicked it to the other side of the bars. Elmiva grabbed it with lightning speed and hurried away, shaking her new trophy in the air and laughing aloud before Cecee could bat an eyelid. She quickly turned around to face her brother.

He looked hard at her. "It's only a pouch, Cecee, get over it!"

His sister answered with fear and dread both in her voice and in her heart.

"Tross, you have *absolutely* no idea what you have just done!"

Outside the caves, Elmiva sat on the edge of a well to study her new treasures. Tucking the two empty Royal pouches into her belt, she inspected the real prize. 'Cecee was so insistent on keeping this golden one!' she thought. 'Hummm, quite heavy for its size, must be pure gold. I wonder how that little fairy manages to carry *this* everywhere! It must be valuable, but does it hold something even more valuable inside?' Elmiva pulled at the strings to open it, but the more she pulled, the tighter the strings became. She struggled, now tearing at it, frustration making her strike it against the side of the well. And then followed something totally bizarre! Out from the bottom of the pouch came tentacle-like strings, as thin as silk thread, twisting their way around her fingers and then her hand. To her complete dismay, she realized the tentacles would not stop as they moved along her arm and then around her neck! More and more they grew, until they enveloped her entire body... she was becoming part of the pouch! Elmiva screamed as she frantically tried to rip away the tentacles and in her terror, fell backwards. Down into the well she tumbled, pouch, Seed, and all. A short silence then... SPLASH! Followed by complete calm.

Cecee sat in the prison, exhausted with worry, the Seed now in the clutches of an evil fairy. She soon came to the frightening conclusion that it must now be truly lost.

Bill came to Cecee's side. "Don't worry... your father will get you another one." But Bill spoke only of the pouch, he, too, having no idea about the precious Seed resting inside.

Cecee couldn't reply. All was lost. Her nerves shattered, her throat dry, she needed water. Walking to the bucket in their cell, she found it empty.

"Bill, would you please call a pixy to fetch something to drink," asked Cecee, as though each word caused her pain to speak.

Bill shouted for help. Eventually, a very grumpy pixy appeared, holding a long, pointed stick which he poked through the bars.

"Who's making so much noise at this hour? Go to sleep!" he snapped.

But Bill persisted, and at the risk of being poked in the eye, approached the bars to plead with the pixy.

"Please, this fairy needs water and our bucket is empty. She is very thirsty and could die, in fact, we all could! Do you want Viperla to return and find us dead? She can't use us for whatever evil plans she has if we're dead! I'm sure she'd be looking for someone to blame…"

The pixy carefully thought this over. Yes, he had felt Viperla's wrath before and certainly did not want to again.

"Alright!" he said, as he picked up an empty bucket beside him.

Quickly, he went outside to the well and attached the bucket to a hook, winding it down into the gloom. As he did so, he looked around guardedly – a pointed stick wouldn't help him fend off an unfriendly dragon! After a while, he heard a soft splash – the bucket had reached the water. Feeling from the rope that the bucket had filled, he began to wind it up. He puffed and panted until it was fully rewound and lifted it from the hook. But wait, it felt far too heavy to contain only water... He could see it was full but *why* was it *so* heavy? He looked closely and there at the bottom, he could see a lump of something green and slimy. Not wishing to reach in to pull it out, he peered at the horrible looking object. He wiggled a finger in the water and the green mass seemed to disappear. 'Humm... maybe it was just a reflection of my very handsome green face,' he thought, nervously laughing to himself. 'I will lose too much water if I try to tip it out to check. Then I'll have to stay here longer to refill the bucket!! There could be dragons about! Oh never mind, a bit of slime never killed anyone!' He hurried back to the cave with pointed stick at the ready, just in case.... Relieved to be inside once more, he grabbed a couple of goblets, made his way back to the prison, placed the bucket on the floor just outside the bars of the gate, threw the goblets into the cell and left, shaking his stick at the prisoners.

"Drink all you need then go to sleep, or else!" he grunted, before turning to leave.

Tross picked up a goblet, squeezed it through the bars, dipped it into the water and carefully eased it back again, passing it to Cecee. She thanked him and put it to her lips. But before drinking, she noticed something green reflecting through the water! She looked closer.

"A lump of slime!" she said aloud, "Ugghhh!"

Disgusted, she threw the water aside. But as it splashed onto the ground, something golden shone from underneath the horrible green mess. As nasty as it was, Cecee carefully wiped away the slime to reveal the shiny object. Her heart pounded. Could it be possible? Were her eyes playing tricks in the dim light? What *was* underneath that horrible, green, cold, slimy goo. Could it be? She looked even closer and… YES! There it was! How and why it came to be there, she simply didn't care, but shining back at her, was her golden pouch! She shot a glance at her brother.

"Tross! My pouch! It's back!"

Turning away from him, she picked it up and secretly tried untying it but to no avail. She struggled with the knot, pulling this way and that. Still nothing happened – Cecee was now more than a little desperate! Could it be possible that the pouch would now turn against anyone who tried to reveal the Seed, even Cecee! Then, to her complete relief, the ties magically moved undoing the knot, allowing the pouch to fall open! There inside, was the precious Seed, glowing with life! She gasped and quickly closed it, just as Tross approached her.

"Cecee, I have never seen you covet something so closely, but thank all the Wizards that pouch is safely back. If you'd lost it for good, I don't think I would ever have heard the last of it!"

"Oh, Tross, I can promise you" she replied, while picking up her vine belt and securing it once again to her waist, "you would have heard about *nothing* else!"

As Cecee re-attached the pouch to her belt, she wondered if it possessed magical powers of its own. Could it possibly judge the character of whoever carried it? Would it do whatever is necessary to return the Seed to its rightful owner? She reflected upon the narrow escape the Seed had with Ace's wife. The seagull's intentions were good, it was true – she only wanted to feed her babies, but supposing she had swallowed the Seed? Who knows, maybe the pouch would have somehow guided the bird to the planting site and made her deposit the Seed through a natural function... She giggled at the thought, but then wondered where the all-important planting site may actually be. Either the pouch, or someone, would need to guide her because, at this very moment, she did not have a clue! And, where was that awful Elmiva? Why would she just disappear? Could it even be, for some unknown reason, she had somehow turned into the green slime that clung to the pouch? But why and how? Cecee looked down to where the pouch had been covered with the disgusting mess. It was now slowly disappearing as it dried upon the prison floor, soon to be no more. Elm brought her back to the moment.

"Cecee, I am glad you have the pouch again, but it's hardly going to save the World, is it! Now it's safely returned, we must concentrate on getting your Crown as well!"

How little did Elm, Bill, or Tross for that matter, really know...

The four settled down in a circle, Tross slowly pointing his Sceptre north, south, east and west before laying it on the floor, after which, all entered into a deep meditation.

Sound asleep in her bed, Sevilla snored so loudly the noise echoed around and around the bedroom. The Crown, resting on the top of her nightstand, suddenly moved a little, making a piercing, scratching sound and stirring Sevilla, but she only snorted and resumed her sleep. Again the Crown moved, this time further, toppling over the edge and landing on the floor with a loud crash, smashing into pieces, the noise carrying through the caves. Sevilla again snorted, opened one eye and sat up, just in time to see the pieces scattering everywhere. Petrified, she stared mesmerised as they twinkled brilliantly but then liquefied, all coming together to reform the Crown. At once, it turned on its side and sped out of her room and along the corridor! As it rolled further and further, bumping its way along and then down a flight of stony steps, Sevilla suddenly realized the urgency of the moment and whinged in her usual whiny manner, "My Crown! My beautiful Crown is rolling away!"

The Crown continued its relentless journey, spinning and tumbling faster and faster along the corridors, past other caverns, quickly finding its way to its destination, finally crashing against the prison gate's strong bars with a loud clang. A faint humming emitted from it as though it were trying to perform something more, but nothing happened and, unable to go any further, began to slowly roll backwards. Grunting as he stretched, Tross shot his arm through the bars in an effort to retrieve it and, by a stroke of pure luck, just managed to grab the Crown in time before it rolled out of reach! But trying hastily to pull it through the bars, the Crown slipped from his fingers! Down it fell once more to the ground and rolled, this time, out of reach, leaving the four to stare helplessly.

"Cecee! Is there anything you can do to bring it closer, maybe through the bars, or at least close enough to grab?" asked Elm.

Her answer was not what Elm or the other two hoped for.

"I don't know!" replied Cecee, in frustration. "I still have no idea how the Crown fully works!"

Bill's ears pricked up, then Elm's. Both could hear footsteps in the distance, growing louder as they hurriedly made their way to the prison cave.

"Cecee, by all the Wizards, *please* do something!" Elm begged.

But all she could do was plead, "Crown, please help us! We desperately need your help!"

Tross picked up his Sceptre and pointed the crystal end towards the Crown with an order, "WEAKEN THE BARS!"

By all the powers of magic, a blinding flash of light instantly shot forth and hit the Crown's centre crystal. The whole Crown began to melt, the clear fluid running in one narrow stream into the cell and, once inside, transformed in seconds! All watched in complete fascination as a strange yellow vapour curled upwards from one of the 'Yellow Mellow' stones, quickly drifting behind each of them and entering their wings to unlock Sevilla's spell in a flash of light. Delighted, they all flexed their wings, but with little time to celebrate they could fly again, Cecee picked up her Crown and all examined it closely, seeing the mysterious writing on the inside. The echoing sound of footsteps getting even closer, Tross suggested they quickly try to interpret the letters. Cecee looked hard at the writing.

"It's not Runic and it's not Latin. What *is* it!?"

Bill looked at it. "I know what it is… it's Wizard!"

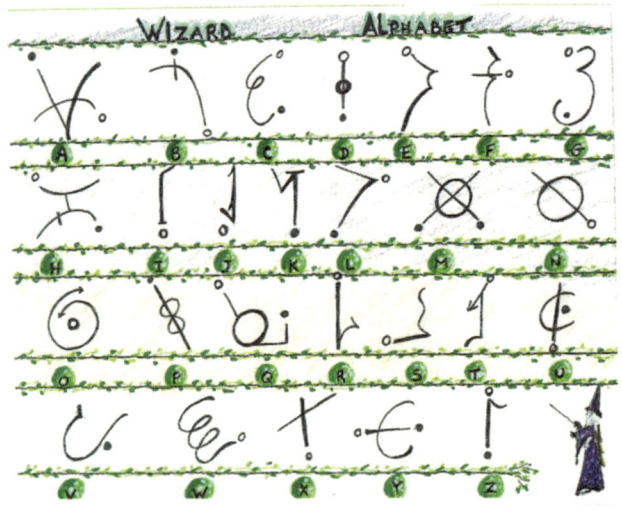

Tross looked too. "Yes! I learned some at school but not very much, but Bill's right, it *is* Wizard. How do you know that, Bill? Can you read it?"

"My father owned herbal shops. He was an apothecary, and the recipes for his medicines were all in Wizard. It's definitely Wizard. Let me read it."

He took the Crown from Cecee and expertly read aloud. Even though the four were convinced something would happen, nothing did…They stood in further anticipation as Cecee now repeated the words... but again, still nothing.

"Cecee, perhaps the Crown has to be in *your* hands?" suggested Bill. "Hold it and repeat the words again!"

Cecee took the Crown and read aloud.

"Beneath the Earth, within the dark, I call to one bright stone. Hearken to me and awake from your slumber."

The Crown briefly shuddered. All gazed in amazement as it then began to shudder once more, this time with a loud buzzing sound. Suddenly it stopped, and a strange, dull, eerie light began to glow from it. Cecee knew enough by now to know something beyond their imagination was about to happen...

Back in her room, Viperla awoke, troubled. She sprang out of bed and rushed towards the door but stopped dead in her tracks, sensing all was far from well. She couldn't believe it. A powerful spell was being read aloud and from, of all places, her prison!

"*How dare anyone!*" she shrieked, her face growing purple with rage. "But wait. I recognize that voice. It's that pesky, irritating, trouble-making, good for nothing, stuck-up little fairy called Cecee!! How can *she* possibly know the words to such a potent spell! She'll ruin everything!"

Viperla became even more hysterical, laughing, screaming and shrieking uncontrollably as she raced towards the prison, imagining what she would do to Cecee and the others.

Cecee was unaware that her words had awoken the master crystal, the very one that would bring life to all the others in the Crown. Viperla felt a sudden pain of weakness that brought her crashing to her knees. She screamed, not in pain, but in desperation.

"NO! The crystals! They *MUST* stay asleep! They must not be brought to LIFE!"

But her screams were in vain for all the crystals had indeed awoken. And now, their true, unimaginable powers, would be unleashed upon the wicked sisters…

Almost reaching the cell, Sevilla stopped and gasped when she saw the reflection in a pool of water – her once pretty face, now old, haggard and wrinkled.

"Noooooo! What is happening to me? I don't deserve this! Viperla, do something to help me! QUICKLY!"

But Viperla crawled to a pool and nervously peered at her own reflection to see a bony, ugly image snarling back at her. As her strength rapidly waned, all the great powers she possessed began to evaporate. Levira, awakened by all the commotion, joined Sevilla, both now puny and bent double. They struggled to reach their eldest sister knowing too well all would be lost if Viperla was left entirely powerless! Finding her on her knees, her face withered and her body shaking violently from head to toe, they watched as every power she had burst from her fingertips. Her magic swiftly shot from her body and exploded above her, scattering into nothingness. As a last resort, she tried bringing to life the snake-hat she so dearly loved. But it gasped and choked before shrinking away to nothing but thin strands of oily, limp hair. The destruction of her magical powers complete, a now weak and frail fairy knelt pathetically whimpering with exhaustion. Sevilla, being the youngest, still had a little strength and flew unsteadlly and clumsily further along the corridor leading to the prison. She tried to scream, but only a croaky whimper was heard.

"Cecee, I beg of you, please don't read any more!"

At last she reached the prison where, seeing Cecee, she was just able to grasp her Wand and point it towards the fairy. She again tried to scream but could do no more than cackle an order to her Wand, "Kill her, kill her, kill her!"

But with her powers drained and no magic left inside, the Wand broke in two, leaving Sevilla holding one piece in her hand, and looking heartbroken at the other laying in pieces upon the ground. She watched mortified as the broken, jagged end of the piece she held, puffed out the last remnants of a weak, smoky, powerless spell. Falling to her knees, she summoned the energy to speak but could only snivel, "Cecee, have pity on us. We were not going to harm you... By all the Wizards, look at me. What have you done? How could you be so cruel? Even Ian left us with our good looks!"

But her pleads were in vain, and the expressions on her captives faces told her all was lost. Panicking, and with the thought of a dreadful future, she tried another plea.

"It was Viperla's fault. She forced me to follow her wishes. I had to do as she commanded. I am the youngest!"

Finding the energy to crawl their way to the cell, Levira and Viperla heard the accusations Sevilla so readily poured forth.

Viperla choked out her words.

"How could you betray me, you spoiled little fool! You will regret those lies. I have been loyal and good to you, but now you have betrayed me. If it is the last thing I ever do, I promise I will make you pay dearly!"

However, Sevilla, upon hearing this, was no longer afraid, laughing aloud and mocking what she considered to be no more than idle threats. But the sisters' bickering soon ceased. To them, the Crown's work seemed relentless as suddenly, the prison bars became thin and weak and with one pull, Elm bent them wide apart.

"Cecee, Bill, Tross, we can escape! Come on, there's no time to waste! Let's go!"

At last they were free from their cold, dank cell.

Bill approached Viperla, circling her thin, frail body before stopping to look her straight in the eyes.

"Pitiful," he said, "*just pitiful!* Remember how you spoke these words to us, Viperla!"

Viperla cackled in reply, "No, you remember something, elfin! Don't ever forget who I am!"

Tross spoke to Cecee with some urgency.

"Your Crown will help us lock them in the cell until we can find help. But before we leave, we must decide what we are going to do about our other big problem, the dragons guarding the exit – they listen to only Viperla!"

"Don't forget we have the Wizard dust!" Bill said, carefully shaking Elm's pouch in the air for all to see. "I picked it up after Tross used it to change my looks!"

Elm checked his back pocket, finding it empty. 'Oh yes, I forgot', he thought.

Seeing Elm's worried look, Bill patted him on the back.

"Don't worry, Elm, there's plenty left. Here, it's yours. Take it."

But Elm refused.

Bill insisted. "Elm, you must take at least a little!"

"No, Bill, you keep it."

"Are you sure?"

"Yes, I'm positive."

"Well, Elm, it will be put to good use, I promise."

Elm was a very proud Seven Oaks soldier who valued his weapons beyond any magical trickery, despite what he had already seen with his own eyes. He thought to himself, 'I have my rose daggers and have every faith in what I can achieve with these.'

Viperla and her sisters, by now looking quite wretched, rested against the far wall of the cell in which they had been securely locked.

"Where is our sister, Elmiva?" asked Viperla, struggling to speak her words. But no one knew. Cecee turned her head to see the three sad sisters and couldn't help but feel just a little sorry for them. She was certain the pouch had something to do with Elmiva's disappearance. But could she say anything? No, of course she couldn't. Elm put his arm about her.

"Cecee, don't fret. Remember how they treated us when they had total power and could spare us, but chose not to?"

"Yes, Elm, I remember."

"Then continue to do so. What you see now is what's known as poetic justice. Serves them right. Come on, it's time we all left."

Leaving the awful prison, Cecee could hear Viperla's haunting voice, calling in the distance.

"Come back! Stay with me, Cecee, don't leave me. I need you, please stay with me!"

But even in the quietness, Viperla heard no response. Realizing all her influence and powers had vanished, she could find just enough strength to wail only threats. "You'd better hope and beg all the Wizards that you make it back Cecee! You'd better hope that you make it safely back to your *own* World!"

The four made their way to the exit without any interference from the pixies. Looking outside, Tross realized they had been in the cave all night, and though visibility was restricted because of a thick, white fog, morning was beginning to break. Finding there were no guard-dragons to prevent their escape, they ventured into the open, but the fog was suddenly eclipsed by huge, dark masses moving in front of them.

Elm shouted as he stopped them going any further.

"Danger! I think there could be dragons out here after all!"

All retreated back into the cave. Tross studied his Sceptre, wishing he knew how to use its full powers, while Bill and Elm looked towards the fog.

"I think I should go on ahead of you all and clear the way," said Elm.

"No, I'll go," Bill argued. "After all, scouting is what I do for a living and it's time I proved how good I am."

Tross butted in. "I should go because I have special understanding beyond scouting."

Cecee had heard enough and stopped the three arguing.

"Wouldn't it be a good idea," she suggested, "to *choose* who goes? We can decide by playing the old 'blade of grass' game. Whoever picks the shortest, shall be the one to go. Tross, you're not to be included as you are next in line to the Throne."

"Cecee! You can't be serious! We're in this mess together, and I'm going to help to get us out of it! I *will* do what I ne…"

Bill shouted above them. "This is not helping – we shouldn't argue. Especially now! Tross, if you want to join in, then so be it. Let's find some grass and play the game!"

All set about the task, ensuring all but one of the blades they found was the same length. Cecee hid them all in her cupped hands. Then, one by one, Bill, Elm and Tross, each chose a blade and held it up.

"Who has the shortest?" asked Cecee.

Holding the shortest, was Elm…

CHAPTER FIFTEEN

WE ARE ALL GOING TO *DIE!*
AND THE SWORROMOT

With a little time to spare, and to rest from the vigours of flying, the Unicorns, together with Ian and Darcy, walked to 'The Great Hall of The Seniors'. Fiero followed some distance behind, deep in thought, his main concern focusing upon Cecee's safety. But something else occupied his mind – he had to admit, within the herd of Unicorns, a pretty female had caught his eye. He thought to ask his father about her so galloped over to him.

"Father. I couldn't help but notice the Unicorn with a very striking, pink mane. Do you know her name?"

His father gave a little smile as he replied, "Yes son, her name is Cloud and she's the daughter of a friend of mine. Comes from an excellent family... a good choice for you. But you will have competition as she is already the centre of attention of two others."

Fiero bowed his head and rolled his eyes – this was not what he wanted to hear. Talking with his father was never easy. Why couldn't he just answer a question without introducing a problem?

"Well, now she has three admirers," replied Fiero.

With this thought weighing heavily on his mind, Fiero walked away to speak to other Unicorns in the herd.

Even though they arrived at the Hall early, they could see dominating the surroundings, an enormous, shining table which stood proudly in the centre. Wizards already seated around it argued, groaned, and grumbled as they debated with one another the ruling of the magical Island. King Foxglove, Tizzy and Remik soon arrived inside the Hall, but Tizzy stood still, awestruck by the sight which met her eyes. The Hall was massive, oval in shape and white in colour. The table, also oval to complement the Hall, was made from a magnificent, single, rare crystal, placed at the centre of which was a grand carving made from many aqua-green crystal shards of various shapes and sizes. Each was arranged to point in a different direction to the others, while a much larger centre crystal was the only one placed to point straight towards the roof which formed a splendid dome. Through this, a tall, crystal funnel towered into the sky. Unicorns entering through a far door lined the white walls of the Hall. With their wings folded down, a breath taking display of many coloured manes and glittering horns took away Tizzy's breath. She could not count how many there were, but ohh, how she longed to have one as a friend! As she followed her father, the pungent smell of spices made all her senses spin. Darcy was now seated with Ian and the King sat opposite them with Tizzy next to him and Remik next to Tizzy. Monitor Elves busied themselves, noisily securing all the doors after which an eerie silence fell upon the Great Hall. All focus was now upon the King as he slowly rose from his seat, making ready to commence proceedings.

"I will open this gathering by coming straight to the matter in hand."

The King paused before beginning. Many glanced at one another, wondering what he would say next.

"My son, Prince Foxglove V11, the only male heir to the Throne of Seven Oaks Woods, and my daughter, Princess Citrina Carmilina Foxglove, chosen to plant the 'Fairy Rowan Seed' this year, are both missing, along with two elves who are also very, very, dear to me."

A gasp sounded throughout and some began to mumble between themselves. The King raised his hand to keep the silence. He continued.

"Ian and I have studied the crystals thoroughly, and it causes me great pain to announce there are very strong reasons to believe all four may have been captured.

I need not tell you how grave the situation is and that time is of the essence. More than ever before, I am asking, no, pleading, for your help to rescue them." The King, looking physically shaken, took another pause before continuing.

"My friends, I will now ask the Wizard Ian to speak."

As the King sat, his face appeared drained of all emotion. Ian stood, briefly casting a reassuring eye towards the King.

"I do not need to remind you all of 'The Great War of Wands' in which we fought in the many tunnels and caves and at the top of 'Snowy Mountain Impasse'. The struggle to crush and finally lock away the evil Viperla, nearly overwhelmed us all. But my friends, through our courage and determination to defeat and imprison her, at last we were victorious. But now the most terrible news… I am shocked to tell you, she has escaped!"

A sudden hubbub arose as the deepest of concern was expressed by all.

"I call for silence!" Ian commanded, before continuing. "I would imagine she, with the support of her three wicked sisters, has sought the protection of her caves. We all know what this means. This time, her capture will be even more difficult. Before, we managed to trick her from her lair. This time, I don't think she will leave so easily. The burning question is, does she beyond any doubt hold captive the King's son and daughter along with the two soldier elves? We know by escaping the Tower, all her magical powers and terrible tricks have returned to her. I call upon every Senior Wizard here to put aside any argument you may have with each other and take the vow of unity to help with this 'Great Matter'. We must go forward as one."

All forty-nine Senior Wizards seated around the table thoughtfully stroked their long beards. By all reckoning, each was completely set in his own ways and the vow of unity would call for each to forgo his absolute stubbornness. Without a word, each removed a purple and yellow coloured robe from his special bag and, unfolding it carefully, wrapped it around himself. Down the back of each robe were sewn triangles of purple cloth edged in gold, each representing one score years of Wizardry. Sewn to some robes were many triangles… To the Wizards, these were a great source of pride and were called by them 'The Tiers of Years'.

Some of the student Wizards who struggled to fully master all magic, daringly referred to them as 'The Years of Tears'!

The Seniors picked up their hats and placed them upon their heads, the crest of Middlesborough sewn onto the front of each hat seemed almost animated in the brightness of the room. Each Wizard rose and stood perfectly upright. Again, silence reigned throughout, this time in anticipation as the ages-old 'Ceremony of Unity' began...

Then, the entire Great Hall was filled with Ian's roaring voice as he commanded, "ENTER THE SCEPTRES!"

All at once, forty-nine Elves marched in from a door that at first sight did not appear to be there. Each carried a large, shining Sceptre, expertly decorated with precious stones in a style to suit the Wizard to whom it belonged. But all were alike in one way – each had silver owls' claws holding a crystal at both ends, one pure, clear green, the other a milky, sky-blue. The Elves circled the table, laying each Sceptre in front of its Master. Tizzy overheard one disgruntled Wizard grumble, "Elf! This isn't *mine*! You have given me the *wrong* Sceptre! Find mine before you incur my wrath!"

After a certain amount of bustling between a few Elves, a deep sigh of relief was breathed by all as Sceptres were now placed in front of their rightful owners and harmony, once again, quickly restored.

All was now in place, and in a grand gesture of great and binding trust between every Wizard, each with his own Elf, turned away from the table, leaving his Sceptre unguarded. Despite the ties that bound together all Wizards, who knows, when given the chance, what cunning magic each could weave to cause mischief with another's Sceptre. This was, perhaps, the ultimate test of their most precious, trusted brotherhood since the 'Great War of the Wands' and the mistrust thereafter Viperla had so evilly sewn.

Following this ritual, each Wizard turned to pick up his Sceptre, pointing the green crystal towards the centre-piece upon the table. All at once, streams of coloured light burst from the large shard that pointed upwards to the roof and shot into the crystal dome, creating a giant wheel of colour which in a flash, bounced back down, disappearing into the crystal! The enormous table shook violently as the wheel of colour then shot straight back out, soaring up into the dome, swirling round and round, gaining more and more in both strength and speed.

All but the King and Wizards cowered as the giant wheel hurtled back down and around the walls of the Great Hall, now so powerful the Hall itself shook to its very foundations, the walls themselves bending back and forth, clouds of white dust falling from up above! Was the power too strong? Had the Wizards lost all control! Suddenly, the mass of energy spiralled upwards, again into the dome. Where would it go? If it couldn't escape, what damage could it cause? Could this be the destruction of the Great Hall! But no, this time, with a mighty, roaring whoosh, the whirling, spinning wheel, entered the funnel, shooting straight out to disappear into the sky! All was now calm. The Wizards slowly lowered their Sceptres, placing them carefully upon the table.

Tizzy had watched, terrified of the immense power she had witnessed. Still feeling in her eyes the brilliance of the light, she turned to hear her father expressing his deepest gratitude to the Wizards for their loyalty, trust and faithfulness. With that, the gathering came to an end.

Everyone moved around, talking in huddles while the King spoke alone with Ian. Wizards discussed the King's 'Great Matter' while Elves carefully gathered the Sceptres to return them to 'The Keep'. They then set about the task of clearing dust, polishing scorch marks from the crystal table and making sure the Great Hall was tidy once again. It was then Tizzy realized just how dangerously hot the light must have been! She looked for her father again, finding him with Ian, both now joined by the fairy Darcy. As she approached, her father was rapt in discussion with Ian how, in the distant past, the centre piece upon the crystal table was a gift from Viperla. But after the then fifty Senior Wizards inserted their magic into the crystal, she learned of its great powers and decided she wanted it back at any cost! The Senior Wizards refused, fearing what she may do with something so formidable. It was her anger and greed that inevitably lead to 'The Great War of Wands'.

Tizzy had not heard of Viperla, so asked if she could sit with them to listen.

"Of course you can, Tizzy. Please sit with us," Ian answered.

Tizzy made herself comfortable. There followed a brief pause. Tizzy thought this would be her opportunity, so asked the Wizard questions of which she had a few…

"Ian, was all that light part of a plan to find Cecee and Tross, or is there another idea? I have magic – I can use it! Will you let me use it? And why do all Wizards have white hair?"

So many questions all at once! Her father smiled at her innocence and enthusiasm. To be fair, if he were Tizzy, he would no doubt ask the same! As yet, he had no idea about the magic Florie had given Tizzy. Perhaps he should have known but he had not spoken to anyone about Florie, her magic, or anything else about her for that matter. He was just so glad Tizzy was alive and well and that he, himself, had survived from drowning. Now he could fully concentrate on finding Tross, Cecee, Elm and Bill. That dreadful day he nearly drowned had muddled his mind. In all the confusion on board ship, he hadn't really taken in what Tizzy had said to him. Afterwards, he thought she had somehow smuggled herself onboard, but he did remind himself to question exactly how she had saved his life. Seeing, close by, a group of Wizards he had not seen in a while, the King excused himself and left to join them.

Ian tried answering Tizzy's questions.

"The answer to your first question is simple. There is almost nothing more powerful, or travels faster, or has more energy, than light. There is no need for another plan."

Tizzy listened carefully, remembering the awesome light that came from her finger.

"Crystals shed light similar to that in our Sceptres, but the crystal light we used today is different – the light returns as images and places them into our crystals! The colours in rainbows do the same thing and we've used these many times. This is why you should never enter a rainbow as you may disturb the balance of the colours."

Tizzy stole a glance towards her father, remembering how she flew through the rainbow!

Ian continued. "The light you saw leaving through the dome is alive and on a journey, secretly exploring at this very moment. Oh, I could tell you so much about space and dark energy that warps back on itself and produces speeds far in excess of light itself. But all will become clearer once you are old enough to fully understand."

Tizzy was now so confused she was totally lost! Words she had never heard before – 'What do they all mean?' she thought. 'I hope they *will* all become clear when I am older! So much to learn! These Wizards must be soooooo clever!'

Ian paused to stroke his beard.

"We hope the light does not come up against 'block troubles' like those in the labyrinth. If there are no hiccups, it will return to the Sceptres with news very soon."

'Ohhhh, there he goes again!' thought Tizzy, but nodded in agreement as though she had a new-found understanding… "So what now?" she asked.

Ian stared at his Sceptre's crystal. There was no sign of any news.

"Now my dear, Tizzy, we must be patient and simply wait," he replied.

He turned to look deeply into the mind of this young, inquisitive Princess.

"And I will now answer your second question, Tizzy. I know you have magic. There is a wizard called Patrick who has given me the news. He always acts with good intentions and you may describe him as being nice. But it is wise to be careful when meeting anyone new… 'Nice' doesn't always mean 'good'. I know you have met him, I see it in your eyes. However, you should never fear Patrick as he *is* good and will teach you all you need to know about magic – when, where and how to use it and so on. I see your power, Tizzy, you possess much in one so young. Your father cannot see all that Senior Wizards can see and it seems to me of late he is still unaware of the magic you possess. Tell him of your new powers as soon as you can, seek lessons from the Wizard Patrick but, above all, always use the utmost caution when using it. So, at this moment, Tizzy, the answer is no, we cannot allow you to use your 'magic'."

His face smiled as he lightheartedly answered Tizzy's third question.

"Wizards' hair… well, it turns white at an early age owing to the magic we perform in our learning years. The reality is, the shock we suffer from the first correct performance, removes the colour, never to return. However, our hair is left as fine as silk and as soft as duck down."

Ian was tall and Tizzy had to stretch to touch his hair. Unbeknown to her, it held powerful static and in one mass, the ends instantly drew towards her hand! A prickling sensation running through her fingers, caused her to draw away quickly, while Ian sighed, trying to flatten his hair!

"Oh yes, that… that can be *quite* a problem!" he said.

While the wizards waited for the light to return with news, King Foxglove, his soldiers and Unicorns all gathered to begin their journey to Viperla's caves. A dense fog had not cleared, making it difficult for those who were to go on foot, so the Unicorns would carry them high above. Before they left, to Tizzy's surprise, she noticed part of the huge outside walls of the Hall had crumbled, almost as though someone or something had attacked them. Alarmed by what she saw and fearing the Hall would collapse, she flew to her father to tell him. He explained the magic performed that very day had caused it, and warned the use of such power carried huge risk… a few crumbling walls could be repaired and were nothing compared with what might have happened – Tizzy should always remember this as a lesson.

***

Back in the caves, all appeared safe to Elm as he stood looking outside. The dark shadows he thought may have been dragons had gone, but the question bothering Elm was where? Regardless of what the answer may be, Elm slowly ventured outside, the rest following into the cold, damp, dismal fog.

Suddenly, Bill cried "Wait! Hold on a sec. Elm, your dagger may not be enough. You won't take back your dust, so here, take my bow and arrows. Cecee, it might be a good idea to tie a long piece of vine around Elm's waist. Then he can find his way back quickly and safely. Tross can stand behind you to check the rear and I will stay in front of you to act as a guide. You will be between us, threading out the vine while we have you safely covered."

Everyone thought this a great idea and soon found plenty of vine. Tying it all together, making one long strand, they looped one end around Elm's waist while Cecee held the rest in a neat coil.

Elm slowly walked into the blanket of fog, Cecee threading out the vine as she watched him slowly disappear. All straining their eyes to keep watch for further dark shadows, Cecee felt a sudden tug on the vine and called out, "Elm, are you alright!"

Out of the fog ahead, a muffled, barely audible voice answered, "Yes, I'm fine, I just stumbled on something!"

Cecee carefully released more, the three slowly creeping a little further forward behind Elm. Suddenly, Cecee felt another tug while at the same moment, a large, monstrous face emerged from the fog above Elm who they could now see standing rigid in front of them! Their worst nightmare now menacingly appeared – a red-finned dragon! Red and white fins buzzed a constant warning as a blood-red mouth opened, shooting out a long, evil-looking, forked tongue. Needing lungs full of air to release a white-hot stream of fire, the dragon reared back, fading into the fog, lifting its hideous head with a roar and sucking in all the air it could hold. Shaking with fear and as fast as he could, Elm loaded the bow, pulled it back so far it bent into a perfect 'u' shape and released the arrow! All four hoped the target would be found. A scream from the dreadful monster followed by an enormous, loud thud, was enough to confirm Elm had made a solid strike, but how deadly? Was the dragon slain? Elm loaded another arrow and drew back the bow before taking a few cautious steps forward, carefully watching for any further danger as best he could through the fog. And then... relief! There, in front of him, lay the beast. Elm could not have wished for a better shot – his arrow had fatally struck the dragon straight between the eyes.

Alarmed, Tross called out, "Elm, is everything okay? Speak to us! Is the dragon dead?"

Elm answered in a quietened voice, "Yes, I'm fine. It's safe to come forward. I have killed a flying dragon but there could be more hiding. They may sense what has happened – best we keep quiet, just in case."

Tross kept close to Cecee, guarding her back, his Sceptre at the ready. Bill, in front of them, eyes ever alert, ventured forward. All sensed danger lurking in the fog. Ahead, Elm carefully advanced. Bill, being the next in line, continued walking forward when all of a sudden, he stumbled over something. He bent down to see a dragon's sharp tooth, long, curved and very mean looking! Tripping on one end, Bill had flipped the sharp point upwards, nearly cutting his leg wide open. Shocked at the size of the tooth, he bent further down to pick it up. 'Cor, this must be what Elm stumbled over!' he thought. Holding it in both hands, he looked through the fog and, in the distance, could see the faint outline of Elm. From within the swirling mass, Elm turned in Bill's direction and called, "Come on everyone, it's all clear."

Bill admired Elm's courage and whilst wondering if one day he could possibly be as brave, a vision of terror, without warning, met his eyes. To his left and looming out from the swirling fog, was the head of a second dragon, towering above Elm! Bill could just make out its red eyes were staring down in Elm's direction. 'Elm was right!' thought Bill. 'There's more of them! This one must be after him for killing the other!' In that same second, Elm's faint image turned away from Bill, seemingly unaware of the danger. Bill shot upright, dropping the tooth.

"Elm!" shouted Bill. "Dragon behind you and staring your way – watch out!"

But as the words left Bill's lips, the dragon lunged at Elm, blowing a white-hot stream of fire straight at him! Elm instantly disappeared and in a triumphant display, the beast spewed forth further fire onto the very spot where Elm had stood, fire so hot, it evaporated all the fog around. With that, the dragon turned, spread its mighty wings and flew into the distance. The long vine once tied around Elm's waist now hung slack in Cecee's hands.

The three stood in total shock. Where was Elm? Cecee's eyes quickly searched all around but could find no sign. She threw down the vine and turned to her brother, looking for an answer, but Tross couldn't find one. He put his arms about her, but she screamed while struggling to release herself.

"No, not Elm! Please, not Elm!" she sobbed.

She broke free and ran into the fog which was now rapidly returning. Cecee reached the spot where Elm had stood, but all that was left, was Bill's magical bow and arrows, lying on the ground. Tross ran to his sister and quickly grabbed the weapons as Bill remained motionless, his mood changing to blind rage. Tross and Cecee could barely see through the blanket of fog, but saw enough to know that Bill stood as still as a statue. What was wrong with Bill! Was he about to do something?! Slowly and very precisely, Bill took the Wizard dust pouch from his belt, opened it and shook some into the palm of his hand. He paused to study it and to think. Then, past the point of caring if too much would harm him, he quickly tipped more of the dust into his hand before throwing the pouch to the ground. He tossed the dust into the air, standing completely still as it dropped down over him, immediately entering his body. As it did so, he concentrated with all his effort, imagining himself to be the biggest dragon that had ever lived. The change was almost instant. He grew enormous legs with massive scaly feet, webbed toes with long, razor-sharp talons growing from them. His head grew larger and larger, a shiny black horn emerging from his forehead. In a flash, his entire body transformed into a monstrous, fire-breathing, winged dragon with a huge, powerful tail.

The fearful monster that had just taken the life of his friend, now returned to destroy everyone else, but its attention was immediately drawn towards the fearsome creature standing on the ground which roared a challenge, sending waves of sound vibrating through the fog.

When the dragon realized it was about to be confronted by a much more formidable foe, it thought the better of it. Quickly, it turned to flee before it met certain doom. Tross and Cecee watched as before their eyes the dark shadow of the dragon roared another challenge from the ground. Instantly, both knew what Bill had done to himself. Before taking flight Bill stopped and breathed a stream of fierce, white-hot fire towards the ground to make sure he could do so. He then spread his mighty wings and chased the murderous dragon to engage in a ferocious battle.

Bill soon caught up with the monster and the two tangled in mid-air. Through the fog and to the ground they crashed in a fight to the death. Ear-shattering screams of pain came from each so loud, everything around shook. The rumbling and shaking of the ground caused Cecee to fly up and hover.

"Tross! What's happening?" she screamed in terror.

But Tross had no time to answer his terrified sister. All at once the fog had begun to clear, giving him a complete view of the awful battle taking place right in front of him. Loading Bill's bow, he had to be absolutely certain about what he was going to do next.

"Cecee, is Bill the dragon with the horn?" Tross asked.

"Tross, wait! Don't shoot! I think so... I'm not sure!"

Suddenly, a deathblow was dealt by one of the dragons. The victim staggered and crashed to the ground. Slowly, it rolled over and lifted its head, groaning in agony, steam puffing from its nose and its eyes slowly closing. As hard as it tried, its efforts to hold onto life were in vain. Its injuries were so severe, life was at an end. With one final gasp, its head fell lifeless to the ground with a huge thud, a cloud of dust rising into the air. The creature was no more.

The victorious dragon turned its head slowly towards Tross, folding back its huge wings against its body. It stood staring, sharp, pointed teeth glinting through the grin of a fire-red mouth. Drawing back its huge head, it gulped in air, and with a deafening noise, blew a stream of steam towards the sky as if in celebration of its conquest.

Tross held the bow and loaded it, carefully aiming straight at the dragon's exposed throat but paused.

"Cecee, could this be Bill! What do you think? It was foggy, I couldn't see very well and I need to be certain!"

The dragon's head lowered, steam still puffing from its nose, its yellow eyes blinking as it stood motionless. It was as though the creature was trying to communicate with Tross through its eyes.

"Cecee, get the pouch with the letter 'W' from my belt and take it out… but slowly!"

Cecee flew down. Reaching for the pouch while keeping her eyes firmly on the dragon, she searched in vain.

"Tross, are you sure it's here? I can't find it!"

She took her eyes off the dragon and hurriedly looked around the ground. There it was! She quickly grabbed it, "Tross, is this it?"

Tross risked a quick glance, taking his eyes away from the beast.

"No, it's not mine, it's Bill's! I forgot, I left mine on the ship! Hurry, Cecee, take some out and blow it towards the dragon. I think it's going to attack any second!"

Trembling, she clumsily opened the pouch but was shocked to find very little left! Was there enough to do the trick? What remained, she blew as hard as she could high into the air towards the fearsome creature. Bright, violet clouds surrounded the huge monster, sparks shooting from within as the dragon reared its head to turn away. Tross again pulled his bow taut. Almost immediately, the dragon's huge bulk began to shrink and wither, moans of pain coming from within the clouds. Cecee and Tross stood watching, amazed as more and more sparks began to fly everywhere, even greater moans escaping. Before long, the sparks ceased as the clouds reduced to a thin mist hovering above the ground. Very soon, Cecee and Tross could see something moving within. To their great joy, they realized it was Bill who sluggishly crawled towards them before coming to a stop, gasping for air. Lifting his head, he managed to sit upright, gazing around in total confusion. Cecee and Tross rushed towards him. Finding the energy to speak, Bill stared up at them and asked, "Did I kill that dragon? Tell me I killed that Dragon!"

"Yes you did, Bill, you did!" they replied together.

Bill attempted to stand but couldn't, groaning, "Oh! I think I'm hurt!"

"Not so fast, Bill, just wait one second," Tross insisted, before gathering armfuls of blue leaves which he hoped would cushion the ground for Bill to lie upon.

"Rest on these for a while to get back your strength."

Bill rolled onto the warm, comfortable leaves, collapsing face down with a satisfied grunt. He turned and struggled to sit up, but his heart sank for, in the distance, he could see where Elm had been standing the last time he saw him alive. With head in hands, Bill broke down and sobbed at the tragic loss of not only one so brave, but one he regarded as a true friend.

"My friend Elm is dead! I can't believe it! It's all my fault," he spluttered.

Tross knelt by his side. "Bill, it's not your fault. Elm was a special breed of Soldier Elf, the sort who put his life in danger to ensure the safety of others. He would have been so proud of you Bill, and you will be rewarded for your bravery by my father."

Bill's saddened, tearful eyes looked deep into Tross's.

"You don't understand. I tripped over a dragon's tooth and picked it up. If I hadn't stopped to pick up that stupid tooth I might have seen that dragon sooner. I don't deserve any reward. Don't you see? Elm was like a big brother to me. He even reminded me of my father...yes, like my father...I just want them back."

"Bill, I was on watch too, you know. Isn't it just as much my fault, then?"

But in Bill's mind, he was the one who was supposed to scout and that included looking out for them all. He was far too upset to answer.

After Tross helped Bill to his feet, all three solemnly walked over to where only ashes remained. Bill felt nothing but absolute grief. Tross and Cecee held onto him as the three stared at the heart-rending reminder of what had happened. But then began something quite beyond their understanding. Before their eyes, the ashes began to rise, forming a bright cloud, a mass of sparkles appearing from within! All at once, it shot skywards and out of sight, perhaps even into the far reaches of space. Tross, Cecee and Bill stared in total bewilderment, expecting something else unimaginable. Lost in wonder, the sudden roar of a dragon in the distance brought all three back to reality with a start.

"One thing is certain," Cecee said while checking her pouch, "we must get away from here!" She was relieved the Rowan Seed was safe but how she wished beyond anything, the task of planting it had not fallen upon her. "We've killed two dragons, and since we have looked away Viperla, she won't be able to feed those left. That means they'll soon be starving and looking for tasty morsels like us! Now, isn't *that* a sobering thought?"

The fog had completely cleared revealing the beautiful purple mountains towering in the distance. Small plants and little creatures had made their homes under and around huge boulders strewn across the ground through which they followed a path leading away from Viperla's caves. Looking back, they could see tall trees partially covering the cave's entrance and bushes with pink blossom offering a gentle relief against the different shades of the trees' blue foliage. It was hard to imagine that behind such a beautiful sight there lurked within the caves, something so vile and hideous.

By now, all three were hungry and thirsty but could find nothing. While searching for berries, Tross noticed a lake a little further on and decided to investigate to see if the water was good to drink.

"I'm going to fly over to that lake. Keep your eyes open you two, we don't know what's around and there's not much cover over there. Cecee, you have your Crown and I have my Sceptre. And, Bill, here's your bow and arrows. With all these, we should be able to protect ourselves."

However, a frown of doubt creased Cecee's forehead.

"I hope so, Tross. I'd feel better about you going if I were *certain* how the Crown works!"

While Cecee and Bill kept watch, Tross flew to the lake and looked around. Having tasted the water, he quickly returned.

"It's very tasty – like sweet grape juice! I couldn't find anything to eat, but the juice will give us the energy we need. One problem though, we can't bring it here and it's far too dangerous for us to go there together… Bill, do you have any ideas?"

But Bill's energy had waned and he was tired, really tired. He answered wearily, "No, Tross, sorry to say I haven't. The leaves may be big and soft, fine for lying on, but they're porous… useless for carrying water. We'll have to take our chances and all go together. Better watch out for each other, that's all."

As his tired eyes looked around, an idea came to him.

"See the small cave over there, not far from Viparla's caves? If we run into trouble, we could fly into it. It looks quite small and I really can't imagine it belongs to her. Whatever we do, we still need to be careful of those ever present dragons."

Cecee recalled earlier experiences with lakes. "No, it might not belong to Viperla but it might belong to the Thunderbirds. There may be other dangers too, perhaps predators *under* the water!"

She quickly tied back her hair in a braid and made sure her formidable Crown was placed firmly on her head. Off they flew, away from the protection of the bushes, soon arriving at the lake. Within no time at all, dark shapes loomed above them…

"Take a drink quickly!" Tross shouted, while they hovered over the water. At the same time, Bill looked around the sky. The shapes above them became alarmingly clear – Thunderbirds, a whole flock, flew above them! They swooped down, one sending out a high-pitched shrill as if to alert the others, "prey available!"

"Quick, follow me to the cave!" shouted Bill, over the noise of the squawking birds.

Cecee and Tross were on Bill's tail in seconds, flying headlong to safety as they reached the small cave. Cecee and Bill flew through the narrow entrance but Tross's Sceptre somehow caught on a protruding rock, preventing him going further – he was stuck fast and the birds were drawing nearer! Bill realised Tross had not made it and immediately flew back to the entrance where he found him struggling to free himself. Quickly, he freed the Sceptre, dragging Tross through the entrance just as a Thunderbird swooped down to attack. The rest of the hungry birds made a rush for the narrow entrance but were too large to enter, the head of the first already stuck fast, its sharp beak snapping in anger. Struggling more and more, it finally managed to pull itself free and with one final shriek, flew away with the rest of the flock.

Now safely inside, Tross, Cecee and Bill collapsed to catch their breath and to rest. But just as they settled down, they heard a noise from deep within. It seemed their intrusion had disturbed a colony of bats which flew in a noisy mass to surround the unwelcome visitors. Before they knew what was happening, the bats grabbed all three, carrying them from the cave, across the lake and dropping them onto the far shore. The bats, in one thick, dark, fluttering mass, then flew off to return deep within their cave, leaving all around eerily still and quiet.

Bill whispered, "Did they save us from something?"

Tross got up, shook dust from his hair, brushed himself down and flexed his wings. "They just wanted us out of their cave, I suppose Bill! You saved my life!

How can I ever repay you! You are one of the bravest elves I've ever known!"

Bill replied simply, "Think nothing of it, Tross, you would have done the same for me."

Tross looked at Cecee and asked, "Are you okay?"

"I'm fine but a little shaken. How about you, Bill?"

"Same with me," came the reply. "Anyway, I think we're safe for the moment."

"Oh no we're not!" Tross shouted, as he noticed, up above, something horribly familiar.

High in the sky, several dragons flew, peering down to see what may be their next meal! Lower and lower they circled, closer and closer they came…

Cecee watched and wondered to herself, 'After all we've been through, have we been brought here simply to become a meal for dragons! Are we to be eaten as an offering from the bats, just to save *them*?! If I can't plant the Seed, what will *that* mean? Could this be the end, to die in this strange land, and like *this*?'

Cecee couldn't wait another second – there was too much at risk! She felt the power of her Crown suddenly surge through her. Was it willing her to fly without fear, headlong into the circle of dragons?

Tross and Bill looked on aghast as she did so! What *was* she doing!

In the distance, massive, pale-white clouds, rapidly rolled towards them, blown along by strong winds. In that same moment, a dragon flew straight for Cecee, its outstretched wings beating frantically against the oncoming wind. Cecee froze – the dragon was next to her, hovering and drawing in air. She could feel the heat radiating from its gigantic body and could see its red eyes fixed solely upon her as it drew back its head. Cecee knew full well what would happen next. Thoughts raced through her mind. 'Why have I done this? What urged me to face danger such as this? What can possibly protect me now?'

In what may be the last few moments of her existence, she froze in time, yearning for the love of her dear family and the safety of home. She wondered how it had come to this as her short life flashed before her.

But wait! She could feel the Crown move! What would it do! All at once, it shot from her, changing shape as it spun around, covering her entire body with blue, fluid-like dust before once more changing shape, this time into a helmet, protecting her head and face! The now mystified dragon became even more confused when silver armour began to appear over Cecee's legs, arms and body! It circled again to study its tasty morsel, while Bill and Tross watched terrified to see it pass so close to Cecee. Then, as if in slow motion, it shot a powerful stream of white-hot fire towards her, engulfing her entire being!

Tross was horror-struck. "No! Not my sister!" he cried in anguish.

The flames lifted from her in seconds. What would remain? Tross and Bill could not find the strength to look – all was lost…

But no, what was that hovering in the sky? Had she somehow survived the terrible ordeal? Yes, there she was! It seemed a miracle, but Cecee was alive! The helmet lifted from her head, changing shape into a fearsome, sharp-edged, rapidly revolving disk. Even faster it spun before hurtling through the air toward the dragon! The beast sensed what would happen and attempted to fly out of its way, its huge wings working desperately to turn, but the disc was set upon its mission and would show no mercy. Reaching the monster, it spun this way and that chopping the wings from the huge animal. With a spine-chilling yell, it plunged helplessly to the ground, but the disc had not fulfilled its shocking task. Before the dragon reached the ground, the disc span back and chop – off came the creatures head!! Back to Cecee the disc flew, hovering as it came to a stop. Cecee carefully plucked it from the air and in an instant, it returned to a gleaming, crystal Crown. Even though it had saved her life, Cecee could not help but to feel afraid of what this object could do – its powers appeared limitless, perhaps even beyond her control.

She looked down to see her brother and Bill below, but no! Not all over again! Cecee could see a dragon approaching an unsuspecting Bill, but Tross had seen it, removing his Sceptre to use against the monster, but in his haste, it slipped from his grasp! Instantly, Cecee placed the Crown on her head and flew down to help. Suddenly, as well as her armour, a silver bow, along with arrows in a golden case, magically hung from her shoulder.

"Tross! Grab these!" she called from above, throwing to him the weapons. He quickly flew to catch them as Bill caught Tross's Sceptre. Bill thought he could fight the dragon without anyone's help and bravely flew at the huge scaly fiend, pointing the magical Sceptre and ordering it to kill.

"KILL!" he shouted.

But nothing happened. Bill stared at the Sceptre in disbelief. He tried again. "KIILLLL!" he bellowed.

But again, nothing. With mighty beating wings, the dragon was now upon Bill! The fire-breathing monster reared back its head to fill its lungs. It was determined to reduce this little prey to absolutely nothing!

Having removed a silver arrow, Tross slung the golden case across his back, loaded the bow and took aim at the fearsome beast, pulling back the arrow as far as he could. Without hesitation, he let the arrow fly, slicing its way through the air, striking the dragon fully in the throat. Down to the ground the creature fell, landing in a twisted, broken, lifeless heap. But there was more to come. A terrible noise came from behind. Tross turned but couldn't believe his eyes. Unable to count exactly how many, he estimated at least thirty more of the monsters were flying directly towards them! This was now a fight they had no chance of winning!

Then, from Cecee's Crown, light flashed as if it were a warning for them to get away immediately and not to be foolish enough to challenge the oncoming clan. The heavy, white clouds that at first seemed to be finally passing over, changed direction and returned at speed. The storm was now on top of them. Lightning flashed and thunder boomed, causing the oncoming creatures to suddenly stop and hover in fright. Despite their undoubted ferocity, they didn't like storms, especially this one. They seemed to sense something was not quite right – a huge mass of soft, white clouds inside of which raged a fearsome storm. They turned to flee. It was at that very moment, more than forty magnificent, white, winged Unicorns carrying Wizards upon their backs, burst from the huge, white mass. The dragons knew they would be destroyed if they withdrew – their only hope was to stay and fight to the end! Wizards cast forth fireballs which the dragons devoured, only to return them in great blasts from their fiery-red mouths. Tross, Cecee and Bill were now witnessing a battle like no other – a truly dreadful sight for all to see! Slain dragons tumbled from the sky, whilst severely injured Unicorns desperately beat their wings, preventing themselves and the Wizards they carried from colliding with the ground. They landed as steadily as they could – all they could now do was to watch the battle raging up above. But, in their place, other Unicorns emerged from within the clouds, each as magnificent as the others, bold and noble, but one was particularly striking, a female with a beautiful, long, flowing, pink mane. Much to Cecee's surprise, mounted upon this wonderful creature, was the last fairy she'd expect to see – none other than her sister Tizzy! Their eyes met for only an instant when a monstrous dragon reared up behind Tizzy, ready to blast its fiery death towards her. Cecee screamed, "Tizzy, behind you!"

Cecee watched stunned as Tizzy and her Unicorn at once lurched to one side, instantly turning around. Tizzy thrust her arm forward to send a bolt of white-hot light shooting from her forefinger to slice through the body of the vile creature. Cecee had no time to wonder from where her little sister had found so much power as from the clouds, appeared her father, Remik and Fiero! The sight filled Tross, Cecee and Bill with such great relief as the onslaught between Wizards and dragons raged on. The battle continued for over another hour. Finally, the dragons could last no longer, the only two survivors finally turning to flee the terrible carnage – they had well and truly lost the battle.

From the sky, Cecee watched Wizards and Unicorns settle on the shore of the lake to join those injured. Immediately, she flew down to land next to her father.

"Cecee!" her father cried, "Thank all the Wizards! Ian saw all of you in his Sceptre and sent a message, a sympathetic vibration message, telling your Crown to light the centre crystal's beacon."

Cecee recalled describing to Johnny and Ace how she could receive messages herself, but was amazed to learn that her Crown was capable of receiving them also! Her father took her hand.

"Cecee, we needed you high in the air so Ian could activate your Crown's beacon. You were incredibly brave to fly into the circle of dragons, but the centre crystal's light was the only way to find exactly where you were."

Cecee fell into his arms and the familiar smell of the woods, flowers and magic, filled her senses. Finally feeling the comfort she had so longed for, she asked, "Father, what is the date today?"

"Don't fret my child, we have two days left, so you have time to rest from what has been a terrible ordeal for you," replied her father.

Had she really been gone that long? Cecee could not believe it had been months. Tross and Bill flew to the King, stood in front of him and bowed low. The King patted Bill on the shoulder, instantly identifying the handsome elf. It was a sobering thought that looks you can change, but the aura of one remains the same. The truth was, he was fond of Bill and saw him as a fine soldier. He told them to rise and then turned his attention to Tross.

"My son! Thank all the Wizards of Middlesborough, you too are safe. Come now, we need to talk. Do you know the whereabouts of those evil sisters?"

371

"They are locked up in their own prison. Cecee's Crown has writing on it that Bill understood and, after Cecee read it aloud, it took away all the powers they had."

Tross then broke the tragic news to his father of Elm's sudden, heroic death. His father could see how much Tross, Cecee and Bill were suffering from the loss, but he also knew his son would be the only one among them able and bold enough to perform the magic which changed Bill. Realising again his son had broken a trust, he felt unable to lecture him now and had little time in which to offer comfort. Having learned the fate of those wicked fairies, he must remove them from the prison cave before the 'Sworromot' arrived...

The 'Sworromot' caused fear in the minds of most. Everyone but the Wizards would hide from them. Ian, upon hearing Viperla and her sisters were locked away, agreed to help the King rescue them from the caves. Yes, they were evil, but he, too, would not let them die a horrible death and secretly hoped the wicked, greedy Viperla would one day mend her ways! Before the King left, he ordered his children and Bill back on board ship. Leaving Tross and Bill to fly together ahead, Cecee, with Tizzy, would follow on their Unicorns. All flew off towards the coast, unaware that the ground below was now slowly moving! The King and Ian felt the ground roll as they walked towards Viperla's caves where she, too, felt the strange movement as she sat in her cell. The time had come, and the 'Sworromot' would soon arrive.... She knew they would come... Of course they would come! Her powers were lost – what could she do to stop them and save herself? Viperla struggled towards the solid bars of her cold, uninviting cell, trying pitifully to scream through them.

"Someone help us! We are all going to *die!*"

***

As the Unicorns took Cecee and Tizzy towards the ship, the ever-caring Cecee felt she wanted to go back to Viperla's caves to see if she and her sisters were all right. Despite their wickedness, she felt guilty ever since leaving them. 'What harm could come of it if I went back?' she asked herself. 'After all, father and Ian are going there.' She wanted to say something to the forlorn sisters to make them feel less wretched before being taken away. So, Cecee persuaded Tizzy to go with her and, together with their Unicorns, soon found themselves returning to Viperla's caves. Of course, in such little time, the caves had not changed. The pixies who were guarding the crystal caves so carefully, were still nowhere in sight. Surprised to find no sign of their father or Ian, the two sisters, along with Fiero and Cloud, walked into the caves. Cautiously making their way along the corridors to the very end, they found Viperla and her sisters huddled in a corner of their cell.

Very softly, Cecee whispered, "Viperla…"

There came no response.

"*Viperla,*" Cecee whispered louder.

The bad fairy opened one eye, and shocked at who she saw, opened the other wide, anger obvious in both.

"Cecee! You… you… you… little… well… have you come to *save* us?" she asked, cynically.

"No, it's too late to *save you,* Viperla, but my father is on his way to get you out."

"OH *GREAT*! Well, he's not here yet, so we are all going to die in this prison then!?"

A puzzled Cecee looked at her.

"No one's going to die, Viperla!"

Tizzy stood back afraid of the old, ugly looking hag who seemed to know her sister so well. She stared at the other two. "Cecee, who are they all?" she asked.

Viperla rudely interrupted. "Oh, she hasn't *told* you? *We* are the result of *her* folly! And do tell us, what is *your* name, little one?"

Tizzy looked to Cecee for support. "I don't like it in here, let's go!"

"Yes," Viperla snapped, "go! Take your little friend and you had better do it fast! The 'Sworromot' are coming and you must hide! In fact, Cecee, hide in my caves – go to the crystal caves, you will be *very* safe in there."

Cloud, though gentle, was a brave and protective Unicorn. She nudged Tizzy. "Tizzy, fly onto my back. Whatever happens, I will look after you and take you away from here."

Fiero heard Cloud's wise words. "Cecee, we are leaving with Cloud. Get onto my back – you're coming with us now!"

But just at that very moment, the ground again shook, this time with greater force.

Viperla, with all the energy she could muster, shouted, "See, I *told* you they're coming! Hide in my crystal caves! Go there now! Ha, ha, ha!"

Tizzy begged Ceeee to leave with them, but her sister could only glare at Viperla. How dare she try to

374

frighten Tizzy. And to think, they had come to comfort them all!

"Take no notice, Tizzy, Viperla is just trying to scare us."

All the same, Cecee flew onto Fiero's back to leave, but too late – now the caves shook, small pieces of rock falling from above! Despite the rumbling sound, they could hear voices… it was their father and Ian! Seeing his daughters, a mixture of terror and anger filled the King.

"What are you doing *here*? Why aren't you safely onboard ship? Don't my children *ever* listen to me?!" He barked.

'My children!' Viperla thought to herself. '*My children!* So, Cecee is *Royal!* Oh great! She and her little friend are sisters and clearly Princesses! TUT! I might have known! This will make my plan a little harder, but if it's the last thing I do, I will get that trouble making little Cecee, she will pay dearly for the harms and snags she has caused me!'

Just then, the King's Sceptre flashed a white light. A message from the Wizards had finally come to confirm Viperla was in her caves' prison!

The King clucked, "A bit late, we are already here! Fiero, Cloud, when I tell you, take my daughters out of here as fast as you can!"

He pointed his Sceptre to unlock the prison gate, but nothing happened! He now tried pointing it at the bars to bend them apart, but again to no avail.

Ian yelled at Viperla, "Where's the key!"

"It's back in my room, down there!" she tried to scream, pointing along the corridor.

Ian aimed his Sceptre in the direction of her room, speaking a few words of magic. The key jumped off her bedside table, shot along the floor, down the steps, through the corridors and finally into Ian's hand! He unlocked the gate, grabbed Viperla by the hand while the King held onto her sisters. The roof of the caves now shook violently as the King shouted, "Wait! Fiero, Cloud ignore what I told you! Cecee, Tizzy, you fly along with me. Ian jump onto Fiero! Viperla, get on Cloud with your sisters. Do it *now*!"

The King and Ian helped the three old fairies onto Cloud. Ian then climbed onto Fiero, and all left as fast as they could, speeding past the crystal cave just before it exploded into the air! Pink quartz flew everywhere. The once hidden crystal cave was now open to the sky! Shards of quartz continued spewing out. The Unicorns knew all were in serious danger so they flew in a shallow swoop along the bottom of the caves and their connecting corridors. On towards the exit the King flew, holding his daughters hands as tightly as they could bear. They flew past the amethyst cave which in seconds also erupted, sending pieces in all directions! As Cecee looked back to see the Unicorns following close behind, she screamed, "Fiero, Cloud! Keep with us! Fly as fast as you can! Fly!!"

Passing another cave, a further explosion sent emerald shards hurtling along the corridor. They ducked, dived and weaved their way through sharp, flying debris. Viperla's sisters, sitting on Cloud, held on with all their might, but Viperla was concerned it was too cramped. With all the twisting and turning, someone could easily fall and she would make certain it wouldn't be her! As they approached the sapphire cave, Viperla thought to herself, 'There little Sevilla, you like pretty blue gems, have all you want! And you Levira, are just a waste of my time!' As quick as a flash, she kicked both her sisters from Cloud's back! Unnoticed by anyone in all the confusion, the sisters landed on the ground directly in front of the sapphire cave. Sevilla tried to scream, "No, Viperla! Help us," but too late. Cloud had flown on too far for her to be heard... The wicked Viperla smiled to herself as she looked back to see the sisters disappear amid a huge blast of sapphire.

'Ha!' she scoffed to herself. 'That will teach them both not to be disloyal to me!'

Nearing the exit, a strange sound like the beating of a heart, could be heard in the distance. The sound grew louder and louder – Ba-boom, ba-boom, ba-BOOM, BA-BOOM! At long last and to their great relief, they burst from the caves, only to be greeted by a strange, frightening, whooshing sound. Cecee looked up and gasped as Tizzy screamed, "Father!"

There, high above them in the sky, long, dangling, pointed tentacles, waved all around. The time had come...the 'Sworromot' had arrived!

CHAPTER SIXTEEN

NOT HOME YET! LAST WORD AND ICICLE

On their way back to the ship, Tross and Bill stopped to drink from a small lake. While Bill cupped his hands for a scoop of the delicious strawberry flavoured water, a red flash reflected across the lake's surface and in the distance, a rumbling sound caused him and Tross to look far down the right side of the lake towards Viperla's caves. But a thumping sound diverted their gaze towards a mystical ship with the word 'CIGAM' written along the bow. Strange looking creatures flew from every porthole, their long, dangling tentacles seeming to search the air for something as they flew in slow motion by the hundreds. Tross watched while they passed slowly overhead. "What *are* those things?" he asked Bill.

"You're asking me! No idea, but they look like flying jellyfish and are heading towards those caves!"

"Viperla's caves! Bill, father and Ian will be there by now. We must go back to warn them!"

The Caves eruptions and explosions seemed unending, filling the sky with many colours. As the two drew nearer, they could see the cave's entrance and carefully approached, just as the King, Cecee and Tizzy burst into daylight! Directly behind, followed Fiero carrying Ian and Cloud carrying only Viperla. The Sworromot had already descended, one of the creatures hovering close to the King. Tross still had Cecee's silver arrows, so quickly loaded his bow, aiming at the strange creature. His father cried out, "Tross, *NO!*" But too late, the arrow had been released. Off it sped with a SWISHHHHH, cutting through the air with ease. All too soon it hit the poor creature, bringing it tumbling to the ground with a thud… The dull, beating sound suddenly stopped and all froze in silence. The Sworromot which had witnessed the killing broke the silence with an awful, sad wail. The King shouted, "Everyone, take cover as best you can in what remains of the caves!"

Tears ran from all the Sworromot's small eyes, melting everything they touched. In the safety of the caves remains, the King hurriedly explained.

"You must all understand, Sworromot are harmless! They may appear disturbing, almost menacing, but remember, some things in life are never as they first seem. Their tentacles collect crystals from the caves and take them to CIGAM. When they see danger, they cry acid tears to defend themselves." Viperla smirked as the King explained further.

"Viperla placed a formidable spell over all the crystals so she could possess them and prevent anyone or anything else from using them. With Bill's help, repeating the words written inside the Crown, Cecee unlocked the mystery that has taken years to try to decipher. It is clear, the meaning of the Crown's writing was a secret Roddy took with him to his grave. At last, Viperla's spell is broken and the master crystal will send a message to other crystals, exposing them for the 'Sworromot' to collect. As the name 'CIGAM' read backwards means 'MAGIC', 'Sworromot' backwards means 'Tomorrows'. Understand, they are our destiny! They collect the crystals into which Wizards insert magic, then to be used to fight all evil. Without these crystals containing their powers, evil fairies such as Viperla and her sisters will deny us a future worth living!"

Tross felt an overpowering sense of shame and remorse. Although he had done what he thought was right, he now understood he had killed an innocent creature which bore no harm and existed simply to help protect others from greedy, selfish, makers of evil.

"Father, I am so sorry…" he choked, barely able to speak.

Cecee glared at Viperla, remembering how she told her and Tizzy to run to the crystal caves where they would be safe. As events had proven, Viperla would have gladly seen them die! Even for Viperla, Cecee thought to herself, 'such *wickedness* is beyond belief. But wait! Where are Viperla's two sisters?'

"Father, Sevilla and Levira! Where are they?" she asked.

Viperla tried to scream as she looked around to find them. Feigning a deep sadness, she whined, "You, Cecee! *You* unlocked the spell, and *you* have killed my sisters. You must have somehow killed them in my caves! My beloved sisters are gone because of *you*!"

Tears rolling down her face, she turned to the King while shaking a bony finger in the direction of Cecee.

"She, *she* should be put on *trial* for killing my two sisters, *and* my poor Elmiva is still missing! I just *know your* daughter had something to do with all of this!"

Even though most of Viperla's caves lay in ruins, Ian decided he would search to see if he could find her sisters. Risking his life, he looked everywhere but could not find one of them – he assumed each must be lying dead, deep within the ruins. Struggling back alone to rejoin the group, he found Viperla still distraught with grief.

"Ian! NO! You are alone! My dear, beloved sisters! Didn't you find them? *Where are they*?!"

Her deceitful sobbing had now become a tragic wail – this was, beyond doubt, one of Viperla's most convincing acts!

With a sorrowful face and quiet voice, Ian replied, "Viperla, I am so sorry. I searched as far as I could, but found nothing of them."

Ian felt her deep grief – she looked absolutely hysterical. She was a wicked fairy, the worst, and locked away she must be. But while she would spend the remainder of her life in prison, he wondered how he could somehow make up for her tragic loss.

Viperla collapsed to the ground, so grief stricken she could sob no more. Holding her face in her hands, she cunningly disguised a broad smile as she thought to herself, 'My wonderful plan is working. Ian is feeling so sorry for me and my 'tragic loss', he, he! Maybe this time he will give me a more comfortable prison. Even better, a little bit more excellent acting and I may even convince them all that Cecee *did* kill the worthless pair! Ha! I am truly the *best*!' But... there was one thing uncertain. Where was Elmiva? Viperla silently worried, 'Was she perhaps hiding and happen to witness me kick our sisters from Cloud? I simply *must* determine where she is!'

A little time had passed and all seemed peaceful outside. The King ventured into the open and could see the Sworromot busily collecting any crystals they could find. He beckoned to the others to come outside. Flying over puddles of the Sworromot's steaming, acid tears, they left the ruins behind and made their way back to Tiddlesworth.

On the way, Fiero couldn't help but gaze at Cloud, thinking she was the most beautiful Unicorn he had ever seen – it had been love at first sight and he wanted to spend the rest of his life with her and would do his best to make this come true. However, before any of this could become reality, Fiero knew, above anything else, he must concentrate on the vital task. Cecee must plant that magical Seed and there was still a long way to go – she was not home yet!

***

All were now at the Castle and everything was as it should be – well, almost. Having been greatly thanked by everyone, the widely respected Wizards and Unicorns left Tiddlesworth with a little regret but much satisfaction they had been of service. Tizzy loved Cloud and heard the best news ever – Cloud was allowed to remain and was more than happy to have Tizzy as her owner! And of course, Fiero was delighted Cloud would be staying with them…

Leaving Tiddlesworth to board the ship, the King stopped abruptly. He could see all the Wizard flags missing and some of his crew and sailors tied up! What could have happened? Looking harder, he could see trolls everywhere! There was only one thing he could do. He left the others with strict orders to stay where they were and flew to his ship. But as he tried to board, the trolls shook their weapons in protest! Even though he knew they couldn't understand his language, the King raged at them, "Remik! What have you done with my great elf, Remik, I ask you?"

His mood and overwhelming presence were enough to make the trolls immediately stand aside, allowing the King to board his own ship. Over to one side, although they tried hard to disguise him, the King could see soldier Remik tightly bound and unable to move. Pointing towards him and forcing his way through the crowd to where Remik sat, he bellowed, "I demand an explanation for this complete outrage!"

Remik spoke up. "Majesty, they say they need to use the ship for protection. They are from the west side of Wizard's Eye Lake, and request you preside over a summit with the trolls from the east. They are losing the War over control of the Lake, and think it's unfair."

"Preside over a summit! Losing a War to control the Lake! Unfair!" yelled the King, now very red in the face. "By *ALL* the Wizards of Middlesborough! Unfair indeed! Remik, you speak their language well, tell them I sympathise with their cause but am unable to assist with any of this right now. We must return to Seven Oaks Woods by tomorrow." He turned to a nearby troll and growled. "Untie my elf or by all the Wizards, you will regret it… and that goes for each and every one of you!" he quickly added, waving his fist and casting his eyes back and forth over the assembled mass.

Of course, the trolls had not understood a word. They looked at each other with a mixture of confusion and anger. Was now the King *himself* declaring war against them? They beat their fists on their chests in protest, each looking directly at the King!

King Foxglove could speak many languages but theirs, 'Langtroll', was not one of them. Unlike Remik, he had not spent much time with them in which to learn. Infuriated at their reaction, he roared, "Remik! Tell them I demand the return of my ship and impress upon them it is critical I have it immediately!"

Remik relayed the message after which there was a short exchange of words. But before he had a chance to speak to the King, the trolls gave a response which was not one the King would find acceptable. They repeatedly thumped their poles and stout, heavy sticks on the deck, almost drowning Remik's voice as he tried to explain,

"Majesty, they boarded early this morning, hundreds of them. They said they are taking over the ship until tomorrow evening. The east side trolls are due to arrive in the morning, and the summit they've already arranged will probably last all day. They also mentioned, in their opinion, the ship should not be on their Lake in the first place! Further, Majesty, they thought you spoke their language. As clearly you do not, I will have to act as interpreter during the summit."

This was more than the King could tolerate. He ordered Remik to tell the trolls he would return and then flew from the ship, leaving the poor elf still tightly bound and talking to his captors.

Landing on the beach, the King scoffed "*Their* Lake!" He looked back at the ship before flying on to rejoin the others. After greeting them he announced, "Something must be done! Trolls taking over my ship! Tying up Remik! Making demands of *me*! Never!" He explained what had happened.

Cecee anxiously stared at her father. This would leave only tomorrow night to get home for sunrise! She asked, "Father, can we recall the Wizards to help with all this?"

"Cecee, you are in my care so please don't worry," he replied, putting his arm around her shoulder.

Taking his Sceptre, the King studied closely its crystal in which he saw Ian's flag flying high on Tiddlesworth Castle's centre turret showing he was 'In Residence'. He then sent a message through the crystal – "Ian, your help is urgently required. Trolls have taken over my ship!"

The Wizard appeared in a flash, white hair and beard flowing in the wind as he walked the plank to board the ship. Instantly, the trolls welcomed him and crowded excitedly around. From where he stood, the King could see Ian had arrived. For a while, the Wizard seemed in deep discussion. The King began to feel a little optimistic – it was a good sign he could hear no shouting or see the waving of weapons in anger. Had Ian somehow resolved the issue with the insolent little fellows? King Foxglove quickly flew to the shore. Ian suddenly held his hand high in a gesture of peace, turned and walked back down the plank towards the King.

"Your Majesty," Ian began, "There is reason to feel a little more confident. The trolls will definitely leave after their gathering with the others has ended."

"But *when* will that be, Ian?" asked the still anxious King.

"Tomorrow morning, if all goes well," replied Ian.

"Ian, all *must* go well between the two sides. You know the reason for our great urgency."

The Wizard stroked his beard slowly, deep in contemplation.

"Your Majesty. There are other measures I could use but, at this stage, I am unsure how successful they would be. Now, I must return to G.H.O.T.S to prepare."

"Thank you for your help, my friend. Can we all go on board?" asked the King. "It will be easier for us to sleep on the ship tonight so we are ready early in the morning."

"Yes, you may board. There is enough room for you all, but a word of warning, do not talk to the families –

they'll twist everything you say!" This was Ian's parting advice as he left to return to his Castle.

On board, Remik was untied and later joined Tross, Cecee and Bill to dine with the King. While they ate, there came a knock on the door and a troll entered their cabin. He walked straight to the King and spoke perfect 'Seven Oaks' language, announcing himself, "My name is Holgart, and I'm the Head of my family. I want you to know that it was not our intention to upset anyone. We simply needed neutral ground to meet, and your ship seemed ideal. The reason for removing the flags was to show no favour to anyone in particular... after all, it is *our* Lake!"

The King sighed while thinking to himself, 'If only these trolls had more manners. He could have waited to be invited before striding in!' His appetite lost, he thanked Holgart for taking the time to inform him. The satisfied troll bid the King goodnight and left.

"Well, not much of what he said was very useful! And what's more, he can speak our language! Why didn't he say something earlier!" the King asked Remik.

"I was unaware he could understand our language, Majesty, and, just like everything else, that's how they are. You never know what they understand or what they're thinking. They feel the need to justify all they do, even if it's wrong or misinformed, and they won't stop arguing until you admit to seeing their point of view. Above all, they must have the last word because it makes them feel their views are the most important. That is why the east and west side of the Lake will always be in deadlock – the Head of each must *always* have the last say!"

***

The following day, all rose very early to prepare. Cecee and Tizzy went to fetch their Unicorns, while Tross went with his father and Bill to the upper deck. There they discovered the east side trolls had already arrived. They, together with the west side, were everywhere, all in a state of excited anticipation, discussing in groups what they expected from the summit. To the King, they all looked alike and it was only their clothing which distinguished one side from the other. Remik was already there, mingling among the trolls, attempting to bring some order but failing miserably! Seeing the King, he flew over to him. With a deep frown across his forehead and with an exasperated sigh, he moaned, "Majesty, this is, without any doubt, a *complete* disaster!"

"Ohh, that's just perfect!" the King replied, as he sat down on a wooden bench to observe the trolls. Thankfully, he saw they had at least allowed the Monitor Elves to attend their chores. Needing something sweet to drink, he looked around to catch the attention of an Elf.

"Can one of you *please* fetch me some peach nectar tea."

The tea was quickly delivered and as he sipped the refreshing brew, the King resumed his watch over the trolls. Fearing they may soon once again be locked in a pointless argument, he considered the wisdom of recalling Ian.

The clouds hung heavy and low, passing quickly overhead in the strong wind. Suddenly, it began to snow, falling thick and heavy! But this was not the usual common white snow, this was bright pink! For reasons known only to themselves, the trolls began to panic, some quickly disappearing down below ship, while those who remained on deck, threw open cupboards and large boxes in search of blankets, sheets, towels, anything with which to cover themselves – on no account must the snow ever cling to their fur! The Head troll of each family, already covered in blankets, ran down the plank and off the ship, shouting, "Between us, we have agreed to cancel the summit! This weather is *definitely* not funny!"

Shouting at the top of his voice, the Foogart's Head accused the Hagarty's Head, "For some reason, you've caused this!"

"No I haven't!" came the equally loud reply. "I bet it was you! Oh never mind! Let's just run for cover and we can debate this later!"

"Yes, let's!" agreed the other.

Remik approached the King with a broad smile.

"Well, Majesty, listen to that! That's *got* to be a first! The two Heads have actually agreed on something! You see, it's the snow! Not that they mind when it's white, but when it mixes with purple dust blown by the wind from the mountain tops, that's entirely different. It turns from white to bright pink before reaching the ground! The effect looks beautiful, but if it falls onto a male troll's furry feet or hands, the pink colouring remains for months!" Remik shielded his mouth and whispered into the King's ear, "This causes plenty of amusement among the female trolls, ha, ha!"

The King laughed heartily along with Remik as they watched every troll hurry from the ship to join his leader, but the last ran towards the King, peering out from under his blanket.

"This is not the end of it, Elf King, you will hear more!" he growled, before leaving the ship to promptly rejoin his family.

To avoid further delay, King Foxglove did not wish to argue the fact that another troll clearly speaks Seven Oaks. He gazed into his Sceptre to see Ian's face shining back and asking with some urgency, "Your Majesty, tell me my crystals are not deceiving me... it *is* snowing there, and it is *pink* snow?"

"Yes, Ian!" replied the King, "pink snow is falling and the trolls are rapidly leaving!"

Ian's face beaming back, he gave an excited laugh.

"Then my magic *has* worked! The trolls are leaving because of my weather! I *can* make weather! Ha, ha, I can actually *make* weather! I knew I could do it!"

After the ship had been made ready for sail, all left Middlesborough at midday. Allowing for the time difference, this meant the time in Seven Oaks was nine o'clock in the evening. Once again, all secured themselves safely for the journey ahead. To help pass the time, they recounted their adventures, together with the sadness the strange Island Middleborough had brought them. Time quickly passed and before they knew it, they had arrived at Seven Oaks Lake. Upon arrival, they found the weather calm with a clear sky full of bright, shining, silver stars. The air had a smell Cecee recognized – it had been snowing at Seven Oaks as well, leaving a thick, deep blanket covering the ground. She had only ten hours before the Sun would rise, and she still had no idea where to plant the Rowan Seed! She hurried home to ask the most important question she was to ask in her whole life – exactly *where* should she plant it?

After a short but joyous reunion with her mother, Cecee, along with the others, refreshed themselves with food and drink. After this, the Queen took Cecee to one side and placed a map in her hand. With a seriousness in her voice Cecee had seldom heard, she explained how the task should be completed but, because of the snow, finding the correct place would be difficult. However, once there, she would receive help from a Boy Human named Michael…

'*Michael*!' thought Cecee. 'Could this be the same Boy Human who appeared in my disturbing dreams?' She studied the map intensely, trying to memorise every detail before saying goodbye and flying off at great speed. Tightly clutching the map, she flew hill by hill, lake by lake, tree by tree, eventually finding her way to where the old Seven Oaks trees had once stood. She was saddened to find some of the beautiful old oaks had blown down in the Great Storm, but reasoned to herself, 'This can't be the place! It's too near the old Oak trees. The Seed will not germinate amongst such huge roots!' Convinced, despite the map, she must be lost, she decided to return and start the whole search again! Several more times she tried but could not find the correct place. Cecee was now in a panic with only fifteen minutes in which to complete her vital task!

"This map! Why doesn't it *help* me!" she cried aloud, "It's useless! Why didn't mother explain things more clearly?" A snow flurry came and went. Cecee looked to see the sky had clouded a little. "Oh no, this snow isn't helping!"

Scrutinizing the map once again, now in a state of complete confusion, she heard someone call to her.

"Cecee, over here… hurry!"

In the centre of a small clearing, was the Boy Human who she instantly recognized from her dreams – Michael! There he stood, waving in the air a yellow crystal. Time was quickly running out – only five minutes remained as Cecee flew to him.

"Here! Dig here!" he shouted, excitedly.

Cecee looked to where he pointed. With the snow deep and the earth becoming harder, she had no time for questions as her tiny fingers worked furiously to make a hole. Quickly retrieving the Seed from her pouch, she was about to plant it when Michael, kneeling beside her, grabbed her arm.

"Cecee, wait, not yet – you must give me the vial of liquid the Queen gave you. Please hurry!"

By all the Wizards, she had completely forgotten! There it was, still hanging around her neck. Only sixty seconds remained. But, under the snow, something moved – something strange and heading straight towards them! Cecee wasted no time, snatching the vial from around her neck and handing it to Michael who broke off the top and placed exactly three drops onto the yellow crystal, drinking the remainder. Thirty seconds to go… With a shock, Cecee recognized the little monster in her dreams as its head unexpectedly popped out from under the snow some distance from them! She knelt, petrified, as Michael studied his yellow crystal. "This *is* the correct place!" he shouted. "*Now,* Cecee! Plant the Seed, *now!*"

Twenty seconds… and the little monster disappeared beneath the snow. It sped towards them, a hump in the snow marking its whereabouts! Michael shouted, this time in sheer terror.

"Cecee, help me! Plant the Seed *NOW!*"

With trembling fingers, Cecee placed the Seed in the hole, quickly covering it with soil. She looked up to see the awful little creature from her dreams emerge again from the snow.

"Michael! The creature! It's coming to get us!"

With only ten seconds remaining, Michael ran towards it, waving his arms in the air to distract the creature, but he tripped and fell. He sat up to bravely face the oncoming little monster, the jaws of which were now wide apart. This time, the sharp teeth Cecee remembered so well from her dreams, were real! Five seconds, and again Michael pleaded.

"Cecee, help me! Has the Seed been planted?!"

Quickly making certain, she shouted with great satisfaction, "Yes, Michael, I've planted it! My task is complete!"

The creature twisted its ugly head to gaze towards the planting spot, its bright red eyes then flicking to peer at Cecee. With a shrill of disapproval that tore through the air, rustling the leaves of the trees, it burrowed back under the snow and simply disappeared. While Cecee stared in amazement, Michael sat back with a deep sigh of relief.

"Michael, I saw you in my dreams, but I have no idea who you are. By all the Wizards, can you tell me, what *was* that horrible thing?"

Michael stood up, brushing snow from himself.

"Well, Rowan didn't get his 'subros' Seed, did he! Phew Cecee, that *was* a close one!"

"What is that? What does the word 'Subros' mean?" asked a very curious Cecee.

"Well, firstly, that creature is called Rowan. A 'Subros' is Rowan's pet name for the Seed you planted. Spelt backwards, the word reads 'Sorbus' – it's Latin for Rowan Tree. As for me, I'm your Human brother! Ugh, I can still taste that liquid! Tell you what, it's worse than any medicine I know! Let me explain some of my history… The job of helping to plant the special Seed has been passed down from father to son for many years. It would have been the death of us if I had not helped… You see, I own the 'Sun Crystal'" He held out his hand. "This has the power to show me information from the 'Moon Crystal'."

"Sun Crystal? Moon Crystal? I know nothing of these and what is the badge you wear on your jacket?

What magic does it contain? Can it help us in the future," replied Cecee.

"Oh no, Cecee" Michael replied. "That's my school badge. There's nothing magical about that, I can assure you!" Michael took out a round, sparkling, silver crystal from his pocket and held it out to her. "Now, *this* is magic! This is the 'Moon Crystal'," he said. "This and the 'Sun Crystal' *are* magical."

Cecee took them both and peered into each, expecting to see a sign.

"But they are empty, Michael!"

"Yes, they are now as everything has been completed. Even though you can't see them at the moment, the swirly shapes from the vial are now inside the Sun Crystal, getting ready for their next reading in four years. I drank the liquid to stay connected. Oh, I know, all very mysterious, but these Crystals have been in my family for generations, so it is all quite 'matter of fact' to me. It started for us a very long time ago. They were gifts to a very distant grandfather of mine, all because he helped one of *your* distant relatives, an Elf Prince called Hawthorne."

Cecee gasped – she knew of him!

"Well," Michael added, "his reward was a pouch of gold pieces. Returning home with them, he felt pleased. However, upon opening the pouch, no gold pieces were to be found, just the Sun Crystal! Certain he would find the gold, he looked deeper into the pouch but found a piece of paper on which was written, 'He who can read the Sun Crystal can find the Moon Crystal – find this and follow its commands every leap year, and your family will have a future full of health and happiness. Refuse this challenge and the gold pieces will be yours.' The challenge was accepted and the secret of reading the Sun Crystal was discovered. The ability to read the Crystal has been passed down to each generation. We accept this is a huge responsibility, but are honoured to have so generous a gift. Since that day, my family have lived happy and healthy lives. Cecee, to have wealth in gold for us Humans could be wonderful and we can all work to achieve that, but without health and happiness, even owning all the gold in the World, well, that would mean nothing."

Cecee stared in awe at the spot where she had planted the Seed.

"But, Michael, you say the gift was the Sun Crystal, which if you can read, you can find the Moon Crystal. Where *was* the Moon Crystal found?"

"It's in the 'Silver Crest of Middlesborough', hanging on a wall inside the eighth turret of Tiddlesworth Castle, and is hidden well. It is, in fact, the first 'o' of the name Middlesborough. The planting of the Seed is the only time a member of my family is taken by an owl and allowed to enter the Island to collect the Crystal."

"Michael, I was there at Tiddlesworth and counted only seven turrets," replied Cecee.

"The eighth is invisible Cecee. It is seen only when powerful Wizard dust is sprinkled into the top chimney of the centre dome and finds its way to the huge, central crystal upon the oval table in the Great Hall. The danger is, the fairy Viperla has turned against all that is good. As part of Patrick's family, she had great power, but I know what has happened to her. She knows of these Crystals and would have stopped at nothing to find them.

With these, she would have dominance over all, including the Wizards! *Imagine that!* For now, the Moon Crystal is safe where it is. To some, it may seem an obvious hiding place, but sometimes that can make an object harder to find!"

"Where does this special Fairy Rowan Seed come from?" asked Cecee.

Michael hesitated before replying, "You may think it comes from the last fairy Rowan Seed planted four years ago. The last was in Ireland, before that Scotland. I think the next in four years' time will be in Wales. Where the original Seed comes from, I'm not allowed to tell you. This is a secret that can never be told by me and must be protected forever. My advice is to seek the answer from your parents or a High Wizard."

"Can you tell me what or even who, was that awful creature? Why was it trying to harm us?"

Before Michael answered, he wondered why this fairy had so little knowledge when the others he had met before, knew everything.

"Cecee, you seem to know little of your own World. What happened to you? Why weren't you told anything on your birthday?"

Cecee explained how, on that day, she was swept off in a storm to a distant land and perhaps this is why she was not made aware of everything. She told Michael of her recurring dream about the ugly creature. It was then he realized how very close they had come to disaster and how lucky they had been.

"Yes, 'The Rowan', a terrifying little thing," Michael said. "An odd coincidence, it's the same as the Seed. But Cecee, had the Rowan Seed not been planted at exactly the right time and in the right place, the creature Rowan would have taken it! He exists only so he can destroy these precious seeds! Had he been successful, drought and famine would have lasted everywhere for five years. Can you imagine, five years without food or water? It would be the end of every living thing!"

Cecee stared at a little robin that came to land on a nearby branch.

"Yes, Cecee, even that little bird perched over there – all would be gone! Even though Wizards, with their tremendous powers, created Middlesborough as a place to safeguard your magic, they can't maintain nature's balance alone. If we did not come together and do things in the right order, even their Island would soon crumble and be no more… You must understand, our two Worlds are connected in many ways, Cecee. Whatever part of the World we are from, we must come together as one to keep this beautiful planet healthy and alive."

Cecee paled, recalling how close she came to failing.

"Can we ever destroy Rowan?" she asked.

"No," replied Michael. "Finding enough power to do that would be as impossible as trying to destroy thunder and lightning! You see, Cecee, he is a warning, nature's warning, telling us to keep the balance of everything in order, or else! Fortunately, we have now planted this year's magic Seed. It will grow into a tree which will help pollinate all other plant life by its mystical wonder. And the creature Rowan? Well, he will find a place where he will sleep for four years and, as you fairies and elves often say, "Thank all the Wizards for that!" Ha, ha!"

Cecee closed her eyes and laughed aloud. Opening them, she expected to see Michael's cheery face, but he had vanished! It was then she understood another and even more startling secret – for survival, a Human must enter her World, a World she thought was for her kind only. The snow had stopped falling and she sat contented as the morning Sun rose in a clear, blue winter's sky. The surrounding snow glistened while, as if by magic, a fresh, little green sprout, peeped through the cold blanket. In the peace and calm, the little red-breasted robin she had seen earlier ruffled its feathers, while singing a merry winter's song. 'Sing little bird,' she thought, 'the time has come and gone and everything is going to be alright.' She realized how many living creatures on Earth must be unaware of what an enormous challenge it is for a chosen few to maintain the balance of nature. She turned her face to the Sun and stretched her wings, the power of its light streaming into her very being. She folded down her wings before turning her attention to where the Seed was planted. The most important tree on Earth, the 'Fairy Rowan', had already started to grow. It seemed to stretch towards the sky to absorb the Sun's life giving light and love. She thought of magic and, depending who used it, how it could be so wonderful or could bring nothing but pain, misery and destruction. She took off her Crystal Crown and saw the writing inside had mysteriously vanished. Studying its embedded crystals, she wondered about their names and true purpose. A hole left by the missing stone – a Red War Crystal – caused her to recall the labyrinth and where it may have been lost. Cecee felt eager to do what she thought correct. Soon, she would return to Middlesborough to search for the stone and promised herself she would, somehow, find a way to return the complete Crown to the fairy Icicle.

CHAPTER SEVENTEEN

WIND, LEAVES AND ALMOST RED

The King held a grand party in his gardens to celebrate the joyous outcome. Cecee had been summoned to meet with her elders and, arriving astride Fiero, everyone gasped at the grand spectacle. Fiero wore upon his back a royal blue, open-weave cloak, decorated with many precious stones. On his side hung a shield displaying Cloud's family crest in the centre of which was carved a pure, white Unicorn rearing upwards, ready for battle. This magnificent shield displayed to all his acceptance by Cloud's family as her future mate. His coat had turned a shimmering, silvery colour. Cecee, wearing a suit of blue and silver armour adorned with shiny knee and elbow shields, was a sight which could not fail but to impress. A long, royal blue cape, trimmed in white with pure gold weaving around the edge, flowed from her shoulders. Into her hair were woven tiny flowers and upon her head, she wore Icicle's splendid, mystical, crystal Crown. In one hand she held a spear, attached to which was the striking flag of Seven Oaks Woods. She dismounted and proudly walked with Fiero to the King and Queen. With one thrust, Cecee dug the end of the spear into the ground next to them, signalling the triumphant completion of her secret task. In so doing, her parents accepted she was every bit a deserving Princess. Her proud father whispered to his Queen, "My dear, what an absolutely magnificent sight Cecee and Fiero make together!"

At that moment, Tizzy and Cloud entered, both looking their very best. The Queen turned to the King and with a contented smile, whispered, "My darling husband, how wonderful both our daughters and their Unicorns look!"

The King took the Queen's hand and nodded in agreement.

All attended the party, except for Violet and Rosie. Upon learning the news of Elm's violent but heroic death, Violet was left heartbroken. The King had sent two of his Elves to find her and, arriving at her home, she agreed to leave with them without any fuss. Although concerned the King had sent them to arrest her, she accepted this was only just. But what about Elm and those stolen bows and arrows she had given him? Even if it was the last thing she ever did, she would do her utmost to preserve his good name.

Before long, the poor fairy was brought before the King, collapsing at his feet. Forgetting to disguise her Scottish accent, she said, "Your Majesty, the bows and arrows – *I* gave them to Elm! I am sure you know by now they were stolen. I feel so terribly guilty. I must have brought bad luck upon poor Elm, selfishly counting those wee daisy petals to see if he loved me... his death was my fault!"

Violet could no longer hold back her tears.

"My dear Violet! I know it was Rush who stole the weapons from the armoury at Middlesborough, and I'm sure an elf such as he was impossible to argue against. But you no longer need to worry about him. As for bad luck and omens, don't believe in these – they're nothing but old, distorted tales! I know who you are, and why you disguise yourself, but there is no need to do so. While I appreciate you wish to protect a family member, you are not the direct descendent of the fairy Princess from Scotland. It is Rosie and it is *she* who must return the magic shawl. Rest assured Violet, your secret is safe and I will help where I can to lift the curse from Rosie." The King leaned close to her ear and whispered. "Violet, I *am* the King and not much escapes my attention!"

"Your Majesty," replied Violet, "there's something you may not know. I accepted Wizard dust in return for mead and I think Rush stole it at the same time he took the weapons. I planned to return it, but now I can't find it anywhere! I also have the Wand Tizzy left behind in my home! It was not her fault, she wasn't feeling well or thinking with a clear mind. But I am guilty of threatening Todd with its powers."

"Hmmm, it's Tizzy who has some explaining to do," replied the King. "She is my youngest and, as with my other children, she seldom listens. Sometimes, I wonder if all fathers have the same problem with their children! However, she owes you an apology. This may come as a surprise, but being my daughter doesn't make her perfect!"

Violet responded with a confused frown.

"Violet, my daughter Tizzy took the Wizard dust from your home and, in so doing, saved my life. Of course, that doesn't *excuse* the theft, but if she hadn't

403

taken it, I wouldn't be here now. Please worry yourself no longer – the Wizard dust is back with its rightful owner, the Wizard Patrick. Now, I would like to speak about why we have searched high and low for you. Come, sit next to me and I will explain."

Violet sat next to her King, feeling much more relaxed, but wondered what more could he say to her.

"Violet, Elm left instructions, should anything happen to him, you are to receive all he owned, his riches and rewards… everything is to be yours. His endeavours left him well rewarded which means you are now a very wealthy fairy. Violet, do you understand what all this means?"

"Yes, I think so, Your Majesty," she answered softly, her heart almost bursting now realizing how much her dear Elm truly loved her.

"A celebration is planned, and I would like you to take part."

"But, Your Majesty, I'm too upset at the loss of Elm. I feel unable to be there."

"Violet, I insist, and it is time you attended Court. Elm was a great soldier and by your presence, you may honour his memory and rejoice in his life. You have my permission to bring Rosie but she must not make herself too obvious."

Violet covered her face with her hands and sobbed. The King gently touched her shoulder.

"Wipe away your tears, Violet, don't cry your life away. Elm would want you to carry on without him and be happy, and that my dear, is true love. Take comfort from his bravery and live your life the way he would have wished. Who knows what your future may bring!"

Violet thought about poor Rosie and how she misses so much in her life. She would bring her to the celebration and together, they would enjoy themselves as the King wished. Violet wondered how she could use her newfound wealth to help Rosie find that cursed shawl and clear her family's name forever! She thanked the King before flying home with the exciting news and, finding Rosie, explained all the King had said. Rosie was very excited as they both dressed for the grand celebration. She arranged flowers in Violet's hair, making her look every inch a Royal fairy, but made certain she herself would not look too noticeable, agreeing to keep out of sight. Then, as fast as they could, both flew excitedly to the Royal Court.

Tross and Bill stood together, discussing over a cone of mead, how Bill could put his fortune to good use. While they spoke, Bill noticed a beautiful fairy standing almost apologetically in a shaded part of the Court.

"Tross, who is that *stunning* fairy? She looks vaguely familiar…" he asked.

"Her name is Violet."

"You mean… *Elm's* Violet?"

"That's right. You know her, she used to be in charge of the 'Two Sevens Inn', but I've only just heard talk of her building a new Inn for soldiers and Royalty where they can stay for free on their travels. Someone overheard she is calling it 'Elm's Retreat' or 'Elm's Manor', something like that, and her friend, a very pretty raven-haired fairy called Rosie, whom I have to say, I have *already* noticed, will take care of it for her."

"Tross, Rosie isn't Royal. In fact, no one knows much about her. *Should* you get to know her?"

"Oh yes, Bill, it is not the first time I have noticed her! Beyond her natural beauty, she is shy and quiet – my type, exactly!"

"Well, Tross, you know best…" replied Bill. In an attempt to tidy himself, Bill ran his fingers through his hair.

"I must make a point of speaking to Violet," he said.

Tizzy returned once again to the place where she always saw Patrick. But, on this occasion, all that remained was just a very strong smell of magic and a pure, green crystal hanging from a vine over a short branch of a tree. Her wings were now strong and she quickly flew to collect it. Taking the crystal from the vine, she couldn't believe her eyes. There, tucked into a crevice in the branch, was her Wand! Tizzy took the magical crystal and attached it to the vine holding the smaller crystal around her neck. But how on this Earth did her Wand get there? Was it Patrick who had returned it to her? And what of the gift of magic from Florie? She had been told she couldn't yet share this secret with anyone. Of course, her father knew and was fully aware of her gifts, trusting her to keep the secret. But Tizzy was still young, and although she knew she could approach her father at any time with whatever question, she never did, always finding him too busy with this or that. The truth was, if only she had realized, he wanted her to interrupt him however busy he may have appeared. What's more, he was certain he had told her so – if only children listened…

The time had come for Patrick to leave for Middlesborough, but before he bid farewell, along with her wand, he had left a message which read, 'Tizzy, I am going to arrange something with your father. When you are seventeen, you must come to Middlesbrough's 'Ridge Edge' School. There, the Wizard Ian will instruct you how to use all the powers given to you. A great obligation is upon you and although you are still young, I trust you to keep your magical gift a secret from anyone other than your mother or father – do not attempt to practice any magic alone – I know you will not disappoint me. Until we meet again little winged one, stay well. The Wizard, Patrick.'

But alas, when she removed her Wand, she did not see the message fall to the ground. Patrick's wise words, along with the leaves, blew away in the wind…

***

Once again, Ian locked up Viperla in his Castle. Her days were spent aimlessly walking around a large, protected part of its grounds where she recalled her days of old. There were times when even a tear gently trickled down her face as though, perhaps, she felt remorse for what she had done. Nonetheless, she seemed to enjoy tending her herb garden complete with a little frog pond, a gift from Ian. He thought the creatures may give her an interest in life, however remotely, as she spent her days imprisoned. Through her loving care, the herbs and frogs flourished, bringing Viperla a sense of joy and contentment despite the 'tragic' loss of her 'dear' sisters. Had she finally learned the error of her ways? Could it be possible the evil, ruthless Viperla, was changing for the better? She often sat, almost gloating at the splendour of her garden. What could she possibly do with such an abundance of herbs and frogs? The truth was, she often pondered to herself, 'Do I now have enough ingredients to mix in the correct proportion to make my 'Magic Bubbles'? *He, he, he!*' Since the end of 'The War of The Wands', the making of her bubbles was strictly forbidden by the Wizards, but when had Viperla ever cared anything about what she was or wasn't allowed to do? Ian often heard her mumbling to herself while tending her cherished garden or stroking her adorable pet frogs. To hear her screeching laughter or miserable moans were as certain as the arrival of the morning light. Ian still felt pity towards her – she had lost everything and now, it appeared, even her mind. But ohhh, could anyone *ever* possibly imagine what new evil was being planned in the mind of that dreadful fairy? Viperla kept her thoughts and plans close to her, remembering how she once made, in days gone by, bubbles of many different colours and strengths, the strongest of which being the bright, cherry red. Inside these, she could trap anything and send it floating off wherever she wished. What particular fun those bubbles were when she placed something scary inside, to drift away and suddenly burst in front of her poor, unsuspecting victims. This made her laugh until she cried, stopping only when her stomach hurt so much she thought she would be sick! So, every day, she mumbled away, trying to arrange her magic words in the exact order. On occasion, she would be cruel to her frogs, poking them with a sharp stick to make them blow the bubbles she so desperately needed, always hoping for that perfect specimen she could turn into a special, bright, cherry red by the use of her secret herbal potion. But the question foremost in her mind was this – even if she could find that *perfect* specimen and make a bubble large and strong enough to carry her weight over the Castle wall and safely away, could she ensure it would not be too strong to burst easily when she wished to escape? This was her devious plan and she vowed to stop at nothing to make it happen…!

It was now early spring and late one night, Tross couldn't sleep. He got up and went to sit all alone upon his father's Throne, quietly thinking and staring through an open window into the night sky. Strangely, it was snowing but he felt very relaxed and comfortable on the enormous chair, knowing that one day, all before him, would be his. His mind wandered back over the past months and an aching feeling tugged at his heart. There was one thing Tross promised himself – he would find out exactly what had happened to Elm after he was so violently struck down by the dragon. He had seen death before but not quite like that. What was the swirling glitter? Was it in fact Elm and, if so, where did he go when an unseen force shot him into the sky and out into space?! He recalled the day Viperla slapped Cecee's face, and the condition in which he had found his sister haunted him. Sisters… he loved his, but what had really happened to Viperla's? Had even *she* loved hers as much as she had said? Now, locked in prison, she had all the time in the World to reflect upon the events in her caves. Back then, all she did was to scream at Cecee accusations of her sister's demise. But with no trace of them, many wondered if they were truly dead and gone. Tross, for his part, wanted to find out for certain. Viperla's imprisonment was not enough for him. She had shown before she could escape, and then there was the added insult – being the former Queen of Middlesborough, gave her certain rights… Ian looked after her well, and she may possibly live for many more years. To Tross, it all seemed so unfair! One day he would be King and was content knowing, when that day came, he would make certain Viperla would *personally* answer to *him*. His eyes now growing heavy with tiredness, he left the Throne to walk in the fresh air outside. The snow now lay heavy and his footsteps broke its even carpet as he dodged clumps falling from tree branches. He sat upon a toadstool, breathing deep the cold, misty night air. Blowing out white breath, he playfully made small white fog rings and smiled watching the breeze scatter them. Now staring up at twinkling stars and gazing at a silver crescent moon, he thought further about his future. As he rested, a strange sight met his eyes – in the moonlight, a large, clear bubble floated by in the distance. He smiled at the thought of a fairy-child, chuckling and blowing bubbles into the night air. But as he watched the breeze carry it along, his smile turned to a puzzled gaze. It appeared a pinkish colour and didn't burst or splatter into nothing, unlike all other bubbles.

'What's this!' he thought to himself.

Chillingly, it changed direction and slowly floated closer and closer towards him as though it had a mind all of its own, knowing exactly where it wished to go. The nearer the bubble came, the darker in colour it grew, now a deep, reddish pink! Unsure of what to expect, Tross took no chances and withdrew the dagger from his belt. The bubble now nearly upon him, he thrust his dagger forward into the eerie object. To his complete amazement, nothing happened! He withdrew the dagger and thrust it forward again but still to no effect. Tross anxiously tried a third time, plunging it with all his strength into the bubble and… BANG! This time it burst, but at that exact moment, he awoke to find he had fallen asleep upon the Throne! He realized a strong breeze must have blown shut the window with a bang. It had been nothing but a dream! Tross felt relieved as he stood, rubbed his eyes and yawned. He walked outside into the fresh air to stretch his arms and legs. But there, just in front of him, he noticed something shining on the surface of the snow. Standing rigid, the more he looked, the more he realized, to his horror, what lay there before him, appeared to be the possible remains of a large, burst bubble! Tross leaned forward and saw the shiny substance had a definite, deep colour, almost red! "By all the Wizards!" Tross called aloud, "It can't be! The remains of a *RED* bubble! But that was in my dream!"

Tross took several steps back, trying to reassure himself all was well, still staring at the red remains upon the snow. 'So what *is* that on the ground in front of me if it was just a dream? *Was I out here*? If so, how did I wake up *inside*, still sitting on the Throne?' In a state of total confusion, Tross nervously tried to reassure himself… "It was just a dream" he said. "That's it, those weird bubbles were the result of a silly dream… *weren't they?"*

The Story Teller's Tale at Welcome Inn

"Why It Always Rains Over Loch Lomond"

A young Cloud Fairy of Loch Lomond and a King Elf from the Land of Scotland were in love. They would hide among the clouds telling of their undying adoration for each other. But unbeknown to them, the jealous, loveless Evil Fairy of Caledonia soon heard of this eternal affection and flew at great speed to spy upon them. Witnessing their embraces, she immediately cast a powerful curse over them both. Her anger knew no bounds as lightning struck and thunder crashed and great holes appeared within the clouds - it was indeed the worst curse ever pronounced. But her fury was still not satisfied as she cast a further spell upon the King Elf, paralysing his wings. He fell through a hole in the clouds and crashed to the ground. Her spite knowing no bounds, the Evil Fairy then cast her final spell. Only when the Cloud Fairy was no more, rain would, whatever the season, forever return to fall over the beautiful Loch. Finally satisfied with her shocking deeds, a horrible, screeching laugh came from the heartless creature as she flew away knowing the King would be helpless to save the young fairy from crying herself to death.

Left all alone, her tears unstoppable, the Cloud Fairy cared little for the warning known to all fairies – a crying fairy is a dying fairy. Looking through the clouds, her love was nowhere to be seen. It was clear to her the King had fallen under a terrible spell. Broken-hearted, her tears continued to rain down over the Loch.

A day had passed when she thought she could see her love by the Loch's edge. Overjoyed, her crying stopped to allow most of the clouds to disappear and the Sun to shine beams of light all around. Now seeing clearly, she realized it was not her love but a 'Selkie', a seal which sheds its skin to become, for a while, Elf-like. Once again miserable and weak, she lay in her cloud, and with all the strength she could find, summoned fearsome winds to bring back the black clouds to spread them over Loch Lomond once more. The following day and close to death, it occurred to the Cloud Fairy that if she allowed the rain to fall over the Loch for two continuous days, she may trick the wicked fairy of Caledonia into thinking the rain drops were her final tears and would surely mean her death.

Caring nothing for her life, she flew through the violent storm to the ground in search of her love. There she met the Selkie who told her of a place by the Loch where her love might be, a place known as 'Fairy Glen'. She made her way, struggling through the wild weather. Her clothes ragged and torn, she found the sheltered Fairy Glen where she did indeed find her one and only love. But alas, she saw him holding the hand of another! Utterly distraught, she tried to fly back to the clouds where she would willingly die of a broken heart, but her wings were too heavy with rain and she found it impossible. Hiding from the King and his new love, she waited for her wings to dry. All too soon, her curiosity got the better of her. Hiding behind a bush, she watched the King and the fairy. It was then she overheard her love beg, "Please, please use all your powers to heal my wings! Before it is too late, I must return to the clouds to find and save my true love, the beautiful Cloud Fairy". Thrilled, she ran from her hiding place to be with him, but as he caught sight of the thin, bedraggled fairy covered in mud, he failed to recognize her and, thinking it was yet another evil trick, turned away. Grief-stricken, she fled from him, but the love in her heart was too strong and would not be denied.

Under the shelter of a bush, for two days she patiently waited for the storm to finally pass. Her wings dry, she found a pool of crystal clear rainwater and took a long, refreshing drink. Her thirst quenched and her strength restored, she washed her face and cleaned her pretty wings. Her beauty restored, she flew to find the King still pleading with the fairy for help. Softly calling his name, the Cloud Fairy flew to him and took his hand. The overwhelmed King embraced the love of his life as she called to the fairy, "Please gather your friends and with all our powers, we can do what is needed to break these awful curses!" The fairy produced a flower trumpet and blew a plea throughout the land. Countless fairies soon gathered within the Fairy Glen. With their magic combined, they chanted a spell and the wings of the King suddenly and mystically recovered their former strength, while the holes in the clouds magically disappeared – the evil curses had been broken!

The King and the Cloud Fairy together once more, their love re-affirmed, thanked the fairies and left to find the Selkie... With a farewell wave, they flew into a sunbeam which took them to the clouds where they both lived happily ever after.

Content they were, never forgetting the wise words bestowed to them by the Selkie... "Cloud Fairy, the Evil Fairy of Caledonia thinks you are dead and the King can never again use his wings. To trick her into believing all her curses remain forever, never forget how to use your magic to summon the clouds to rain down again and again o'er the bonnie banks and braes of Loch Lomond."

GAME OF 'PIP IN THE POT'

The game of Pip in the Pot is played on a checkered playing field once a year to celebrate the start of summer or for special occasions. It is played by two opposing teams, each consisting of eight players with eight flying frogs. One team is dressed in white, the other in black.

The playing field is divided into thirty equally sized black and white squares arranged in a chequered pattern. A red centre line divides the playing field into two equal halves of fifteen squares each. The first team to place twenty plum stones (hereafter referred to as a 'pip' or 'pips') into its own pot which is secured behind the centre square in the blue box of the opposing team's half of the field, is declared the winner. If neither side has a total score of twenty then the team with the highest score will be declared the winners.

RULES

1.   Whilst a game of celebration, it must be accepted it is very dangerous. Therefore, every player and his flying frog must pass a stringent physical and endurance test before entry into the competition is allowed. As the pip can fly at great speed, and after the fatal accident of the infamous Hitter Elf, 'Lief', in 2003, the Sporting Committee insists all players must wear acorn shell safety helmets.

Note 1: There have been numerous requests made that teams are allowed to paint on their safety helmets the crest of their Woods. This is allowed and indeed encouraged.

2.   Only the frogs are allowed to fly. To prevent an Elf from flight he is required to have his wings pinned under the supervision of the Elf Willow.

3.   Each Elf is to be secured to his frog to help prevent falling.

4. There is a total of eight referees consisting of four side-line referees holding red, yellow and green flags, two centre-line referees holding red and green flags and two score referees, one standing at each pot and holding one blue flag. In the event of a dispute between the referees, a hawk called 'Eagle Eye' will be called to settle the dispute.

5. There are various coloured flags in use: Red to stop the game, green to start or continue the game, yellow to signify a warning, red and yellow held together to signify a disqualification or the awarding of extra pips, a blue flag to signify a score of one pip in the pot.

6. There is bound to be a degree of frogs and their riders bumping into one another. Any unintentional colliding is acceptable without penalty if the referees and/or Eagle Eye so agree. However, if the referees and Eagle Eye agree there was deliberate colliding then they will, following their mutual agreement, award three pips to the team whose player they consider suffered from the deliberate collision.

7. To decide which team plays first, both teams of eight elves must, in their own half, stand back from the centre red line. The 'Hitter Elf' will prominently display across his back the letters 'HE'. HE must stand at the centre of his team's

line-up and position himself a little forward from the rest.

8.   The current May Queen Fairy will enter the arena accompanied by her Maids of Honour.

Note 2: All the usual pomp and ceremony must accompany this grand entrance.

9.   The May Queen Fairy will stand at the centre of the red line and throw a pip vertically into the air. The side of the red line on which the pip falls designates the team to commence play.

Note 3: 'Eagle Eye' will decide whether or not the pip was thrown vertically without any deviation to either side of the line. To indicate a 'Miss Throw', he will fly in a circle, a red flag will be held high by each referee and a re-throw will take place.

10.   Subject to no Miss Throw, a green flag will be held high by each referee and the May Queen Fairy will then pick up the pip and throw it high into the air for the Hitter Elf of the team to start the game to catch. Making certain she and her Maids of Honour quickly retire to their seats in the arena, they will keep a close eye on both Score Referees' blue flags in order to record the number of pips placed in each pot. They will

continuously hold up large score cards for all to see.

11.   The Hitter Elf is the first allowed to fly on his frog to catch the pip. This is the only time a pip can be caught in the hand and not the scoop net.

Note 4: The 'catching of the pip' is vital, as failure to do so will lead to instant disqualification of the Hitter Elf's team, leaving the opposing team to be declared the winners. This will result in a lot of booing and hissing from the disappointed crowd.

12.   If the pip is successfully caught, the remaining members of both teams will take to their places astride their frogs. To commence the game, the Hitter Elf must throw and, with his 'Ash Stick', strike the pip in the direction of any one of his seven 'Net Elves' comprising three defenders and four attack elves.

13.   The Net Elf will direct his frog to fly so that he can catch the pip in his scoop net. Using this net, the Elf will throw the pip towards the Hitter Elf who will then use his Ash Stick to hit the pip to another member of his team who he feels is in the best position to help advance the pip towards their team's pot. At this point all players can be airborne.

14.   Any Net Elf can place the pip into his team's pot.

15. The Hitter Elf cannot hit the pip into his team's pot. If he does, this will be declared 'Out of Bounds' and the referees will show red and yellow flags to award the opposing team two pips counting towards their total of twenty. The blue area is out of bounds and any player who enters this will be shown the red flag and disqualified. A player in this case may or may not be substituted at the discretion of the referees and/or Eagle Eye.

16. A Net Elf cannot hold the pip within his scoop net for longer than a count of four seconds. Failure to observe this Rule will result in a red flag being shown and will lead to disqualification of the Elf.

Note 5: A disqualified Net Elf may or may not be substituted at the discretion of the referees and/or Eagle Eye.

17. The pip must be placed in the pot by a Net Elf who is in flight upon his frog and not while landed on the ground.

18. Following the successful placing of a pip into the pot, the game must be restarted from the centre red line. The Hitter Elf of the team which has just scored can place himself anywhere along that line as long as he remains within the centre square. He will throw and hit the pip in the direction of a Net

Elf in his team who he feels is in the best position to advance the pip towards their pot.

19. Three 'Defence Elves' (the letters 'DE' will be prominently displayed across their backs) are required in each team to guard the opposing team's pot. They are allowed to prevent a pip entering the pot, as long as they do not cover or block the pot's actual opening. If a player is guilty of covering the pot's opening at any time, he will be accused of committing an F.B.P (Frog Before Pot) and the referees will show red and yellow flags awarding the opposing team three pips counting towards their total of twenty.

20. The Defence Elves are allowed to defend only when there are at least two members of the opposing team in their half of the playing field.

21. There is to be no contact with the pip other than as provided for within these Rules. The Hitter Elf is allowed to use the following hits: Top spin, under spin, curve pip, fore hand, back hand and lob.

22. A frog is permitted to catch a pip with his tongue and place it into his rider's net only while flying over the same coloured square as his team. Following a breach of this Rule, the referees will show red and yellow flags and award the

opposing team three pips and the game will be restarted in favour of the opposing team. The Hitter Elf will throw the pip into the air and hit it in the direction of a Net Elf in his team who he feels is in the best position to advance the pip towards their pot.

23. A frog can land to pass the pip as long as he lands in the same coloured square as his team.

24. A frog cannot place a pip into his team's pot.

25. If the pip is not caught and falls to the ground, the game is restarted by the team who did not have possession of the pip. From the spot where the pip fell to the ground, the Hitter Elf's frog will retrieve the pip with his tongue and pass it to the Hitter Elf who will throw it into the air and hit it in the direction of a Net Elf in his team who he feels is in the best position to advance the pip towards their pot.

26. If the pip falls outside of either of the two side lines or either of the two inner rear lines of the playing field, the game is restarted by the team who did not have possession of the pip. The Hitter Elf's frog will retrieve the pip with his tongue and pass it to the Hitter Elf. From the spot where the pip left the playing field (Eagle Eye to decide on this), the Hitter Elf will throw the pip

into the air and hit it in the direction of a Net Elf in his team who he feels is in the best position to advance the pip towards their pot.

27.   The game is played in two equal halves of thirty minutes. At the end of the first half there will be a refreshment break of fifteen minutes after which, the game will recommence. The two pots are emptied so that the total number of pips can be counted in order to check the score with the May Queen Fairy. Elves with their frogs will now change to the other half of the playing field and the two pots repositioned.

28.   If after the second half each team has scored the same number of pips there will be a further twenty minutes break after which Elves with their frogs must change halves again and the pots emptied of any pips and repositioned. The first team to place three pips into its pot or to score an overall total of twenty pips will be declared the winners.

29.   No magic sceptres, wands or other flashing items are allowed in the arena, not even for a second!

30.   Have fun and shout for your team as loud as you like as the players will appreciate the support!

Fairy Tumbling Competition

Rules

1. A minimum of ten Woods required to take part for the Competition to be held.

2. Any Wood wishing to enter must be represented by a team of six fairies chosen from the Wood and consisting of two from each age group – see Rule 4.

3. Please arrive at least two hours before the competition is due to start.

4. At the entrance to the competition area, competitors will find three Tumbling Log Books, one for each of the following age groups - eight to eleven, twelve to fifteen and sixteen to nineteen. Each competitor must enter into the appropriate Log Book, her name, age and the names of the tumbles she will be attempting in each of her two dives. Any fairy older than nineteen will not be allowed to compete.

Note 1: proof of age is required. The Sporting Committee has concerns that the fairy tumbles become more difficult with every passing year, and considers senior competitors may be placed in danger of serious injury. Note 2: A senior competitor is a fairy who has been competing for six or more consecutive years. Though not mandatory, a senior competitor is advised and encouraged to join a team of teachers and coaches instead of taking part in any further competitions. A list of such teams can be found in your pink crystal under, 'Fairies in Motion School of Tumbling' (There is one located in every Wood and the pay is great!)

5.   Three years of regular practice is mandatory before any fairy is allowed to compete.

Note 3: Evidence of such practice must be produced upon request by the Judges.

6.   A team of eight Judges consisting of fairies retired from active competition will be chosen by the Sporting Committee. A Judge must be selected from only those Woods not taking part in the competition.

7.   The same age group from each Wood will complete its dives before the next age group is allowed to compete. For breaks, see Rule 16. Order of competition in age group – first, eight to eleven, second, twelve to fifteen, third, sixteen to nineteen. Each competitor is allowed two dives in order to perfect three tumbles over the two dives. Once a competitor is in the air, the start height of each dive must be fifty times the height of the competitor.

Note 4: At no time before completion of the third tumble is a competitor allowed to use her wings for flight. The Judges will award points for each tumble. The maximum score for three perfect tumbles per competitor is seventy five points (25 points for each perfect tumble). If a competitor scores the maximum of seventy five points in her first dive she does not take the second. A total maximum of 150 points can be scored by the two fairies in each age group. The team (consisting of three age groups) can therefore achieve a maximum score of 450 points - see Rule 13.

8.   Each team must provide two Safety Elves who are allowed to 'spot' from the ground for that team only. Note 5: To 'spot' involves the learned ability to determine at which point a competitor is in imminent danger of causing herself injury from an uncontrollable tumble and/or dive. These Safety Elves will immediately fly to catch her and return her safely to the ground.

Note 6: This is a direct result of the intervention from the Joint Committees of the various Wood's Department of Safety and Health.

Note 7: Any elf who decides to catch the competitor in mid-tumble and/or dive, may incur for the team a deduction of ten to twenty points depending upon the decision of the Judges. It will be for the Judges to determine which tumbles were successfully completed before any Safety Elf intervened – Judges' decisions are final and binding.

9.   A competitor can only use her wings to return to the ground once she has completed her three chosen tumbles for each dive. Flying before three complete tumbles will mean she will be committing an F.O.E. (Flying Out Early).

Note 8: The committing of an F.O.E will result in the offending competitor losing any points awarded for any tumble in that dive and will also result in forfeiting the second dive if one remains. If she is taking a second dive and commits an F.O.E she will lose half of any points awarded to her in the first dive.

10. The coaching of a competitor is permitted only during practice. Any coaching of a competitor during the competition is prohibited and if discovered will lead to either instant disqualification of the competitor from the competition or to immediate arbitration – decision of the Arbitration Committee is final and binding.

11. Any fairy who has an injury to her wings or cannot fly in an acceptable manner, will not be allowed to enter the competition.

Note 9: A test flight to determine her fitness to compete will be undertaken by each fairy one hour prior to the start of the competition.

12. Any fairy fit to compete does so at her own expense. However, the Royal Courts of each Wood have promised to consider financial assistance should any unfortunate competitor become injured during the practice time allowed or the actual competition.

13. The new tumbles (including head dive victory rolls, one and a half double loops and treble tumbles) introduced by Princess Cecee, may be included by any participating fairy if declared in the Log Book – see Rule 4. If successfully completed, additional points may be awarded at the discretion of the Judges but within the maximum overall score of 450 points per team. In the event of a dispute the matter will be referred to the Arbitration Committee for their final and binding decision.

14. Courtesy from each team to all other teams must be demonstrated at all times.

15. Etiquette is expected from all competing fairies and their Safety Elves. All are reminded to remain still and silent while a competitor is performing her dives and tumbles.

16. No spectator may enter or leave the competition area while a dive is in progress. Any spectator can leave or enter only during a break, which follows after each age group from all Woods has completed its dives for that age group. The break will be for a period of forty five minutes only - no spectator will be allowed to return to the competition area after this time, so it is advisable to return within this period otherwise, return will only be allowed at the next break. Food and drinks are to be kept out of the competition area. Refreshments are free and can be found by the many Refreshment Trees in the spectator's area. King Foxglove VI's Master Chef Cameron and his team, will be providing this year's selection of delicious food and drinks including his famous 'Honeyed Fruit and Coconut in Juice'.

17. No flying around the competition area is permitted except by the competitors or their Safety Elves and then only when a dive is not taking place.

18. Spectators are welcome to bring along pets, such as small frogs, beetles, bees, butterflies, ladybirds, dragonflies, etc., but these must remain silent and/or grounded otherwise they, together with their owners, will be asked to permanently leave the competition area. Competitors are participating in a dangerous sport and can easily lose focus and or concentration if distracted by noise or other flying beings.

19. Anyone wishing to place daisies on the ground of the competition area in order to assist with the soft landing of a competitor after her dive is welcome to do so, but

this must be done only during a break – see Rule 16. The throwing of victory flowers is permitted only after the announcement of the winning team. As a courtesy to the winning team and the Clean-Up Elves, please use flowers with no thorns on their stems.

20. The winning team is the team who accumulates most points subject to a maximum of 450 – see Rule 4. In the event of a dispute the matter will be referred to the Arbitration Committee for their final and binding decision. In the event of a tie between teams a further competition will take place in order to decide the overall winner and at a date to be announced.

21. Last rule of all: Have lots of fun and please remember to keep King Foxglove VI's Woods tidy!